BOOKSELLERS LOVE
THE REVOLUTIONARIES TRY AGAIN

"*The Revolutionaries Try Again* is a daring novel that pits youthful idealism against persistent and inescapable corruption. Mauro Javier Cardenas is an exciting new voice in Latin American literature, and his debut crackles with an exuberance that readers of Valeria Luiselli, Julio Cortázar, and Horacio Castellanos Moya will love."

—*Stephen Sparks, Green Apple Books on the Park*

"Written in rapid-fire, playful, musical prose, Mauro Javier Cardenas's riot of a debut, *The Revolutionaries Try Again,* follows three longtime friends who are facing the evils of dictatorship in Ecuador. It's one of my favorite books of 2016 and one I'm eager to share with other readers. I would tattoo lines from Mauro Javier Cardenas's brilliant debut on my body."

—*Caitlin Luce Baker, University Book Store*

"Fans of dense, brilliant, and mind-bending Latin American lit have a treat on their hands in September. *The Revolutionaries Try Again* is a marvel."

—*Mark Haber, Brazos Bookstore*

"A tremendously skilled storyteller and monologuist; his writing is so exuberant."

—*Paul Yamazaki,* Publishers Weekly

"*The Revolutionaries Try Again* transfixes on every page—across every world-devouring sentence—with a rigorous, incandescent language rarely seen in contemporary fiction. It's a bit early to say, but Cardenas's debut is either the jubilant beginning or the rapturous end of the Latin American novel: a fucking revelation of a book."

—*Hal Hlavinka, Community Bookstore*

THE REVOLUTIONARIES TRY AGAIN

THE REVOLUTIONARIES TRY AGAIN

/ MAURO JAVIER CARDENAS /

COFFEE HOUSE PRESS
MINNEAPOLIS
2016

Coffee House Press books are available to the trade through our primary distributor, Consortium Book Sales & Distribution, cbsd.com or (800) 283-3572. For personal orders, catalogs, or other information, write to info@coffeehousepress.org.

Coffee House Press is a nonprofit literary publishing house. Support from private foundations, corporate giving programs, government programs, and generous individuals helps make the publication of our books possible. We gratefully acknowledge their support in detail in the back of this book.

Library of Congress Cataloging-in-Publication Data

Names: Cardenas, Mauro Javier, author.
Title: The revolutionaries try again / Mauro Javier Cardenas.
Description: Minneapolis : Coffee House Press, 2016.
Identifiers: LCCN 2016006300 | ISBN 9781566894463 (paperback)
Subjects: | BISAC: FICTION / Literary. | FICTION / Political.
Classification: LCC PS3603.A7346 R48 2016 | DDC 813/.6—dc23
LC record available at https://lccn.loc.gov/2016006300

Printed in the United States of America

23 22 21 20 19 18 17 16   1 2 3 4 5 6 7 8

To Lilia & Klara

/ CONTENTS /

PART ONE: ANTONIO & LEOPOLDO

I / LEOPOLDO CALLS ANTONIO 3
II / ANTONIO IN SAN FRANCISCO 16
III / LEOPOLDO AND THE OLIGARCHS 33
IV / ANTONIO EDITS HIS BABY CHRIST MEMOIR 49
V / ANTONIO IN GUAYAQUIL 66
VI / ANTONIO'S GRANDMOTHER GIVES ADVICE 87
VII / ANTONIO & LEOPOLDO AT DON ALBAN'S 90

PART TWO: ROLANDO & EVA

VIII / ROLANDO & EVA 117
IX / ROLANDO LOOKS FOR EVA 138

PART THREE: DISINTEGRATION

X / ANTONIO AND THE PROTESTERS 151
XI / FACUNDO AT SAN JAVIER 163
XII / LEOPOLDO'S GRANDMOTHER GIVES ADVICE 169
XIII / LEOPOLDO & ANTONIO AT JULIO'S PARTY 172
XIV / EVA ALONG VICTOR EMILIO ESTRADA 205
XV / ROLANDO FINDS EVA 225

PART FOUR: FACUNDO SAYS FAREWELL

XVI / FACUNDO SAYS FAREWELL 239
XVII / ANTONIO EDITS HIS BABY CHRIST MEMOIR 249
XVIII / THE NIGHT BEFORE ALMA'S FIRST VOICE
OF WITNESS INTERVIEW 256

THE REVOLUTIONARIES TRY AGAIN

PART ONE

—

ANTONIO & LEOPOLDO

I / LEOPOLDO CALLS ANTONIO

Everyone's saying that lightning struck the phone on Palm Sunday, Don Leopoldo. The one public phone at the Calderón that didn't filch your coins. At least not all of them. That soon after hordes were pilgrimaging to it and lining up to dial their departed. That the single witness of the fateful strike, who's the custodian at the Calderón — you know that park? The one by that gas station caught watering its diesel and dumping burnt Pennzoil in the Salado, imagine that, as if that river needed any more muck, a bit more and the stench won't let us breathe, hopefully you don't live by the Salado like I do, luckily León's in charge and he'll send someone to rinse it soon. That's why I voted for your boss, Don Leopoldo, you know I've always voted for León. So the custodian hears thunder and sees lightning and he's spooked. Brimming with liquor Patito, too. Apparently he's known as a drunk and a troubadour. Little Jaramillo they call him over in El Guasmo. Apparently he serenaded his second wife at the Calderón and still shoulders his guitar to serenade the domestics that stroll by on Sundays. Cuando tú / te hayas ido / me envolverán / you know that pasillo by Julio Jaramillo?

An answer will only encourage Pascacio but no answer will not discourage him. Not that Leopoldo minds listening to him. Or that Pascacio doesn't already know that Leopoldo doesn't mind listening to him.

Las sombras?

That's the one, Don Leopoldo. My Grandpa Lucho used to Pancho it for us while he fried his famous yapingachos. God keep him. He'll never forget what you did for him. So while the rain's pouring, Little Jaramillo's running for cover with his guitar tucked inside his shirt, but of course its head is still protruding out of his shirt and scratching his beard with its pegheads, though my sister's neighbor says he was running because he had seen strange shadows after him, shadows seeking retribution for his insatiable womanizing, though my sister says her neighbor's a prude old cow who's probably inventing this part, on the rest everyone agrees. That's the neighbor I've been telling you about, Don Leopoldo. The one who thinks her jars have a different spirit than her cans. Everyone says that at night she Ouijas tin spirits with spoons. That her cabinets are like marimbas from ultratumba. Strange shadows or no shadows, Little Jaramillo's running for cover and then he hears the loudest thunder he's ever heard in his life. Under the ceibo by that public phone he squats and hopes lightning won't strike him. If you ask him about it he'll show you the mud on his sailor pants. He'll even walk you to that shriveled ceibo and make you crouch. From right here, he'll tell you in that Polo Baquerizo squawk of his, you know how those people talk, Don Leopoldo, from right here I saw a flash of lightning with twigs on it, ñaño. It was like a hand descending from the sky to hoist the roof off that phone. And the torched telephone still works. I know because after the storm's over the first thing I did was call Conchita to tell her of how the lightning nabbed the phone instead of me. The phone's ringing and ringing because Conchita's big on sleep, and when she finally picks up I'm reckoning the phone's dialing on no coins so I'm like Conchita, I'm calling you for free, finally we netted us a real miracle, and before she can rooster me for waking her I'm hanging up and dialing my brother up in El Paso and the long distance call goes through and I'm jumping and screaming Jorgito you wouldn't believe what just happened.

Phone's still broken?

You're not going to report it, Don Leopoldo?

Of course not, Pascacio. No.

Still busted. I'm heading there again tomorrow to call my cousin Jacinta up in Jacksonville and my sister, you've met my little sister? She's calling our Aunt Rosalia up in Jersey. Both had to flee after the last Paquetazo. You probably have a call or two to make too, eh?

Leopoldo does. And yet admitting it would reveal that his family is also vulnerable to the periodic catchups between downturns and shocks. Therapies of shock everyone calls Los Paquetazos. Thanks for the tip, Leopoldo says, finalizing their exchange as they reach León's office with the rolltop oak desk they've been pushing along the hallway. The one desk remaining on the third floor. Or on any of the five floors. A relic from the times when El Loco and his cohorts emptied the municipal palace of everything but the doorknobs, the wallpaper, the one rolltop oak desk that was too heavy to haul.

After Pascacio picks up his bucket and mop, after he wishes Leopoldo a good night, after the metallic sound of his oscillating bucket fades down the stairs, Leopoldo checks his watch for scratches, though in the dark this isn't easy to do, the only working light is down the hall, from the lamppost out the window, which he approaches with an industrious trudge and inflated chest, ridiculing himself for the servile diligence he adopts when León's around, hearing the mottled collision of bugs outside, fireflies and moths and mayflies, those leeches of light, smashing themselves against the incandescence. Pascacio's trying to rack up favors by helping him. Don Leopoldo, at the registry they're asking my sister for a bribe she can't afford. Don Leopoldo, at the social security they've pocketed my grandfather's pension. With one call Leopoldo can fix these. He's León Martín Cordero's chief of staff. He has that kind of pull. And yet his pull is at odds with the digital watch he's been sporting since high school, a gift from when his godfather scored his father a minor post in the prefecture, a clunker with shortlegged blip buttons and a rubber strap, sure, but an advanced machine back then, before his father fled in the wake of an embezzlement scandal. No new scratches from pushing the rolltop. Good.

Though he's exhausted he will not wait for the bus at the stop nearby, even though at this late hour Pascacio's the only coworker who might spot him there, but instead he will navigate through Pedro Carbo, Chimborazo, Boyacá, and at the crossing between Sucre and Rumichaca he will catch and ride a different bus along Víctor Manuel Rendón, Junín, Urdaneta, past that gas station that used to dump burnt Pennzoil in the Salado River, past La Atarazana and La Garzota and up the slope on Alcívar, where the bus driver will downshift abruptly and the bus will rattle like a can in a long trail of cans dragged across the asphalt of this canned city by the

(tonight Leopoldo's dinner will consist of canned chili beans)

and along Alcívar the people already crammed inside the bus will be forced to stomach another round of house painters, domestics, fruit peddlers, hop in, people, lots of room in the back, and at least one of them will fake a panic attack to snatch a decent seat, a panic attack that will further dispirit everyone because those who disbelieve its authenticity will jostle with those who are trying to make room for the poor old woman who's having the panic attack, and their sweat will not drip on the tin ridged floor but will be absorbed by thousands of pores that will regurgitate the smell of their daylong labors, which will not disgust Leopoldo because this time he shall will these people into a nonexistence that will not deject him then but later, when he will be reminded yet again of how uncharitable he can be toward those less fortunate than he is.

Leopoldo forestalls his bus ride by Tupa & Mera. On the window display silvered arrows point at televisions. On one of them a farmer guides his tractor with a remote control. On another the interim president, a protégé of León, praises the recent coup and announces another Paquetazo. On another the arrival of a helicopter promises yet another triumphant return of El Loco, who has already run for president twice. On another the young and the rich are behaving badly again, this time in Salinas Beach (isn't that Torbay, his classmate from San Javier?). From the shuttered entrance of Tupa & Mera the watchman steps out onto the sidewalk and tries his most pugnacious glare on Leopoldo.

Good evening.

He does not answer Leopoldo's greeting. Perhaps it's too dark for the watchman to notice his tailored suit pants, his embroidered silk tie, his gold cufflinks with the San Javier logo?

Salvador's not on duty tonight?

The watchman shakes his head.

Tell him Leopoldo Hurtado said hello. I work over at the mayor's office, by the way. Tupa Mera's a friend. Not sure if you've met him. He's the owner of this and five other electronics stores across Guayaquil.

Leopoldo hands him his business card. The watchman holds it up with both hands, angling it, trying to lamp it with the TV screens. Now you can see?

I'm so sorry, Economista Hurtado. I'm so new at this job I didn't even . . .

You're for El Loco.

Never, Economista Hurtado. Always for León I . . .

On the bus Leopoldo does not yet think of calling his grandmother from the busted phone at the Calderón. He does think of her though. Not as she is now, he wouldn't know how she is now, three weeks after fleeing to Pensacola because of the last Paquetazo, but as she remains in his memory, on her farm in the outskirts of Manabí, where he's still ten years old and she's teaching him how to drive her green John Deere, a one seater, sliding forward on her lap and holding on to the giant steering wheel while her rubber boots ram the pedals and she says that's my Leo, drive it over those Jesuits if they give you trouble at San Javier, you hear, drive it over your pansy classmates if they heckle you for being smarter than them, which of course he proves to be, seven years later he's up at the podium of San Javier's coliseum delivering his valedictorian speech, the one he'd endlessly rehearsed in Antonio's living room, we are the future of Ecuador, debating with his friend the meditative pauses, the stormy passages, the unrestrained warnings they'd learned from the sermons of Father Villalba, how are we to be Christians in a world of destitution and injustice, although Father Villalba wouldn't have cared if they'd learned anything from him because while he was still alive he'd spurned them and cursed them and told them he knew they were going to sow misery like their fathers had sown misery, and while Leopoldo delivers his valedictorian speech he sees his grandmother among the crowd of senators and diplomats and of course León Martín Cordero, former president of Ecuador and current mayor of Guayaquil and the greatest oligarch of them all, carajo, and Leopoldo knows his grandmother has said to them or will say to them that's my Leo, always the brightest one of them all, and he'll go far, they'll lie to her, he'll go far.

Leopoldo asks the bus driver to slow down. He's getting out. The driver doesn't hear him so everyone in the bus relays the message that one's coming down, chofer, mount the brakes, chofer, free the hangar, chofer, and when at last Leopoldo reaches the exit he jumps out of the moving bus and lands, at a gallop to avoid plunking forward, between the Salado and the Calderón.

By the busted phone there's a long line, thirty people at least, he should've anticipated a line before jumping out, who knows how long before the bus drives by again at this late hour. Leopoldo proceeds to the front of the line, not hearing the voices saying I haven't talked to my father in more than two weeks, I haven't talked to my sister in four, strangers sharing with each other stories about those family members who had to flee after the most recent Paquetazo because the price of gas shot up, the price of butter, the price of rice, ladrones de mierda, because for the good of the economy the interim president tripled their bus fares, doubled their phone bills, because the Progreso Bank shut its doors after its owners absconded with the accumulated savings of those of us without any government friends to warn us ahead of time, qué hijueputas, outside the Progreso Bank my cousin Marta and hundreds of others screamed at the guards, hanging from the metal bars of the bank's entrance, not knowing the bank was empty, not knowing the bank had already been sacked, and as Leopoldo advances to the front of the line, fast enough to parry what he already knows they're saying, someone says hey, where do you think you're going, oye, where to compañero, hey.

Leopoldo Arístides Hurtado, raising his wallet like a badge, addresses the crowd. My name is Leopoldo Arístides Hurtado and I'm with the office of León Martín Cordero. This telephone is in violation of code 4738 of the telephony guidelines established by the city council in 1979. This telephone is therefore deemed inoperative until it is compliant. Those who continue to operate it can and will be prosecuted.

What he say?

Can't use the phone.

Kidding?

Someone walks up to Leopoldo and squints at his raised wallet as if it were a plaque next to a sculpture.

He's not kidding.

Doesn't look like he's from León's office to me.

A young woman in line decides to intervene. She unruffles the hemline of her polka dot dress, rubs the mud from her high tops, curving her left one atop her right one, a swift canvas peck, and then tittups to León's envoy, whose name she recognizes because her brother Pascacio has mentioned him before, yet she doesn't want to implicate her brother so instead of mentioning his name she smiles at Leopoldo, a smile that her brother says is almost as comforting as the yapingachos of Grandpa Lucho, a smile that the shintacklers who soccer on her street like to whistle at, Malenita, mi amor, where are you going with that sassy smile. She offers Leopoldo the scribbled numbers on her lilac notepad. We're all calling our families, she says. You know how impossible it is for us to afford these calls. Couldn't you wait to issue your order just a tiny little bit?

Leopoldo tries not to flinch. He pockets his wallet. No.

He's not kidding, Malena informs the people in line, recklessly raising her voice so that Leopoldo can hear her saying that her brother Pascacio works nights at the municipality and has heaped praise on that piece of lastre for whatever reason.

Slip him a twenty, someone says. A man takes off his cap and hands it to his son, who begins to collect change from the people in line. Leopoldo did not expect this. In his mind this little caprice of his ended without resistance, with the crowd quickly vanishing from the Calderón. The boy shambles toward Leopoldo and tries to hand him the coinfilled cap.

Please. Please don't. No.

The boy runs back to his father after leaving the cap, asprawl, at Leopoldo's feet. He could concede. All right, he could say, just this one time, go on and call your families. Later Leopoldo will convince himself that he'd arrived at his decision not by impulse but by deduction, because Pascacio's sister is here, Leopoldo will think, and Pascacio likes to gossip, and gossip spreads fast at the municipality so León, who does not tolerate corruption in his subordinates, could eventually hear of this, which is unlikely, but perhaps not so unlikely, either way the country's too unstable for him to allow even for the prospect of León hearing about it so he will have to cover himself and follow through by reporting the busted telephone first thing tomorrow morning.

I don't take bribes. Please vacate the premises.

After securing enough witnesses that she was already at the front of the line, an old woman approaches him, bowing to him as she sets down her pineapple by the coinfilled cap, showing him she has nothing left in her grocery bag except lettuce and a bag of rice, shuffling back to her place at the front of the line.

Everyone tallies what else they are willing to part with. Should they send the boy again? No. One by one for greater impact? Who should go first? Who will account for their place in line? Malena rips a page from her notepad, hands numbers to everyone in line. The boy claims he and his father should receive a better number because of their cap collection idea. But it didn't work, someone says. One by one they deposit their belongings in front of Leopoldo. Green mangos, ripe bananas, photographs of their loved ones, plastic rosaries, a bag of lentils.

If Leopoldo were Antonio he would cry of embarrassment and hurl their belongings back at them and leave them to their ridiculous phone calls. Why don't they just assault him? Wouldn't that exonerate him from deciding anything?

I don't take bribes. Please vacate the premises before I summon the squadrons.

No one moves. In line someone shushes someone until everyone's shushed. The crowd seems to be waiting for something to happen. For someone to appear before them and rectify this.

Let's get out of here, Malena says. We'll find some other way to call our families.

A collective groan. Whistling. As they collect their belongings some are muttering desgraciado, others holler descarado, malparidos like him are what's sinking this country, rata de pueblo, moreno de verga, just wait till El Loco returns.

No one's left at the Calderón but him. From his wallet he tries to pull out his phone list, which includes the numbers for his grandmother, for his friend Antonio, for the economics department at the University of Indiana, where according to his contacts, scholarships for Ecuadorians might be available through the ministry of finance. The phone list's lodged inside a pocket where his fingers almost fail him. He pulls the list out but drops it, swatting for it in vain on the way down. If you ask him about it he won't show you his muddied phone list. Or tell you he was surveilling the withered ceibos of the Calderón to check if Little Jaramillo was lurking behind them, checking the sky for lightning too, although this telephone does not look as if it has been struck by lightning. Not that he would know what that looks like.

Leopoldo dials his grandmother.

No estoy, deje un mensaje, y si no hablan español me importa un pito, por su culpa mismo estoy aquí así que no voy a aprender su inglish del carajo.

Leopoldo's relieved that her answering machine picks up. He would have been embarrassed to talk to her. He hangs up without leaving a message. He has expelled those people for nothing. Does the mud beneath him smell like vinegar, sulfur, or piss? Did the mud already absorb Little Jaramillo's piss? Was it softened by it such that children could frolic in it? Make mud balls and snowmen benosed with carrots? The next number on his list is for his friend Antonio, known at San Javier as the Snivel, Gargamel, Drool, Saber Tooth. Leopoldo hasn't talked to him since he left to study abroad, a month after their graduation, almost ten years ago. At Stanford, Antonio was supposed to breeze through a double major in public policy and economics and then return. At the Universidad Católica, Leopoldo was supposed to enlist the luminaries of their generation and then run for office with Antonio. Together they were supposed to do — what? what did you think you were going to do? — so much.

Leopoldo dials Antonio. Through the decrepit phone line Leopoldo hears the first ring, the fourth, and then an alien blare interrupts the sixth: banging on a piano, frantic strings, the crackling of shortwave.

Hello?

Barely hear you.

Why don't you shut your vacuum? Unplug it, if that's the less strenuous option.

Messiaen's Quartet for the End of Time. Which you're interrupting. Here to end your end times. So to speak.

The hell's this? Hello?

This, Gargamel, is your father.

Microphone Head?

Drool?

Microphone Head!

Drool!

So a vacuum is your best metaphor for avant garde music? Surely nonretrogradable rhythms haven't reached your village yet. Rarely has the term yet been used so dubiously.

Pardon me for neglecting to profit by your remark. Leopoldo hears Antonio laughing. Antonio remembers that quip. Of course he remembers.

Oh Drool. Always shortchanging your kind. Is your window open?

Is his window open? Yes. Right. Leopoldo's buying time to prepare a comeback. A common tactic from Who's Most Pedantic, their game from San Javier. During recess by Don Alban's cafeteria they would refute each other about everything, spoofing the pompous language of demagogues, priests, themselves, digressing manically upon premises like compatriotas, let us applaud León's proposal to privatize our toilets, compañeros, let us consider that if El Loco wins, Facundo's maid will lop off his maid killer in his sleep, if she can find it, although rules are rules, digressions earn you top points but they have to eventually boomerang to the original premise, the audience permitted to interrupt only to call out for vocabulary clarifications: badinage!, what is?, sapidity!, what is?, and they halt their sciolisms and provide definitions, magniloquent inventions, on the spot. Is his window open? Antonio chooses not to block Leopoldo's question with a question. He wants to hear what Leopoldo comes up with.

Why yes, my window is indeed open.

You see my friend, well you don't really see, that's why I'm about to inculcate you, your vacuum not only absorbs the detritus on your carpet but also the particles that float through your window, particles that carry inside of them the alarm of ambulances, the clang of cans, the tenor of the toll collector, all your troglogradables that are, in short, inside your artifact of . . .

Troglo what?

Gradables.

Chanfle. Do you own a vacuum?

Why yes. Indeed I do.

And you change its filter often?

Every two months.

You see, Microphone Head, well you don't really see 'cause you're as blind as a microphone, I haven't changed the filter of my Red Devil in years. Therefore it has ceased to absorb anything. Neither detritus nor particles and absolutely no clang of cans. Oh Microphone Head: always faltering between the general and the specific. You know the one about Glenn Gould and the Hoover? Of course you don't.

On the Salado side of the Calderón a domestic appears along Bolívar Street, too far from the busted phone for Leopoldo to know if she was one of the expelled. It is likely that more people will appear again soon. At San Javier their Who's Most Pedantic game had served them well. On the national academic quiz show broadcasted by Channel Ten they had excelled in the debate section. And the Q&A section. They'd swept the city rounds and the interprovincial rounds and the finals against Espíritu Santo. At school everyone recognized them. During recess the appeal of Who's Most Pedantic widened. Why I'm a better presidential candidate than you became a favorite premise.

Still flatlining the currency at the Central Bank, Microphone?

Been following the news?

About the twilight of the IPOS?

About the recent coup.

Another one?

Rumors that the interim president might be loosening the electoral requirements so El Loco can run.

El Loco's returning again?

And the stronger candidates . . .

Stronger? You mean burlier? Dollarized at the gut, if you will.

. . . don't want to run. The situation is irredeemable, so what's the point? They'll get ousted anyway. Ever considered returning?

Absolutamente never. I'm too busy wading in stock options. Money? Paper, yes.

There's massive protests all over the country.

Again?

The indignation of the people has reached its limit.

Now that definitely hasn't happened before.

Leopoldo doesn't respond. Antonio interprets Leopoldo's silence correctly. Leopoldo isn't playing anymore. Antonio turns down Messiaen's Abyss of the Birds.

And yet with the right strategy someone . . .

–Juana we're out of eggs!

I think the lines are crossed, Leo. Typical of our backward . . .

. . . an outsider could sweep the elections and effect real change . . .

–Juana I gave you enough change for eggs.

He yells at you because he loves you, Juana.

. . . at last our chance to . . .

–Juana, carajo, quit eavesdropping on the politicians and go basket some eggs.

Hello?

Barely hear you.

–Quit clowning and hang up already. Juana?

Vote for us, Juana's husband.

We always wanted an audience and here at last . . .

–How much for my vote?

Free milk?

Free housing?

–I'm voting for El Loco.

El Loco's not coming back, sir.

–That's what you people said last time.

How come we haven't heard from Juana?

Juana's husband and his imaginary wife, Juana, are voting for El . . .

–I'll track you two conchadesumadres and . . .

Hang up and call again?

I think we have a chance, Antonio.

–Quit my phone line already!

Hello?

Everyone thinks they're the chosen ones, Masha wrote on Antonio's manuscript. See About Schmidt with Jack Nicholson. Then she quoted from Hope Against Hope by Nadezhda Mandelstam, because she was sure Antonio hadn't read her yet: Can a man really be held accountable for his own actions? His behavior, even his character, is always in the merciless grip of the age, which squeezes out of him the drop of good or evil that it needs from him. In San Francisco, besides the accumulation of wealth, what does the age ask of your so called protagonist? No wonder he never returns to Ecuador.

Why had her comments in Antonio's manuscripts been so mean spirited? She'd been transferring the contents of her closet to boxes that will be transported to her new apartment in New York soon and she'd come across Antonio's manuscripts inside a hatbox, where she'd also come across the compendium of contemporary classical music he had recorded for her, which she was listening to as she read his manuscripts again. She hadn't seen Antonio or thought about him in at least twelve months, since around the time of his farewell party, and because she doesn't remember marking his manuscripts with such virulence, reading them now was akin to discovering that while she was asleep or away someone who turns out to be her had defaced an entrusted room with a red pen. Had she somehow subscribed back then to the asinine notion that one couldn't just barge into art, as Antonio had been desperately trying to do, without a lineage that justified one's so called artistic inclination? Her father was a physicist and her mother had been a violinist and unlike Antonio she grew up alongside the Western Canon but she hadn't become a great painter.

—

D Sharp Minor Etude, No. 12, Opus 8 by Alexander Scriabin: Horowitz wrong noted the D sharp etude in Moscow, Antonio said to Masha, listen, toward the end, Vladimir must have been nervous, or overwhelmed, or trying to both perform and watch himself perform because he's eighty three years old and hasn't been to Russia in sixty one years, and yet what's amazing, or perhaps not so amazing, I know you'll grumble if you don't think it's at least mildly amazing that, if you put on your headphones and scan every second of that recording of Horowitz in Moscow, you have to conclude that he's not crying, unless he's a silent weeper, now listen to this Valentin Silvestrov piece called Postludium, Antonio said — I absolutely agree with you, Masha, Silvestrov's concept of the postlude, of a nostalgia for tonality expressed as a dissipation of tonality, sounds more interesting than his music — now listen to this piece by Arvo Pärt called Tabula Rasa, Antonio said, recounting for her what he knew about this music with so much glee that she began to think he couldn't even believe he knew so much about a repertoire that just a few years ago had been foreign to him. She might have found his glee appealing then, or maybe she hadn't, but since she had been new to San Francisco and hadn't known anybody yet she had allowed herself to find his glee appealing (his glee and his excessive focus on researching the music, as if to atone for the deficiencies in his musical training he was trying to become a librarian of sounds   did you know that Messiaen composed his Quartet for the End of Time in a German war camp? — I don't care I still don't like his monotheistic bird music, Antonio —), but now she chooses to dismiss his glee and his librarianism as a noxious attempt to differentiate himself from others, no different than a dentist sporting heavy metal tank tops emblazoned with creatures that could extirpate Messiaen's birds on earth, although the need to differentiate themselves had been what brought Masha and Antonio together: their contempt for those who stopple their lives for the promise of stocks, for instance, their unstated belief that what really matters exists in a parallel San Francisco of performances and paintings and poetry readings and yet unlike Antonio she detested poetry readings: why undermine your quiet text with your loud, needsome voice? At Antonio's farewell party the loud voices of the women there had confused her. Were these not the same philistines they had targeted with what they liked to call, in homage to Nabokov, their plumed opprobrium?

All the guests at Antonio's farewell party had been women. A blond American had opened Antonio's door. She seemed to know that she needed to pull the door extra hard against the bristly carpet, although she looked confused about why her pull also spilled her drink, and either because she was drunk or because Masha refused to smile at the girl's performance of cute bewilderment, the girl interrupted the welcoming skit that she'd seemed ready to enact for Masha, and yet as the girl in the tight jeans and pink pumps retreated down the hall, holding her Styrofoam cup as if it were a pet soaked in pee, and as the teleological dance beats coming from the living room concluded in a collective singalong — we want your soul! — Masha didn't keep Antonio's manuscripts rolled in her hand but returned them to her messenger bag, stashing them among his copy of A Werewolf Problem in Central Russia and her new palette knives and what was left of a bottle of corner store Pinot, the same brand that Antonio had offered her on the night they first met. She shouldn't have come unannounced. That she'd felt entitled to because she wanted to know if the fictions Antonio had given her were true seemed ridiculous to her now. That she'd been trying to make herself believe that was the real reason she'd come was even more ridiculous. She knew then as she knows now, as she listens to Scriabin's D Sharp Minor Etude from Antonio's compendium, that her five or six months with Antonio entitled her to nothing. She also knew, because he'd told her, that not only were all of his friends in San Francisco women, but all of his relationships with them lasted less than six months. Why return to these moments at his farewell party then? Just toss his manuscripts and his tiresome compendium. Does she find solace in reminding herself that the moment's over and she's become the only spectator of that embarrassing moment, Masha in her black turtleneck by Antonio's front door, trying to decide whether to leave what turned out to be Antonio's farewell party, or wade into the party and confront him with absolutely nothing? On the other side of his living room Antonio was dancing in the exuberant way he probably thought American women expected from him, just like his exuberant clothes were probably what Antonio thought American women expected from him, a South American in San Francisco, although his clothes were so outlandish that they looked more like a parody of what Antonio thought American women expected from him, or perhaps his clothes were a rebuff for expecting him to dress like this, or perhaps the extra slim white bell bottoms with the crimson flowers printed on them and his extra tight white linen shirt abloom with ruffles were simply a ploy to make American women think that he wasn't vain; that he favored the absurd not the vainglorious; that his clothes just happened to be tailored to accentuate his body and just happened to be expensive and that, unlike most Russian immigrants she didn't associate with, he wasn't brandishing these clothes as proof of European membership. On the other hand the more obvious possibility: Antonio had been having fun. Don't you wish Antonio would have taken you to at least one of those all night dance parties, Masha? Yes. Maybe I would have tolerated the dumb trochaic rhythms of his electronic dance music just to watch him twirl in his slim flower pants inside a warehouse in the South of Market, no, I wouldn't have tolerated it. I would have countermanded the excesses of the evening, which is probably why he never invited me. Or I would have drunk too much to thwart my tirades about his absurd costumes and a generation of young men hexed by, oh, enough, Mashinka. Enough.

—

I wanted to become a Jesuit priest, Antonio wrote, hoping his impulse to become a Jesuit priest when he was fifteen or sixteen and still living in Guayaquil could sustain a novella or at least a short fiction about youth and god and so on, the kind of fiction that would rhapsodize his volunteer work with Leopoldo at the hospice Luis Plaza Dañín and would exalt their roles as catechists to the poor in Mapasingue, and yet a week or two after writing down that first sentence about wanting to become a Jesuit priest, a week like every other week for him in San Francisco (happy hour at 111 Minna on

Wednesdays, a launch party for a new technology startup on Thursdays, an all night warehouse dance party on Fridays, and because he lived right behind Davies Symphony Hall and the War Memorial Opera House, and because he wanted to see and hear everything in the world — to become an expert on the unconscious one needs to know everything, Carl Jung said, and Antonio liked to believe that applied to becoming a writer, too — a symphony or an opera on Saturdays), Antonio concluded that although he wanted to write about his impulse to become a Jesuit priest when he was fifteen or sixteen, he wasn't interested in dramatizing his impulse to become a Jesuit priest through scenes and reversals and recognitions from the time of Aristotle, yes, let us please not follow the pious Ecuadorian boy who, after a series of intense religious experiences, including the apparition of La Virgen del Cajas, which Antonio was absolutely not going to write about for anyone in the United States (Leopoldo had been there, too), loses his faith as everyone eventually does, no, dramatizing his impulse to become a Jesuit priest with scenes and reversals and recognitions seemed to him contrary to everything he valued about fiction (his first adult encounter with fiction had been Borges, and it was only after he enrolled in an introductory fiction class at the Berkeley Extension that he was shown the flat world of Best American Realism — I discovered Borges because of Michaela from Sweden, Antonio would have liked to tell Leopoldo over the phone, a fellow economics student from Sweden who allowed me to stay with her during the winter break of my senior year at Stanford because I didn't have any money to fly anywhere that resembled home — listen to this, Leopoldo, a Mexican grad student who also had a crush on Michaela had handwritten a dedication on Borges's Ficciones that read Dear Michaela, after reading this book, you'll finally understand me — how does anyone understand anyone via Borges, Leo? — fiction that unfolds solely in Judas's head was how Antonio liked to think of Borges's fictions), so Antonio discarded his first sentence about wanting to become a Jesuit priest when he was fifteen or sixteen just as he had discarded his first sentence about wanting to become the president of Ecuador or at least the minister of finance and coming to the

United States to prepare himself to return and run for office with Leopoldo because what he had come to understand was that he didn't know how to write the kind of fiction he wanted to write, didn't think he had another option but to continue to work as a database analyst during the day and read as much as he could during the night until one day maybe he would come to know how to write the kind of fiction he wanted to write (to manufacture a sense of daily anticipation during his workweek at the check cashing technology startup where he ran database queries he would order novels without tracking numbers from different websites and wait for them to arrive before lunch so he could read them during his two hourlong lunches outside South Park Café), and then one day Leopoldo called him and said come back to Ecuador, Drool, and despite Antonio's copious explanations to himself about why he was no longer interested in returning to Ecuador to run for office (if the goal of running for office was simply to increase people's income — people we don't even know, Microphone — then he wasn't interested because playing the piano or writing fiction was more challenging and for him more personally rewarding — dilly dally all you want, Leopoldo would have countered, have your fun, we'll wait —), he didn't tell Leopoldo he wasn't interested in returning to Ecuador anymore, didn't explain anything to Leopoldo but instead said let me think it through — what exactly do you have to think through, Leopoldo would have countered if the phone lines had been less crossed   and the week or weeks after Leopoldo called him Antonio was surprised and not surprised that he'd been expecting Leopoldo's call even though he hadn't talked to Leopoldo in years (even on his deathbed he would still be expecting Leopoldo's call — out of bed, old man, the time to revolt is now — I do receive discounts on air travel now that I'm old and decrepit, Microphone —), even on his deathbed he would remember wanting to become a Jesuit priest when he was fifteen or sixteen because the logic of his impulse to become a Jesuit priest had been inarguable to him: if god was the pinnacle of life, one should dedicate one's life to god, but that hadn't been the last time he was inarguably certain about what to do with his life: the impulse to come to the

United States and study at a school like Stanford to prepare himself to return to Ecuador and run for office had been as inarguable a plan as wanting to become a Jesuit priest, and what he told himself to explain the evaporation of his impulse to return to Ecuador to run for office included the discovery of Borges and Scriabin, Merce Cunningham and Virginia Woolf (Antonio liked to tell his American acquaintances that if he hadn't come to the United States he would have never discovered Pina Bausch and Stanley Elkin, for instance — quit it with your Elkin and your Pina Bausch, Drool, what really changed your life plan was that you underperformed in your macro-economics class at Stanford and discovered women, or rather you discovered that, unlike in Guayaquil, here women actually pay attention to you, the exotic Ecuadorian), Cortázar and António Lobo Antunes, Claude Simon and Leonid Tsypkin, discovering the possibility of an alternative life in which he did not have to submit to embarrassing myths about himself — everyone thinks they're the chosen ones, Drool — although he had approached fiction and piano playing the same way, thinking of them not simply as activities to pass the time before he died but as transcendental callings, which was an exhausting way to live: but what I really wanted to tell you is that I loved Annie, Leopoldo, loved driving up to the Berkeley Hills to take piano lessons with this stern, elderly French lady named Annie, loved her two grand Steinway pianos and her tall bookcase with shelves like mail slots for sheet music only, her high heels clacking on the floorboards between her piano and her front door, loved how I tried to please her every week by switching on her metronome and showing her how much faster my fingers had become and at the same time displease her by picking piano pieces I wasn't ready to play, her husband, Bruce, a composer who praised my imprecise yet according to him tempestuous rendition of Scriabin's D Sharp Minor Etude and allowed me to practice in his piano shop by the Gilman Street freeway exit, loved hearing about Annie & Bruce's Evening Games in which she would play different records of the same piece for him, Chopin's Ballade No. 1, for instance, and then her husband had to guess who was the pianist, and one night, at the annual Halloween recital she organizes for her students, I showed up shirtless, wearing shiny red leotard pants and a boa around my neck, ready to perform Brahms's Ballade No. 1, and afterward one of her students, an Austrian psychotherapist who favored Maurice Ravel, said to me I couldn't concentrate on your Brahms because I kept imagining you in my bed, Antonio, to which neither I nor her husband had anything witty to add, and just as Antonio had intermixed two of Borges's fictions to come to think of Borges's fiction as fiction that unfolds solely in Judas's head, he'd also intermixed Annie with his impulse to return to Ecuador, Annie frowning at him like she always did after he attempted to play Scriabin's D Sharp Minor Etude and scolding him and saying you are a foolish one, Antonio José, for what made you think you were going to be allowed to stay in San Francisco and not return to Ecuador?

—

After a twenty one year absence my father returned to the church. The pious boy I was back then had convinced him to attend Christmas Mass, and, according to my grandmother, his return that night was what led to the baby christ's tears. Most in my family readily adopted my grandmother's version, as I was to do in the years that followed, sharing it with my American friends as another example of the quaint superstitions of my Third World country, which would often prompt in them comparisons to eyewitness news reports of Virgin Mary sightings on trunks of trees or mortadella sandwiches. Of course I suspected my grandmother's version was far too simple, but nothing ever compelled me to elaborate on it by implicating others or by including events that began long before that night.

Masha had forgotten to ask him about his grandmother's baby christ, just as she'd forgotten to hand him his manuscripts at his farewell party despite the inordinate amount of time she spent reddening them with recommended readings, allusions, panels of question marks, imagining a late night at Antonio's in which she was to hold forth, by Socratic questioning, like Akhmatova must have done with Osip — Akhmatova never piled obloquies on Osip, Masha — on the defects of his work. Did Antonio really witness a baby christ cry? Did his classmates at Stanford really mistake him for the son of the dictator of Ecuador? How could anyone expect her to have been the one to convince him to stay if he didn't even share anything about his life in Ecuador?

—

I enrolled in piano lessons soon after graduating from Stanford and accepting a lukewarm job at an economic consultant firm with absolutely no ties to Latin American development, Antonio wrote, hoping that by writing about the life he had chosen in San Francisco he could counter his impulse to return to Ecuador, an impulse that he knew was imprudent to pursue outside of his imagination and that was extensively documented in literature as a terrible idea — just because I was born in a poor country doesn't mean I'm obligated to return, right? I can become something else: why not a pianist? — so Antonio tried to write about his attempt to become a pianist after graduating from Stanford, beginning with his first piano lesson, Annie guiding his index finger to middle C, for instance, Annie tapping his knuckles with a number two pencil, him fumbling through his first le petit pieces to the delight of the Japanese premed students who happened to be studying in the common area where he'd found an upright piano and who happened to interrupt his clunkers with their variant of American snark, which of course drove him to practice longer and louder, and then he tried to write about how after just a year of practicing three hours a day he was able to play challenging pieces like Scriabin's D Sharp Minor Etude, and then he tried to write about how exhilarating it had been to discover Olivier Messiaen, who used to voyage to canyons and forests around the world to transcribe birdsongs, some of which can even mimic the city sounds around them, a French composer called Olivier Messiaen, who meticulously inked all of his birds, which he called, without irony, little servants of immaterial joy, into an opera about San Francis of Assisi: at the North American premiere of San Francis of Assisi, from the balcony section of the War Memorial Opera House,

I watched San Francis praying about what he calls the perfect joy, Leopoldo, in other words about the acceptance of suffering, which the orchestra and the ondes Martenots and the xylophones granted to him by performing an insistent, nervewrecking squawk of every single birdsong Messiaen had ever transcribed — can you imagine what Father Villalba would have said about calling such racket the Sermon of the Birds? — in unison all instruments mimicking a different birdsong, instruments with names as thrilling as the names of Messiaen's composition methods: nonretrogradable rhythms, limited modes of transposition — why shouldn't I be able to compose fiction or music or anything with names like that, Leopoldo? — and then a Russian painter called Masha said I can't take this racket anymore, Antonio, and Antonio said to hell with these birds, let's get out of here, standing up, the disapproval of the audience around him enlivening him so he laughed and tarried on purpose, pantomiming a clumsy, sluggish retreat along the row of wincing footwear, and then back at his apartment, emboldened by the champagne he'd ordered for them at Absinthe, Masha surprised him by taking off all her clothes except for her underwear, ambling toward him with her arms crossed to cover her chest, purposefully exaggerating her shyness so as to conceal her shyness, both of them outstretched on his sofa, the lights off in his apartment but on outside his windows, hearing the drunk tenors stumbling back to their station wagons because the night had been surprisingly warm so the living room windows were open, or perhaps he has ascribed the drunk tenors to that moment in retrospect because the San Francisco Opera's parking lot happened to be in front of his apartment building on Fulton Street and late at night he could often hear the drunk tenors stumbling back to their station wagons, wailing their arias in self mockery, and as Antonio tried to write about his attempt to become a pianist he came to realize that just as he used to think of himself as the boy who taught catechism to the poor and vowed to return to rescue them (he still thinks of himself as the boy who teaches catechism to the poor and vows to return to rescue them), he now also thinks of himself as the Ecuadorian who listens to extravagant classical music, and isn't it wonderfully freeing that no one here expects an Ecuadorian to know anything about Silvestrov's post-ludes or Messiaen's birdsongs?

—

I drink so I can bear talking to people, Antonio wrote. I acknowledge my conversational alcoholism. The more people converse with me, the more alcohol I am bound to imbibe. My liver, that most handsome of organs, was heard gossiping to my other organs about the absurdity of my social neurosis. Thank god my kidneys stood up for me and said shut up liver, you're drunk again. So your narrator drinks at parties, Masha wrote along the margins, then what? Yet another tale about the agonies of partying in the USA? Why not include some of your actual travails?

One morning she'd commented on the expensive red leather pants strewn on his bedroom floor and he'd whispered to her, as if they could hear them, they're uninvited guests, Mashinka, crashing for the night. Can you believe I allowed my cheap Acura Integra to be repossessed not only because I didn't need it anymore but because I wanted to use the monthly payment to buy more clothes? Can you believe I was fired from my first job at an economic consulting firm for falsifying receipts for meals I did and didn't have? Antonio behaved as if he'd come from money but that morning he told her his only income was his junior database analyst salary. He also told her that after all the startups in the South of Market ran out of cash and were forced to shutter their businesses, including the startup where he collected his paycheck, the only company hiring in San Francisco had been Bank of America. I interviewed for yet another database analyst position at Bank of America last week, Masha. A former marine who's now in charge of managing twelve million checking accounts asked me about challenges I've faced. Weaknesses? Where do you see yourself in five years? Sir, to tell you the truth, sir, this job would be temporary: I'm going to become the liberator of the Americas so I can only stay twenty to forty years tops.

Months later, at his farewell party, she enticed him away from the other women by telling him she had carefully read his manuscripts, avoiding at first any references to the actual travails he'd shared with her. So what do you think, Mashinka? Any hope for me as a writer? Wait, let's have another round of shots first. Antonio finished his shot and hers. She had forgotten that, although she didn't hand him his manuscripts with her comments, she did tell him what she thought of them, paraphrasing most of the red comments she has been rereading while listening to Tabula Rasa. You claim to despise so called conventional fiction, she said to him, you mock me for listening to Bach instead of John Cage, and then you write this extremely conventional fiction about a miraculous baby christ who cries because of the corruption of the narrator's father. She looked away while she said this, although she knows she's softening her defiance so she can feel better about herself. She knew Antonio had been writing for less than two years. Would he have stayed in San Francisco if she had lied and told him his fictions showed promise? Hints of brilliance? You seem to purposely exclude any clues as to why you're throwing all these words at us, Masha said. How can we distinguish the important and serious from the less important? Neither the festive atmosphere nor the shots lessened the impact of the harsh words she was foisting on him. Had she expected him to banter about her critiques? To refute her comments amusingly? He didn't. He looked embarrassed that he'd disappointed her. I'm sorry, Antonio. I wish I would have told you back then to wait, keep going, no one can write decent fiction in less than two years. The other day the televisions at my gym were showing a special about astronauts, Antonio said. Did you know my neon gym is my one link to American pop culture? I was on the Treadmaster watching all those silent televisions, and in spite of their muteness I could easily tell what the shows and the commercials were all about because they had cued up all their moments for me. Here's the moment of truth. Here's the moment of cereal. Plus some of the televisions had subtitles. What does it mean, Masha? When all our narratives have been cued up for us? Here's a moment for you: There was a radical old priest at my Jesuit high school and we were all in awe of him and for years I used to think of him as my mentor but I only spoke to him once, maybe twice. By the time I arrived at San Javier he had abdicated his role as a spiritual counselor because he thought my classmates and I were the problem. I wasn't the exception, but for years I imagined he'd been my spiritual sensei, my Narcissus, my Mister Miyagi. But it doesn't really matter, right? Our faux narratives affect us just the same. Here's a narrative for you: one time I stayed on the Treadmaster for more than two hours because the music channel was showing a documentary about a former member of Menudo, a Latin American boy band that was popular when I was in middle school. This represents at least a hundred words I was not counting on. Come, Antonio said, pulling her to his bedroom, I want you to meet Alvin Lucier.

—

Not yet asleep on her living room sofa, as she listens to Tabula Rasa amid boxes she still needs to retape and ship to her new life at NYU's film program, boxes where she may or may not toss in Antonio's reddened manuscripts, she wonders if years from now she will only remember Antonio because of Tabula Rasa, the only piece out of all the contemporary pieces he'd included in his compendium that turned into a favorite (in a few days she will move away from San Francisco like everyone else, leaving behind friends who were really acquaintances who paired up with her simply to avoid going out at night by themselves and who will not remember her just as Antonio won't remember them and she won't remember him — every moment is an ending, Arvo Pärt said, every five minutes there's an ending do you understand? — no, I don't —), and perhaps all that will remain of San Francisco for her will be Tabula Rasa and the vague contours of Antonio at his farewell party (why hadn't she interrupted his drunk ramblings with questions or asides or by shouting at him why are you leaving? — you didn't want him to think you cared? — I did and didn't, do you understand? — on the one hand everything will pass and on the other nothing will pass and I miss Antonio's dumb sprint toward everything in the world —), and perhaps she will also remember that first night with Antonio at Bistro Stelline, and afterwards how surprised she'd been at how much he'd revealed about himself and how quickly she'd accepted his invitation to come to his apartment, although he didn't phrase it as an invitation but simply slipped his hand on hers and said come, Masha, no, Antonio, she didn't say, I just met you, no, Masha thinks as she listens to Tabula Rasa, she will toss Antonio's ersatz fiction in her recycling bin along with her unused canvases and be done with a life in San Francisco she will not remember once she settles in New York.

—

I'd never listened to classical music before, Antonio wrote, at home in Guayaquil no one unwrapped the classical cassette collection compiled by the Encyclopedia Salvat because on the one hand my mother favored the melodrama of José José, not melodrama, no, let's call it pickled fatalism, while on the other hand I favored the pickled nihilism of Guns N' Roses: to me symphonic music as elemental as Tchaikovsky's Pathétique sounded like sap from soundtracks, so to train my ear I started listening to easy Satie piano pieces, then I moved on to Mozart sonatas, a movement at a time, which Annie was glad to supply for me, sharing her recordings of the complete Beethoven sonatas by Richard Goode, of Schumann's Symphonic Etudes by Alfred Brendel, everything by Sviatoslav Richter and nothing by Glenn Gould, and after I exhausted Annie's music stash I ventured out on my own, driving to the shopping outlets in Sonoma or Saint Helena and listening to Scriabin's sonatas or Prokofiev's piano concertos or whatever I'd purchased at random from the classical music section at Tower Records that same afternoon, no, not at random, those listening / driving sessions were life projects to me so the recordings had to be of (a) longer piano pieces and of (b) composers I didn't yet know, and perhaps because I didn't yet know too many classical pieces besides the ones that Annie was introducing me to through analog recordings of Sviatoslav Richter and tapes of master classes she'd attended at Berkeley, which I was borrowing from her because I'd refused to play the little Bach pieces she'd assigned to me from the Notebook for Anna Magdalena Bach and therefore needed to know what else was out there, purchasing a recording before setting out to Sonoma or Saint Helena still felt like a chance activity, and although Annie had cautioned me against listening to piano music while driving because the onrush of road underneath obfuscates the nuances that I should be listening for, especially when the markings of a phrase demanded pianissimo, I did it anyway, purchasing Prokofiev's piano concertos because Annie frowned upon Prokofiev — if you would have lived in San Francisco with me I would have immediately shared with you that as a young student at the St. Petersburg Conservatory Prokofiev would sneak into the concert hall before a performance to pencil wrong notes into the scores, Leopoldo — and then one night at Annie's house, after she examined the cover of my sheet music binder that read Antonio's Piano Career, and after she laughed at it as one laughs at the silly refrains of children, I parked outside Gordo's Taquería on Solano Street and cloistered myself inside my car, forcing myself to listen to the first movement of Tchaikovsky's Pathétique until it made sense to me, which must have been a long while because the burrito folk started eyeing me suspiciously: by the time I was done training my ear, I had to accept that it was too late; that there was more to playing the piano than pressing the right notes; that I would never achieve a competitive level of pianism and would never become a pianist: well, why not a writer?

—

I Am Sitting in a Room by Alvin Lucier: I am sitting in a room, Alvin Lucier said, different from the one you are in now. I am recording the sound of my speaking voice, and I am going to play it back into the room, again and again, until the resonant frequencies of the room reinforce themselves. Was this Antonio's idea of a prank? Or was his insistence to have her listen to this piece just a pretext to seclude himself with her by his bed? Antonio wasn't laughing, and the door to his bedroom wasn't locked, but neither was sufficient evidence to refute her hypotheses. So that any semblance of my speech, Lucier said, with perhaps the exception of rhythm, is destroyed. What you will hear, then, if you ignore the reverb and the space sounds of the electronic dance music coming from his living room, where his farewell party wasn't ebbing yet — can you believe it? Antonio's going back to do the Peace Corps in his own country! — are the natural resonant frequencies of the room, articulated by speech. What you won't hear is Antonio relaying his unspoken expectation of her to her: concentrate, Masha, music isn't just counterpoint and variations. But I regard this activity, Lucier said, not so much as a demonstration of a physical fact, but more as a way to smooth out any irregularities my speech might have. I am sitting in a room, different from the one you are in now. After the seventh or eighth iteration she stopped listening in for surprises. Lucier was simply shearing his voice and what remained was metallic noise. His fingers surprised her by grazing her lips. She didn't smile so he did it again, this time acting as if he was clearing bread crumbs, stepping back, drunk like the rest of them — all of my friends here are party friends, Mashinka — turning his left hand into a bird, fingers like antlers, as he had done the night they stormed out of the premiere of Messiaen's San Francis de Assisi. Whatever he saw in her face saddened him but he was a quick one, raising his index finger in mockery, as if he had just remembered something important: aha, yes, he had to stop his double decker and tap the other portable player to check that it was still running. Are you recording this, Antonio? He nodded, motioning with his hand to please recite something for him. Sure, why not? She could recite something he wasn't likely to know: here is my gift, she could recite, not roses on your grave, not sticks of burning incense: alone you let the terrible stranger in, she could recite, and stayed with her alone: only my voice, like a flute, she could recite, will mourn at your dumb funeral feast: but she didn't feel like giving him that satisfaction. Later that night, at her apartment, she was to recite those lines out loud to herself. They're opening a new crêpe place on Gough, she said. I'm sorry I didn't call you about the party, Masha. I figured you would hate it anyway. Or that you would expect to find painters like you, pianists and poets, a salon. All last minute anyway. I'm leaving. I was going to call you and tell you. To Ecuador? Where else, Masha? Berlin, Barcelona, New

York? Guayaquil has one performance arts center named after one of our presidents who was praised by Reagan for his strong armed tactics. The shows mostly comedies there? Antonio laughed. Then he sat down on the bench by his bed and cried. Was this another ploy of his to embarrass her? To expose her callousness? To repulse her with his self pity? No. He probably would have cried even if she wasn't there. Or wouldn't have cried if she was there but hadn't dismissed his manuscripts. Or if she would have asked him to tell her more about Alvin Lucier. How easy it is to discourage aspiring writers. Because of his flower pants and his ruffled shirt she still expected him to turn his crying into a joke. He didn't. She didn't know then that this would be the last time she would see him. That her last gestures toward him would be nongestures: no sitting next to him on his bench, arms around his shoulders, trying to convince him to stay. Imagine a different life in Berlin or New York, where you could walk out of operas like Messiaen's every week. Goodbye, Antonio.

III / LEOPOLDO AND THE OLIGARCHS

Along the empty municipal hallway León Martín Cordero dashes to a press room that will have no chairs, no lamps, no bouquets of microphones like those favored by El Loco, no podium but instead a rolltop from where he will enact Leopoldo's idea of summoning the two thousand four hundred and ninety pipones that El Loco indiscriminately added to the previous payroll. Prostitutes and junkies who would only materialize on payday and whom he wiped from the books on his first day as mayor of Guayaquil, carajo, summoning them now under the pretext that they'll be reinstated to the payroll, please bring your official letter with you, not knowing that he has also summoned the press so that their cameras will remind the nation of El Loco's repulsive brand of graft, and yet as Leopoldo waits for León Martín Cordero to finish dashing along the hallway, Leopoldo's sure León's not thinking about Leopoldo's idea or about the lawsuit against him for his alleged human rights violations during his tenure as president, no, not thinking that now they have the nerve to complain, conclave of ingrates, now because they think that I've been enfeebled by a minor eye surgery (his right eye was replaced by a glass one) or by a routine coronary bypass (his third in ten years) or because of rumors that I have lung cancer and even

(Doctor Arosemena cannot yet confirm to Leopoldo if León has Alzheimer's)

all of which I've survived just as in my youth I survived three bullets unscathed, carajo, now they have the nerve to complain instead of thanking me for ridding this country of terrorists like Alfaro Vive Carajo, now they like to pretend they weren't panicking about what could've happened to their husbands, ay mi Luchito, ay mi Alvarito, all of whom were at risk of being kidnapped like Nahim Isaías had been kidnapped by that tracalada of thieves who called themselves guerrilleros, ay Mister President, ay Leoncito, do whatever it takes to weed them out, now they like to prattle about so called truth panels instead of thanking me like Reagan thanked me by gifting me a miniature .38 caliber automatic that I still carry under my

(an articulate champion of free enterprise)

and yet as Leopoldo waits for León Martín Cordero to finish dashing along the hallway, Leopoldo's sure León's not thinking about Leopoldo's plan or about El Loco's graft or about the lawsuit against León for his alleged human rights violations but about Jacinto Manuel Cazares, who an hour earlier had asked for permission to write León's biography, arriving precisely when Leopoldo opened León's door, as if this Cazares individual, a former classmate of Leopoldo who nevertheless looks like the son of a horsekeeper raised by law clerks, had synchronized himself to León, courtesy of some municipal snoop who'd relayed the data from León's wristwatch, some sneak who shook León's hand and managed to extract León's data to the millisecond, some groveler or someone posing as a groveler just like this Jacinto Cazares individual who showed up with Volume III of León's Thoughts and Works, which had been published by the National Secretariat of Public Information when León was president and that León probably overlooked as a prop of ingratiation because that impossible to find volume describes the most ambitious highway system the country had ever seen, plus it was tagged with so many sticky notes that it looked like a flattened sandwich or a

(León's daughter Mariuxi used to collect centipedes)

look Son, three foreign publishing houses and one international television network have offered me large sums of money to allow them to write about me and I've always refused because I'm not going to begin at this stage in my life to have the vanity of having someone write about my life when the only merit I presume to have is that I have fulfilled my duty and above all other considerations have abided by a strict respect for the law.

Mister President the reporters are here.

But you are the one leader of this nation who could serve as an example for our youth.

Mister President?

From afar León's leaning on Leopoldo's shoulder probably looks like gesture of camaraderie, although of course Leopoldo doesn't care if this is what it looks like, nor does he care that unfortunately no one's around to witness what this looks like, León's right hand man here, folks, Leopoldo Arístides Hurtado, nor does it matter if he cares because everyone at the municipality already knows he's León's right hand man. What Leopoldo does care about is León's tubercular coughing. Not that he knows what tubercular coughing sounds like. Although he's heard something like it before. At the hospice Luis Plaza Dañín that Leopoldo and Antonio used to visit when they were sophomores at San Javier the coughing of the old and the infirm sounded tubercular. Like a calling, too: talk to me, visit me, and at the same time like a refusal: we're still here! Today León's coughing is partly Leopoldo's fault though. Leopoldo knew that if he didn't intercept León on the way to the press room, if he didn't slow him down with administrative checklists, León was likely to swagger down the hallway at an overtaxing speed. The same speed León's been brandishing since he was prefect. The same swagger of someone who could afford to leave his post as head of Industrial Molinera to become senator of Guayas, president of Ecuador, mayor of Guayaquil, of someone who once campaigned on horseback, who once ordered tanks to flank a congress that wouldn't stamp his decrees, who once traversed the country atop caravans that would quadruple in size from Machala to Naranjal, from Babahoyo to Jipijapa, who toward the end of his presidential campaign gathered at a stadium abloom with signs and flags and chants of bread, roof, and employment in which he swore, in front of god and the Republic, that he will never betray them. Leopoldo grew up with those words. That stadium. León wreathed by a procession of children. Sweating as if inspirited by his people or by a sorrow he must overcome to swear, no, in that stadium León's voice breaks off, as if allowing the echo of his voice to reach as far as Esmeraldas and Calceta, Macas and Junín. I swear, in front of god and the Republic, but then León breaks off again, as if taking in the gravity of his promise. I swear, in front of god and the Republic, that I will never betray you. On the field and on the stands the crowd bursts. Some are chanting León / León / León. Others are jumping in unison and waving their flags. On his father's shoulders, Leopoldo waves his flag, too. It's yellow like the others and tiny like his hands. His father isn't waving his sign though. He'd been flapping it tirelessly since they boarded a pickup at La Atarazana but now he doesn't move. Because of the commotion around them Leopoldo cannot tell why his father shivers as if he's cold. It's not cold. It's hot and humid and the headlights are exacerbating the heat and everyone's soaked and screaming along or in spite of the loudspeakers that are unburdening themselves of songs. His father's sign is staked on the grass and his hands are resting on it as if it's a waypost that has appeared just for him. His father's about to rest his forehead on his hands, oblivious to his son on his shoulders, who's instinctively tilting backwards as his father tilts forward, but then his father straightens as if he's been pricked and shrieks. Anda que te parió un burro. My back. Bread, roof, and employment. With León it can be done. The rally ends. León wins. His father flees in the wake of an embezzlement scandal. Leopoldo finds himself one night, groggy and cold, in the dark living room of the old Centenario house. His mother is gone and the bald domestic is watching troglodytes on a screen that flickers like a lantern on a boat. They're clobbering each other and sniffing the bark of giant palm trees. The living room smells like burnt veal. Then a tidal wave rises like a hand that's also a spider and swallows everything. The end. Go back to sleep, Negrito. León's tubercular coughing worries him. And yet today Leopoldo didn't intercept León dashing down the hall. He had too much to coordinate before the press conference about El Loco. Besides, León was busy giving audience to that Jacinto Cazares individual (known at San Javier as Funky Town, Excrement, Thief).

León tries to contain his coughing with his fist, which seems pointless, although this thought strikes Leopoldo as pointless too, for what else can anyone do? How ungenerous of him. And how ludicrous to make yet another vow of compassion toward his fellow men. As if to rebuke him, León's coughing ends. He grimaces, irritated at having Leopoldo witness his coughing, or trying to discern why this dark kid's standing so close to him. León shakes Leopoldo's hand with both hands as if campaigning at a kindergarten, but before Leopoldo has time to consider the absurdity of León's gesture he starts coughing again. Down the hall two reporters are peering at them. Leopoldo shields León from the reporters by shifting sideways, placing one hand on León's shoulder and the other on León's back, patting it three times, soothing him, before Leopoldo realizes what he's doing. León doesn't mind or hasn't noticed but Leopoldo pulls back nevertheless. The reporters still need an interpretable gesture. Leopoldo leans to León's ear, cupping his hand as if blinkering them from what he's conferring about with León, and if Leopoldo could he would blinker himself from seeing León like this, for even the most generous bystander would agree that León looks like a disheveled Santa, or a one eyed wheezer, or a strained Lear unlike the King Lear that Leopoldo's grandmother, on her farm in the outskirts of Manabí, would perform for Leopoldo after baking him his favorite sugar rolls, tying a white plastic bag on her head like a wig and then hobbling while she proclaimed, in unintelligible English, blo win, crack you cheek, rage!, blo!, her voice steeped in the same excitement she will use years later when Leopoldo's about to deliver his valedictorian speech, sharing with the distinguished parents in the audience how as a boy, barely reaching the veranda of her balcony, little Leo would spend hours giving speeches to the passing trucks and sometimes even an ambulatory salesman would stop and clap and try to sell little Leo pink ceramic piggy banks — los chanchitos la alcancíaaa — and while Leopoldo delivers his speech his grandmother hears León saying to his wife carajo, that kid sounds just like me.

El Loco's people are arriving as planned. I have everything under control.

You? You have everything under . . . ?

León sidesteps him so Leopoldo has to scramble behind like a domestic who should've known better, a domestic who's carrying León's briefcase, which contains the Cohiba cigars that Fidel still ships to León, a recommendation letter so Alvarito Rosales can be admitted into Babson College, a stockwhip from León's ranch that León plans to unleash on El Loco's people, brown shoe polish for his cowboy boots, double chocolate wafer crumbs from La Universal, called Tango for no good reason.

How are the horses, Mister President? Marcial still on a winning streak? How are the Dobermans? The bonsais growing nicely? Shooting at the range this weekend?

It's never easy to tell when León's in the mood to chat with reporters. Definitely not today. The reporters and the film crew arrange themselves on the floor, by the one rolltop oak desk.

León preempts questions about the human rights lawsuit against him by lecturing them about antiterrorist practices around the world.

Leopoldo, following the press conference from the side, by the wall with the chomped wallpaper, has heard all about it before. By now everyone else has, too. León had secretly contracted an Israeli antiterrorist expert during his presidency and together they eliminated so many people that, unlike in Colombia and Perú, we have no more of those terrorists here, no more of those antisocials whose dissatisfactions were irrelevant because that's why we installed a democracy here, carajo, if they wanted change they should've run for office, a strong hand had been needed and that was the end of it, and yet if Leopoldo never hears another word from strong armed despots like León (no, León isn't looking over this way), if he doesn't read another word about these autocrats or caudillos or patriarchs or whatever you want to call them, he would be the, bah, he doesn't know if he would be the better for it. He just doesn't want to hear about them anymore.

León's strong arm performance, interrupted by his coughing, continues. Leopoldo tries not to think about El Loco's people waiting outside. What does he care about El Loco's people anyway? With his handkerchief he wipes his face slowly, careful not to appear desperate, but not too slowly so as to appear like he's applying face powder. Should he have his initials embroidered on his handkerchief? Light gray would be the best color. Because light gray goes with everything. He could do it himself, too. Unlike Antonio, whose longhand was as uneven as his flare ups, which ranged from sobbing on the soccer field after losing a game to hurling his calculator against the back wall of their classroom after supposedly botching a physics exam — hey, the Snivel's here, watch your calculators, fellows — Leopoldo excelled in calligraphy. He still has a few of those lined notebooks with the translucent paper. Though of course excellence in calligraphy does not equate to excellence in embroidery. Just as excellence in history does not necessarily equate to being chosen to write León's biography. Just as extreme intelligence does not necessarily equate to a nomination from León for the upcoming elections, or any elections, even a little one, ever. There's even a rumor that Cristian Cordero, also known as the Fat Albino, that pretentious agglomerate of flab, one of the laziest students at San Javier, who would only show up at Leopoldo's doorstep to borrow the answers to their calculus homework, and who also happens to be León's grandson — don't think of you groveling after the Fat Albino to obtain a recommendation for the post as León's domestic, Microphone — might be running for president. At San Javier, Antonio lost two out of three fights against the Fat Albino. Does Antonio remember those fistfights at the Miraflores Park? Does he remember teaching catechism in Mapasingue with Leopoldo? Does he remember their work at the hospice Luis Plaza Dañín? From a wicker basket they would hand bread to the bedstricken inside rooms the size of hangars. The elderly waited for them along the hallway, one of them waiting for Antonio at the farthest end. Rosita Delgado? Once, before Antonio arrived at the hospice, Rosita unwrapped for Leopoldo a photograph Antonio had gifted her: Antonio as a boy in a cardboard penguin costume. Years later that boy in the costume became a Stanford economist who has come back to discuss their role in the upcoming presidential elections. Leopoldo checks his watch. He will be meeting with Antonio in thirty two minutes. They're just meeting to talk, nothing definite yet, the country's too unstable for León to find out, not that he's going to let León find out, that he's conspiring with Antonio to run in the upcoming presidential elections. Antonio's probably expecting an audacious plan from him. Which Leopoldo actually has.

Sort of. He pockets his handkerchief. Calligraphy and embroidery are probably not related at all.

Mister President, are you reconsidering your party's position of not nominating a presidential candidate for the upcoming elections? Mister President, are you ever going to run for president again? Mister President, are you ever going to buy furniture for this building?

I won't buy anything for this building, Leopoldo hears León say, indignant as ever, narrowing his eyes, or at least one of them, and like a priest denouncing the stench of sin he points at the vacant corners of the room, as if the corners had anything to do with it, as if once upon a time León flunked geometry just like his grandson flunked everything but flute lessons, although of course Leopoldo knows that León never flunked anything and that this pointing is just León's theatrical way of enumerating the missing clerk desks, reception desks, oak chairs, tin chairs, white paper, brown paper, air fresheners, copy machines, washing machines, phone lines, phone cords, everything that was carried away by the friends and family of El Loco. Except the rolltop. That'd been too heavy to haul. Everyone had seen the looted palace on television. And yet to most people the images of the sacked rooms had not seemed surreal or incredibly despairing but funny. Everyone's saying that they found nothing but a pig chomping on the wallpaper, Don Leopoldo. That the pig's tiny ears made her nose look unnecessarily big. And on top of that she smelled like garbage. Oh but Elsa the Pig did not care. She munched on the municipal wallpaper and did not care. That's how the idea of summoning El Loco's people occurred to Leopoldo. People weren't outraged, he'd told León. Everyone thinks it's funny. Extra, niño Leo, read it here first: León's Right Hand Man Pockets Pensions and Roars to Miami. Check it out, Microphone Head, Fraud Forces Francisco Swett to Jet to Florida. Extra, Don Leopoldo, Jeffrey the Hutt Escapes Prison Order and Flees to Miami. Jeffrey Torbay did look like Jabba the Hutt, which made his embezzlement during León's presidency even more sinister. Everyone's saying that Jeffrey the Hutt opened a nightclub in Miami Beach, Don Leopoldo. That they're calling it Ecuador Bar & Beer. Although more likely it was called The Palace or The Cathedral or The

Mansion and its doors were probably flanked with pit guards spurnful of dark Mexicans and blacks. The other thing Leopoldo didn't tell León is that everyone still remembers El Loco lashing a stockwhip out the window of the municipal palace, promising to flog oligarchs like León during El Loco's tenure as police chief.

I won't buy anything for this building until the people realize the extent of that man's corruption, Leopoldo hears León say. That swindler shouldn't be allowed to return. Accomplished and honest professionals are what our country needs.

Is León showcasing Leopoldo as an example of an accomplished and honest professional? The reporters seem to be wondering the same thing because they're turning to appraise Leopoldo. Do they remember what Leopoldo has accomplished for the city? Do they remember that El Loco and his cohorts had also emptied the city's coffers and that that's the other reason León can't buy anything for this building? Or that León had shut down the empty palace and jumpstarted a tax collection campaign to replenish the coffers but what he collected he had to immediately disburse to avert an epidemic because the sewers had clogged somewhere and black water was inundating the streets and the rainy season hadn't even started and on the way to work people were seeing rats splashing for life? Leopoldo approaches the window on the other side of the room to check on El Loco's people. To keep it manageable Leopoldo had only summoned two hundred out of the two thousand four hundred and ninety pipones, and yet outside more than two hundred are already crowding the courtyard, spilling onto the streets and gardens, he should've anticipated that more than two hundred would show up, although perhaps his arithmetic is off? One by the oyster stand, two by the juice vendor (hey, is that Facundo Cedeño?), three by the, well, don't worry too much, Leo, no one's going to notice in any case. Across the room Leopoldo signals León. Let us begin.

—

Facundo Cedeño, sporting cream polyester pants and a brown SPAM tee shirt, which barely covers his ventripotence, or as his classmates at San Javier used to call it, his bus driver beer bulge, I'll show you a bulge!, he would retort to them, adopting a leader of the hencoop posture, a poultry falsetto, a mock priapic strut along with grabfuls of his storied maid killer under his school jeans, the same cotton butt jeans that used to be an indefatigable source of school hall badinage, the latter word, incidentally, being the kind of word that Facundo would often call out for clarification during Who's Most Pedantic: ba the bleet of sheep, di the circus interlude, nage the Vader belch: baah, dee, NAAAAAGE, transmogrifying their recondite words as payback for their mocking of his shabby, ill fitting jeans that would drop on him just as his cream polyester pants, two sizes too big, are dropping on him as he stands on the steps of the municipal palace.

Buying a belt is a passing thought amid the Saharan heat. No sand here though. No Arabian ghost masks either. A limerick about camels and parasols is a passing thought as he spots a juice vendor on the other side of the courtyard. A pint of papaya juice would be swell. Not as swell as my belly here, eh? Eh? Ha ha. This round fellow here, his grandfather used to say as he petted his whale of a belly, is worth thousands. Everyone always laughed at that joke. And yet when Facundo tried it on his audience at La Ratonera no one did. Pretend you're old and still living in a mud hut and they'll roar over, Facundito, Grandpa Paul had explained. Facundo straightens his hands like a visor, eyeing the courtyard like an explorer overseeing the Americas. A limerick about Cortez is a passing thought as he spots an oyster stand, a tricycle of sorts, which also looks promising as relief from the heat. A catfish look alike is placing his oysters by his ear before slurping them, as if expecting to hear their last words. Don't eat me, catfish! Kiss me, catfish! Mrkrgnao. Too many people are thronging the courtyard. Too many people are beached on the stairs. Some of them are grousing about the long wait, others about the jump in the price of lentils, others about weevils in the rice imported from Thailand by a minister who fled the day before his prison order was issued, about the probabilistic that El Loco might return to squash those corrupt oligarchs conchadesumadres in the upcoming presidential elections. Shush it, Fabio, León might hear you and pop your eye. You think weevils are crunchy, compadre? To traverse the crowded courtyard for some juice of dubious sapidity, not to mention its dubious coldness, for even if the juice vendor had the strength to carry the weight of the buckets plus juice plus ice blocks, he probably loaded the ice early in the morning so it must be all melted by now, yuck, well, hold on, why do I have to traverse anything? Hey juice man. Psst. Over here. At a miraculous speed the skeletal juice man approaches him.

How much for your punch?

Twenty five, patroncito.

Getting sly on me?

Fifteen and fresh from the fruit, patroncito.

Say again?

Ten and to the brim, patroncito.

Facundo pulls a photocopy of an official looking letter with the municipal seal, waving it like an eviction notice in front of the lanky juice man, whose roasted body reeks of shrimp, and whose veiny arms are overtensed by the buckets' weight.

I'm with the municipality. This juice's probably a health hazard. Let me see your permit.

The defeated look of the juice man seems like an obvious exaggeration, no? As if he's not used to it? Right. What an actor. The juice man squats to set the buckets down but right before they touch the cement he changes his mind and lets them drop. Flatly they land on the step. The skinned bean jars clink against each other. Splashes of red juice land on his rubber sandals. He submerges his hand into the water bucket, the one where he rinses the jars, retrieves one, and then inserts it inside the other bucket, the one with the juice and the ice.

Free for you, patron.

Ah. Much better. Nice and cold.

A limerick about gluttony is a passing thought as he swills the juice. The juice man is eyeing the smoke clouds nearby. Hoping for what? The smog of retribution? The avenging thunderbolt? Facundo tries to appease the juice man, sticking his teeth out, bunnylike, diligently wiping his curd from the rim of the jar. Nothing. No funnybone on this one. Facundo hands him back the empty jar. At a miraculous speed the juice man vanishes inside the crowd.

More arrivals stream to the front, by the stairs, mostly because there's no line but eventually there'll be a line and then they'll be first, not knowing there's probably a long wait ahead, not caring about crowding the courtyard further, hey, stop pushing, quit shoving. A green balloon escapes from someone's grip but doesn't drift up. Facundo swats the limp balloon, which tries to float, like an eyeball above them, toward a magician who's selling lottery tickets and stuffed pets. The magician releases the balloon as if it were a dove on a mission, find the fig little one, fly. The balloon lollops by the magician's feet, landing by three businessmen in blue suits. One of them scoops the balloon from the floor, careful not to scratch his cufflinks, holding it from its knot and fretting it against his fist. The other two businessmen are comparing his municipal letter with theirs. The businessmen inspect their surroundings, confirming their suspicions that everyone but the street vendors, those cholos and lowlifes, are also carrying a municipal letter, some of them carrying the original document, others probably carrying a counterfeit of the original document, which states that all municipal employees hired by El Loco will be reinstated to the payroll, your one time appearance is required at the municipal palace. Something's fishy, one of the businessmen says. I don't think El Loco loaded this many riffraffs into payroll. I couldn't get ahold of El Loco today either. The other two businessmen agree. Something is fishy. Shield your wallets, gentlemen, and let's get the hell out of here. The magician tells someone who tells someone who tells someone what they overheard those businesspeople say, and as the something's fishy rumor spreads some are saying I don't care if El Loco's Loco or Sapo, at least he cared enough to write us a check, which I desperately need to buy textbooks, someone says, to buy powdered milk, someone else says, to pay the water truck, someone else says, to rent a washing machine, someone else says, and I've traveled far, someone says, I've traveled far. No one flees. Everyone remains in place. The oyster man turns the dial of his portable radio, skipping from song snippet to static to the interim president has just announced a new package of tightening measures, to Wilfrido Vargas and his papi no seas así / no te pongas guapo / ese baile les gusta a todos los muchachos. The balloon wanders back to Facundo. This time he picks it up. As he reaches the oyster stand, he digs his nails on the balloon and . . .

An explosion. A shot? A gunshot? No one's down. Everyone hunts for the origin of the explosion. Where? Where?

Now folks please direct your attention over here, Facundo says, displaying his balloon shreds like a flight attendant. Just the balloon popping here, folks. Nothing to worry about. No one laughs. Everyone's so frazzled here, Facundo thinks. Well. He'll find a way to make them laugh. He towels his hands with his tee shirt, as if purging himself of his streak of lame jokes, and then he says to the oyster man oiga ñañón, turn that tune up. The oyster man shrugs and turns up the dial. Wilfrido Vargas is singing El Baile del Perrito. Everybody knows this merengue. Ladies and, okay, gentlemen too, my impression of our current mayor, our lion and grand patriarch, the one and only León, Martín, Corrrrrrdero. The doors to the palace are still shut so the crowd's free to gather around the fat man, who's dropping on all fours and is imitating the fast barks of the merengue, shaking his rear as if he's the mayor eagerly wagging his tail for El Loco, who must have ordered León to reinstate all of them to the payroll, someone says, and although León has never been known for following anyone's orders, especially those of El Loco, the crowd claps and hoots and sings if something I owe you / with this I repay you / if something I owe you / with this I repay you. Hey fatty, someone says, do you think El Loco ordered León to throw us a party? Hey SPAM man, someone else says, do you think he hired Los Iracundos to sing for us? Do you think El Loco ordered that oligarch to raise our salaries? Do you think?

The doors to the municipal palace finally open. About time, someone says. León, trailed by a film crew, dashes out. The television cameras are aiming at the courtyard, scanning them from side to side like security cameras. The reporters are mouthing into their microphones as if chronicling a flood or a raffle. Someone at the bottom of the stairs waves his arms at the cameras. Someone by the oyster stand waves her letter. Others next to her wave theirs, too. Hundreds wave their letters like handkerchiefs at a ship. But what's wrong with León? He's just standing there. Covering his mouth with his fist as if about to inflate himself? To knock someone out? He looks pissed. Hey fatty, someone says, why don't you go talk to León and see what's going on? Yeah fatty, someone else says, go. What? Me? Ha ha. But apparently they're not kidding. The crowd parts for him, forming a passageway through the courtyard, up the stairs, to León Martín Cordero. An old woman who's pressing a rag to her nose reminds Facundo of the smell of burnt tires. Someone pushes him forward. Okay, fine, I'm going. Facundo tries to underplay his assignment by highfiving the crowd. Not everyone plays along. The ones that do smile at him too effusively, like parents congratulating their son for coming in eleventh place. On the stairs the party's over. Behind him the crowd goes silent. Facundo extends his hand to León but León refuses it. Hey there's Leopoldo! Leopoldo's approaching him but he's shaking his head discreetly at Facundo as if saying no, Facundo, you can't know me here.

How many of you are there?

Uh, not enough?

On the courtyard everyone sees León gesticulating and shouting but what's León saying?, someone asks, what's he so angry about?, someone else asks, and then they see León brush the fat man aside so the fat man stumbles, sideways and backwards, tripping down the stairs, where some of them are already shouldering their way out, which is unworkable because most of the people by the stairs are staying put, wondering if perhaps the fat man offended León somehow, if perhaps the fat man's drunk, if perhaps the agape briefcase that León's assistant is presenting to León contains their paychecks, and yet what León removes from his briefcase isn't a wad of paychecks or a scroll with a welcoming speech but a whip that he's uncoiling as he points at them as if they're the scum of the earth, snapping the whip as he charges down the stairs, where most of them recoil but do not move, as if they still can't believe the slashes and imprecations

are meant for them, but then the whip cuts them and they're fleeing now, pushing each other as León calls them leeches, cockroaches,
bloodsuckers. On the far end of the courtyard the crowd seems to
have caught wind of what's happening because they're running in
all directions now, and because those cramped in the middle of the
courtyard cannot run yet they're jostling each other even more. Later
they will see their stampede on television and hear that on top of trying to swindle the city El Loco's rabble trampled seven women and
three men in front of the municipal palace.

The courtyard has been cleared.

The overturned tricycle, the spilled juice, the cracked jars, the
scattered oyster shells, the stained lottery tickets must seem unfortunate to León. Ill omens of some kind. Not the time, however, to be
indulging in superstitions. It probably isn't clear to the senator from
Guayaquil, to the governor from Guayas, as he tries to breathe, what
the time is for, or whether he

—

Leopoldo should've had a firmer grip on León's briefcase. After León
charges down the stairs and inadvertently pushes Leopoldo, the briefcase lands facing down, away from Leopoldo, as if resentful he'd let it
drop. The business of collecting its contents, of crouching after shoe
polish amid a commotion he'd rather not see, of squatting and toil-
ing after a recommendation letter so Alvarito Rosales can be admitted
into Babson College, so that Alvarito can pretend to study business administration at an institution that won't flunk him, so that
Alvarito can then return to run his father's prawn business or run
for office with promises of bread, roof, and employment — Alvarito
Rosales, the candidate of the poor — has to be done. But when does it
end? Leopoldo's father like Antonio's father like Stephan's father like
Nelson's father like Carlos's father like Eduardo's father had embezzled and fled the country because they knew that was their one shot at
getting ahead. Leopoldo and Antonio had refused to accept that. And
then one day the newly appointed minister of finance fired Leopoldo
from his hard earned post as a senior economist at the Central Bank

so that the minister could hire his wife's nephew instead. And then for months Leopoldo couldn't find another job. The end. Go back to sleep, Negrito. Leopoldo crumples Alvarito's letter and tosses it but then picks it up because what if someone finds it and tells on him? León has emptied the courtyard. His hands are shaking. The damp back of his guayabera has unaccountable streaks of soot. Leopoldo cannot see León's vacant face but he can easily imagine it. He hurries down the stairs to steer León away from the cameras before León turns back toward them. On his way down Leopoldo slips on a compact mirror but he's all right, yes, he didn't fall. One of the cameramen, who has already broached the subject of a special favor with Leopoldo, isn't filming León. He seems to be giving Leopoldo the chance to take León away. Does that moronic cameraman think Leopoldo doesn't see the other cameras? Some of the reporters, as if they know Leopoldo's about to obstruct them, are urging their cameramen down the stairs. By one of the garbage cans Leopoldo takes his time disposing of Alvarito's letter. Ándate a la verga viejo hijueputa. Let El Loco's people see León's in no condition to block El Loco from returning. León turns and faces the cameras without looking at the cameras, as if lost in someone's kitchen. Leopoldo checks his watch. Antonio's waiting. It's time.

IV / ANTONIO EDITS HIS BABY CHRIST MEMOIR

For first, there is not to be found, in all history, any miracle attested by a sufficient number of men, of such unquestioned good sense, education, and learning, as to secure us against all delusion in themselves. — DAVID HUME, AN ENQUIRY CONCERNING
HUMAN UNDERSTANDING, SECTION X

After a twenty one year absence my father returned to the church. The pious boy I was back then had convinced him to attend Christmas Mass, and, according to my grandmother, his return that night led to the baby christ's tears. Most in my family readily adopted my grandmother's version, as I was to do in the years that followed, sharing it with my American acquaintances as another example of the quaint superstitions of my Third World country, which would often prompt in them comparisons to eyewitness news reports of Virgin Mary sightings on trunks of trees or mortadella sandwiches. Of course I suspected my grandmother's version was far too simple, and yet nothing ever compelled me to elaborate on it by implicating others or by including events that began long before that night or that decade.

—

Everyone was implicated, Antonio writes along the margins of his baby christ memoir, meaning everyone he'd once known in Guayaquil (Cristian Cordero's grandfather, Espinel's father, Julio Esteros's mother, his own father) plus everyone else in the world (and here Antonio wishes he wasn't inside a plane so he could search online for an essay by Leszek Kołakowski, a philosopher Antonio had been drawn to because he was from Poland like John Paul II, the first pope to visit Ecuador — we can never forget the existence of evil and the misery of the human condition, Kołakowski wrote —), and so to write about implicating others before that Christmas night and that decade seems redundant to him since it was implied everyone was implicated, although he could argue against himself and state that most of us need reminders that we're implicated with the existence of evil and the misery of the human condition, okay, so let's say that you encounter these reminders in the leisurely world of memoir or fiction: wouldn't you ignore them, Antonio, or at most be smote by yet another round of deep urges to change Ecuador that might impede your reasoning and compel you to board a plane back to Guayaquil without much of a plan or money?

—

Before my father agreed to attend Christmas Mass we were at my grandmother's house. My father had announced I was old enough to sit with the adults, and since my grandmother's dining table could seat only eight, and since neither my aunts nor my grandfather wanted to sour our Christmas by starting another pyrrhic battle, ten of us struggled to pass the potatoes and slice the pig without elbowing each other. And we did so in silence. My father was in an awful mood, and we knew that whoever spoke during dinner risked being savaged by his sarcasm.

—

But perhaps he has been equating Leszek Kołakowski with Father Villalba, Antonio thinks, perhaps he has been drawn to certain novelists and philosophers not because they're from Poland like John Paul II but because their work reminds him of Father Villalba's sermons, even though he doesn't remember Father Villalba's sermons anymore (once Antonio searched online for texts by Clodovis Boff and unbeknownst to him he later ascribed them to Father Villalba — never purchase a painting of your favorite landscape because that painting will come to replace your favorite landscape, one of W. G. Sebald's narrators says, but what choice did Antonio have if his favorite landscapes have, for the most part, vanished? — bless me Father, Clodovis Boff recounts, Father we are dying —), or perhaps he hasn't been drawn to certain novelists and philosophers because of Father Villalba but because he likes to believe intricate association mechanisms subtend his mind like in the novels of W. G. Sebald, drawn to Father Villalba like Jacques Austerlitz is drawn to fortresses that contain the seeds of their own destruction, for instance, and whether on that Christmas night at his grandmother's house they stuffed themselves with potatoes and pig he doesn't remember anymore either, so he should just delete the porcine and potato details or acknowledge he doesn't remember them anymore.

—

My father had assumed that his appointment in the administration of León Martín Cordero had entitled him to arrogance, and perhaps because of his airs of infallibility we did not consider something could be troubling him.

—

He had also assumed that his father's appointment in the administration of León Martín Cordero had entitled him to arrogance at San Javier, Antonio thinks, but who could blame such a skinny teenager with acne on his face for assuming airs of infallibility for just a tiny bit? (And here Antonio recalls some notes he'd written about Your Face Tomorrow by Javier Marías — one never experiences genuine self disgust, Javier Marías wrote, and it's that inability that makes us capable of doing almost anything — or, in Antonio's case, of doing almost nothing — I'm on a plane on my way back, isn't that enough? — no.)

—

My grandmother, restless amid our silence, seemed to be counting rice grains with her fork, though most likely she was deliberating whether to talk. She loved a seated audience, and Christmas was the time of the year when everyone was more receptive to her stories. She must have reminded herself that she was, after all, the most inured to my father's jabs because she began recounting for us the storied origins of her dining table. The story was not a new one (none of them were) yet we were relieved someone other than us was talking. After her father sold a small fraction of his plantations, she said, he had decided on a whim to throw out all their furniture and start anew, contracting for the job all the carpenters available in Portoviejo at the time. For a week, on their cobblestone patio, the sound of hammers and hacksaws merged with the sound of poor families carrying off the old furniture her father was giving away. The dining table my grandmother had inherited from those days had knotted flowers carved on its thick width, which matched the dense Guayacan patterns of the four adjacent cabinets, immense cabinets stuffed with more plates and teacups and sugar bowls than anyone could ever use in a lifetime, all of them burnished at least monthly, most of them handpainted with landscapes no one wanted to see.

—

Before Antonio's grandmother squandered what remained of her father's plantations in Portoviejo, Antonio would stay with her during the summer, and what he remembers of those summers in Portoviejo are the black bats that would appear outside the immense windows in his bedroom like apparitions from Monstruo Cinema, the weekly horror TV hour he wasn't allowed to watch, the black bats that he knows he hasn't invented in retrospect because he'd asked the laborers in his grandmother's plantation and they had confirmed that yes, niño Antonio, vampires love bananas, and clouds of them do swarm us at night, and although the black bats had terrified him they hadn't traumatized him irreversibly, or at least his nightmares about the black bats by those immense windows did vanish eventually, and what Antonio also remembers of those summers in Portoviejo is the chained monkey at an outdoor grill by the side of the highway, Antonio hurling rocks at the squalid monkey chained to what looked like a giant nail sledgehammered into the mud, the monkey charging toward him and choking himself before he could reach him until the one afternoon the monkey managed to grab his hair and wouldn't let go, someone help that little boy, for god's sake, the monkey thrashing Antonio by his hair and Antonio thinking then or later that he got what he deserved, the monkey not letting go of Antonio's hair even after a pair of brooms descended on him, the monkey probably thinking we're both going down, carajo, you and me to the grave.

—

My father did not interrupt my grandmother's story. He remained silent, concentrating on the uneven horizon inside his wineglass. I could not tell if he had been staring at it for long, or if it was just a passing gesture of wine connoisseurship because I was too distracted by my upcoming speech. After participating in my father's reckless lifestyle the summer before, I had decided it was my duty to convince him to attend Christmas Mass with us, and for this delicate task I had prepared a speech. I had spent quite some time contemplating not the exact words to deliver but my father's reaction to them, envisioning a sudden conversion like Saul on his way to Damascus, god's light passing through me so as to inspirit my every word. In a mixture of rosary prayers and feverish writing, I'd finished my speech the night before. Perhaps a resolute argument, perhaps a series of unconnected allusions to the theological texts I was studying in school, either way, I'd accumulated at least seven or eight pages wrinkled by my scribbling and crossing and waiting for the light to shine. I would address my father after dinner.

My Aunt Carmen, the only one in my father's family with enough good looks to marry a bold, young politician, brought up the headline news. The mayor of our city, or perhaps some other elected official that I can no longer recall, had defrauded the municipality and fled.

Just another crook, my father muttered, aware that my grandmother had urged everyone to vote for that crook during election time. We waited for my father to riff on his remark. He didn't. This did not imply his mood was improving. Under the table I could see his hands stroking his gray suit pants, as if reassuring them of their own fine tailoring and fabric, which he had once explained to me by pointing at the minute violet stripes that had been woven into them.

—

His father never explained those minute violet stripes to him, Antonio thinks, crossing out the passage about the minute violet stripes, but his father did drag him along to splurge on Italian business suits at the most expensive boutiques in Quito, no, not drag him along, Antonio loved sauntering into those expensive boutiques where the voluptuous saleswomen would dote on both father and son, his father flirting with them and the saleswomen saying your son's so handsome, Don Antonio, he's going to stir the cauldron as much as you, a prediction that didn't come true while he lived in Guayaquil — hide your Smurfs, here comes that ugly Gargamel — but that came true once he arrived in San Francisco — good one, Menudo Boy — and although Antonio likes to believe he has inherited nothing from his corrupt father, he knows he has inherited his father's penchant for expensive clothes because he splurged even when he couldn't afford them (and likely will continue to splurge because the realization that a behavior is inherited isn't strong enough to counter the inherited behavior — you could simply stop buying expensive clothes, Drool — easier to continue to splurge and blame it on my corrupt father? —), and of course to his American acquaintances his penchant for expensive clothes was a source of amusing anecdotes, courtesy of Antonio from faraway Ecuador, but to him his penchant for expensive clothes dispirited him because if he hadn't splurged he could've quit his database job and returned to Ecuador sooner, although he would have never returned to Ecuador without owning a sizable amount of expensive clothes — you're fated either way, Gargamel — fine, let's not delete the minute violet stripes since my father did purchase a gray suit with those minute violet stripes, Antonio writes along the margins of his baby christ memoir, and I did notice the minute violet stripes without my father pointing them out to me (though possibly the saleswomen had been the ones who had explained the minute violet stripes to them?).

—

Heartened by what she mistook as my father's unusual restraint, my grandmother loosed tale after tale about our great ancestry, ranches and islands and heroes of the Independencia, eventually landing on her favorite story: about how the baby christ materialized into our family. In a dream, she said, a voice had guided her grandmother. Buried on the far side of her father's plantation, the voice had said, by the tallest oak tree with the knifed bark, she was to find resounding evidence of god's existence. Her grandmother awoke, soaked in sweat despite the force of her ceiling fan. She was not the gullible type, no sir, my grandmother said, but when god calls, our lineage answers. Her grandmother sprang out of bed, and with her mosquito net still entangled around her knees she ran across her father's field, one of the largest ones in Manabí, and despite the bats and the Pacific coast wind, she fell on her knees and with her hands she pierced the earth until she found him: our baby christ. He was intact, lying in a wicker basket like the one Moses must have been in when the Egyptian princess found him. He was wrapped in a purple and gold shawl, his wide clay eyes contemplating the heavens.

—

No tallest oak tree with the knifed bark, Antonio writes along the margins of his baby christ memoir, no mosquito nets, no bats (or rather, yes, bats but not in his grandmother's baby christ story), no Pacific coast wind, no force of the ceiling fan (his old bedroom in Guayaquil did have a poorly installed ceiling fan that spun like a moribund turbine above his bed): the dream guiding her grandmother to the baby christ, on the other hand, had been recounted enough times by his grandmother for him to still remember that the function of the dream had been to guide his grandmother's grandmother to where the baby christ was buried, and yes, he understood the narrative purpose of telling details, and he also understood the need to add concrete details for the sake of verisimilitude, but there has to be another way to revisit his past without him pretending he remembers the whole of it.

—

I had heard my grandmother tell the baby christ story many times before. Sometimes her grandmother pierced the earth with a shovel, sometimes she rushed out at noon, either way, I wasn't judging her inconsistencies this time because I knew she was feeling slighted by the rest of us. After Christmas Mass, as long as I could remember, we had always driven back to her house for our gift exchange. This year we were driving back to my Uncle Fernando and my Aunt Carmen's newly built home instead. Along with my Aunt Carmen, I had openly rooted for this change of location, so out of guilt and solidarity I listened to my grandmother's story attentively, as if riveted by the alternatives (the lord not choosing us, the baby christ not being there).

—

No riveting alternatives could've existed for me because we believed we'd been fated as a family to receive the baby christ, Antonio thinks, and although he likes to believe he no longer believes he's fated, chances are he will forever be tied to semblances of those childhood beliefs, which shouldn't matter that much to him except how can he get anything done if he's always waiting to receive fateful instructions on what to do with his life, how can he make himself less vulnerable to interpreting so much of his life as fateful signs just as he'd done when Leopoldo called him and said come back, Drool, because even though he's returning to Ecuador as requested, if they accomplish nothing and he flees back to San Francisco and then ten or fifteen years from now Leopoldo were to call him again, Antonio's likely to still be vulnerable to interpreting Leopoldo's call as a fateful sign — this time the time really is right, Drool — but what are the alternatives: Do atheists rationally scrutinize every potential turning point in their lives? Do agnostics run logistic models to predict whether a phone call or an email or an article in the newspaper could become pivotal to their lives? How can he be expected to scrutinize what might constitute a symbol or a sign after seeing the sun move in Cajas? After seeing his family's baby christ cry?

—

As if searching for a better position from which to pounce, my father straightened himself on his chair. Perhaps tired of imitating himself, he dropped and dangled his forearms from his armrests. He nevertheless said to my grandmother too bad that voice didn't advise you and your father on how to keep all that land. This was true. They had squandered it all. Half of my grandmother's house was now for rent. The other half was crammed with handcrafted armoires.

My father downed his glass of Concha y Toro, my grandmother's favorite wine. He knew what he had just done. He always knew. And yet his facial expression (his brown contentious eyes at odds with his downcast glances, although it's possible that over time I have layered these features on a face I can no longer remember) informed us that for him this knowing was punishment enough.

Uncle Fernando, who despite being young and short always looked at ease next to our dignitaries, said what are you, the Grinch? Lighten up, Antonio. You're scaring the children. My Uncle Fernando was the only one in our family who could reproach my father. Three or four years earlier, after a series of my father's business ventures floundered, my uncle had secured my father a post as head of a minor government agency in charge of shipping office supplies to government bureaus across Ecuador, and so of course my father could not yell or swear back at him like he did with the rest of us. I liked Uncle Fernando. He sent my mother good presents even after she divorced my father, sported slim Italian suits, raced European sports cars despite the ban on imports. He also worked as a personal advisor to the minister of finance, whom he had known since his days at San Javier High School.

—

So many hours of his summers with his father in Quito were spent under long, empty office desks inside that minor government agency, Antonio thinks, playing with a calculator that must have had games on it because he probably spent all eight office hours a day under those long, empty desks along empty hallways instead of wandering the city on his own, instead of writing love letters to the neighbor from Sweden at his father's apartment building whom his father was to introduce him to and whom he was to date the summer after, when he was already too tall to bury himself under those long, empty office desks (and what he remembers most about that neighbor from Sweden is how proud he'd been of declining to sleep with her because he was fifteen and intercourse before marriage was a mortal sin — anyone want to guess what the Drool was doing with the pigeon from Sweden? — I didn't have the heart to inflict that kind of pain to our Madre Dolorosa — with the same hand you masturbate you stab a dagger into our Madre Dolorosa's heart —), and sometimes the secretaries who were probably his father's lovers would stop by his lair under those long, empty desks and ask him if he wanted or needed anything, hoping to ingratiate themselves with Antonio as if he had any sway at the minor government office his father managed, bah, on the contrary: if he could go back in time he would have denounced them — or you would try to sleep with them? — probably.

—

My father's smile tried to mask any signs of strain. He echoed my uncle's jovial tone and said isn't it Mass time already? You Cristianitos are going to be late.

My father lit a cigar, and my grandmother, with synchronic urgency, as if cued by his silver lighter's snap, tolled her tiny porcelain bell, which to me sounded like a poodle's. In restaurants she would deploy her bell if she did not receive immediate service. At home it was part of her daily meals. Maria, caramba, pay attention, she said. An ashtray for Don Antonio.

Since my grandmother sat at the head of the table with her back to the kitchen, she could not see Maria, her most recent maid, trying to suppress her scowl. In a country where more than 60 percent of the population lives in poverty, any family with a decent income can afford a live in maid. And my grandmother went through them as if they were a disposable breed of humans. At first they came the safe way, recommended by her fellow obstetricians, but after the recommendations ran out, my grandmother had to hang a Maid Wanted sign outside her gate, which of course lured strangers, who eventually absconded with her silverware. My three aunts liked Maria, though, and as she approached us, my aunts' glances pleaded with her: patience with the old woman, please, patience. I had never seen my aunts' pleads before.

—

So what that I hadn't seen my aunts' pleads before, Antonio writes along the margins of his baby christ memoir, crossing out the sentence about not seeing his aunts' pleads before, he doesn't remember that seeing his aunts' pleads for the first time carried any significance for him, so perhaps he's mindlessly following the narrative convention of these coming of age stories in which the first time the boy sees something out of the ordinary he undergoes a transmogrifying shock or revelation, the word transmogrifying, incidentally, which rhymes too much with the word ogro, should only be unfurled to mock transformative feelings, the word unfurl, Antonio writes, likewise.

—

Without raising her gaze Maria placed the ashtray by my father, whose eyes became fixed on the curvy silhouette beneath her white uniform. Her one piece uniform was several sizes too small (we could see her brown shoulders and thighs, although we were not staring), not out of coquetry but because it was the same uniform the other maids had had to wear and hand wash every other day. Maria hurried back to the kitchen, leaving behind her scent of talc and sweat. We did not know it at the time, but that night was to be Maria's last.

My grandmother laughed and clapped at something my grandfather had said. I grew thankful at the possibility of merriment, hoping that it might calm my father before it was time for my speech. I cannot tell you what suddenly lifted my grandmother's mood. Her moods swung as widely as my father's, and so it could have been nothing at all, or the tiny sound of her porcelain bell, or the way her Christmas lights reflected on our faces so as to make us look happier, or my grandfather holding her hand, or too much Concha y Toro.

There are family members whose roles in one's memories, through no fault of their own, become so inconsequential that eventually one is free to remember them in whichever way one chooses. This is how I choose to remember my grandmother: dancing a cumbia on her seat during our family dinners, raising her wineglass and singing tómese una copa / una copa de vino / ya me la tomé / ya se la tomó / ahora le toca al vecino, which translates to drink another cup of wine, and, when you are done, it is your neighbor's turn. By song's end my grandmother would turn to my grandfather and call him mi perrito, my little doggy, and my grandfather would reciprocate by barking or asking her to dance. Much later, after the cocktails and the dance, they would lie on the sofa like exhausted lovers, my grandmother bunched against my grandfather, who would have fallen asleep without fanfare sometime earlier. My grandfather was the only one in the family who prayed to the baby christ regularly. He had built a wooden altar for this purpose, and since he had placed it by the entrance to their bedroom, we always had to be careful not to swing their door open, lest we bump the door against his worn kneeler and disrupt the order inside his altar. Every space on his altar was crowded with rosaries, scapulars, fringed crosses, miniature images of saints too fragile to be taken out of their plastic sleeves, so many of them that sometimes we wondered if my grandfather bought a new one every week, and whether he did so in honor of the baby christ or to keep himself company in those long hours of fasting and prayer. Most of the time we didn't have to worry about bumping the door against my grandfather because, when he was by his altar, my grandmother would always tiptoe out of their bedroom, and like a guard who thinks her task is as important as that of whom she guards, she would admonish us and ask us to keep quiet. Silence. Grandpa Antonio is praying.

My father did not touch his coconut flan. After Maria cleared the pig's skeleton, he was still chewing on its hard skin, gnawing at it with such force that I could see his grimacing teeth like a dog's.

With rushed signs of the cross we stood up and readied ourselves to leave. My father, sprawled on the sofa closest to the exit, examined us with feigned amusement, as if preparing to taunt us out of my grandmother's house.

We had to start heading to Christmas Mass, and I, without much time left, had to start convincing my father to come with us. This was my only chance till next Christmas. For his government post my father had moved to Quito, and although I visited him during the summer, his lifestyle in the capital did not allow for much church talk. I know I wouldn't have ventured my speech in front of my family (my grandmother would have asked me not to pester my father), and I know they wouldn't have let me stay behind. In that brief space between the house and the garage, I must have told them I had forgotten my rosary or my bible. My grandmother must have given me her house keys because my father did not open the door. He had moved to the sofa farthest away from the door. He had crossed his legs like a professor about to lecture himself, but he had sunk the rest of his body inside the sofa. He was holding up his cigar backwards, with the burning end facing him, and he was staring at it as if inspecting a live snake or an alarm clock that should've gone off.

He noticed me and said qué, flaco, you're not going to Mass?

He asked this without ridicule or annoyance. He asked this with sincere concern. I was sixteen at the time and steeped in love with our Madre Dolorosa. That year I had successfully avoided any impure thoughts that could have marred my love for Mary. I do not know why this was so. At San Javier, I used to advertise the daily rosary service my friend Leopoldo and I had founded and our classmates would ridicule us because they thought we were just brownnosers. But my father did not make fun of me. I do not know how he found out about my religious fervor (I didn't tell anyone about my rosary prayers or my volunteer service because I was following the precept of not letting one hand know what the other hand was doing), but around me he tried to keep his disdain for religion to himself. I am not sure if I knew it then, or later, or if I had guessed it all along with that intuition that binds a son to the defeated aspirations of his father, but in his last year at San Javier my father had decided to give everything up and become a Jesuit priest.

I delivered my father no inspired speech. I stuttered and asked him to please come with us. Without grumbling an okay or an all right my father stood up. He nodded absently, walking toward me and then beside me like a surrendered fugitive. On the front seat of her car my grandmother, who was carrying the baby christ on her lap, silenced the Christmas carols with a careful turn of the stereo's dial and contained her tears as if afraid the merest peep would change my father's mind.

Nothing unusual happened during Mass. As always, we drove to the Iglesia Redonda, the round church with four entrances distributed equidistantly around its circular perimeter, and in between these entrances, rows and rows of arched benches facing the elevated altar on the temple's epicenter. Following tradition, my grandmother placed our family's baby christ on the altar's steps, next to the other family effigies, but not without spending some time hogging the best spot and patrolling it until everyone sat down. Because we did not arrive early enough we seated ourselves as best we could. Parallel to the front of the altar, by the confession booth, far from the rest of the family, my father and I sat together. I must have felt triumphant. Or perhaps humble and grateful to the Virgin Mary for answering my prayers. Surely I felt compelled to concentrate on the Christmas sermon, ignoring the subdued elegance of the faithful and the perfumed smells of Ecuadorian women intent on becoming European damsels. The priest delivered his last blessings. The crowd that minutes before had been silent became festive, friends and families searching for each other in circles and laughing heartily upon finding one another. My father remained in his seat. I did not stand up either. By the front row, near my father and me, men in distinguished suits were walking up to my Uncle Fernando. They were grinning stupidly and shaking his hand with the same vigor they were using to chat him up, probably sending their best regards to the minister and joking that they had some deals they would like to discuss further. My father tried to avoid them. He stood up, covering his face by pretending he was wiping sweat off his forehead, but as he walked away someone next to my Uncle Fernando shouted out his name. My father stopped, hesitated, but then he turned and saluted the man by cracking a joke across the aisle. My father was a joker. Outside our family, everyone seemed to relish seeing him on the street or at restaurants. He would put people at ease simply by changing their name from Roberto to Roberticux or from Ernesto to Ernestinsky. I had seen him do this many times before, especially when I visited him. At first I would take the bus up the cordillera to Quito, but from the second summer on my father bought me a plane ticket as well as imported clothes and the expensive sneakers I had wanted to show off at school. One early Sunday evening, during my last summer there, my father said he wanted to show me where my Uncle Fernando worked. He said this with obvious pride, so instead of reminding him that Sunday nights were our chess nights, I went along with him. A huge slab of cement, darkened by mold on most of its windows' edges, a sight that I was to see again many years later in the soviet buildings of Warsaw: this was the ministry of finance. My father and I entered the minister's office without knocking. I had never seen so much lacquered wood or as many fur rugs inside an office. My father locked the door behind us. As we glided by, emboldened by my father's knowledge that we were special guests, I could see our reflection on the thick edges of the bookcases lined with edicts and regulations. On the far end of the room, by the windows overseeing our capital, the minister, my Uncle Fernando, and a few others were already gathered by an oval table. The minister greeted my father with one jolly clap, then stood up and delivered a mock address: We are gathered here today. The minister placed a black leather briefcase on the table. He squinted and concentrated on aligning the briefcase's three tiered code as if trying to open a safe, and after the gold fastenings popped and the minister rearranged the knot of his silver necktie, he began to serve us wads of cash as if giving away free money for a game of dice. Some of the men accompanied their cheers by playing with the rubber bands gripping their cash. I can still remember the sound of scrunched rubber against paper. We should all thank our chief of office supplies here, the minister said, although of course he should thank us. Someone poured champagne as if it were meant to be spilled, and later that night, at La Cueva, a traditional Spanish restaurant dug under a new downtown skyscraper, everyone swigged champagne and wine and whiskey. During dinner my father stood on his chair. Up there, his head almost touching the low brick ceiling, he removed his gray suit jacket with the minute violet stripes, placed it over his shoulders like a cape, and as he slurred his toast his tie dangled like a reptile and his splotched white dress shirt consumed the liquor overflowing from his glass. He flashed his wads of cash and said tonight, gentlemen, the women are on me. Everyone else at our table puffed their cigars. Clapped. The service had no choice but to celebrate us. My father patted me on the back, and since I did not readily smile he increased the force of his greeting. After downing half a glass of Chivas he thrust it toward me. This, it occurred to me as I sniffed his drink, is the kind of life my father leads. But I did not question my father about what type of deal he was celebrating. I knew that the answer would be unpleasant. I also knew that any questions might alter my father's mood and ruin my chances of getting more expensive sneakers out of him. And so I ate and laughed and drank his stiff drinks and by night's end I, too, must have been drunk.

At the Iglesia Redonda, as my father walked across the aisle to join the others, I recognized the man who had yelled my father's name: he had been at the minister's office, too. He was the father of Maraco Espinel, one of my classmates at San Javier.

I did not wait for my father to call out my name across the aisle and introduce me to his friends. I walked the other way and searched for the rest of my family. Eventually we all found each other. As we gathered to leave, my grandmother realized that my father and my Uncle Fernando were missing. Despite my protests, my grand-mother sent me to look for them. She was still visibly excited about my father attending Mass, clutching the baby christ's basket with one hand and fanning herself with the other, and I could tell that she'd cried and that she would continue to cry whenever she remembered this Christmas. When my grandmother found out my father was serious about becoming a Jesuit priest, many years before I was born, she grounded him. When he wouldn't budge, defying her by pray-ing loudly in his room, she took him on a trip to Paris, Milan, and other European cities where she showered him with the traditions of luxury. At the lobby of the Hotel Saint Jacques he met a girl from Norway. My grandmother suggested he should travel with her for an extra month or two. He accepted my grandmother's money and did. He must have been seventeen years old.

I trudged back inside the church, which was now empty, walking around it and peeking out of every exit, and when I reached the third door I found them. They were alone now. My father, with his arms crossed, kept his gaze down while listening to my uncle's instructions. My uncle was smiling, insouciant, as if telling a story at a cocktail party where everybody knew him. He was saying don't waste any time, Antonio. Resign first thing Monday morning and don't worry about a thing. Take a long vacation, in Miami, for instance, and before those bastards get a chance to issue you a prison order we'll have it all sorted out.

My father noticed me first. He tried to discern whether I had heard what my uncle had just said. He must have concluded that I did because he closed his eyes and crossed his arms further, as if trying to wake himself up by squeezing his chest. These motions did not last. He opened his eyes and said what were to be his last words for the rest of the night: What the hell do you want? What is it, Antonio José?

They're waiting for you.

Come, my uncle said in a conciliatory tone. Let's join them. We'll chat more after the gift exchange.

V / ANTONIO IN GUAYAQUIL

To sleep, Antonio thinks, so exhausted by the long flight from San Francisco to Guayaquil that he doesn't roll down the window of his Taxi Amigo to examine what has changed about his miserable hometown in the last twelve years (plus he doesn't want the horrendous humid air outside to wade through the air conditioner vents inside), doesn't wonder too much about why Leopoldo didn't show up to welcome him at the airport (or rather why was he expecting Leopoldo to show up to welcome him at the airport), doesn't think about the two old indigenous women who were embracing each other and crying as the plane landed, isn't disheartened by the familiar images of El Loco on every telephone pole and every billboard along whatever this airport road is now called, on the contrary, feels embarrassingly reassured that while he was away, his country has remained as backward as ever, El Loco for President becoming less ubiquitous as his Taxi Amigo approaches his old neighborhood, where no one has ever voted for El Loco, and whether anyone here will vote for El Loco this time, if he manages to return from his exile in Panamá, wouldn't be difficult for Antonio to predict, although since this is the first time in twelve years that Antonio has been back to Guayaquil he doesn't yet know whether the neighbors who used to pile on El Loco for being an uncultivated thief still live in the neighborhood where he grew up, or whether they would still be alarmed to see a caravan for El Loco just like the one they'd seen on Bálsamos Street the first time El Loco ran for president, or perhaps it was the second time El Loco ran for president when the caravan for this self proclaimed leader of the poor alarmed the neighbors and his mother but not him, although of course in retrospect he's likely to downplay any threatening aspects of that unfortunate caravan, and as he unloads his luggage from his Taxi Amigo, a private car service his mother suggested for security reasons, it occurs to him that without the unfortunates of his country, without the 60 percent of Ecuadorians who live in perpetual poverty (why always sound like a demagogue when invoking the poor?), he would have had to fabricate a new reason as to why he thought he was different from his fellow Saks Fifth Avenue shoppers in San Francisco, oh, but unlike you materialistic North Americans, I'm going back to Ecuador to help my — nice scarf, Drool — and yet by returning to Guayaquil he has ruined it for himself: he could've spent the rest of his life in San Francisco thinking of himself as the boy who once taught catechism to the poor, or as the teenager who once vowed to return to save the poor, and it would've been okay, yes, from the corporate headquarters of Bank of America during the week, or from an armchair inside his neighborhood coffee house during the weekend, his bountiful inner life would have shielded him from his bountiful inaction, and perhaps he still has time to fly back to San Francisco and pretend his return to Guayaquil never happened, and as he enters the apartment on Bálsamos Street where he lived with his mother until fleeing to the United States, he's relieved that nothing has changed since he left, although so much time has passed that perhaps it's not possible to claim that nothing has changed, or perhaps he wants to believe that nothing has changed to avoid the onrush of nostalgia he imagines most emigrants feel upon returning to their hometown after a long absence, or perhaps he wants to avoid thinking about all those years his mother had to live alone in this apartment after he fled to the United States — the light left the house after you left, Antonio — or perhaps he's too exhausted for onrushes of nostalgia or to start thinking about that one Christmas when his mother visited him in San Francisco and shared with him what had happened to her in Guayaquil, disrupting the convenient emptiness of all those years his mother lived alone by telling him about the first time she was robbed right in front of our apartment on Bálsamos, Antonio José, recounting the robbery for him with a voice attuned to a peace that was foreign to him and that surprised him more than any details about the robbery (during her visit to San Francisco his mother had also revealed to him that not only was she involved with transpersonal yoga and the Catholic meditations of Father Davila but with Reiki and rebirthing, too — I knew this was what they called an express hijacking, his mother said, where they take you with them until they're done robbing others because normally those big Land Rovers have a tracking device —), and perhaps the elegant air conditioned cabin of the Land Rover had made it easier for his mother's friend to believe she was safe to parade her luxury car through the miserable streets of Guayaquil, or perhaps he's entertaining such embittered thoughts to avoid considering that in that same elegant cabin his mother was probably terrified, and so the one thief on his mother's side pressed the unlock button so that the other thief could open the door on the driver's side, and Monsi became hysterical, not again, Monsi was saying, not again, screaming at them hijueputas, malparidos, leave us alone, jostling with the thief on her side who was pulling her up by her hair and beating her with the butt of his pistol so she would stop shrieking (no, Antonio thinks, to him that caravan for the self proclaimed leader of the poor hadn't looked like a threat but like an outburst of celebration, as if earlier in the day El Loco had announced that if he became president not only was he going to provide the people with jobs, as he had promised in his ads, but with meals and free housing too, and in their excitement at this incredible news they had rallied up their neighbors, had rounded up their motorized belongings, had set out all over town to flap their signs and shout their hymns and bounce on their flatbeds, eventually losing their way and ending up on Bálsamos Street, a mere block from León Martín Cordero, carajo, the one ex president his mother still rooted for, the one who had been anointed by Reagan because of his strong arm tactics and his free market packages and who would have had no qualms about outfitting his grandson with a BB gun to shoo El Loco's people off his street), and as he sets down his luggage in the living room of the apartment on Bálsamos Street where he lived with his mother until fleeing to the United States he remembers his mother emerging onto her balcony to find the caravan for El Loco blasting its songs of hope from a megaphone fastened to a Datsun's roof with rope — the force of the poor / Abdalá / the clamor of my people / Abdalá — and on her balcony on that day like in those years before she steeped herself in transpersonal yoga and the meditation exercises of Father Davila, his mother seemed ready to order everyone to shut the hell up, which was exactly what Antonio refused to do in those days, although sometimes after he argued with her he would refuse to talk to her for three, six, seven days in a row, or until she would threaten to send him to military school, and in those days he would often hear his mother complaining about how even people with only a smattering of education knew that El Loco was a joke, and whether Manuel, our domestic, was in on the joke worried my mother so much that from her balcony she was checking to see if Manuel looked enraptured by El Loco's caravan, but no, Manuel wasn't, although later my mother was to assume so, Manuel was just hosing the parking spots in front of our apartment building, and yes, El Loco was a joke, but what wasn't a joke were the alternatives, because our cultivated ministers and prefects and mayors and even my own father had been too busy defrauding our government to care about the poor, and what was even less of a joke was the precarious conditions in which so many people in Ecuador lived, and so I raised my hand and gave the caravan a thumbs up, a gesture that confused them because they seemed to be trying to determine if I was mocking them, although it's possible they were just observing me because I happened to be sitting there, a lanky teenager sporting his Emelec soccer uniform, and yet Antonio wasn't mocking them, he was smiling and clapping and ignoring his mother on the balcony who yelled come inside right this second, Antonio José, and as he opens the empty fridge rusted along the edges in the apartment on Bálsamos Street where he lived with his mother until fleeing to the United States, he considers how loud his mother must have yelled at him because the people in the caravan heard her, hesitating as to whether to heckle her because on the one hand her voice carried an authority they acknowledged, and on the other hand she was a woman, either way Manuel diverted their attention by waving at them, water splashing on his feet and sprinkling on his stone colored jeans, which he had rolled up to his knees as if he were about to catch carp at a rough river, wiping his hand on his tee shirt and waving at them again, which to me seemed innocuous enough, as if Manuel was greeting a traveling circus, a circus that then surprised him by returning his greeting, some raising their fists as if promising to fight for him, others stretching their arms toward him to shake his hands, and as the last pickup passed him he did not take the three or five steps required to shake their hands, which should have counted in his favor but didn't because later that night Antonio's mother said I want you to watch him, or perhaps she said keep an eye on him, or perhaps she didn't say anything and in retrospect her statements have surfaced as manifestations of what he didn't know then that he was intuiting about her fears about El Loco, we need to be careful, his mother said, we need to keep all entrances locked, his mother said, and as he contemplates the empty walls of the apartment on Bálsamos Street he thinks of all the fistfights at San Javier that his mother had to account for when Father Ignacio would call her to inform her that her son had been suspended or placed on probation yet again (and once, during semifinals, Antonio swiped the yellow card from the referee and tossed it at his face — red card! you're out! — fighting for the ball with elbows and knees and taking off through the outermost flank at an incredible speed, the goalkeeper yelling stop him, Antonio yelling ábranse hijueputas, propelling the ball to the goal minimally when the ball was inflated maximally so that from afar his mean sprints looked like pranks — pata floja —), and what Antonio said to his mother after she told him to keep an eye on Manuel was I don't know what you're talking about, or leave me alone, or whatever he used to say to her when he wasn't ignoring her, don't play stupid, his mother said, because of course she knew that Antonio knew she was worried about El Loco, the self proclaimed leader of the poor who was talking the class talk, demonizing those people with money, those oligarchs who steal from the poor, those aniñados, and what worried my mother and her clients at her nail salon wasn't that El Loco was known for disregarding the sensible limits of public fraud but that our domestics might take El Loco's rhetoric to heart and revolt against us, rumors circulating among them about servants lurking inside our houses to slash our throats, and what Antonio said to his mother that night was you, all of you, are overreacting, raising his voice and saying something about our country needing a revolt, anyway, to rid us of thieves, sensing or thinking he could sense that his mother wanted to nod in approval because what he'd said was an oblique swing at his father, who'd fled the country for defrauding the government during the administration of León Martín Cordero, but instead his mother admonished him for raising his voice, an admonishment interrupted by a telephone call, or perhaps the call came later, and as Antonio heads toward his old bedroom he wonders what they could possibly have said to each other in that interval between her admonishment and that telephone call — the light left the house after you left, Antonio — and it occurs to Antonio that he had never noticed how empty the walls looked in the apartment where he grew up with his mother, how emptied one feels after a long plane ride, how easy it is to assume he has never noticed something before instead of considering that what has become an absence in his past might include an evening in which he noticed the empty walls of his apartment when he was seven or fifteen or twelve years old (when Antonio was twelve he made a vow of silence to atone for whatever had been prescribed by the Jesuits as sin), how reassuring it was to find the old rotary phone on his way to his bedroom, not ringing now as it had rung that night when his mother admonished him for raising his voice, the phone ringing and reminding his mother that she was too exhausted to squash his bluster, ringing and announcing that one of her clients (Marta de Rosales or Veronica de Arosemena or one of the wives of our dignitaries whose proximity allowed my mother and I to pretend we were the kind of people with money El Loco was railing about and not the kind of people who would have slipped to a faraway low income neighborhood if my grandfather hadn't allowed us to stay in the apartment building he'd built before our neighborhood became a good one) was probably calling to request a last minute appointment to swap a broken acrylic nail before heading to a social function we hadn't been invited to, and yet even after all these years in which he has amassed what he considers to be an inordinate amount of memories that have interposed themselves between that time and this time, he's almost sure his mother didn't end their exchange that night by saying you're supposed to be the man of the house, Antonio José, start acting like one, no, he's almost sure she simply picked up the phone and waved him away, and as Antonio heads to his old bedroom he wonders if his scapulars are still there, his poster of our Madre Dolorosa, his handwritten pamphlets with his interpretation of the Joyful Mysteries of the Rosary, which included the presentation of jesus in the temple, the annunciation of Gabriel to Mary (one summer when he was sixteen he didn't incur a single bad thought that could mar his love for Mary), his comic books about San Bosco, his comic books about El Chapulín Colorado, a parody of a superhero from a popular television show brimming with catchphrases that everyone at San Javier used to repeat to each other — recontra qué? — chiro — chanfle — his pocket edition of the Imitation of Christ, his rosary with the sunflower sized beads, all of which was stored inside a long row of cabinets that had been built by a carpenter who looked like Cantinflas, a sunburnt sixty five year old Cantinflas who would show up drunk at their apartment on Saturday mornings, ring the bell, and greet my mother gently and ask her if there was any work this week, Doña Ceci, I could really use the work, how's niño Antonio, is he still growing like a tree, and it surprises Antonio to remember his mother addressing their carpenter without scorn, maestro, you've been drinking again, she would admonish him playfully, un poquitín nomás, Doña Ceci, he would say, and while Antonio still lived in Guayaquil their carpenter installed the iron gates by the glass doors in his mother's balcony, the sturdy cabinets in Antonio's bedroom, his bed and the sliding bed underneath his bed where Leopoldo would sleep when he stayed over, and perhaps by his old bed the immense poster of The Cure that used to spook his mother is still there, spooking no one now (although perhaps his mother still sometimes thinks about that black poster with the phosphorescent eyes and remembers those Saturday mornings when she would open the door to his bedroom and complain about his room reeking of whiskey, or about those Saturday mornings when she pretended she was or wasn't heartbroken because of him, as if he'd slighted her somehow, and I would plead after her in the kitchen and ask her what's wrong, Mom, and she would eventually tell him that when she opened the door to his bedroom that morning he had insulted her, had cussed at her, but he didn't remember, Mom, he'd been asleep, or perhaps she still thinks about those Saturday mornings during the last months before he was to flee to the United States in which something changed between them and they were at peace), the immense The Cure poster in his bedroom that he'd purchased in Gainesville, Florida, where he spent the entire summer before his senior year at San Javier scrubbing dishes at a restaurant near his maternal grandparents' house so he could afford to bring back a suitcase filled with impressive sneakers and jeans, mopping floors for a frumpy ladies' man who would sniff Antonio's bucket to check for the pine fresh (the grease on his hands wouldn't come off), vacationing with his maternal grandparents in Florida was what he told his classmates he had been doing during the summer so on the first day of school they were not surprised to see him sporting aerodynamic sneakers and Iron Maiden tee shirts with hirsute monsters that were later banned by Father Ignacio, and as Antonio enters his old bedroom he finds that his room has been emptied, that yoga mats have been spread on the floor, that nothing remains on the walls except a photograph of Paramahansa Yogananda, that on the other hand at least the ceiling fan is still there (during the rainy season mosquitoes would buzz his ears despite the breeze of that poorly installed fan that spun like a turbine set on unhinging itself), and as Antonio considers switching on the fan, or opening the curtains, or approaching the photograph of Paramahansa Yogananda to maybe draw a mustache on it, or lying down where his bed used to be to listen to someone practicing scales, although that's ridiculous because no one has ever practiced scales in his grandfather's building, or perhaps not so ridiculous because he's sure he can lie down where his bed used to be and imagine he's hearing someone practicing scales and to him that imagining would be just as real, well, it doesn't matter, he's exhausted from the long flight from San Francisco to Guayaquil and just needs a bed and a room with an air conditioner so he switches off the light of the bare, warm room that used to be his bedroom and shuts the door carefully, as if trying not to wake himself, and then climbs up the wooden stairs to his mother's room (when he was little the stairs had no handrails or balustrade so his mother worried about him falling down to the storage floor that during the rainy season would flood to the waist like a pond, and when he was seven or eight or twelve he would sleep in the guest room next to his mother's room and at night he would hear rats scraping his door as if trying to burrow inside, and in the dark he would shoo them away with a clap and the rats would scramble down the stairs so often that even now he can evoke the sound of their nails clacking down the wooden stairs), and in the week or weeks after the caravan for El Loco appeared on Bálsamos Street the rats returned, although my mother assumed it was something else, we were having dinner or about to have dinner, and before or after she defrosted a bag of lentils, we were startled by the sudden noises coming from the patio, which sounded as if someone was searching for something among our plants, but this someone couldn't have been Manuel because Sunday was his day off, and of course I could tell that my mother was thinking that Manuel had come back to rob us, or that he had brought back people with him who could rob us, or that he had told people who could rob us that despite the locks and bolts and metal bars on every one of our windows the service door facing Bálsamos Street could be jumped (his mother had been meaning to ask their carpenter to install longer spikes atop that door because it led to a passageway that led to the patio that led to the dining room, where his mother was rushing to the front door to call his Uncle Jacinto, who lived in the apartment upstairs — your Uncle Jacinto rescued us from your father, Antonio José —), and when his mother visited him in San Francisco she told him that when they were still living with his father in the Barrio Centenario his Uncle Jacinto had showed up one night in his jeep with his fellow firemen because his father had barricaded the house and wouldn't let us leave him — your uncle banged on the door and your father screamed at us and when it was over I found you trembling under your little bed, Antonio José — and what surprised Antonio that night in San Francisco when his mother seemed determined to confess everything wasn't that he didn't remember any of it but that his mother was telling him all of it as part of a transpersonal project she seemed to have been planning for years, because after she underwent something called holotropic breathwork therapy, she said, after she underwent Gestalt and rebirthing and constellation therapy at Centro Pachamama in Chile, she had liberated herself from what the two of them had gone through and now it was time for him to liberate himself too, and although he doesn't remember what he went through when he lived with his father, he does remember what he went through when he lived with his mother (Antonio's not going to think about that now (one morning during recess when he's seven or six or eight years old and still at Jefferson Elementary School he's running through a park that looks like an island planted with green bushes like gnomes and he's discovering a scrap of plastic like something knifed from the edge of a refrigerator, a long scrap of plastic that has hardened and bent like a bow, cutting the air like a boomerang when he wields it, running back to his classroom and hiding it inside his desk, running back to his mother after school and presenting it to her as a gift and saying look at this funny stick, Mom, perfect for you to beat me with)), and although he doesn't remember his Uncle Jacinto showing up to rescue them in his jeep, he does remember driving with his Uncle Jacinto in that jeep one morning and stalling because of the downtown traffic, his uncle banging on the steering wheel and saying the hell with this, switching on the siren on top of his jeep so the two of them could speed through, arriving to our apartment immediately after my mother called him on the night we heard noises outside, armed with a flashlight and his rifle, my mother clinging to his arm and saying out there, ñaño, out there, my uncle shrugging her off with his elbow and saying don't be hysterical, Cecilia, my uncle unlocking the sliding fence rail and unbolting the door to the patio, his flashlight barely catching a glimpse of the runaway culprits, rats, which were scurrying away and there, right up there on the wall, a rat was climbing on a pipe so my uncle aimed his rifle and shot, warning us, as he held the fallen rat by its tail, that more of them would turn up, as in fact they did, sneaking inside our kitchen and hiding behind our stove, where we could hear them struggling against the heat and the wiring and where, days later, the stench of their decay would prompt my mother to order Manuel to remove them, banging on the side of the stove to check if any of them were still moving, and after my Uncle Jacinto packed his rifle and left, my mother stood still by the dining room table, or perhaps she stood still by the stove, or perhaps she didn't stand still at all but paced around the living room, considering whether it was prudent to finish our dinner and risk hearing noises again, eventually saying let's go watch television, Antonio José, to which I probably replied something like there's nothing on, Mom, nothing at all, and as Antonio enters his mother's bedroom in the apartment on Bálsamos Street he doesn't remember if that night his mother rushed to her bedroom to turn on the television, or if she waited for him to come along with her, either way he remembers following her and finding her checking the locks to the balcony, drawing the already drawn curtains and fastening them with a pin, sitting on her bed without removing her Egyptian sandals, her back upright against the headboard as I pulled her dresser bench next to her bed, careful to not bump her dresser and disrupt her collection of perfumes, which are no longer there, some of them with only a mist left, water lilies and carnations and mari-gold all jumbled into one soothing scent (one evening when she couldn't find the scrap of plastic he'd gifted her she pulled the cur-tain rod from the guest room's wall and used that to beat him instead), and as his mother flipped the channels she chided herself for not anticipating that with only a few weeks left before the presi-dential elections the political ads had of course usurped most of the evening's programming, some of them showing El Loco promising to fight the oligarchy and free the land, others showing León's candi-date promising sound macroeconomic policies, others showing El Loco returning to save his people in a helicopter, others warning viewers about El Loco by showing El Loco pouring a glass of beer over his head, others showing El Loco addressing thousands of followers, mops and brooms and cardboard signs alive and wild everywhere and is there a parent in the crowd?, El Loco asks, please raise your hand, let's see you, gentleman, here with your son, let's talk the truth, no tales, I'm going to demonstrate to you that you are not the same for León, sir, with the greatest respect, if your eighteen year old son falls in love with León's daughter would they let him in their house?, no, no, no, but if León's grandson were to leave your daughter pregnant, oh, ha ha, it's just our boy being a rascal, is this not the truth, yes, yes, yes, or she would be imprisoned and forsaken with a bastard child like they have forsaken and imprisoned my beloved country, and as Antonio tries to rest on his mother's bed he cannot recall which ad finally drove his mother to fling the remote control across the room, the triple A batteries crashing against the TV stand and rolling on the floor, and although he knew others would have been alarmed at her violence he stood up as if nothing had happened, turning off the television, picking up the remote, and not finding the batteries anywhere, searching for them under her bed, sticking his whole body in there, casting away spiderwebs and crawling on his elbows and finding the batteries by a stack of books on transpersonal psychology, yoga, meditation, discovering for the first time she owned these kinds of books, which he was to secretly read in the last months before he fled to the United States (the Autobiography of a Yogi by Paramahansa Yogananda, for instance, which contains scientific footnotes underscoring the legitimacy of levitation and out of body migrations), and as he resurfaced with the batteries his mother smiled at him, a steady, gentle smile that she seemed to be trying on and that she seemed unwilling to unsettle by wiping the sweat off her eyelashes or swatting away her red locks of hair from her cheeks, resting her warm fingertips on his wrist and smiling and saying thank you, Antonio José, next time I'll have to remove the batteries beforehand, and as Antonio lies down on her bed and closes his eyes, unable to remember the warmth of his mother's body when he would bunch next to her in her bed but able to imagine her warmth by placing his hands flat on his chest, feeling at last how exhausted he really is from the long flight, he irrationally expects different of himself, as if perhaps this time he could become the one who could console her, no, he's yanking his arm away from her, tossing the batteries on the empty side of her bed and saying, before slamming the door on his way out,

I told you there wasn't anything on, Cecilia, yes, he's really exhausted, he should try to sleep (and on Saturday afternoons during their last year together she wouldn't turn on the television but would lie down quietly on her bed, sick from the methacrylic acid she was using to glue those acrylic nails, although he didn't know then or pretended he didn't know then that she was sick), and on those Saturday afternoons Antonio used to dispatch his mother with a curt goodbye Mom, I'm off to play soccer at school, which wasn't true, every Saturday afternoon Antonio boarded a bus to San Javier, where he boarded Don Alban's bus to Mapasingue, where along with the other members of the apostolic group he taught catechism to the poor (don't let your left hand know what your right hand is doing, the Jesuits had taught him, and yet even after all these years in which he likes to believe he has disavowed anything that sounds like a precept, he still can't share with others anything remotely good about himself: no one at Stanford knew that he taught catechism in Mapasingue for four years, no one in San Francisco knew that, despite barbing his memories of Mapasingue with inquiries like do you really think that your paltry exposure to the poor has marked you instead of just serving as an excuse to feel like a chosen one, he still thinks of himself as that pious boy standing on the hills of Mapasingue atop the stairs that lead to Guayaquil), and it occurs to him, as he tries to sleep, no, how can he sleep without first taking off his clothes and turning on the air conditioner, which is revving up and canceling the noise of the utility vehicles speeding along Bálsamos Street and of the people watching television upstairs, the decrepit air conditioner that used to consume so much electricity that his mother wouldn't switch it on unless the heat was as unbearable as it is now, and as he lies down again and tries to sleep he wonders if perhaps the reason he thought his mother was overreacting about El Loco turning Manuel into a threat to them at home was that he rarely interacted with Manuel, rarely saw Manuel, barely remembers anything about Manuel except sometimes, during dinner, the sound of his dinner plate vibrating on top of the dryer when the dryer was on, or Manuel's soft voice saying yes, Doña Ceci, right away, Doña Ceci (one day when his mother was out Antonio sent Manuel on an errand to rent pornographic videos featuring Ginger Lynn), or perhaps he thought she was overreacting because it was convenient to behave as if nothing threatening was happening in Guayaquil since he was leaving this miserable place anyway, or perhaps he thought she was overreacting because Manuel, who must have been fourteen or thirteen years old and was even skinnier than Antonio had been back then, looked harmless, or perhaps he thought she was overreacting because at school everyone portrayed El Loco as a coarse loony who couldn't even incense fruit flies into revolting, a coarse loony with a raspy bus driver voice who flaunted his chest hair and said ridiculous things like León has watery sperm, and one day during recess what the Fat Albino said about that coarse loony was if that pest wins we'll have him out in less than a week, to which we all hooted and clapped because the Fat Albino was the grandson of León Martín Cordero, carajo, the ex president my mother still rooted for, the one we've seen that week or the week before or the year before on television saying that only prostitutes and junkies have ever voted for El Loco, and yet as everyone hooted and clapped the Fat Albino turned toward Antonio and said I don't know why the Drool here's laughing, we're talking about ousting his dad, to which everyone hooted and laughed, relishing the opportunity to pin El Loco to Antonio as some of them had already tried to do by linking Antonio's erupted face with El Loco's pockmarked face, calling him La Baba Loca or La Baba Bucaram to see if those nicknames would stick, and yet Antonio thought he'd succeeded in squashing those nicknames with threats to beat up his classmates, but no, that day during recess everyone was waiting to see if Antonio would threaten the Fat Albino or leave himself wide open so of course Antonio said shut up Yucca Bread, or perhaps he said shut up you lazy piece of crap, to which the Fat Albino replied something like watch what you're saying, hijueputa, which is what everyone expected the Fat Albino to say because he was the kind of fellow who liked imparting mockery but not receiving it, which was the same kind of fellow Antonio was, and so the pushing and shoving began, the pushing and shoving that everyone usually attributed to freshmen who feigned a willingness to fight but never did, goddamn cowards, and although neither Antonio nor the Fat Albino wanted to look like cowards they were both on probation, whatever, probation or no probation, as everyone crowded around them yelling grab that caraeverga by the neck, Yucca, kick that fat ass in the balls, Don Buca, they had no choice but to end their freshman sideshow and fight, not that they didn't hate each other to begin with, during their sophomore year they'd both made the soccer team and because they lived close to one another, and because Antonio's mother didn't have a car and soccer practice started at six in the morning, their coach had suggested that the Fat Albino give Antonio a ride, to which the Fat Albino had agreed to earnestly, putting on a show of being so happy to help the team, coach, driving Antonio grudgingly three times a week until the morning when the Fat Albino asked his chauffeur to race up on Bálsamos Street to pick up Antonio in reverse (why did that backwards driving feel like such a putdown?), and as everyone crowded around them Antonio lunged at the Fat Albino and the Fat Albino swung at Antonio and Antonio stumbled and Father Ignacio broke up the fight, and although both of them were on probation only Antonio's mother received a call from Father Ignacio informing her that he needed to talk to her in person because this time he was really going to expel Antonio, and that night his mother said I've had it with you, Antonio José, I'm not finding you another school, after all the sacrifices I've made to keep you there, now you'll end up graduating from some antro in El Guasmo, looking defeated by what she heard herself saying because she knew that Antonio loved San Javier, knew that when their green cards had gone through during his sophomore year she'd asked him if he would rather stay and wait to graduate with his friends before moving to the United States and he'd say yes, Mom, please, Mom, and what he said to her that night after Father Ignacio called her was I think this time Father Ignacio is serious about expelling me, Mom, help me please, tell him it had something to do with my father, tell him my father came back and we had an altercation, anything, please, tell him anything, Mom, and the next day in Father Ignacio's office his mother did lie to him so Antonio could stay in school and graduate with honors but without medals and then leave her, and when his mother visited him in San Francisco she told him that after he left Manuel started bringing her soup, that Manuel learned to cook so she would have more time to rest, that Manuel had volunteered himself when she needed someone on whom to practice the nonordinary states of consciousness therapies she was learning, and what Antonio didn't tell her then or later is that one Sunday in the weeks or months after the caravan for El Loco appeared on Bálsamos Street he'd ventured to the patio outside to check on Manuel, knowing that on Sundays all domestics in the neighborhood had the day off, sneaking inside the cement box that had been built into the patio for live in domestics and that seemed to have been forgotten long ago because the bottom part of the door, hollowed by mold or rain or moths or mice, no longer reached the floor, because the door had a hole instead of a handle, because inside someone had stored piles of bathroom tiles and splotched cans of paint, because the mattress on the squalid bed was as thick as a straw mat, because squashed mosquitoes blotted the walls, because the whole place wasn't bigger than a tool shed, and as Antonio tries to sleep and free himself of the caffeine he ingested on the plane from San Francisco to Guayaquil he cannot remember if the miserable conditions in which Manuel lived moved him, no, they didn't, he was too focused on his salacious pursuit, although even if he hadn't been so focused on finding pornographic magazines he probably would have found a way to overlook the implications of this sight, searching through Manuel's things without disrupting them, as if demonstrating to whoever could be watching that he had good manners, and what doesn't amaze Antonio is how easy it was for him to actually believe he was searching for posters or placards or any evidence that Manuel was a Bucaram subversive, searching and finding a black and white photograph of an old woman who could have been Manuel's grandmother or his mother or an aunt, searching and finding a bundle of letters written with the same meticulous calligraphy and the same florid language that did not detract from the wistfulness of the contents, all of them mailed from Calceta, a small town in

Manabí, searching and finding under the mattress a page that had been ripped from Diario Extra, a sensationalist tabloid, and yes, a picture of El Loco was on one side, but the kind of picture he'd hoped to find was on the other (a voluptuous woman in a green bikini who was nestling her forehead on a palm tree, holding it with both hands as if it were a placeholder for her lover to be, you, inviting you to admire the tan of her thighs and the flow of her hair, which Antonio did, then and later in his room), returning the ripped page from Diario Extra before Manuel came back that evening because Antonio liked to think of himself as the type of person who wouldn't have just used that scrap of picture without returning it or praying the rosary right after he was done, and although Antonio doesn't remember if a rosary prayer was part of that Sunday afternoon, or that Sunday evening a week or two later when Manuel was supposed to come back but didn't, Antonio does remember that while he was worrying about whether through the mysterious hand of god Manuel had found out that he had searched through his things and had therefore decided not to come back, his mother was worrying that with only a week or two left before the election Manuel had defected to join a group of Bucaram subversives, although on the Monday or Tuesday after Manuel didn't come back she tried to make it into a joke by saying that Manuel was probably inflating balloons for the caravans for El Loco in Esmeraldas, and yet by Wednesday or Thursday the joke was over because someone had informed her that two or three other domestics down the block hadn't come back either, and then on Saturday morning Antonio heard the bell ringing, the door opening, his mother saying where the hell have you been, Manuel, less as a question than as an accusation, as if him being anywhere but here was an outrage, her voice as hoarse as always, careful not to reveal that she might be scared, holding on to the doorknob in case she had to slam the door shut, although the brass chain was still fastened, my grandmother, Manuel was saying, she couldn't get out of bed, Manuel was saying, couldn't eat, couldn't stop sobbing, Doña Cecilia, at the bus stop on Sixth Street the domestic for Doña Elena had been waiting to tell him that his grandmother was sick, that his grandmother was asking for him, and it was only when he was already on the bus to Calceta that he'd realized he didn't know our phone number, hadn't memorized it, and while Manuel spoke Antonio approached his mother but she did not acknowledge him, you're lying, his mother said to Manuel, relieved by the finality of her verdict, didn't they teach you not to lie in school, you never said anything about a grand-mother in Calceta, which was true, of course, except that Manuel had never said anything about anything because we'd never asked, in frag-ments Manuel repeated himself, perhaps hoping to make his sad journey more real to her, sensing that my mother wasn't listening because his voice started to lose conviction, you can't come in, she said, you don't work here anymore, and as I stood next to her, express-ing my solidarity with her decision, Manuel said talk to the señorita, niño Antonio, tell her I'm not lying, and yes, I had leafed through enough of his letters to at least confirm he had an ailing grandmother in Calceta, and yes, Manuel did look as if somewhere along his return here he had declined to exist and what remained of him stood before us, a skeletal child of fourteen or thirteen who was clearly grieving, and although it is easier for Antonio to imagine himself pushing Manuel away and slamming the front door and saying don't come back, you hear, which allows him to distance himself from the pathetic thing he actually did by deploring the violent thing he didn't do, what actually happened was that Antonio said he does have a grandmother in Calceta, Mom, he does, which made his mother wince, as if Antonio was interrupting a scene in which he didn't belong, and perhaps anticipating her reaction he had said what he had said without much conviction, less as a fact but as a distant possibility, and so Antonio didn't insist and walked away, and so his mother shut the front door and that was it for Manuel, and a few weeks later El Loco lost the elec-tions by an alarmingly small margin, and a few months later Antonio graduated from San Javier and fled this miserable place, and in the next twelve years more of our cultivated prefects and ministers embezzled our country and fled, and more people were forced to live in the most precarious conditions, and more children of the self pro-claimed Ecuadorian elite who barely managed to graduate from third tier American universities bestowed upon the country the useless wisdom that we must not give the poor the fish but teach them how to fish, and twelve years after leaving this miserable place Antonio decided to return because Leopoldo called him and said come back and let's run for office, Drool, and a few years before he decided to return his mother told him about the night two armed men robbed her outside their apartment on Bálsamos Street, Antonio José, the thief on the driver's side was pulling Monsi up by her hair and beating her with the butt of his pistol so she would stop shrieking, and the next thing I remember is the car speeding us away from the city, and the man in the backseat next to me pointing his pistol at me, and Monsi insulting them and me trying to calm her down, she didn't want to budge so she was stuck between the two front seats, I was trying to calm her down and then one of them yelled at me to shut up already, I am trying to calm her down because I want to avoid a tragedy, I said, I was very calm, following Father Davila's advice that in times of need one should invoke one's ancestors and becalm oneself by inhaling, exhaling, in those days I was meditating at least three hours a day, Antonio José, saying to Monsi come back over here, my dear Monsi, pulling her to the backseat because the man up front was hitting her, don't let him hit you, my Monsi, come back here, hugging her so she would calm down but she kept screaming not again, I've had enough of this, and then the thief next to me asked for my handbag and I said to him this bag is old so if you want to take it, take it, but I am not going to give you my documents because they're tough to reissue, give me your wallet, he said, no, I said, I am going to give you my money, I have money that I took out of the bank this morning that's going to benefit you, because I know what interests you is the car but also the money and the others that dropped you off are not going to know you are going to have this cash, but leave us some money for the taxi for the way back because otherwise how do we get back, and please don't leave us somewhere dangerous, we're two women alone, so I gave him my money and he let me keep enough money for the ride back, I think he was more scared than I was, they were both between sixteen or seventeen, apparently they hire these kids from the street and they make them do these robberies for a little bit of money, the newspapers recommend not fighting with them since they are likely to be nervous and can inadvertently shoot, plus we've heard they are often given drugs to bolster their courage, and the next thing I remember is the car speeding us away from the city as I held Monsi's hand and I was saying to her it's okay Monsi, they won't hurt us, right?, you won't hurt us, they just want the car, Monsi, there's no need to point that gun at us, and then, as if tired of listening to me, the thief in the driver's seat stopped the car and said take off your shoes and get out, viejas del carajo, and of course we did, exiting as fast as we could and finding ourselves in a barren field where someone must have detonated something because it was strewn with shards of glass and broken rocks, walking for at least an hour before we encountered a small house where an old man who made a living by scavenging metal scraps committed himself to driving us back to the city, Monsi's feet were permanently damaged, Antonio José, sleep now, Antonio, sleep since tomorrow you'll be meeting with Leopoldo for the first time in twelve years, and after I arrived home the memory of the robbery settled on me and I couldn't sleep in my room anymore, his mother said, I had to switch to the guest room where I felt more protected even though the panic attacks didn't ebb, and in San Francisco his mother told him that a year after El Loco lost the elections Manuel showed up at their apartment on Bálsamos Street again, pleading for a second chance, this time I won't disappear, Doña Cecilia, I promise I won't disappear, and soon after she agreed to give him a second chance Manuel started bringing her soup, learning how to cook so she would have more time to rest, volunteering himself when she needed someone on whom to practice the nonordinary states of consciousness therapies she was learning at Centro Pachamama, and what surfaced during these therapies astounded me, Antonio José, when Manuel was born his mother had to abandon him by the side of the road because his father had vowed to drown him, I don't know, Antonio José, maybe that man thought the child wasn't his, thankfully a good soul picked him up and tried to raise him, Grandma Angela, Manuel called her, poor Manuel, his troubles didn't end there, somehow his father found them and burned Grandma Angela's house, little by little Manuel began to liberate himself from the past, Antonio José, Manuel and Grandma Angela had to escape and find refuge in a different province, little by little I began to encourage him, he was seventeen years old and hadn't even finished elementary school, Antonio José, I offered him meditation lessons, Reiki, Bach flower remedies, and one day Manuel enrolled himself in night school and bought himself a pair of dress pants and said to me I've always wanted to wear pants like these, Doña Cecilia, and before I was to leave he was almost done with trade school, Antonio José, before I was to leave Guayaquil for good he had tears in his eyes and said what am I going to do without you, Doña Cecilia, what am I going to do without you now.

VI / ANTONIO'S GRANDMOTHER GIVES ADVICE

Tu tío Manolo rentaba sus caricaturas, Antonio's grandmother said. Ataba una piola en las barras de hierro de las ventanas de afuera y ahí rentaba sus, ah? ¿Qué pasa ahora, Enrique? ¿Qué? En la mesa de noche, Enrique, adónde más? Siempre tu abuelo lanzando gritos que adónde están mis remedios y ahí mismo siempre están. Tu tío Manolo solía arrastrar las sillas del comedor hacia la entrada de la casa y ahí rentaba sus caricaturas a los niños del barrio. No quería que yo supiera pero claro que sabía. Yo lo escuchaba forcejeando con las sillas del comedor, esas sillas que en ese entonces eran el doble de su porte, a mí nunca me gustaron esas sillas, Antonio José, cuando tu abuelo y yo nos casamos tuvimos un peleón sobre qué juego de comedor comprar y no llegábamos a un acuerdo hasta que un día Enrique se apareció en la casa campante con camión y cargadores y dice aquí están tus cachibaches, Primavera. Manolo solía arrastrar esas sillas por el pasillo oscuro donde tu tío Edgar una vez le disparó una flecha a tu mamá y casi le zumbó el ojo, ese fue el final de Indios & Vaqueros para los chicos, Antonio José, tus tíos siempre la andaban cazando a tu madre con arcos y flechas pero ella era la preferida de tu abuelo, la única niña entre seis varones, y esa noche Enrique se dio cuenta que el ojo de tu madre estaba hinchado entonces dice ¿qué es que está pasando aquí? Tu madre no quería decir. Tus tíos tampoco. Tu tío Cesar nos delató haciendo barullo de indio bajo la mesa. Enrique les quebró las flechas y les dobló los arcos y les dio correazos a todos y dice se quedan sin merienda estos mamíferos. Para mí que tu abuelo exageraba. Porque el ojo de tu madre no estaba tan hinchado. Un día encuentro una de las sillas del comedor de cabeza en el pasillo, en ese pasillo que nunca recibía luz, por eso es que nunca instalé cuadros en las paredes de ese pasillo, Antonio José, Enrique me jorobaba y decía por qué tan vacío el pasillo, Primavera, por lo menos pon fotos de los chicos. Pero para qué, Enrique? La silla estaba tirada boca abajo ahí y yo voy diciendo Manolo, Cesar, Edgar, las sillas en esta casa no son para estar bobeando, quién arrastró esta silla, salgan en este instante. Nada y nadie. Encuentro a tus tíos en mi dormitorio, encerrados en el clóset. ¿Qué están haciendo ahí? Somos cavernícolas. Manolo arrastraba las sillas por el pasillo y luego por el patio ese grande que teníamos repleto de animales. ¿Qué? Deja de gritar, Enrique, le estoy contando a Antonio sobre el negocio de caricaturas de Manolo. No te escucho, ¿Enrique? ¿El control remoto? En el primer cajón de la cocina. ¿Cuál era el nombre de nuestra chancha, Enrique? ¿Enrique? ¡Enrique! Sí. Cuando vivíamos por La Universal. Rosa. Eso mismo. La Chancha Rosa. Míralo al abuelo. En su vida veía telenovelas cuando vivíamos en el Ecuador y ahora el doctor Rodriguez no para de ver estas telenovelas gringas. ¿Sabes por qué estas telenovelas gringas nunca se acaban? Eso mismo. Teníamos un venado, Cesar, perdón, Edgar, digo, Antonio, Antonio José, teníamos un venado, Antonio José, pollos, tortugas, perros callejeros que Enrique traía sin consultarme, tucanes, el venado al que los chicos llamaban Bambi, el cual se nos murió por un descuido de dejar una ensalada con demasiada mayonesa afuera, y la Chancha Rosa, claro. No sé por qué teníamos tantos animales. A los chicos les gustaba tenerlos. Tu madre quería a la Chancha Rosa y así mismo la Rosa lo adoraba a tu abuelo. Cuando tu abuelo llegaba del hospital Rosa era un bólido a darle la bienvenida. Rosa era enorme, una de esas chanchas que engrandecen a diario, parecía rinoceronta. Y un día la asé. Llegó el día en que la asé, sí. ¿Qué? Ay ya cállate, Enrique. Sigue viendo tus telenovelas tepidas. Tu abuelo todavía cree que la horneé a Rosa porque yo estaba celosa de tu madre. Vaya a creer. Tu abuelo ni pasaba en la casa. Rosa era otro juguete para los chicos pero también era una cerda. Una chancha, Enrique. Tu madre no se enteró que la habíamos asado hasta que la cocinera la sirvió en bandeja para la cena de graduación de César. Teníamos visitas y me dicen bien gustoso el puerco, Primavera, pero por qué los chicos no prueban bocado? ¿Nos quieres envenenar? Rosa se embestía contra tus tíos cuando los veía persiguiéndola a tu madre. Hubieras escuchado los chillidos que le salían a Rosa cuando los perseguía. Como ¿qué tipo de cantante? Ah, no. Yo no sabría. Tu abuelo nunca me llevó a la ópera. Tampoco hay óperas aquí en Gainesville. Por eso mismo me hice miembra del grupo de iglesia hispano. Muy buenas gentes. Con excepción de los cubanos, claro, esos nacieron bulliciosos. Tu tío Manolo ataba una piola en las barras de hierro de las ventanas de afuera y ahí colgaba sus caricaturas para rentarlas. Lo que ganaba lo ahorraba para comprar caramelos de La Universal, la fábrica de caramelos por dónde vivíamos. Compraba unas cestas en miniatura y las llenaba de caramelos y chocolates para después regalárselas a los niños pobres de nuestra calle en Navidad. ¿Qué? Cómo vas a saber tú que era negociado lo de Manolo si ni pasabas en la casa, Enrique. Tu abuelo cree que Manolo se guardaba la plata. Eso no fue así. Los niños limpiabotas y los que vendían chucherías en el mercado se aparecían en nuestra puerta en Navidad y tu tío Manolo les entregaba sus cestas con chocolates. De mis siete hijos Manolo fue el único que hacía esto. Yo no era religiosa, Antonio José, tu abuelo tampoco, ninguno de nosotros lo era. Tampoco le dijimos que lo hiciera. Él lo hacía solito nomás. Todos los años lo hacía solito.

If Leopoldo were a woman I would know what to expect, Antonio thinks, how to dress for our first meeting in twelve years, what to omit about my life in the United States, because if Leopoldo were an attractive woman, for instance, Antonio would know his objective was to impress her with a carefree disposition so on their first meeting he would pick a casual outfit and free associate for her about everything except of course death and desolation and Father Villalba saying how are we to be Christians in a world of destitution and injustice, and if Leopoldo were a former girlfriend Antonio would know his objective was to pretend he hadn't missed her and that life had gone on without her so on their first meeting after years or months of not seeing each other he would wear new clothes she hadn't seen before and listen attentively to her but avoid any references to their time together, and if Leopoldo were his mother he wouldn't know his objective but he would at least know to adopt a confused detachment toward her, and yet in his entire life in the United States he did not have to prepare for a meeting with anyone like Leopoldo, in other words no one with whom to argue about the future of Ecuador, no one to remind him of their time together handing bread and milk to the old and the infirm at the hospice Luis Plaza Dañín, of their time together catechizing the poor in Mapasingue — you and I by the stairs atop Mapasingue, remember? — of their time together at San Javier playing Who's Most Pedantic by Don Alban's cafeteria, and as Antonio rushes along Rumichaca Street to meet with Leopoldo for the first time in twelve years, he wonders if their brand of bantering, which they both defaulted to when Leopoldo called him and said come back to Ecuador, Drool, is perhaps the only option allowed for men to show affection for one another, a performance of how television sidekicks interact with one another (Starsky and Hutch or the Dukes of Hazzard, for instance — I got your back, man — don't touch my back, homo —), except he and Leopoldo haven't been sidekicks in twelve years, and it occurs to Antonio that perhaps their game of Who's

Most Pedantic had been a ritualization of their brand of bantering, and although Antonio doesn't remember the exact content of their Who's Most Pedantic exchanges by Don Alban's cafeteria, he does remember that their game consisted of refuting each other about everything, spoofing the pompous language of demagogues, priests, themselves, digressing manically about the reforms they would enact to transform Ecuador — external debt, what is? — Leopoldo shaking Antonio's hand whenever he won and declaring Always Above You, my friend, and if Leopoldo were a woman Leopoldo would have been at ease in Antonio's life in San Francisco because all of his friends in San Francisco had been women, as opposed to his former life at San Javier, where all of his friends had been teenage boys who expressed their affection by taunting each other with homophobic insults or misogynist interpretations of the language between husband and wife — where's your husband, Drool? — Microphone's at home ironing my shirts, where else? — and if Leopoldo were a woman Antonio would be able to say I've missed you, Leopoldo, even though I didn't think of you since I was occupied trying to forge a new life in San Francisco, I've missed you, and what worries Antonio more than whether Leopoldo's plans to run for office are realistic or not is whether he's capable of meeting with his dear old friend Leopoldo without slighting him somehow — I'm back from the First World, you provincial nincompoops — although perhaps it's too late: Antonio's already wearing his most expensive black suit.

—

Don Alban!

Muchachón!

Leopoldo didn't tell me we were meeting at your restaurant. I didn't even know you had a restaurant. What a wonderful surprise, Don Alban. Looks great.

De a poco we jumpstart the franchise.

Now that I know your place's here I'll be coming back every day.

My restaurant is your restaurant, niño Antonio. Leopoldo lunches here daily. My sopa de bollo he loves. One time when your classmates were here he stood up, you know Leopoldo, always the speechman, and delivered his Ode to Don Alban's Sopa de Bollo. The bollo here does have heft, niño Antonio. I ask Hurtado, Economista, where's your friend? Ah Don Alban, he says to me, still hooked on blondes up north. Your other friend I still see on Saturdays.

Mazinger?

Rafael, yes. That's the one.

He's not going to Mapasingue still, is he?

To Mapasingue and to the dumpster, too. The apostolic group never ended for him. Every Saturday before sundown he and Father Cortez head to the city dumpster to deliver antibiotics and bread. That boy used to be quite the kicker.

Had that robotic speed.

See him sometimes on the soccer field on Sundays. Your classmates still play together.

Rafael's still kicking the ball into outer space? Monkey Shooter we used to call him, remember?

We're out of monkeys, muchachón. How about you, niño Antonio? Did you show the Americans how it's done?

I stopped playing soccer when I got there and . . .

I remember your fast finta dribble. You would grab the soccer ball and bolt. Unstoppable. Staying for good?

For a little while. Longer, maybe.

Let me clear a table for you. Sit, niño Antonio, sit.

I've called Rafael a few times but he hasn't . . .

I remember driving you and Leopoldo and Rafael to Mapasingue every Saturday, remember?

The apostolic group bus. How could I forget?

—

DROOL: First we raise their salaries.

MICROPHONE: Can't. Inflationary.

DROOL: Enforce a minimum wage.

MICROPHONE: Cost goes up, can't compete, factories shut down and reopen in Colombia.

DROOL:	We pact with the Colombians.
MICROPHONE:	Shut down and reopen in Perú.
DROOL:	Pact with the Perúvians.
MICROPHONE:	Remember Paquisha?
MAID KILLER:	Paquisha / es historia / saaaagraaadaaa.
DROOL:	Screw borders. Petty maps.
MICROPHONE:	The impact of cartography on the onanistic tradition. Let us
MAID KILLER:	Ona what?
MICROPHONE:	Nistic.
CHORUS:	Chanfle.
DROOL:	Tax incentives. For factories to stay.
MICROPHONE:	Excellent.
MAID KILLER:	He's got you now, Microphone.
MICROPHONE:	Time?
MAID KILLER:	Two till.
MICROPHONE:	We can be late for Berta's class.
MAID KILLER:	Bobeeeeerta.
MICROPHONE:	Drool wants to keep his milk program?
DROOL:	That's a bovine question.
MAID KILLER:	Bovine! What is?
CHORUS:	Your mom.
MICROPHONE:	Your tax incentive just holed our budget. We'll have to axe your milk program.
DROOL:	You wouldn't do that.
MAID KILLER:	Seen the Microphone do worse, Drool.
MICROPHONE:	Milk for the kids or jobs for the parents. You decide.
MAID KILLER:	With León it can be done?
DROOL:	Don't have to decide. Both.
MICROPHONE:	No problem. Just cover our hole, sir.
MAID KILLER:	Nasty girl.
MICROPHONE:	Privatize the phone lines.
DROOL:	Free milk for a year. Then what?
MAID KILLER:	Think of the children.
DROOL:	Privatize electricity.

MAID KILLER:	Bulb Head, powered by Torbay.
MICROPHONE:	Then what?
DROOL:	Privatize water.
MICROPHONE:	Then what?

—

According to Rafael the Mazinger, Father Villalba founded the apostolic group, a volunteer group that visits the elderly at the hospice Luis Plaza Dañín and teaches catechism in Mapasingue, soon after his appointment to San Javier, an appointment that Father Villalba abhors and that, according to Facundo the Maid Killer, was forced on him by the Vatican after they removed him from his parish in Ambato, where he'd been rallying the flowerpickers against the landowners just as the international flower market was booming, typical of this backward country, those indígenas should be grateful instead of grousing against the hand that feeds them, although, according to Bastidas the Chinchulín, Father Villalba was actually removed because of his diatribes against John Paul II at some conference in Puebla, diatribes that probably resemble the sermons Antonio used to hear from Father Villalba during the Sunday alumni services he used to attend with his grandfather years before he was admitted to San Javier, angry Sunday sermons that would irrupt against the school's alumni, as if the alumni were to blame for him being exiled at a Jesuit school where for decades the same landowners I've been battling against have studied theology, where the sons of the same landowners I've been battling against have studied and will continue to study theology, although, according to Esteban the Pipí, Father Villalba has slowed the inflow of oligarchs by successfully lobbying to axe the school's tuition and hike the difficulty of the entrance exam, and as Antonio approaches Father Villalba's office to request permission to join the apostolic group he's thinking about those sermons in which Father Villalba asks how are we to be Christians in a world of destitution and injustice, how is it possible for a single instant to forget these situations of dramatic poverty, insofar as you did it to one of these least brothers of mine, insofar as you exploited or ignored or mistreated these least brothers of mine, you did it to me, and as Antonio waits for Leopoldo at Don Alban's restaurant he remembers Father Villalba saying that at the supreme moment of history, when your eternal salvation or damnation will be decided, what will count, the only thing that will count, is whether you accepted or rejected the poor. Antonio knocks on the door.

Yes? What is it?

Father Villalba, I . . .

You're interrupting the music, Olmedo. Sit and keep quiet.

On Father Villalba's desk a portable cassette player is transmitting music that follows no distinguishable pattern, roils, seems to progress in a scabrous direction, climbing to an altiplane to toll a bell, and then Father Villalba's music's over and someone in the recording coughs, someone scrapes a chair, and everyone's clapping.

What do you want?

I want to join the apostolic group.

That's for second year students.

I want to join this year.

Next year. You're too young. Next year.

What does age have to do with helping the . . .

You won't get any perks from joining, Olmedo. Let's make that clear. From me or any of the other priests. Or at least not from me. Now go. Shoo.

From his shirt pocket Antonio pulls a page he has ripped from one of his arithmetic notebooks, the white fringe from the ripped page sprinkling on his lap, a sign of some kind, Antonio probably thought back then, just as his abstruse calligraphy, which his classmates will spoof on the blackboard for the next six years, was kind of a sign, too, emboldening him to read out loud what he'd handwritten on the page the night before.

All the efforts of human thought are not worth one act of charity.

Who said that?

You did.

That's Pascal. From my Christmas sermon last year. Is your father an alumnus of this venerable institution?

Father Villalba doesn't wait for an answer but instead attends to the bookcases behind his desk, the three bookcases that if turned sideways wouldn't fit inside the narrow width of Father Villalba's office, which used to be, according to Facundo the Maid Killer, formerly for storing pommel horses, mats, talc, and yet Father Villalba's office doesn't reek of humid leather or rank feet but of dank grass, likely germinating from the mate gourd Father Villalba is sipping as he pulls out what looks like a volume from an encyclopedia, the exhaustive kind, from the eighteenth century perhaps, something out of Tlön, Uqbar, Orbis Tertius, which Antonio will read nine years later during his last winter break at Stanford, Father Villalba riffling through his encyclopedia as if its pages contained disposable knowledge, although sometimes Father Villalba doesn't riffle through the encyclopedia but parts it exactly on the page he's looking for, sliding it across his desk to offer Antonio Pascal's complete quote.

What does your father do, Olmedo?

Father Villalba seems to regret the question as much as Antonio. Does Father Villalba know Antonio's father had to flee the country because of embezzlement charges?

What else have you been transcribing, Olmedo?

Government supplies. My father's . . . away now.

Father Villalba rewinds or fast forwards his cassette, and because the cassette's old and Antonio likes to remember the room and the school as being completely silent, the rewinding or fast forwarding makes quite a commotion, which to Antonio wasn't and still isn't a sign of any kind, and yet after the cassette's done rewinding or fast forwarding — you mustn't listen to a cassette while rewinding another cassette, Antonio José — Father Villalba doesn't press play.

Father Ignacio already knows your name. Better watch it.

Obregon tried to steal the soccer field from us.

So what?

We were there first. You would have done the same. Just because Obregon's a senior doesn't mean . . .

Doesn't matter what I would have done. Don't start any more fights. Ignacio will expel you.

Don't care.

Of course you don't. Did you at least win?

We kept the field. And Obregon lost hair.

Father Villalba leans into the glass top of his desk, examining Antonio, who's sitting upright on the sunken armchair, this scrawny boy whose nose was broken by a senior three times his size, scowling without Christian restraint.

Father Ignacio thinks Mapasingue is too dangerous for freshmen like you. As if your classmates were clamoring to spend their Saturdays teaching there. You and Leopoldo Hurtado are the only freshmen who've come to see me. Have you met Leopoldo Hurtado yet?

—

MICROPHONE:	Then trickles down.
DROOL:	And while the people wait for your trickle, more of them starve.
MAID KILLER:	Apples from a tree, pickles in a jar.
MICROPHONE:	We set aside funds for a safety net.
MAID KILLER:	Mosquito / chicken / gallina / hen.
MICROPHONE:	Free milk.
DROOL:	Free bread.
MAID KILLER:	Roof and employment?
CHORUS:	Shut up, fatty.
MICROPHONE:	We subsidize natural gas.
MAID KILLER:	You just axed that subsidy.
MICROPHONE:	That was transportation, lerdo.
DROOL:	Pay attention, fatty.
MAID KILLER:	How do I get to school with such high bus fares again?
DROOL:	Why come to school? You'll flunk anyway.
MICROPHONE:	Atrasa pueblo.
DROOL:	Mosquito pipón.
MAID KILLER:	I'm voting for Cazares.
CHORUS:	Shut up, Maid Killer.
MICROPHONE:	What about our external debt?
MAID KILLER:	Hoy no fío / mañana sí.

DROOL:	Later.
MICROPHONE:	Pay later?
DROOL:	Leave it for later.
MICROPHONE:	Gentle reminder.
MAID KILLER:	External debt! What is?
MICROPHONE:	60 percent.
CHORUS:	Chanfle.

—

On Saturdays Don Alban's bus transports the apostolic group to Mapasingue at a sluggish speed, not because Don Alban, who at San Javier also administers the school magazine and the school cafeteria and the intramural tournaments ranging from chess to minisoccer and whom the students have nicknamed Motorcito because of the rapidity of his short legs, isn't a very good driver, but because Don Alban's dilapidated bus, which Don Alban borrows from his neighbor on Saturdays from one to six, is a veteran of too many potholes and crowds weighing down its frame, hop in, people, lots of room in the back, although Don Alban justifies his sluggish speed by telling them I've got to watch out for you, muchachones, got to be on the lookout for those reckless pickup trucks that have proliferated because of the national bus strike, but not to worry, Don Alban says as his bus dodges the scorched tires, the protesters, the pickup trucks brimming with their cargo of people, I'm looking out for you, muchachones, and what surprises Antonio on his first ride up to Mapasingue is that even at Don Alban's sluggish speed they reach the entrance to the hills of Mapasingue quickly, an entrance that isn't too far from where Antonio lives, on the other side of Lomas de Urdesa, three short blocks from the home of León Martín Cordero, carajo, and as Don Alban's bus crosses the entrance to Mapasingue a street vendor jumps in and hollers Chiclets, here the ciruelas and Chiclets, the road getting steeper and Don Alban's bus getting slower, échele ganas, Don Alban, pújele, Don Alban, and what does surprise Antonio is how long it takes for them to spiral upwards and how much time will pass before they can see the city below past these hundreds of boxlike houses that look deserted and toylike in their rightangled simplicity, equilateral and orthogonal and

(Antonio's geometry homework is due on Monday)

as unreal as they would appear to him when he would drive to the cemetery with his grandfather and far away he would see thousands of dots, these tiny houses, latching to the hills surrounding the city, and as Antonio waits for Leopoldo at Don Alban's restaurant he thinks that if someone told him his life in the United States hadn't happened, that he was still on his way to Mapasingue to teach catechism to the poor and that it was from atop Mapasingue that he has been imagining his life in the United States (Antonio arrives at Stanford, learns what to do to change Ecuador, returns to this same spot atop Mapasingue where, moved by the perpetual inequities around him, he decides to commit himself to saving his people (Antonio arrives at Harvard, learns what to do to change Ecuador, joins the International Monetary Fund, and pontificates about what to do to change Ecuador (Antonio arrives at Yale, meets a beautiful English major who worships Artaud, decides he has the strength of character to do without expensive clothes, applies to a graduate program in experimental literature))), he wouldn't have a hard time believing he has been imagining his life in the United States, although of course he would have a hard time believing he has been imagining his life in the United States. Don Alban's bus arrives at the elementary school in Mapasingue where the apostolic group teaches catechism and where unfortunately a pipe, the school coordinator informs Don Alban, has burst, flooding the classrooms and infesting the patio with mosquitoes, which from inside Don Alban's bus Antonio cannot see, although later he will imagine clouds of mosquitoes swarming the inundated patio, dark abuzz clouds of mosquitoes that will remind him of the killer bees everyone was saying were on their way to Guayaquil from Africa or Brazil, and as Antonio waits for Leopoldo at Don Alban's restaurant he marvels at how even the most remote association like that high school rumor about killer bees, which he hadn't thought about in years, can, without in any way diminishing the solemnity he has ascribed to his time teaching catechism in Mapasingue, coexist with his time in Mapasingue, flickering on and off every few years to remind him it's still there, orbiting him as Don Alban tells the school coordinator that the apostolic group isn't allowed to teach outside the school, strict orders from Father Ignacio, Don Alban says, not allowed, and of course the school coordinator doesn't ask why because he can guess why these aniñados aren't allowed outside the school, and of course Don Alban knows the school coordinator knows why so they nod and pretend to be agreeable but what a waste, Don Alban says, what a shame, the school coordinator says. Someone's banging on the metal doors, the wide black entrance doors to the elementary school, although Antonio is no longer sure if someone had actually banged on those metal doors or if the recurrence of the memory of those black metal doors opening and closing, opening and closing for him on all those Saturdays for all those years, has begun to generate in retrospect all possible outcomes associated with those doors, including Father Villalba banging on them on the afternoon the pipe burst. Look, the Rabid Gnome's here, Facundo says. Don't call Father Villalba names, Maid Killer. What's the matter? Father Villalba asks. Don Alban explains what's the matter. Nonsense, Father Villalba says, plenty of room to teach on the sidewalks and on the stairs. Everyone out of the bus. Rafael: teach your students by the trees. Olmedo and Hurtado: take your students to the stairs. Rolando: come with me and let's seal that damn pipe. Father Villalba disappears inside the inundated classrooms. Antonio's students follow Antonio outside but then sprint in front of him, aligning themselves like a wall, feigning consternation: frowning, scowling, thumbs down, stomping forward, clenching twigs like flags and saying you talk funny, profe, god isn't proud, some of them inflating their chests and clapping as if at a military parade, others genuflecting and spoofing desperate pleas to god, others making the sign of the cross, their eyes loopy and crossed, trying not to laugh, and although Antonio doesn't remember their faces or their names or anything about them — how can you ascribe so much meaning to teaching catechism to the poor in Mapasingue when you can't even remember anything about the children you taught there? — no, that isn't true, I remember them rushing toward me outside the church after their first communion ceremony and embracing me as if I were San Bosco — you only remember that moment outside the church because you had once been devoted to San Bosco and you still like to think of yourself as San Bosco (before going to sleep Antonio would often reread his comic book about San Bosco rescuing the street children of Turin) — and although he doesn't remember the children's faces or their names, he does remember hoping that Father Villalba would witness how much the children liked him, and he also remembers that, despite his broken nose, which still can't smell anything, he'd been able to detect the scent of perfumes on some of the children, water lilies and marigold from their mothers perhaps, because he'd seen their mothers combing their hair with combs like pocket rulers and fastening the topmost buttons of their shirts as if they were heading to a baptism or a wedding. From atop the stairs Antonio sees Father Villalba driving away. Is it unreasonable for Antonio to still expect Father Villalba to wave him goodbye? To approach him before leaving? To say the lord has chosen you? To say you must set forth? You must prepare yourself for the great task that awaits you? To say Father bless this your apostle? Months or weeks later Father Ignacio announces that Father Villalba has had some difficulties with his heart. A heart attack, Facundo, yes. Not sure for how long, Rolando. Eventually Father Villalba returns with a pacemaker. Two old women start attending Father Villalba's Mass on Thursday afternoons, placing their tape recorders by the altar. Hey is that your grandma, Drool? Is that Mama Robot, Mazinger? Shut up Maid Killer! By orders of Father Villalba the tape recorders are relegated to the side exit. On the way out Facundo knocks on the plastic window of the tape recorders. Knock knock. Who is? Rabid Gnome is. Faith challenges the historical progress of the powerful. Father Villalba's sermons retain their vigor. Lucio was shaking, Father Villalba says. What's the matter, Father Lucio, I said, get ahold of yourself, what has happened? A terrible sight, Father Lucio said. By the side of the road a woman had fainted, and her three small children, he said, but Lucio couldn't go on, Father Villalba says. One of her children was holding on to the woman's braids on his lap, he said, but his hands were limp, Father Villalba, as if the veins in the boy's hands had exhausted her transfusions and they were now resigned to whatever the sun wanted to extract from them. And the other two children looked indifferent to the woman's plight, Father Villalba, but they weren't indifferent, Father Lucio said. I knelt by the woman's side and saw that the children were fainting of hunger like the woman had fainted of hunger. Father, she pleaded, bless me, Father, she pleaded. Father we are dying, Father Villalba says, breaking off to take in the conglomerate of teenage faces, this squat bald priest with the oval shoes, looking for where his warnings are going. We are on the side of the poor only when we. When we. We are not. We. The news of Father Villalba's death doesn't yield widespread consternation. At his funeral, the two old women reappear, placing their tape recorders atop his casket. Which tape should go first? They cannot agree. One of them just starts hers. The other one follows, upping the volume of her artifact. How are we on the side / Christians of the / in a poor world / alongside. A somber old priest next to Antonio dabs his eyes in his handkerchief. He's not from San Javier. Not from Ecuador, either. A scuffed black trunk, abloom with faded tags, separates him from Antonio. The curled corners of stickers for Vallegrande, La Habana, Valdivia, Ambato have been reattached to the trunk with tape. Former pebbles, crag particles, and hair adhere to what remains of the tape's adhesive paste. This foreign priest observes Antonio reading his luggage but fatigue seems to preclude him from smiling at Antonio. From telling him about the stickers, places he's been. There goes the last of them, he says. Father Villalba drives away. Goodbye, father.

—

Doctor Drool.
Mister Microphone.
Economista.
Abogado.
Good flight?
Yes, ingeniero.

Good to hear, arquitecto.

Dígame licenciado.

Licenciado.

Gracias. Muchas gracias.

Antonio and Leopoldo feign a demure stroll toward each other, shaking hands like portly congressmen. They palm each other's back, as if dusting each other, and embrace.

Missed me?

With all my heart, etc. How's the village? Swelling visibly?

Leopoldo steps back to appraise Antonio's black suit, exaggerating a professorial stance.

That's a great shirt, Leo. I favor the French cuffs, too. Pink's still your best color though.

That suit's two sizes too small, Drool. Must be a new fashion. Flypaper for pickpocketers? You must be boiling in there. Last time I spotted a black suit was at Bohorquez's funeral.

Bohorquez's dead?

Out whoring. Got shot. No one told you?

No one told me. And you didn't tell me we were meeting at Don Alban's, either.

Surprise? Surprise!

—

At their spiritual retreat in Playas, during their sophomore year at San Javier, inside a cement structure that looked like a boarding school / beach house that had been abandoned in the 1970s, Father Lucio chastened them with a phrase that, because it was hilarious and true and shameful, and because the chapel was dark and crammed and they had to sit too close to each other on foldable beach chairs, none of them would ever forget, and what Father Lucio said that night was that with the same hand that holds the cross of christ you jack off, yes, that's exactly what he said, fellows, we couldn't have asked for a more punnable phrase, with the same hand that holds the cross of christ you jack off, and what Antonio also remembers of that retreat house is the sand spilling inside the cement patio, the sand creeping under the gates that led to the beach, as if trying to escape from whatever was outside, which was just a beach streaked with algae where Father Lucio had allowed them to play soccer before Mass, the wind blowing sand on their faces, the late afternoon surprisingly cold and bleak, although Antonio didn't feel cold or bleak — pass the ball, nerd monkey — and aside from Father Lucio's infamous phrase what Antonio will remember of that spiritual retreat is that after their evening Mass, disregarding Father Lucio's warning that no one was to leave their rooms upstairs — stay alone with the lord, Drool — Antonio escaped from his room and evaded the Dobermans that had been unleashed by the priests and snuck inside Leopoldo's room, where late into the night they argued about what god wanted from them and we have a responsibility to him, Leopoldo says, the lord has chosen us, Antonio says, the Dobermans barking outside Leopoldo's room as Leopoldo raises a glass toward the light and says we must be transparent like this glass so that god's light can pass through us.

—

Did everyone read the parable of the prodigal son? Noooooooooooooo. Yeeeeeeeees. Who wants to read it for us? Check, check, the Microphone to the microphone. What did you call me? Leopoldo will read it for us. I can declaim it from memory unlike the Drool here. Uuuuhhhhhh. Quiet down, children. One day the son of a wealthy man demands his inheritance. Just like Nebot, profe? Leaves home with it. Squanders it. Oh like El Loco in Panamá, profe? Whosoever interrupts the Microphone again will have to run up and down the stairs twelve times. Someone unplug him, we already know this parable. If you already know it tell it to us, Carlitos. Tell us the one about the broom and your mom, Carlitos. Fine I'll tell it. Says to himself I'll go back to Father and say to him Father I have sinned against you. Sets out on his journey home. Father I'm recontra chiro. His father runs to him and embraces him. Bring forth the best robe, his father says. My son was dead and is alive again. My dad would have said you might be alive now but this belt's going to make you dead in less time than it takes to say parable of the don't take my money again, Son. My father would have said if you were dead, and are alive again, that means you're a ghost, and since Grandma's afraid of ghosts, you're going to have to sleep outside, Ramiro. All these years I've been slaving for you, the oldest son complains to his father, and you gave me nothing. I asked for nothing. Your brother was dead and is alive again, his father says. He was lost and is found. The end. So the young one's the sly one and the oldest the sucker, profe? Check, check, Cain to the microphone. Enough of this nonsense, children. Leopoldo assigns homework. Antonio steps aside and takes in the sights atop the hills of Mapasingue. Far down on the stairs that lead down to Guayaquil, a man's hauling up his improbable fruit stand; his daughter's dragging a straw sack; and an old white haired woman's climbing hundreds of stairs, and far behind her there's the rooftops and bustle of the city, which seem impervious to the thousands of tiny houses surrounding it, single room houses built from whatever could be scavenged: caña, cardboard, hoods of trucks, cracked bricks, desiccated palms like on the wall on Antonio's immediate right, which has been patched with a CFP poster from the times of Assad Bucaram. When the white haired woman finally reaches them, she stops and examines the children, as if she has climbed all the way here to check if they are her own. Antonio tries not to stare at her but it's his duty, he thinks, not to overlook any of this. She has wrinkles on her face like knife scars. Her parched hands are swollen, fisted into lumps. As she fans her scorched feet with her purple skirt she examines Antonio and Leopoldo severely, as if demanding an explanation as to why they're there. And what business did we have there? To say: blessed are the poor, for yours is the kingdom of god? To say: it is easier for a camel to go through the eye of a needle than for a rich man to enter the kingdom of god? To say: from here we will project the good intentions that will sustain us for years? Move along madre, Don Alban says, no bothering the catechists. Catechists? They're with the Jesuits, the children say. Ah, she says, bowing in Antonio's direction. May god keep you, Father. May god keep you.

—

The first course Antonio enrolled in after transferring to Stanford from Santa Fe Community College was the Political Economy of Latin America, a course in which the assigned reading exceeded the number of books he'd ever read in English up to that point, a course in which one day the renowned political science professor asked her approximately one hundred students what was the most stable form of government, and perhaps because Antonio was actually Latin American, he raised his hand confidently and did not wonder why no one else was raising their hands when the answer was so obvious, standing up in a room full of Caucasian American students who would one day attempt to set policies for Latin America and Antonio said dictatorships, Professor Karl, which apparently wasn't the right answer because everyone laughed (everyone he knew in Guayaquil had been in favor of León Martín Cordero's strong arm policies because that was the only way to get things done, just as everyone he knew had been in favor of Pinochet because look at Chile now, although later Professor Karl pointed her students to charts that demonstrated that during Pinochet's dictatorship Chile's inequality had actually risen, a chart he actually shared with his mother so she would stop embarrassing him with her nonsense about Pinochet's economic miracle that he'd once parroted at San Javier — how could my mother turn to yoga and meditation to improve herself and still espouse such retrograde views about that murderer? — would it surprise you if I tell you Professor Karl's course was the kind of course I had always imagined you and I would one day take together, Leopoldo? — you didn't have anyone with whom to pace up and down the hallways of Stanford to debate matters of great importance to the future of Latin America? — those Caucasian American students would have called our debating style pompous populism, Leo —), and what Professor Karl said afterwards to dismantle Antonio's asinine answer he doesn't remember anymore, although he does remember that later someone spread the rumor that he was the son of the dictator of Ecuador, the leaden sarcasm of the original remark frittering away upon repeated transmission so that by the time it reached his dorm, the rumor had acquired the undertones of a concealed fact, and because of the expensive clothes Antonio liked to wear (there was no way he was ever going to tell anyone at Stanford that he was on financial aid and that he'd purchased those flashy clothes with a credit card he never paid off, just as there was no way he was ever going to tell anyone that perhaps the reason he hadn't applied to any graduate programs in public policy and hadn't returned to Ecuador to run for office with Leopoldo right after college was that he didn't mind having a pointless database job if it allowed him to buy the kind of clothes he couldn't afford when he was growing up in Guayaquil), and because he didn't dismiss the rumor about being the son of the dictator of Ecuador, on the contrary, he performed the bored confidence he thought his dormmates expected from the son of the dictator of Ecuador — let us not speak of my past, gentlemen — everyone came to believe Antonio was indeed the son of the dictator of Ecuador.

—

You've worn your most expensive black suit in the humidity and the heat merely to witness Leopoldo's envy, Antonio thinks, although perhaps another interpretation could be that, given that he'd hastily shuffled through his wardrobe options in the closet the night before, he'd actually picked his black suit at random, although he knew he'd hastily shuffled through his options not because he didn't care about what he was going to wear for his first meeting with Leopoldo but because he needed to fabricate the evidence that he hadn't picked his most expensive suit to elicit envy, or that he hadn't picked his most expensive suit because he knew you couldn't find anything like it in Ecuador, and yet all along he'd known Leopoldo would know why he'd worn this suit. It wasn't the first time he'd flashed his meager advantages to his friend. Leopoldo had grown so used to it that he'd turned his reaction into a skit, countering Antonio's flaunts by acting like a father resigned to the pettiness of his wayward son. That Antonio equated resignation with approval allowed him, twelve years after not seeing Leopoldo, to do this to his friend again. He could tell Leopoldo that even at a considerable markdown he'd barely been able to afford this goddamn suit. That month after month he consumed every cent of his paychecks at high end department stores. That to afford orange Italian nylon pants he had to limit his grocery shopping to Chinese noodles and ground beef. That because of his shopping habits he only had enough savings to last him six months. But how to say this to Leopoldo without patronizing him? Even if he found a way he knew he was likely to betray himself with an ostentatious aside.

—

MICROPHONE: Doctor Drool.

DROOL: Mister Microphone.

MICROPHONE: Economista.

DROOL: Do you mind if we start over?

MICROPHONE: Reenact your mom and dad in the act of Drool conception?

DROOL: Greet each other differently.

MICROPHONE: You're asking if we can be something other than what we are?

DROOL: I'll start. All these years I've been imagining this reunion and here we are at last, Leo.

MICROPHONE: You would never say that. You would punch me in the shoulder, feign a demure stroll toward me, shake hands like portly congressmen.

DROOL: I wish we would've gone to Stanford together, Leo.

MICROPHONE: I haven't thought about you in years.

DROOL: We could've spiked our Who's Most Pedantic with courses on phenomenology, econometrics, non-retrogradable rhythms.

MICROPHONE: Only what ends continues, pig.

DROOL: I would've been happier staying in Guayaquil with you and arguing with you about everything.

MICROPHONE: Yet another half truth.

DROOL: I'm sorry Leo I . . .

MICROPHONE: You really think you have to confess all this to me?

DROOL: Everything's implicit and not implicit.

MICROPHONE:	Do you feel better now?
DROOL:	Momentarily. No.
MICROPHONE:	How many times do you have to reimagine a heartfelt reunion until it replaces the memory of our paltry reunion?

—

Let's shut the door.

Aren't we expecting company?

They can knock.

They?

Julio. Others will join later.

Why is that lastre even a part of this? Bet you a sopa de bollo Julio won't show. Popcorn's out hunting for hoyos / so pay up for the sopa de bollo. Does that door even shut?

Of course it does.

Leopoldo tries to shut the door but the frame's too big for the door and the door doesn't have a handle. After much fumbling Leopoldo settles for the least ajar option, changing his mind and searching for a chain and a lock behind the counter. The business of locking the door is a clattery one. Leopoldo can't find the key to open the lock so through the hole in the door handle and the hole in the wall he fastens the chain like a bow.

Is this some kind of secret meeting?

Allow me to select a seat for you, sir.

Antonio sits and Leopoldo playacts at searching his pockets for his proclamation but of course he's kidding because clearly he doesn't need a piece of paper to proclaim anything, although he does need to pace up and down the cramped length of the place as if deliberating about matters of great importance.

Still flatlining the currency at the Central Bank, Leo?

We're gathered here today, Leopoldo begins, but of course he's kidding. Our country is at a crux, he says, the annals of history, he says, checking the door as if worried he will be found out. Leopoldo's speech goes on in this vein for quite some time.

Bravo, Microphone. You've convinced me. Again. Now tells us about our plan.

The plan is for Julio to run for president. Leopoldo and Antonio would act as his invisible advisers. Say what you want about Julio but the guy has charisma. Everyone likes him. Plus the price of tuna is up. He can fund the campaign with the surplus of his father's tuna fish empire.

Very funny, Microphone.

And yet Antonio can tell Leopoldo is not kidding. At San Javier Leopoldo often found ways to include Julio, the oldest son of one of the wealthiest men in Ecuador, for years a close friend of Antonio, or at least Antonio had thought so. Antonio isn't about to admit he doesn't mind Leopoldo has included Julio. Just as he isn't about to admit he's relieved Leopoldo's plan isn't bolder.

Try again, Microphone. We're at a crook . . .

Someone rattles the door. Hangar te sésamo, someone shouts. Putative puerta del carajo.

Leopoldo's blocking Antonio's view of the door. As soon as the chain drops Antonio recognizes the poultry voice.

I reckoned you'd be maggoting here. You Pharisee piece of crap.

Leopoldo steps aside so that Facundo can see Antonio.

Why so miffed, Facundito? The Microphone didn't share his homework with you?

Drool?

Maid Killer!

Antonio jumps up and hugs him. Facundo seems taken aback and does not reciprocate the embrace. Even with his broken nose Antonio can smell sardines and motor oil on him.

What boomeranged you back to the village? Missed the smell of garbage?

A garbologist of folklore, indeed.

Garrrrrboooologiz.

Missed the smell of guayaba, ceviche de concha, your mother. What's with the bloody elbows, Facundito? Getting potatory on me so early?

Pota what?

Tory.

Chanfle. That's a good one. If potatory means betrayed by your potato headed pal over there then the answer's affirmative.

Indignantly Facundo tells Antonio what happened earlier at the municipality.

Leopoldo listens to Facundo's story as if it's simply vaudeville, although every time Facundo raises his voice Leopoldo eyes the door uncomfortably.

You're working for León? I thought you were chief economist at the Central Bank. How come you didn't tell me this? How come no one told me this?

The gringa wanted daily updates?

I think so.

Why's he dressed like a narco?

To harrumph the natives?

To collect funds for his goodwill foundation?

Against droolitis.

Droolcephalitis.

Droolnorreah.

Facundo and Leopoldo shake their heads at Antonio. Facundo punches Leopoldo on the shoulder. Leopoldo pretends to be injured and then slaps the back of Facundo's head.

Don't turn on me again, capullo.

Next time coin me for the newsflash, sorullo.

Check, check, the Microphone to the microphone.

Enough of this nonsense, children.

I have to run, fellows.

Off to clock the maidens?

Check, check, the Drool to the Not Funny Mic. Microphone?

Yes dear?

See you Sunday?

Yes dear.

Bring that piece of Drool if he hasn't turned too much into a blip, blip, I'm alien robot from gaytown, blip.

Facundo kicks the chain on the floor as if trying to score a goal and then slams the door on his way out.

What's Sunday?

Leopoldo explains Sunday's their monthly barbeque soccer gathering at San Javier.

Will Rafael be there? I've been calling him but he hasn't . . .

Your husband had a rough time for several years after Jennifer ended their relationship, Antonio.

How did you end up working for León?

Long story.

Apparently we have time. Because it might be a while before our candidate arrives. What do you do for León?

Chief of staff.

Secretary to mini Reagan. Who would've thought.

I believe the Drool used to be a staunch supporter of mini Reagan? I believe the Drool received a recommendation to Harvard from mini Reagan?

Decent schooling has turned me into a staunch opposer. What happened at the Central Bank, Leo?

Leopoldo picks up the chain from the floor and restarts the business of locking the door.

Who's running for León's party? You?

No one. Cristian Cordero might be running on his own.

The Fat Albino?

León doesn't want him to run though.

León doesn't want his grandson to ruin the franchise? What about El Loco's son? Jacobito has girth, too. What's Facundo up to these days?

Leopoldo tells Antonio that Facundo works as a security guard and sings sad songs at La Ratonera.

Facundo came to visit me one day and asked to borrow my dictionary. What for, Facundito, I said. Apparently he thinks his audience finds it funny when he uses big words.

The legacy of Who's Most Pedantic continues. Even back then he loved misusing big words to entertain us. Julio's having a party at his house tonight, by the way.

Is he?

If he doesn't show we can talk to him then.

Don Alban comes back with his son, Rolando, who's carrying what looks like obsolete radio equipment.

Look who's here.

Both of them feign excitement at seeing Rolando.

Rolando!

It's been a while.

Rolando's been busy starting his own radio station.

That's awesome. What kind of music? Are you a cumbia man?

I love cumbias. La del Garrote. You know that one?

That's Lisandro Meza, no?

No, no, but Lisandro Meza's fun.

He's the one who sings about the Antichrist?

Ahora sí les llegó la hora . . .

. . . y si tú no estás preparado . . .

–Shut up.

Rolando, please.

–Shut the hell up, you thieves.

Antonio and Leopoldo look over to Don Alban for help.

–Goddamn thieves. Get out of here.

Come. Let's . . .

I don't have to go, Dad. They do.

Ya, Rolancho. Come.

Don Alban grabs Rolando gently by the arm and guides him to the back door.

What's wrong with the Gremlin?

How would I know?

PART TWO

—

ROLANDO & EVA

Rolando wanted red flyers — blood red — sickle red with red captions
and etchings of veins promulgating the rebirth of Radio Rebelde on
the hills of — No Rolando no one wants blood or veins and here the
sickle never tickled — why did Eva always have to undermine him
with silly rhymes? — which he thought but didn't say   Besides
the name of your radio's too Cuban — how did she get the Cuban
reference? — because she'd claimed she didn't care and had therefore never read about Castro and Guevara and the pointless gore
they'd craved for the continent — it was only pointless because they
failed! — Look at us now — Boys with guns — ugh — Boys who
ended up dead — And those who didn't had boys who had boys
who now peddle lettuce for a living is that a life? — and he could
have continued and said how about your mother what she had to
go through? — and Eva would have probably punched him in the
shoulder — which wouldn't have hurt — okay maybe a little — or tell
him again — no she wouldn't have told him again about the night she
danced to ABBA with her mother in her single room house with the
forkable floor — the rain thundering their tin or thatched roof — her
mother's skirt like a blanket — a carousel — and Eva interrupting
her ABBA story to ask Rolando if she'd ever told him about the night
her mother took her to see the amusement park on the esplanade of
the Estadio Modelo — about that night abloom in aqua and crimson
lights — the Scrambler Mama — the bouquets of inflatable rabbits
and felt giraffes — the Skydiver — the game of matching the waves of
surprise with the right roller ride — imagining the whir of the cotton
candy machine even from afar — holding hands with her mother as
they danced — as her mother lifted her and spun her around — the
Flying Dumbos — the Teacups — and then the tape player crunched
her mother's tape but her mother said doesn't matter chiquita we'll
hum the songs — the vapors of something boiling in the kitchen — mi
chiquitina — rabbit broth? — rainwater flowing underneath the door
like lava — the plague! the plague! — mi chiquitolina — knowing me /

knowing you — quick the lamb's blood — Yes it is a life Rolando and no one wants it coiled with veins or stained with blood — and so the flyers Rolando and Eva are handing out as they climb the stairs to Mapasingue aren't blood red but grass green.

Rolando distributes the flyers but Eva does all the talking — We'll have a recipe hour at noon Doña Flores — ugh — Good afternoon I'm Rosado Sibambe how powerful is your station? — Rolando here's the expert — Thirteen kilowatts — A lucky station? — A mile and a half of signal — How much for a minute of ad? — This isn't that kind of station — We're just starting out we're open to ideas I'm Eva by the way this is Rolando forgive him he's constipated what do you have in mind? — To promote my business — which consists of a telephone booth she has installed inside her living room and which she rents to her neighbors — Paneled it myself — but she wants to expand her business and add another booth — How much for a minute of ad I can record it myself — Doña Rosado I think your business counts as a service to the community — Call me Rosie — We can advertise your business for free Rosie — For how long? — As long as you want — What do I have to buy? — Absolutely nothing — Soundproof booths / come and call / your cousin Mooch — We can help you come up with a catchier jingle yes — Let's use your voice we could sell eggs to the chickens with that voice — Thank you so much Rosie — What does that mean? — What does what mean? — Could sell eggs to the chickens because here the chickens can't afford to buy anything if someone swiped the chicken's eggs that's it no more eggs for that chicken — Maybe no one swiped her eggs — Right maybe she's just a business chicken who wants more eggs — Or maybe her eggs were lonely — And even if she had no money the business chicken could barter for them — Warm four keep two that sort of thing? — Maybe the chicken wants more eggs so she can feel more motherly — Or maybe the chicken just wants to impress the leader of the hencoop — Or maybe the chicken just wants to eat someone else's eggs — Forgive him he's — I'm not constipated! — In any case Eva you have a beautiful voice — Thank you so much Rosie — Come let me show you the first booth in the booth chain — No we don't have time — Ah come on

Rolandis it'll take a minute — and already she's hurrying along with Rosie down a dusty path — goddamnit — among the cement boxes that the people here call homes — and why shouldn't they? — Speaking of eggs this is Felix Cervantes's home from where he wholesales his eggs — and through the window Rolando sees a room full of eggs — hundreds of them — rows of them on trays stacked atop each other almost to the roof — green and red trays but mostly gray — and amid the eggs a white plastic lawn chair next to a barrel sealed with tape — How does he keep the eggs fresh? — but neither Rosado nor Eva answer him so he hurries behind Eva who seems to be enjoying the neighborhood tour — greeting the people who are slurping caldo de salchicha — at least that's what it smells like — the intestines and plátanos that Rolando likes — waving at the people standing under a parasol by a cauldron of caldo de salchicha — That's Lucila's food stand we're here come inside — Oh Rosie I love your plants — full heads of plants hanging from the ceiling — so many of them that vertically the room looks halved — the kingdom of the plants is above us — and even the walls here look halved — red above the waist and gray below — gray like the crossbars on the window and the clouds of cement smudged around the window but not like the incredibly well crafted phone booth which has been paneled with birch and has been framed with metal as resplendent as the silver doorknob — the words Booth One carefully stenciled on the plexiglass — Just the beginning my booth chain will spread hundreds of them all over town one day you'll see — Look at that garden — Come I'll show you — and through the crossbarred window Rolando sees a puny semicircle of land outside enclosed by a tilted fence of wire mesh — and there's an old woman dressed in a white sheet that's either her pajamas or a ghost costume and she looks radiant there with her long white wet hair to the waist — and she seems to be talking to the plants or petting the plants as if trying to console them — That's my grandmother she's apologizing to the tomatoes and the potatoes because we'll have to eat them soon.

Rolando wanted apocalypse in the dial — 666 AM — to cry out over the airwaves how long will we let this go on? — how long will we let them profit from our poverty? — let us descend on a city that's repulsed by us — let us smash the gated communities that we've bricklaid for them — that we've barbed with wire for them — and for what end? I ask you — and for what purpose? — to protect them against us ladies and gentlemen — let us drag them to Mapasingue — to El Guasmo — to La Perimetral — to El Suburbio — to where according to León Martín Cordero only swindlers and rapists and prostitutes live — and yet unfortunately for Rolando his Ecuadorian apocalypse not only reminds him of the speeches he's been rehearsing since he was a freshman at San Javier but of The Exorcist too — to Las Orquideas — to El Fortín — of being twelve years old and sneaking out to the video store with his cousin Eduardo to rent The Exorcist because Rolando's father had forbidden it — the devil here? — no sir — to the video store by that steep hill where he and his cousin once skateboarded like acrobats — speed down Rolandazo no stopping — scraping the whole of his back on the asphalt after a pebble catapulted him down the hill — and at night before going to sleep he would pick the scabs on his back and think about nothing — absolutely not about The Exorcist — which frightened Rolando and his cousin so much they couldn't even finish watching it — is the sin of watching it sin enough to be possessed? — oh please Mother it burns — Rolando and Eduardo alone in his uncle's bedroom and although the curtains were drawn the room was awash in shadows and the bed looked like Regan's bed — the sheets shaped like snakes look — stop that Rolando — it burns — and then his cousin folded the bedspread and switched on the desk lamp — which was shaped like the beard of our lord jesus christ — stop that Rolando — the devil here? — yes sir — for months Rolando's dreams not dreams but reenactments of Regan's slimed impieties — the impotence of the priests against evil — strike terror into the beast lord — the power of christ compels you — you faithless swine — let our voices terrify them — let our voices deafen them — and one Sunday afternoon Rolando's sister arrived home early and refused to return to the Esteros's house where she had been working as a domestic — and when his father pleaded with her she said nothing — and when her Aunt Celia pleaded with her she cried and said nothing — and after Doña Esteros showed up at their house flanked by three policemen who seemed to be protecting Doña Esteros from her surroundings — and after the three policemen informed his father that a gold pendant encrusted with diamonds had disappeared from Doña Esteros's house — exactly at the same time your daughter disappeared from the Esteros's residence isn't that a coincidence? — and after the three policemen wrecked their house in search of Doña Esteros's pendant   why did you take off missy?   we can't find it these people must have sold it already — and after Doña Esteros shook her head at them in disgust and covered her nose with her handkerchief as if their room reeked of mold or bug repellent — a misunderstanding Doña Esteros my daughter would never steal from anyone — and after his father pleaded with his sister — please Almita — it's not about the pendant it's about the principle — god's commandments — I hope you people go to church — after all I've done for your family Don Alban — and after the policemen said we'll have to take her in for further interrogation — his sister screamed at the policemen — at Doña Esteros — at their father — but not at Rolando because he was hiding in his bedroom — I wasn't hiding! — yes I was — I left that house because Doña Esteros's son forced himself on me — what? — that lowlife is lying — please Dona Esteros — Rolando go back to your room — Doña Esteros reappearing at their house again a week later but this time with Father Ignacio and Doña Esteros said she had sought spiritual advice from Father Ignacio and they had concluded — after a night of vigil — a night of prayer — that the only explanation for your daughter to be lying like this — to be blaspheming like this — is because she's been possessed by the devil — what? — Rolando go back to your room — and then Father Ignacio blessed a vial of water and Rolando's father allowed Doña Esteros to sprinkle water on Alma — out Mephistolo — a misunderstanding Doña Esteros it will never happen again — No Rolando no one wants the apocalypse here no one wants cataclysms or uprisings leave the people alone — and so the dial on the flyers isn't 666 AM but 535 AM and Rolando's radio isn't called Radio Rebelde but Radio Nuevo Día.

The radio equipment has been set up in the living room of Doña Luz — an acquaintance of Eva's grandmother who has been prose-lytizing for her comrades at the Movimiento Popular Democratico since the times of Assad Bucaram — Check — Check — Is this thing on? — Welcome to Radio Nuevo Día — The station of the people — What would you like to hear? — Call now! — Good morning in the news today the interim president — Or whatever you want to call him — What would you like to call him? — Call now! — Whoever comes up with the best presidential appellative wins — Appella what? — Tive — Chanfle — What do you win? — Another package of economic packages — Ha ha ha — That's not funny folks — What's economical about these packages anyway? — All they do is skyrocket our fares to cork their bungles — We should call these emergency packages the — What would you like to call them? — Call now! — Oh but what's this? — Two of our neighbors are dropping in at the station folks — Radio Nuevo Día / la radio de tu tía — Guessing Doña Luz isn't home — She isn't but — Are you her grandson? — No but you're on the air — I'm always on the air — Good one — Neither good nor bad señor it just is — There's a song by Mecano about aire / soñé por un momento que era / aire — I don't think Aurora here is saying she's dreaming of air — That's right don't patronize us we're always on the air but no one listens — Oh no Auroris don't melo-dramatize us just because you're on the radio this isn't the Betrayal of Lola Montero — Don't pile on poor Lola she already has enough with knowing she's going to betray someone someday — What makes you think Lola knows? — It's in the title of her soap opera bobita — Don't change the subject I listen to you been listening to you since — Since? — Since before the plane for your president crashed against the Huayrapungo — He was just so young — Everyone's still say-ing that the Americans blew him up because of his hydro gas laws — He was so handsome too — What with those giant eyeglasses like snow globes? — Remember how on election day the voting lines for the women were so much longer than the men's? — Nothing to do with Jaime Roldós Aguilera being handsome the women just happened to dislike the dictadura more than the men — Remember that woman in line who told us about her sewing a replica vest for her husband like the ones Roldós wore and her husband complaining about it looking like a corset? — Don't change the subject I listened to you after Pancho disappeared on you — Don't bring up that botarate — I'm sorry — Apology refused — I'm sorry I was sorry — I thought you came over to listen to me because you were lonely — What? — Sometimes an inrush would come over me like a teakettle and I would close my eyes and see you all alone in that house and I would talk to you in my head ay Leonorcita I would say if you're feeling lonely come knock on my door — Aurora Castellanos / psychic or loca? — And Doña Leonor would knock on your door? — Yes she always did — What else do you see when you close your eyes? — I see a squalid radio commentator asking me what else do I see — Ay Aurorarora sometimes you're such a — No cursing on the air please — What? why not? — I thought La Luz de America said this was our radio — You know Luz hates it when you call her La Luz de America — You're censoring us on our own radio? — Absolutely no censorship here ladies but children might be listening — Ah that's true okay ay Aurorarora sometimes you're such a — Teakettle? — That's it — I boil all wrong mamacita — Come here viejita — No you come here — and Aurora and Leonor are embracing and Rolando's handing Aurora the microphone that he's been holding up to them and Aurora's singing to Leonor la gallina turuleca / está loca de verdad — Remember that song? — Aurora la turuleca — Ha ha ha — Leonora la desodora — Aurora la encantadora — Ladies that's the perfect segue to our contest about what would you like to call the interim president? — Puppet of the oligarchy — Very nice Doña Aurora — Pompous pajorreal — We're warming up folks — Bestia con terno — Keep them coming comadres — Radio Nuevo Día / la radio al día — Up next how to cook a seco de chivo without the chivo — Baah — Speaking of chivos — El Loco is said to be returning from his exile in Panamá — Who's voting for that thief? — If you tell me you're voting for that Loco I'll go loco — Has anyone seen the mansion of this leader of the poor? — Call now! — Speaking of crazy goats — Here's a family friendly version of La Cabra — la cabra /

la cabra / la loca de la cabra / la madre que la cuidó — Want to feature your goat on our show? — Call now!

After signing off at midnight Rolando drives to his house instead of driving to Eva's house because the night before she'd told him she wasn't going to be home — errands to run she said — at midnight? really? — but because he wanted to focus on his first day on the air — for which he had drafted three segments and had rehearsed them in front of the bathroom mirror — trying on different personas — different voices — which he had to rehearse in silence because his father was asleep in the other room — which was an odd thing for Rolando to do — to murmur the grandiloquence he was after — and if an audience would have been watching they might have said that his voice was refusing to participate in the borrowed theatrics of his face — call now! — no I won't — murmuring — don't make me — murmuring — and because he wanted to focus on his first day on the air he tried not to think about how dubious it was for Eva to be running errands at midnight — at least she could've found a better excuse no? — and Rolando is parking his father's pickup truck and he's surprised all the lights in the house are out — the lightbulbs on the porch — the desk lamps in the living room — which is neither good nor bad — just is — and he can imagine his father sleeping in his armchair inside and operating the lights in his sleep — which is a ridiculous thing to imagine — so what? — his father shutting off the lights so that the darkness around him will filter into his dreams and console him there too — and although it's late Rolando expected — what? — what did you expect? — nothing — because my father doesn't see the point of my radio — because what my father probably wants is for me to chain myself to the Formica tables inside his restaurant so that he has time to transform another hole in the wall into a cheap lunch place — welcome to Don Alban's Another Ton of Lunch — and he can imagine his father's franchise of lunchrooms — thousands of caves underneath busted hotels — and what my father probably wants is for me to man a pickaxe and — what? — do you really know what your father wants? — no I don't — why don't you ask him? — what do you want from me Father? — to slave like you? — I'm sorry not to slave like you to grovel like you? — is that the best you can muster against your father? — there's more — more what? — more ass kissing — so kissing him on the mouth is out? — shut up — and Rolando is parking his father's pickup truck and all the lights are out and Rolando's opening the door and — Surprise! — and the lights are on now and there's a sign that reads congratulations — and there's a cake decorated with candles and cookies shaped like radio dials — and his father embraces him and says congratulations Rolandazo — congratulations — and what Rolando will remember later is the stiffness with which he receives his father's embrace — the abruptness with which he breaks from it — the ridiculous silence he adopts to suppress his gratefulness — and Rolando will see himself stepping out of himself and inspecting what's left of him there — you son of a bitch — but then that night begins again and Rolando's parking his father's pickup truck and he's opening the door and — surprise his father says — surprise! — and the lights are on now and there's a sign that reads congratulations — and there's cookies shaped like radio dials — and Rolando says thank you so much father as if accepting a medal from a bishop or a general — how could I forget Rolandazo — and later Rolando will also think of his sister — of how cold he'd been when he'd said goodbye to her at the airport — not cold — no — absent — because the week before she was to fly to Guatemala to begin her crossing of the border to the United States he had imagined saying goodbye to her at the airport so many times that when the day actually came he had already cried — had already emptied himself and embraced her — mi ñañita — and so repeating what he'd already imagined would have felt like acting so that morning at the airport he patted her too hard on the back and said don't sweat it Alma it's probably not as hard as they say to cross that border — which turned out not to be true — they didn't hear from her for more than six months and when they finally did the news was excruciating — Alma corazón — but then that morning at the airport begins again and he's embracing her and saying I'll miss you so much ñañita — please take care — remember when we used to play topos? — topo / topo / topo — and Rolando is parking his father's pickup truck and — surprise! — and the lights are on now and there's a sign that reads congratulations — and there's confetti sprinkled on the floor and toy trumpets on the kitchen table and Rolando's embracing his father and Rolando's saying you don't know how much this means to me.

Someone bangs on the door — someone fusses with the doorknob although the door is open and — Surprise! — and Eva's sprinting toward him as if to tackle him before Rolando can say what the hell are you — and she's tossing the bouquet of orchids she has brought for him on his father's armchair and she's jumping on him and because she's taller than him — bigger than him — no she isn't — Rolando falls backwards — which doesn't hurt — and on the floor Eva's body encapsulates him and Rolando closes his eyes and places his arms around her and hears the translucent plastic of the bouquet crackling — the faucet in the kitchen running — a vase gently landing on the table — a chair trying not to creak.

Later that night at Eva's house — on Eva's bed — she says I heard it all — Heard what? — Your radio show silly — Ah — That Leonor and Aurora are quite something no? — I guess so — You should invite them back or hire them as neighborhood commentators — I guess so — The people were going wild when Leonor and Aurora came on — What people? — By Lucila's food stand — So like three people — No Rolancho I brought chairs — What? — Ten foldable chairs — How did you carry them up? — Look at these arms and weep machote — Ha ha — Oh and your father helped me carry them — Really? — We arranged them in a circle and we sat by Lucila's food stand and listened to you while Lucila stirred her soup to showcase its flora and fauna to the people who were peering inside her pot and asking where are the bollos Lucila? — And Lucila said abracadabra pata de cabra? — My bollos are packed with so much beef they don't float — and when Leonor and Aurora came on the air she and his father noticed people were hanging around longer than before — They were slurping their soups slowly as if they were only allowed to stay if their bowls were full you should have seen them trying to laugh without displaying the food in their mouths their mothers must have taught them not to talk with their mouths open and you could hear some of them saying sock her Leonor that Aurora's an ingrate and most of them didn't want it to end the way it did — So? — So I had an idea — Did they like anything else besides the Leonor and Aurora Show? — and unfortunately Rolando's question comes out too pleadingly — which is what he'd been worrying about while Eva was talking — but fortunately Eva hasn't noticed because she's steeped in her idea which she's about to — Participation is key — I've been telling them to call now — No Rolancho what I mean is different — Call later? — No Rolandis — Call the day after tomorrow? — I was thinking that we could put on a play in the neighborhood plaza and let the audience participate — You mean like a singalong? — We'll cast and direct the play but we'll let them decide what happens next and then we'll transmit it on Radio Nuevo Día — This radio wasn't meant as entertainment — I know Rolanbobo but the plots of the plays don't have to be about Lola's betrayal or about Ricardo the Rich falling in love with Pepa the Poor or about Ricky Martin's hairless chest but about the people — The people love Ricky Martin Eva — I know that — I know you know that — Did you like my radio voice? — Your voice was perfect the people hate acerbic screeds you were lighthearted and kind of funny — Kind of? — Call me now? — You come here now.

That week they wrote down ideas for potential plays dealing with unemployment — with subemployment — with privatization — with lack of sustentation — with the return of El Loco — with the partial demise of León Martín Cordero — with the rumor that an American transnational was partnering with a local consortium to construct a fake snow sky resort on the hills of Mapasingue — which of course meant leveling what currently exists — and that's the plot they decided upon which begins with the local magnate advising the Americans to hire elements from the local police to evacuate the people of Mapasingue who live there illegally — all of them squatters Mister Kissinger — and since the people of Mapasingue resist the local magnate advises the Americans to hire paramilitary squadrons to squash those cockroaches — and since the people of Mapasingue fight back the local magnate equips his people with crowbars and rifles — and since the Americans don't like to hear about crowbars or rifles the local magnate tells the Americans not to worry — I'll take care of it Mister Kissinger — not telling the Americans about the armed paramilitaries who are approaching Mapasingue and are raising their rifles and are aiming at the crowd but they remain frozen like that — Yes that's it with their rifles raised like that — And now the audience has to decide what happens next — and hopefully the audience will clamor for the paramilitaries to lower their rifles and think differently — for one of the paramilitaries to shout stop — everyone stop — these are our brothers and sisters — we cannot open fire on our brothers and sisters — and after Rolando delivers a moving monologue the paramilitaries see the light and put down their arms and join the people of Mapasingue in their fight against the local magnate and the Americans — Ladies and gentlemen do we have a show for you this Saturday — Come to Roldós Plaza and help us decide what will happen to Mapasingue — Need help locating Roldós Plaza? — Call now!

On the night of their first show Rolando's surprised to see so many people in the audience — some of whom are sitting on the foldable chairs and some of whom are standing behind the foldable chairs — and some of them are unwrapping the humitas that the Humita Lady has sold them from a wicker basket and others are improvising a circus show for a newborn who's being burped and others are arguing jovially about something Rolando cannot hear — and on the tree by the stage the Christmas lights are flickering steadily as if to reassure everyone Christmas will come as it always does — and the generator's burring and the night's hot and humid like every other night — Ladies and gentlemen Los Guapayasos and Radio Nuevo Día present Snowflakes in Mapasingue — and the crowd applauds too effusively — as if they're fans of the playwrights already — which in this case include Rolando Alban Cienfuegos and Eva Calderón and the people of Mapasingue — which means they're partially applauding themselves? — and then a clown sporting a blue business suit that has been spraypainted with the word Pig enters the stage holding up what looks like blueprints — and next to him there's another clown that's dressed in the same kind of suit but without the sleeves and with shredded pants who's obviously the Pig's servant because the words Pig Servant have been spraypainted on his suit — and the crowd's booing and jeering and yelling out with that Pig — Down with the Pig! — Hog! — Swine! — I do like pork chops though — Shut up Ramiro! — and the Pig clown approaches the edge of the stage by the angry audience and the Pig clown hesitates as to whether he should go on — looking askance at Rolando who from the side of the stage nods reassuringly — although Rolando isn't sure if he should go on especially because next to him Eva looks worried — and then Rolando signals the Pig clown to please go on and the Pig clown cups his hand like a visor — Hmm this place looks dangerous — Nevertheless it will do for fake snow — We'll just have to make these people disappear — Do you like magic? — I do — Enough about me — Yes patroncito that's an excellent idea that way I won't have to worry about feeding my pig wife and my pig kids anymore — Puff all gone from Mapasingue — Down with the Pig! — Toss him out! — The audience has spoken! — and some in the audience are hurling their humitas at the Pig and the Humita Lady is clutching her wicker basket to her chest as if afraid the people are going to raid the humitas in her basket but she doesn't leave — and Eva's hands are covering her face to not see but she does see — and Rolando's ashamed he's staring at Eva when she's clearly in a state that doesn't allow her to yell stop staring at me — and Rolando hopes she's not thinking that he's thinking I told you so Eva — nothing changes without violence — and as he reaches out for her hand she flails her arms and yells por Dios Rolando do something — and because the crowd seems ready to jump on the makeshift stage the Pig clown exits the stage so all that's left on the stage is the Pig Servant — who has no idea what to do next — and then Rolando enters the stage and says ladies and gentlemen tonight you decide what happens next and you've decided to have no Pig — That's right mosco — But we can't have a play without a Pig — Improvise something you clown — And get off the stage — Yeah we don't want clown paramilitaries on the stage — and then Rolando exits the stage and the crowd tells the Pig Servant to take off his suit — and thankfully the Pig Servant is wearing boxers without holes though his undershirt does have what looks like moth holes — and the crowd seems unsure about whether to laugh at his puny arms and what looks like a burn mark on his shoulder — as if someone had pressed an iron on his shoulder just for fun — and someone in the crowd throws him a white guayabera shirt and says put it on and pretend you're El Loco — Yes be Loco — Loco! Loco! Loco! — and the Pig Servant looks grateful for the part and turns into El Loco shouting I'll never allow those oligarchs conchadesumadres to take over our land — and someone hands him a glass of water which he pours over his head as if to cool himself just like El Loco used to do during his rallies — smudging the white paint on his face — and as he dries his face with his fingers the red paint of his nose spreads to his cheeks — and as he holds a humita from the floor as if it were a live trout he's about to swallow the crowd goes wild — Bring in the Pig! — I'm not going back there — You're making it worse they're going to come get you — which is exactly what the crowd seems ready to do so the Pig enters the stage but stays on the side of the stage — and of course El Loco runs over and brings him center stage as if to present the people with evidence of how ridiculous his opponent looks — Loco! Loco! Loco! — and the Pig clown complies with the role assigned to him and tries to ingratiate himself with the crowd by impersonating León Martín Cordero who's shouting at El Loco you savage only prostitutes and junkies voted for you — Loco! Loco! Loco! — You disgusting uncultured beast — Loco! Loco! Loco!

That night at Eva's house — on Eva's bed — Rolando doesn't know whether to say that was a disaster or that was amazing — either way they're both trying to pretend nothing much happened at Roldós Plaza — At least now we know what the people want — to which Rolando doesn't reply by saying yes Eva the people want to trounce the same old stories — Yes Eva the people want a swine for president — You misunderstand them — Diagram it for me then — I'm not your schoolteacher — Ever tell you about our grammar teacher at San Javier named La Caballero? — Oh boy stories from boys' school — Everyone pined for La Caballero because she was the only human resembling a female in a three mile radius and during class some of my classmates would install their mothers' makeup mirrors atop their sneakers and when she walked down the rows of desks — That's disgusting — What's disgusting is that swine what's the point of our radio if we live under a system that allows El Loco to run for office again and again? — which is the wrong thing to ask — already he can feel his irritation coursing through his voice — The point is to inform them — already he's angry at how unconvincing she sounds when she says that the point is to make their lives better — that the point is to stop asking what's the point all along the hypotenuse of our lives — Hypote what? — Nuse — Chanfle — That's right — Hypotenuse of our — No Rolando it's annoying and you still have clown paint on your ears — White at last — Not funny — Not even a tiny bit? — It's annoying and it's tiring — Isn't it counter to our idea of ourselves not to question what's the point? — Nothing's ever going to change — Ugh — We both know all of this is futile leave the people alone Rolando — I didn't do anything — No one wants the apocalypse here — I didn't say anything — You think I don't know what you've been up to? — Radio Nuevo Día / la radio de tu — You think people here don't talk? — I don't know what you're — You're a terrorist — You're exaggerating a little — You think the acts of vandalism you're planning are going to help anyone here? — No one Eva — What do you think you're accomplishing? — Nothing Eva but probably more than your stupid little plays — which unfortunately he does say — not unfortunately okay I'll say whatever I want — and after Rolando says whatever he wants Eva shoves him out of bed — and she seems to resent that Rolando isn't taken aback despite almost falling off her bed and that Rolando knows she knows there's nothing she can say to rebut him — we're conscientizing the people — she doesn't say — we're veering the discourse toward a truth they will willingly accept as just — she doesn't say — through art we will transcend our condition — she doesn't say — Get out — she does say — Go away — she does say — Fine — Okay — and he's putting on his boots and storming out of her room and imagining how he will slam her front door and drive away and not talk to her ever again and then change his mind after a few days and call her three and four times a day until she picks up but she won't pick up and his frustration at not being able to know if her anger has irreversibly ended their relationship will likely be greater than his frustration at her unwillingness to concede the pointlessness of their plays so he doesn't storm out of her house but instead remains in her kitchen — hearing her switch off the lamp on her nightstand — although he knows she won't be able to sleep — at least he likes to think she won't be able to sleep — and after a while he likes to think she's not asleep — although the room's still dark and he hasn't heard Eva shuffle even once — and after a while the sound of trucks speeding by and the crickets remind him of nothing — and after a while he thinks about El Loco — about his radio — about the radiant woman who reassured her plants — about silence giving the impression that one has no opinions — that one wants nothing — about his first day at the Universidad Estatal — about waking up on the morning he was to graduate from San Javier and finding that his scuffed black shoes had been miraculously polished — returning to Eva's room and sitting quietly on the chair by her bed and thinking about the morning he found a soccer ball under their Christmas tree when he was five years old — When I was five my father gifted me a doctor's kit and I would go around the house tapping the cement walls with my tiny hammer — to which Eva doesn't reply — and after a while he thinks about his father changing his mind about opening the school cafeteria on the day he was to graduate from San Javier — okay Rolandazo go on and take your seat at the coliseum you're in the first row — And in that short interval between my father's day jobs at San Javier administering the school magazine and the school cafeteria and his night jobs hauling boxes at the harbor he would doze off in his armchair restlessly like a watchman who knew something was up which in most cases meant me not doing my homework — And when it was time for him to leave he would enact the same skit that included my sister until she left — My hair's a mess he would whimper — As if the armchair wouldn't let him out of its grip until someone fixed his hair — And then my sister would rush over to him gleefully — Pretending she was fulfilling some portentous duty — My sister and I both loved Topo Gigio by the way — When we were little she would put me to sleep by singing a / la / camita — Do you know that song? — According to my father on my sister's first day of first grade I propped myself by the living room window and cried inconsolably after she left — And because that week and the week after I didn't stop crying my father had to beg the director of the school to take me in too — And then my sister would comb my father's hair — And then one evening when my sister was no longer with us my father wouldn't wake up from the couch despite me banging my ruler on the kitchen table — Which is the kind of thing my sister would have scolded me for — And I could hear my father mumbling words at random — Nikon — Formica — Un solo toque — My hair's a mess — And while he mumbled words at random I searched for my sister's comb and found it under his pillow — Red with teeth like toothpicks — Which I'd seen my sister trying to soften with her fingertips — And which no longer smelled like her strawberry shampoo — In any case I combed his head while he was asleep — And as I did so my father opened his eyes and looked at me as if thinking the same thing I was thinking — This isn't what men do — But my father doesn't wave me away — He closes his eyes and pretends he hasn't seen me — That he's still asleep — And I go along with him — I go on — Back then my father was already bald by the way — but Eva doesn't comment on what he just shared with her — Eva doesn't move — and after a while the room is still silent and he thinks about finding a new white dress shirt on his father's armchair on the morning he was to graduate from San Javier — about how years before he was a freshman at San Javier his father had included pictures of him in the school magazine — about how during his six improbable years at San Javier there had been more pictures of him in San Javier's magazine than of any other student — about his father changing his mind about opening the school cafeteria on the day he was to graduate from San Javier so that Rolando wouldn't have to serve empanadas to his fatuous classmates — so that Rolando wouldn't have to serve chorizo to that Opus Dei woman whose plastic surgeries couldn't conceal her contempt for everyone who looked as aboriginal as she used to look and who happened to be the wife of a tuna fish magnate — that would be Julio Esteros's mother — and before his father changes his mind again Rolando runs out of his father's cafeteria and runs past the soccer field that will never see grass and what does he care about grass not growing on a field where new batches of conchadesumadres will continue their awkward dribbling unlike his quick dribbling on the mini basketball court — which he's passing now and on which he once scored eight points in less than ten minutes — the outdoor basketball court by the garbage cans that he'll never have to empty again — and as he crosses the forest of eucalyptus and birch trees his tie doesn't flutter because of his new tie clip — which according to his father belonged to his grandfather — and although his sprint from the cafeteria to San Javier's coliseum doesn't last long year after year he returns to this memory just as he returns to his radio — to the radiant woman who reassured her plants — to the first day he arrives at the Universidad Estatal — where by the entrance smoke is still rising from a tractor wheel — where by the entrance the gates are locked but bent enough for crossing inside — where the streets look as if decades ago trucks had dumped the belongings of a slum onto them and no one had bothered to clean up the gnarled tricycle — the spray cans — the tin or thatched roof — the broken glass still attached to rum labels — the rocks everywhere — as if someone had icepicked the moon and here was the detritus of that absurd effort — the metaphysical rebel declares he's frustrated by the absurdity of the universe — the pamphlets glued to cracked bricks — and in its widest sense rebellion goes far beyond resentment — the emptied tear gas canisters — the rocks everywhere — Yankees Go Home — the smell of tear gas — My father used to fumigate the cornfields of a Polish American landowner in Portoviejo and sometimes Mister Henrik would ask my father to wear a brown body suit with tanks like in those movies about chemical warfare — And before heading to fumigate Mister Henrik's land my father would always repeat the same phrase — He loved the sound of Mister Henrik's words by the way — Try to say maaaska — Try to say tlenooowa — Goodbye children I'm off to do the monster he would say — Why are you telling me all this Rolando? — oh — so you were not asleep — he doesn't say — what is he supposed to say? — I'm sharing all these tender memories with you so you'll know — what? — that I am not what I am? — Rolando doesn't say anything and she does not press him or turn toward him — Maaaska — she murmurs — Tlenooowa — and then she does fall asleep — and then he tries to fall sleep on the chair by her bed and he's dozing off and he's running past the basketball court at San Javier and past the line of station wagons heading to San Javier's coliseum — as fast as a chicken in Ethiopia — Rolando being both the fowl and the hungry Ethiopian — good one Facundo! — neither good nor bad señor — approaching the coliseum where Facundo Cedeño and the rest of his classmates are loitering outside and look Satan's here — Guillermo Maldonado says — what's up empanada — Antonio José says — yo empanada — Leopoldo says — looking good chorizo — Cristian Cordero says — empanaaaaaaaaaada — Facundo Cedeño says — diavolo — Carlos de Tomaso says — gremlin — Giovanny Bastidas says — le empanada — Stefano Brborich says — with beef — Juan Lopez says — and cheese — Rafael Arosemena says — and molto chorizo — Jacinto Cazares says — shut up Jacinto! — everyone says — Rolando hurries inside the coliseum — the clanking of chairs — the crowds gathered around León Martín Cordero — empanada — gremlin — diavolo — gizmo caca — with beef — and chorizo — hey.

Rolando leaves before Eva wakes up and he doesn't see her the next day or the next or the day after the next and early on Sunday he rides the bus to El Guasmo and jumps on the back of a pickup truck that's part of a caravan heading to welcome back El Loco — and on the side of the road Rolando sees a small crowd circling a burning tire in celebration of El Loco's return — and on every corner megaphones are transmitting the same songs — the force of the poor / Abdalá / the clamor of my people / Abdalá — and on the flatbed where he's standing everyone's singing along to this unending stream of songs — and on every corner a poster of El Loco adorns doors / windows / lampposts — as if the people here believed they could summon him back with an overabundance of images — quick the lamb's blood — knowing me / knowing you / there is nothing we can — the force of the poor / Abdalá / the clamor of my people — and as the sun goes down Rolando follows a long line of people who are lighting torches — but Rolando doesn't seize their torches and scream wake up you idiots can't you see El Loco is as corrupt as the rest of them? — and on the plaza there are couples dressed as if going to a wedding and families dressed as if going to church and girls with veils and what looks like first communion dresses — and contrary to the rumors he had allowed himself to believe the people aren't coming here for free alcohol because there's no free alcohol anywhere — although of course there's ambulatory vendors selling water and beer and there's so many flags that Rolando has to keep changing positions so he can see the stage — it's getting tougher to move because everyone wants to be by the stage — especially those with signs representing their cooperatives or their neighborhoods — and on the stage Los Iracundos is singing the same old ballads that everyone loves — y la lluvia caerá / luego vendrá el sereno — the force of the poor / Abdalá — and everyone's singing along and it's hard to tell amid the noise if that's the sound of a helicopter behind them — it is! — a helicopter that's descending rapidly toward them and some of the children look scared of the winged machine above them but most people are just waving their handkerchiefs and signs despite the gray whirlwind of dirt that's swirling pebbles off the ground which are pelting them so that Rolando has to cover his face — the force of the poor / Abdalá — and Abdalá lands and he's welcoming them and thanking them and singing and saying I love you Ecuador — and Abdalá's pacing back and forth on the wooden platform and he's sweating — he's angry — his white guayabera cannot contain his indignation because of what the oligarchies have done to the poor of my country — Is there a parent in the crowd please raise your hand — Let's see you gentleman here with your son let's talk the truth no tales I'm going to demonstrate to you that you are not the same for León because they have another god — The god of racism — The god of monopoly — The god of wealth — I'm going to demonstrate it to you and you tell me if I lie — Sir with the greatest respect if your eighteen year old son falls in love with León's daughter would they let him in their house? — No! No! No! — They will beat him and throw him out yes or no? — Yes! Yes! Yes! — exactly yes — Rolando go back to your room — But if León's grandson were to leave your daughter pregnant what would León say? — Oh ha ha it's just our boy being a rascal is this the truth or is this not the truth? — Yes! Yes! Yes! — Would they give that baby their name? — No! No! No! — They would make her abort it or she would be imprisoned and forsaken with a bastard child like they have forsaken and imprisoned my beloved country.

IX / ROLANDO LOOKS FOR EVA

Check — Check — Is this thing on? — It is? — So what? — Anyone out there? — Do you like magic? — Say you're strolling by a — Taking a stroll by a pond where a child's drowning what do you do? — I don't even unstrap my watch you say — I don't even slip out of my penny loafers — I dive right in — Yes quite commendable sir but why are you sporting penny loafers by a pond? — And what if it turns out you're the child in the pond who will dive in for you? — My neighbor you say — My cousins — El Mono Egas because I owe him a crate of bananas — But what if you look around and discover they're in the pond too? — Say we're all drowning in the pond and howling for help but no one comes for us because the perimeter of the pond is said to be dangerous? — the piranhas Mama — Who if we cried out would come for us? — It's silent here tonight — Have we all gone? — Are we still here? — and where is Eva tonight? — Rolando thinks — is she listening to his broadcast from her igloo? — And if one day we manage to crawl out of the pond — To slither out like half men half snakes — Like half women half manatees — Do the ones who didn't come for us have the right to grouse against our torching of their homes? — To plead mercy when we line them up against a great wall and spray them with dark brown pond? — Does anyone have a garden hose I can borrow? — Preferably longish? — Oh what's this folks we have us a caller hello pond repair — That's not funny folks hello you're on the air — Hello I'm always on the air but no one listens ha ha — Aha a regular listener do you have a request? — A question — We're listening — Do you have a father? — Sometimes — And you don't think your father would dive in for you? — He's already in the pond sir — What if he knows how to float? — He does have a whale of a belly but it doesn't at present function as a floating device — What if he knew about the pond beforehand and had floaters strapped around his waist? — Floaters deflate sir — Say you're in the pond and you just found out you're going to have a son — I'm not bringing children into this pond sir — Do you not think you would prepare giraffe floaters for your boy? — I'm not bringing children into the — Don't underestimate fathers Rolando — Dad? — Yes? — I — I don't think listeners of Radio Nuevo Día want to — Dad? — Dad? — Apparently the phone line is down folks but here's an old favorite in the meanwhile — Cuando vuelva a tu lado / y estés solo contigo.

After signing off at midnight Rolando thinks of not driving to Eva's house as he drives to Eva's house — thinks of not thinking about what he'll say to her   not that he thinks he's obligated to say anything special to her — I've missed you — every morning I wake up disappointed if I haven't dreamed of you — ugh — I haven't come here to recite you poetry Eva — just drive Rolando — the surface of the road on the way to Eva's house shifting abruptly from pavement to gravel to craters that rattle the bus that's speeding by with a handsized flag of El Loco attached to its antennae that sounds like the shuffling of cards — which reminds Rolando of nothing — of his father who never played cards backgammon chess — switching off the headlights as he parks by Eva's house — to remain silent is to give the impression that one wants nothing — to shut off the lights in one's house is to give the impression that one wants — a surprise? — shut up — that one is asleep — that one is embracing someone other than Rolando Alban Cienfuegos carajo — stop that — that one has shut one's eyes to the world — let it rot Rolando — winning the chess championship at San Javier three years in a row but his classmates turning it into a joke — Gremlin eat Queen ha — crossing the road and standing by Eva's door and listening in for nothing — irrationally expecting Eva to appear precisely when he steps on her front porch — watched too many soap operas as a kid eh? — my sister Alma loved those horrible Venezuelan soap operas with soundtracks by Timbiriche — corro / vuelo / me acelero — a megaphone in the distance kicks off a Friday night dance party at the plaza nearby — a cumbia rhythm ladies and gentleman — focus Rolando — fine okay — knocking a friendly tune on Eva's door — fuego del amor — nothing — stop knocking like a repentful boy you didn't do anything wrong — a manly knock on the window — nothing — stop don't knock when the cumbia from the plaza ebbs or you'll alert the neighbors — Gremlins!

Midnight! Agh! — the window at the back of Eva's house isn't locked so he opens it and waits for something to happen — don't wait that long moron — climbing through the window and landing in her kitchen where a rubber ducky is floating sideways in her sink with its ear to the clogged water — there's your goddamn pond — shut up — no one in the living room — good — no heaving sounds coming from the bedroom — good — no one in the bedroom — bad? — I haven't come here to serenade you Eva — you've come here to tell me what you haven't come here for? — I haven't stood here to hear what you haven't come here for Rolando — good one — neither good nor bad señor — maybe he should sit on the one stiff dining room chair and await instructions — sit Robot — turning into another stiff item of furniture by the time Eva returns — if Eva returns — hello I am chair cushion — you're too bony to be a cushion Rolando — hello I am monk cushion repent — why do you have a ceramic whale on your dining room table Eva? — because that whale swallowed my doll and I'm waiting for him to cough her up Rolanbobo — the rumble of buses outside — of bulldozers advancing on gravel — of dump trucks hauling dead whales to supermarkets everywhere — don't slump Rolando — this chair's uncomfortable okay? — hundreds of butchers sawing off whales inside factories ablaze with stadium headlights — the music from the plaza no longer audible just the cumbia beat like a galloping horse — the same damned horse for the same dumb cumbias — the same dumb tragedy of their rhythmic perfection — as if long ago someone picked a horse from the Andes and called it a cumbia and then condemned it to gallop mindlessly across the Pacific coast — not a horse but a donkey that was condemned to gallop like a horse — enough — the dining chair is too uncomfortable he's moving to Eva's bedroom — lying down on her empty bed instead of searching through her things as if that absolves him of his breaking into her house — the burglar took a nap but didn't even take a cauliflower officer — once he's accustomed to the dark he can see that all of Eva's plants have been angled toward the bed like an audience — but where's the front of a plant? — because if you don't know where that is how do you know what they're looking at? — who they're looking at? — me? — take off your shoes mister — chlorophyll what is? — sleep Gizmo — what the hell were the Drool and the Microphone Head doing at his father's restaurant? — and why did his father prank call him? — and what hideous cumbia puns are they transmitting at that dance party nearby? — and why are these notebooks which he's never seen before stacked on Eva's nightstand? — and why do they have drawings of stick figures with oxygen tanks and fins? — and why are some of these notebooks discolored and wavy? — did she spill her Fanta on them and try to dry them with a hairdryer? — and why does the thought of opening them and reading them seem like such a terrible idea if they might actually contain evidence of her — of her what? — of where and with whom she is tonight? — dear diary today I met a wonderful someone unlike that grim Gremlin — shut up — fine he won't read them — remember when you read your sister's copy of Little Women like four times? — just her annotations on the margins okay? — okay what now? — sleep but don't drool on her pillow and don't forget Eva has vanished like this before after arguing with you so don't worry too much — for days Eva not answering his calls and then resurfacing as if she'd been simply contemplating life at an igloo unaware he'd been desperate to talk to her remember? — not unaware no absenting herself from the awareness that he was desperate to see her — exiting through a side door before the news of his desperation reached her — these crevices aren't meant for you sir — no — not desperate to talk to her but desperate to know if this time her exit was irreversible — if you knew you were going to feel this way why did you leave Eva's house after you two argued? — you should've tied yourself to her back until she spoke to you again — some people haul hay / some people haul this guy — what's this guy doing on your back Eva? — of course Rolando's worried regardless because the last time she vanished had been unbearable for him hour after hour reimagin-ing all those moments they spent together realizing that real regret is simply the ceaseless reimagining of all those days he could have seen her but didn't — all those moments he could have told her hey I know it sounds corny but I would like you to know I love everything about you — all of those moments turning into reimagined moments in which he does see her and does tell her everything — why are you wearing a Stevie Wonder costume Rolando? — I just called / to say — take off those glasses let me see your evil eyes — my beautiful black eyes? — why are you wearing a grass costume Rolando? — so I can outstretch myself under your feet — why are you looking at me like that Rolando? — so I can hypnotize myself into never forgetting the twist of your mouth when you disapprove of me — enough of that go to sleep Rolando — one sheep — if he had a hole in his sock he could twiddle his big toe like a puppet — hello boys and girls! — Eva's room silent and static which is how he imagines Eva's room when he's not around — which is how he imagines Eva when he's not around — Eva not brushing her hair or draining the sink or sailing her yellow ducky — no — he has never imagined her doing anything when he's not around as if she didn't exist whenever he wasn't with her or existed in an inanimate state of waiting for him — an inanimate object is less likely to cheat on you eh? — shut up — two sheep — in the stiff dining room chair Eva waiting for Rolando to reanimate her — no reanimation is needed when you imagine her exiting from you? — Rolando's sitting up and switching on the desk lamp placing the stack of Eva's notebooks on his lap discovering after a quick glance at her notebooks that the entries are from fifteen years ago — convincing himself that if he doesn't read her entries chronologically he will be less at fault — not only did he not take a cauliflower he didn't even snoop officer — maybe cauliflowers constipate him? — enough with the constipation jokes — opening a black notebook at random and reading Eva's handwriting Hi / I'm Evarista / I collect proverbs and snails / Dear journal I can't glue my seashells to your pages so I will draw each shell from different angles that I will then mark on the shells with my watercolors / Aunt Mercedes brought an extra lock for the front door today and says every night she will come lock it so that no one has to worry about me sleepwalking outside again / Don Carlos the driver of the 22 bus let us in for free again and my mother said to him I don't want your pity Don Carlos and Don Carlos said this isn't about pity now take a seat and give your daughter this candy here on our way out I said thank you to him with a nod my mother didn't see it but I waited until we got home to unwrap the candy cane / Yesterday on the bus to Quito I vomited corn / For her noble and pure gestures Rosa Porteros wherever you are / Halloween again bleh / Today Mama didn't get out of bed but this time I fried her a cheese sandwich before going to school / Dear journal I'd rather see you blank than strewn with pointless words / Either we serve life or we serve death neutrality isn't possible said Arnulfo Romero / Dear Óscar do you mind if I call you Arnulfo I wish my classmates called me Arnulfa the Smurf instead of Eva the Cobra / Today I didn't think of you even once Arsenio / My mother said to my Aunt Mercedes that if at least they had handed over his body because my brother Arsenio wasn't an animal to be tossed in some ditch — enough Rolando — returning her notebooks to the nightstand and switching off the desk lamp — why didn't Eva tell him she had a brother? — and why doesn't her omission feel like a betrayal? — because what's the point of telling anyone anything anyway? — he has never told Eva about his own sister crossing the border to that accursed country — about his sister finally calling from that accursed country after six months of not knowing whether she'd managed to cross the border — about his father answering the phone and calming her — Alma corazón — about Rolando hearing the sound of her sobs from the kitchen — about his father with the phone to his ear sitting down carefully — as if trying not to disturb the balance of the — no such thing as a balance of the universe no — he just didn't want his movements to alter the phone signal so he stood up again slowly — my sister crying of excitement to finally get a hold of Dad I told myself but no that wasn't it — I could sense that wasn't it — or perhaps I couldn't sense anything and I've now turned myself into someone who can sense the grief of a sister thousands of miles away — my sister on the phone crying — Alma corazón — and I standing away from my father and yet trying to listen to what he was listening to — I didn't make much of that moment in the moment or maybe I did how would I know? — sometimes I feel encrusted with moments that recur with or without my knowledge — and I standing away from myself and yet trying to listen to what I was listening to — switching on Eva's desk lamp picking up Eva's notebooks arranging them chronologically reading them in order and after a few hours piecing together that two days before Halloween when Eva was eight years old her fifteen year old brother had borrowed the neighbor's pickup truck to buy talc powder for their ghost costumes and was never seen again — that for years her mother had searched for him in vain — that her mother had been warned by the police to stop asking so many questions or else — that it was more than likely that her brother had been detained by the ambulatory antiterrorist squadrons that had been secretly trained by an Israeli antiterrorist expert who had been secretly hired by that goddamn oligarch known as León Martín Cordero — that just like the brothers Restrepo and hundreds of others who had been detained for no reason during the presidency of León Martín Cordero her brother was probably tortured and murdered and tossed in the Yambo lagoon with the rest of them — Rolando switching off the desk lamp and shutting his eyes — the carousel Mama — four years without you Arsenio — sardines flapping on a gray beach where Rolando's legs are submerged in mud as he trails his father to a fishing boat — today I didn't think of you again Arsenio — your son's a wimp Don Alban even my mutt doesn't get this seasick — I'm so sorry Eva — today I counted how many times in the last year I wrote down that I hadn't thought of you I will make it up to you by thinking of you just as many times today Arsenio.

Eva doesn't come back on Friday or the next morning and by nightfall Rolando gives up his waiting for her but instead of huffing out without leaving her a note or without making her bed he leaves her a heartfelt note and straightens her bed — no I didn't — I don't want to go on without you Eva — okay I did so what? — your expectations of me are so tiresome leave me alone — sometimes I feel like I don't want anything but you Eva — arriving at home where he's surprised to see his father because he'd been expecting to be alone as he'd been alone for the last twenty four hours — What's wrong Rolando? — Nothing — No radio tonight? — Don't think so — You should let Eva host it sometimes so you can rest — I don't need to rest — I don't either that's why I have hemorrhoids ha ha — Come on

Dad — What? — Stop saying hemorrhoids I hate that word — Fine but don't sit on my hemorrhoid cushion — Dad! — Eva has the best radio voice no? — A voice that could sell eggs to the chickens yes — What does that mean? — what does what mean? — Never mind — She sounds like Eydie Gormé — No she doesn't she sounds like Mercedes Sosa — Only when she's mad at you because when I talked to her yesterday she definitely sounded like — You talked to her yesterday? — Last night yes said she was earning extra money for your radio show by taping posters for a nightclub — And? — And that she had to wake up early today to help someone install a phone booth what's the matter Rolando? — She didn't come home last night — How do you know? — Don't want to get into that right now — I tell my son what his woman tells me but he can't tell his father what his — Stop that Dad — You think I'm fond of you not talking to me about anything? — to which Rolando doesn't answer — very funny moron — You want me to call her? — I can call her myself Dad but since you're so good at dialing that phone — That phone dials itself ha ha — Why did you call the radio show Dad? — Don't want to get into that right now — Fine — his father dialing Eva's number and sharing the earpiece with Rolando so they can both hear the phone ringing — No answer? — That's strange her answering machine isn't picking up — did Rolando turn off her answering machine by mistake when he was listening to her messages? — Something must have happened — Nothing Dad she probably just — Something did happen — Don't be melodramatic Dad — You don't know what it is to be a father Rolando — A father's intuition? — That's right — to which Rolando doesn't answer by saying Eva's not your daughter Dad your daughter's at a terrible place far away from here — What do you propose we do? — Look for her what else? — She could be anywhere — The phone booth she was going to help someone with a — I know who that is — Let's go.

His father's driving the pickup truck at a speed that's even more reckless than his father's usual speed — a speed that has always baffled Rolando because in everything else his father is so cautious — so deferential to everyone else — here we go again — shut up — and yet Rolando doesn't say slow down Dad — stop honking at the omnibuses

Dad — don't yell at that taxi that cut you off — anda que te parió un burro — to remain silent is to give the impression that one has no opinions — Rolando has no opinions he just wants to rest his head against the window and sleep and in his sleep dream of nothing at all — the bumper cars Mama — what if something did happen to Eva? — rolling down the window and taking in the wind and the crowds of people who are still celebrating El Loco's victory despite the news reports that his sumptuous inauguration gala at the presidential palace was a disaster thousands of uninvited people trying to get in — What ever did I do to you Rolando? — What? — What ever did I do to you? — Nothing Dad — Did I ever hit you? — No Dad — Did I ever hey stay in your lane ratface did you see that bus driver look at him he looks like a rat I swear what was I saying? — Nothing Dad — Oh did I ever hit you? — You asked me that already — Did I ever raise my voice? — Yes — Okay but not that often right? — Not that often slow down Dad — Not that often's good right? — Why are you — why is his father asking him all these questions? — can his father intuit what Rolando would reply to him? — does his father feel the need to punish himself by hearing his son say to him you should've raised your voice to forbid my sister from leaving? — you should've barred the door so she couldn't come out? — you should've raised your voice when Doña Esteros shat on us because of a pendant I know for a fact her son swiped from her and then used it to barter with his favorite prostitute because in our last spiritual retreat before graduating from San Javier — in our last week of enforced silence in that retreat house in Ambato — on the last day of the retreat when there was a round table and everyone shared what they had discovered within themselves during their week of complete silence — Julio Esteros confessed that one time when he was fifteen his father cut off his allowance so he swiped his mother's pendant and the maid — that's what he called Alma — the maid — had been blamed for the missing pendant but he hadn't said anything about it and poor Julio sobbed in front of us — not knowing that the maid was my sister — not knowing that I knew he had forgotten to mention that he had also tried to rape that same maid — and yet he was right not to mention it no? — because if he had mentioned it who would have felt bad about that? — who among all those schoolboys would have felt bad about my sister? — and you know what I said when it was my turn at the spiritual round table? — nothing Father — nothing at all — god didn't speak to me that week — the holy ghost didn't course through me that week or the week after — and unfortunately Julio's snot and tears might have been coursing down his face on his day of spiritual reckoning but because he was still twice my size and had a red belt in tae kwon do I found a way to pretend he hadn't said what he said so that I wouldn't have to acknowledge that I couldn't topple him — you think the acts of vandalism you're planning are going to help anyone here? — my lame sabotage of Julio's mansion helped me feel better for about five minutes — You've always voted for León Martín Cordero — I would never vote for a prepotente like that Rolando — I've heard you tell the Jesuits at San Javier that you've always — That's what the Jesuits want to hear that's what I tell them — Turn left by the tire place Dad — I miss Alma too Rolando — Second right at Roldós Plaza — Every day I miss her too.

Good evening do you — Hello and welcome to Rosie's Phone Booths where every — Remember me? — No but next time I hey yes you're Eva's downer — Is that what she — No she told me you were constipated and — He's been constipated since he was — Stop it Dad — Forgive him he's — We're looking for Eva and thought you — She told me she was coming to help me today but didn't and I — This morning she didn't? — Not all day no — She didn't come home last night and — You two live together? — No we — He doesn't want to get into that — Aha — I'm his father by the way — I figured that — I figured that you figured but I wanted an excuse to hold your hand — Dad! — Your son's a prude eh? — Look Eva's missing and — We think Eva's missing and we thought you might — She told me she was going to distribute flyers on Victor Emilio Estrada last — Posters she was going to — Right posters do you want to call someone? — Who? — Someone who might know someone? — Father Ignacio knows some people no? — Leopoldo at the mayor's office might be able to — Let's search for her before we go around calling people — Along Victor Emilio let's go.

His father's driving them down the hills of Mapasingue obviously trying to calm Rolando by asking him how did you two meet? — to which Rolando doesn't answer — You and Eva was it at the university? — At a protest? — Did you kick her in the shins at a soccer match? — to which Rolando does answer by saying Eva doesn't wear shin guards Dad — Does she raise her socks all the way or bunch them at the bottom? — Bunches them — aha — Says she wants the other team to see her bruises so that they'll know she doesn't care about bruising them or them bruising her — That makes sense — It's redundant because she's always yelling at the other team so they know not to mess with her — Did her yelling stop you from messing with her? — Of course not — Do they red card her often? — No but she plays her best when someone on our team has been red carded and we're down to ten — The other day Eva told me — How often do you guys talk? — Every day I think — Amazing — What's so amazing you think your father is not good at listening? — What? — You think your father is not good at listening? — What? — Very funny — Sorry — The other day she called me and said she was writing a love letter to the one boyfriend who had broken up with her — What? — From when she was fourteen relax — Ah — She wasn't going to send it she said she just wanted to write him a love letter isn't that amazing? — I guess — He broke up with her over the phone she said and she was so nervous while he was breaking up with her that she fidgeted with the gum she had taken out of her mouth and then fidgeted with the gum wrapper she had taken out of her pocket — And? — And when it was over she placed the green gum inside the gum wrapper and saved it inside a shoe box as a memento — That doesn't make any sense — Of course it does — I would have thrown that gum in the trash — Oh — I would have flung it far away from here so no one would ever have to see it again — You okay Rolando? — Yes fine I'm just — Take my handkerchief — unfolding his father's handkerchief and inhaling the cologne his father dabbed on it in the morning like he has done every morning since he can remember pressing his father's handkerchief onto whatever's happening to his — nothing leave me alone.

PART THREE

—

DISINTEGRATION

X / ANTONIO AND THE PROTESTERS

What ever happened to Bastidas the Chinchulín, Antonio thinks, Bastidas the entrepreneur who at San Javier, along with Rafael, had been Antonio and Leopoldo's closest friend, studying together for the academic quiz show Who Knows Knows, teaching catechism in Mapasingue, sitting at the back of the classroom for six years like a mafia of nerds who would swap or sell answers to tests — remember that math test where no one knew the answer to the last question and Bastidas became so agitated he started shouting someone hand me the answer for heaven's sake please someone? — yes and that time he was caught with a polla taped to his leg? — or that time La Pepa asked him who wrote The Veil of Queen Mab and he stood up and said that wasn't part of the assignment, I don't know what the hell you're talking about? — for years everyone asking Bastidas hey where's The Veil of Queen Mab? — I don't know what the hell you're talking about — bowling together during the summer when they couldn't play soccer because of the mosquitoes and rain, bribing their teachers together (without Rafael though since Rafael didn't approve), drinking in Kennedy Park and somehow a prank ending with a rusted nail inside Bastidas's leg, which they disinfected with Patito, and although Bastidas wasn't keen on performing verbal pyrotechnics during Who's Most Pedantic, he had always been there, their wry audience, their older brother who was amused by them but already suspected neither Antonio nor Leopoldo would amount to anything, although at the same time he wished they would amount to something, yes, Antonio should have asked Leopoldo about Bastidas, what ever happened to his good friend Bastidas.

—

After his meeting with Leopoldo at Don Alban's restaurant, Antonio doesn't call the private Taxi Amigo that his mother recommended for safety reasons but ambles through downtown Guayaquil instead, thinking about Julio, Bastidas, Rafael, even Esteban, all his classmates whom he hasn't seen since he graduated from San Javier. A protest at the corner of Rumichaca and Sucre interrupts him. The people, united, the protesters are chanting, will never be defeated. Antonio grew up with that song. At Edge Fest in Berkeley, he'd also heard Rzewski's thirty six variations on that same song. The protest seems endless, at least ten blocks long, though he cannot see that far back. They've paralyzed all traffic around him. Smoke clouds hover above the protesters. Something had been off with the performance of Rzewski's piano variations, though he did not know what that had been. The protest advances in a tumult of students, plumbers, domestics, fruit carriers, street vendors. And while they march they clap, scream, blow whistles. Rattling their cardboard signs as if warning of a cataclysm or a mattress closeout or the second coming, and as they scream they distend their mouths so wide they look as if they're about to swallow the back of their heads, although of course that's only possible in movies like Pink Floyd's The Wall. Onward they march. United they shout. Not to be defeated again. While he lived in Guayaquil he had witnessed many protests, but only from afar, mostly on television, where at the forefront of the screen a commentator interpreted the meaning of their protest. Never witnessed a protest this close. Unless he counts the protests in San Francisco, where he had often seen the American crowds waving their flags of self importance and gorging themselves with organic cucumbers before returning to their placid homes, diluting in his memory the protests of his compatriots, who on these streets look visibly strained. Protesting to exist. And what is literature which does not save nations or people? Songs of drunkards, Miłosz said. Readings for sophomore girls. Despite the virtuosity of Rzewski's piano variations, despite the transpositions, the inversions, the complex paraphrases, the shouts of the pianist, the song sounds more powerful when sung by these protesters. Rzewski's variations are redundant diversions. Olives on a howl. Three shoeshine boys near Antonio spring from their stools. They're drumming the wooden part of their shoe brushes against their toolboxes, parodying the protesters' hymn. The shoeshine boy who has camouflaged his face with tan polish climbs on his unsteady stool and pretends he's a marionette. The other two, circling him, clap their hands and sing, the people, defeated, will never be united. Antonio watched Pink Floyd's The Wall at the Policentro movie theater on the day a band of paratroopers kidnapped President León Martín Cordero. The ticket woman and the ushers, glued to the apocalyptic news flashes on their portable radios, did not notice he was underage, although perhaps they did notice but did not care. The program notes for Rzewski's performance mention that the complete protest song had been written after a Chilean composer heard a street singer outside the palace of finance shouting the main chorus. Three months later, on September 11, 1973, Pinochet's thugs, financed by Kissinger, bombed La Moneda. A reign of terror swept through Latin America. That defeat doesn't seem to have registered with these protesters, although perhaps the lyrics are beside the point and the singing is what counts, the filling of their lungs, the euphoria of the stadium, meaning as collective noise. At first the protesters passing by the shoeshiners smile and clap along with them. Then some of them realize they're being mocked. Don't they know why we march? The onward push of the crowd dissuades the protesters from running over to the sidewalk and caning those conchadesumadres. Instead they rejoin the soothing sounds of their old hymn. The people, united, will never be defeated.

—

What ever happened to Rafael the Mazinger, Antonio thinks, Rafael the Robot who'd programmed himself to ace every test, to rocket toward anyone who called him Mazinger, no zits on his metal plates, misbehavior set to neutral, unless you pressed the Call Him Mazinger button, devotion to god set to outperform, so he taught catechism at Mapasingue with Antonio and Leopoldo and had followed the logic that led Antonio to conclude he should become a priest — remember all those hours during recess at the San Javier chapel praying to our Madre Dolorosa? — who's this? — and yet the Robot had been drawn toward Antonio the Drool, Antonio the troublemaker, as if the Robot had wanted to compute what it was like to hurl his calculator against a wall, as Antonio had done, what it was like to fistfight the Fat Albino after school, to advertise their rosary prayer from class to class without feeling embarrassed by the sneers and the shouts of lambón, lameculo, but of course the best moments with the Robot came during accidentals, for instance when Rafael would kick the ball into outer space during their soccer tournaments — baja mono — or when Rafael ingested Popov vodka for the first time and couldn't contain his torrent of brotherly love for Antonio and Leopoldo at Kennedy Park, or when Antonio introduced him to Jennifer, a girl from the Liceo Panamericano who guffawed at the formality of the Robot and pulled him to dance corro / vuelo / me acelero with her, and perhaps upon leaving Guayaquil Antonio must have decided Rafael had served his purpose because it never occurred to him to write to Rafael, to call him and acknowledge all those years at San Javier when, overflowing with uncontrollable impulses — watch it, the Drool poured gasoline on our desks — let's burn down the school, why shouldn't we — Rafael's presence would calm him, just as it still does now, even though Antonio hasn't talked to him or seen him in twelve years.

—

Some of the protesters seem revolted by the pickup truck near Antonio, painted with the bright yellow color of León Martín Cordero's party. Inside the pickup truck the driver is reading the paper indifferently, as if he's grown used to these protesters, just as seasoned drivers grow used to sheep on country roads. His passenger seems less fond of the crossing. He's pounding on the horn and shouting move, roaches. Scram. Behind them, on the flatbed, an old man is standing by two signs promoting the presidential candidacy of Cristian Cordero (hey, is that the Fat Albino, his classmate from San Javier?). Cristian's obvious attempt at looking tortured by the suffering of his people can't conceal his smirk, and no doubt this is what some of the protesters are glaring at, those signs, and no doubt this is what makes them squirm, the same damn smirk of the same damn oligarchs. On the other hand Antonio can't help imagining himself on those signs:

Antonio José for President. On a white horse returning to solve the problems of transportation, alimentation, lack of sustentation. But what have you done for your country so far, Antonio? Even some of your American classmates at Stanford have already done more for Latin America than you have. The old man in the flatbed seems to be appraising Antonio's black suit. The old man powers the megaphone atop the roof, banging on the passenger window so they can quit it with the honking. The old man amplifies his voice with the megaphone and proclaims bread, roof, and employment, with Cristian Cordero it can be done. Cristian Cordero for president, vote for Cristian Cordero for president.

A scrawny protester (hey that's the Gremlin!) steps out of the march and plants himself by the pickup truck. Down with the oligarchy, he screams. Twice. Even amid the chanting and the megaphone and the banging of stew pots, some protesters behind him actually hear him. They're joining him by the pickup truck and shouting down with the oligarchy, down with the oligarchy. Encouraged by the shift in the chanting those who have already passed the pickup truck turn around abruptly, colliding against the onward current and exacerbating everyone's anger, signs and sweat clashing, a mob forming around the pickup truck.

—

Every weekend or almost every weekend of their last year at San Javier Antonio the Drool, Facundo the Maid Killer, DeTomaso the Norro, Bastidas the Chinchulín, Leopoldo the Microphone Head, Lopez the Monster, and Rafael the Mazinger would gather at Kennedy Park to guzzle cheap Popov vodka and wail whatever songs Facundo knew how to play on his guitar, and sometimes they howled popular songs like es más fácil llegar al sol / que a tu corazón, and sometimes they whispered rock ballads like quiero que me trates / suavemente, and always toward the end of the night they sobbed along to Silvio Rodríguez's mi unicornio azul / se me perdió, and as Antonio ambles through downtown Guayaquil he wonders if all of them knew that, if it hadn't been for their six years at San Javier, Antonio's mother would have probably scoffed at Antonio's friendship with Facundo, who was dark skinned and lived in La Atarazana, and Rafael's mother would have probably balked at Rafael's friendship with Lopez, who wasn't dark skinned but lived in La Floresta, and Julio's mother would have probably, ah, no, despite sharing the same classroom at San Javier for six years, Julio's mother did balk and scoff at Julio's friendships with all of them, dark and light alike (Julio's family lived in a compound enclosed by tall white walls that couldn't be jumped, except perhaps with a firefighter's ladder — would Doña Tanya Esteros have even allowed firefighters on her premises? — probably not — this place will burn down before I let those lowlifes in here —), not that they saw Julio that much since Julio was always out on his own, picking up loose women at dubious nightclubs or off the main streets in the marginal neighborhoods of Guayaquil, and as their graduation neared, the frequency of their gatherings at Kennedy Park increased and the intensity of their singing grew feverish, knowing that after San Javier was over the Drool was flying to the United States, that Mazinger was studying political science in Spain, that the Microphone Head was going to be too busy working two jobs to afford the Politécnica, that the rest of them didn't have the grades or the money to go anywhere except the public university in Guayaquil, and although they knew or at least suspected that their differences would eventually disband them — remember the first time Mazinger got drunk? how he hugged that shriveled tree trunk? — the Robot in love ha ha — they had allowed themselves to believe those differences did not matter because they had spent six years together in the same classroom and had grown to love each other, yes, there was no other way to put it, they had grown to love each other although Antonio wouldn't have put it that way to anyone in the United States — do you still remember Kennedy Park, Leopoldo? — of course I do we used to call ourselves Los Chop do you remember why? — how many years have to pass before the memory of who we were together dissipates, Leopoldo? — too many — nor did Antonio ever recount to his acquaintances at Stanford that he once had all these great friends in Guayaquil whom he missed until one day out of necessity or callousness or because that's what everyone does after high school — quit making such a fuss about high school, Drool — he didn't miss them anymore, and a week or two after they graduated from San Javier they gathered one last time at Antonio's house, singing songs till dawn and passing out everywhere, as if a wave had washed us up in the living room, look, there's the Maid Killer on guitar, there's Leopoldo on the maracas, Lopez on keyboard, singing songs at the Guayaquil airport the next morning until Antonio boarded a plane to Florida and never saw them again.

—

Would rather be home by now, Ernesto Carrión thinks, undisturbed on his front porch, listening to his grandson Manolito singing along to Eydie Gormé and Los Panchos inside his house instead of listening to these protesters from the back of this yellow pickup truck, y qué hiciste del amor que me juraste / y qué has hecho de los besos que te di, those old boleros that Manolito slips into the tape player because he knows Grandma still suspires to them, singing along to Eydie Gormé and Los Panchos while he flattens plantains with Grandma's rolling pin, and somehow grandma and grandson feel more real to him this way, unseen, as voices from the kitchen like ghosts from the beyond, although of course less spooky. Someone had told him that back in eighteen hundred and something the Catedral De La Inmaculada Concepción had been scheduled to become the biggest cathedral in South America until the builders discovered they had bungled their measurements so that, in the end, they had to shrink it or else the whole thing would collapse, and that, my friends, Ernesto would often say, is why I rarely venture inside that immaculate disorganism, any day now it could still collapse. Even from the courtyard outside La Inmaculada, he'd often told Manolito, while I sold guachitos, I could hear their sad amen canticles. Manolito wanted a guitar for Christmas. Next year, Manolito, next year. More protesters are glaring at Ernesto, likely because he's working for, as his neighbors have warned him, as if his neighbors have the right to warn him against anything, especially about getting a job, not too many of them these days, the country's too unsteady to be refusing a job, even if it's a job working for the one male descendent of the greatest oligarch of them all, León Martín Cordero. A young man on the sidewalk is also staring at him, although he's not glaring at Ernesto but instead seems to be researching him? The young man is wearing a black suit, dressed either for a bank function or a beach house funeral, his moccasins awfully pointy, handy for kicking poodles. The driver of the pickup truck told him that Cristian Cordero had just hired a team of foreign advisors. That they're already scattered all over town, watching the natives for clues. It is not unlikely that the young man in the black suit is one of these foreign advisors and that he's wondering why Ernesto is just standing there instead of spreading the news of Cristian Cordero's candidacy. The old man, asleep at the mic. Ernesto powers the megaphone atop the roof, banging on the passenger window so they can quit it with the honking. Ernesto amplifies his voice with the megaphone and proclaims bread, roof, and employment, with Cristian Cordero, it can be done. Cristian Cordero for president, vote for Cristian Cordero for president.

—

I'll pick you up soon, Julio would say, and when he didn't show up at Antonio's apartment on Bálsamos Street, which happened often, Antonio would call him again and sometimes one of the domestics in the kitchen downstairs would answer and spend ten, fifteen minutes searching for Julio in that immense compound, calling out niño Julio, telephone, niño Julio, asking the other domestics if they had seen niño Julio anywhere, and sometimes during the search for Julio the domestic would put the cordless phone down without hanging up, and either because she forgot about it, or because she was summoned to a different task in a faraway wing, or because she figured the odds of Julio answering the phone were the same whether she searched for him or put the phone down on a side table, she would just put the phone down and leave, and sometimes Antonio would wait and listen to the sounds of Julio's compound, hoping to catch proof that Julio was still there, imagining Julio's invertebrate double floating above the white piano in the living room because according to Julio he'd mastered the art of lucid dreaming, just as according to Julio he'd mastered the art of speed reading, womanizing, piano playing after he'd heard Antonio was learning to play the piano in San Francisco, imagining Julio waiting for his parents to fall asleep and then sneaking outside, putting one of their cars in neutral, and slithering out of their garage in one of their ancient Mercedes Benzes, the kind you still see as evidence that time hasn't passed in La Habana and which the Esteros family preferred so as to not alert thieves that they were one of the wealthiest families in Ecuador, although one time Julio did eschew his parents' cars and borrowed his uncle's Porsche 911 Turbo, and due to the rain and the high speed and Julio and Antonio not knowing how to switch on the wiper washers, they crashed and spun against a small bridge in Urdesa — we're not dead? — verga my uncle's going to be pissed — and later Julio would fabricate the most amazing tales as to why he hadn't been able to pick up Antonio, but of course back then Antonio would believe anything by Julio the Popcorn, Julio the nephew of Father Ignacio, the principal of San Javier, who in the middle of their sophomore year magically admitted Julio to San Javier, ha, Antonio still remembers Julio on his first day, wearing a white tee shirt with a reflective spider on the back he couldn't have possibly purchased in Ecuador, already convincing Esteban, the most studious of them all, whom they called Pipí because he happened to look like a penis, to let him copy his homework, and soon after Antonio called Julio and invited him to attend a heavy metal concert at Colegio Alemán Humboldt, and Julio said why not, and so while a band called Mosquito Monsters or Dengue Dwarfs blared their angry music, Julio screamed like a vulture or a hawk, so loud that the audience, taken aback, turned toward Julio, who pretended it wasn't him, and when the audience wasn't looking he tossed his soda at them, nope, it wasn't him, because Julio had already perfected his look of stunned innocence, as if he couldn't believe you thought he had, for instance, stolen your identity to open a credit card in your name, as Julio had done to Antonio while Julio pretended to study in Atlanta, Georgia — my dad cut down my allowance I had no choice I was about to pay it in full of course I'll pay you back, Antonio — but that was too many years after their first heavy metal concert at Colegio Alemán Humboldt, where Antonio, emboldened by Julio, a better looking, better dressed reflection of himself, tossed his soda at the audience, too, and so Julio and Antonio became good friends, and so one night, a school night, way past midnight, while Antonio's mother slept upstairs, Julio knocked on Antonio's living room window downstairs and said let's get out of here, driving them to downtown Guayaquil, where Julio began searching for streetwalkers by the post office, picking up two of them although Antonio passed on his for religious reasons so Julio and his streetwalker entered a motel while Antonio, who didn't know how to drive, raced Julio's ancient Mercedes Benz past multiple red lights, angry at himself for almost sinning with a streetwalker who looked like a vocalist from Warrant or Mötley Crüe or Ratt, one of those hair bands whose tee shirts were banned at San Javier for being satanic, eventually stopping for the police car that had been chasing him — I'm so sorry my parents beat me, officer, I'm confused about life, etc. — quit it with the sob story, how much money do you have on you? — and when Julio exited the motel he was livid because apparently his streetwalker was a man, ha ha ha, yes, that night had been a watershed in Antonio's teenage life not only because it was the first time he'd seen a streetwalker up close but because his mother discovered he had snuck out with Julio and, thinking he was out doing drugs with this Julio, who according to her already had a reputation for frequenting nightclubs in the red light district even though he was only fifteen, seemed ready at last to ship Antonio to military school, as she had threatened to do for years, but of course Julio and Antonio continued to cause trouble, like for instance during their senior year, when Rosendo, Julio's driver, told Julio's mother that Antonio had stopped their ancient Mercedes Benz on the way up the hill to San Javier and had convinced Julio to skip school with him, and so Julio's mother called her brother, also known as Father Ignacio, the principal at San Javier, and she also called Antonio's mother and said yuck you lowlifes stay away from my family, and so Antonio was expelled for a week and Julio wasn't, and so both of their mothers forbade their sons from seeing each other, which made it all the more fun since that meant Julio had to sneak Antonio into his compound, hiding him in the closet on those rare occasions when his mother or one of the domestics would knock on his door, and of course when Antonio would call Julio he would have to say his name was Leopoldo or Esteban, and sometimes one of Julio's younger brothers would chance upon the phone one of the domestics had put down on a side table and say, as if bemused by the encounter and yet annoyed it required him to speak, hey who's this, or sorry I need the phone, call back later.

—

One of the shoeshiners stakes his stool by the edge of the sidewalk, climbs on it, cups his hands like a horn, and directs his yelling at the crowd around the pickup truck. Chickens! Wipe their windshield while you're at it. The boy grabs his stool and frogs away. The scrawny protester snatches a protest sign and raises it above his head like a sledgehammer. Then he charges against the pickup truck, leaping atop the hood and smashing the sign on the windshield. The blow crushes the cardboard part of the sign. The windshield does not crack. Not even a tiny bit. The splintered cane is light so he hammers on the windshield rapidly, like a teenager at his grandmother's piggybank. The other protesters do not join him. They seem to be relishing their roles as spectators. Which doesn't last long. When the men inside the pickup swing their doors open, the crowd charges forth. The driver and the passenger escape from them. Protesters climb atop the flatbed. This sudden invasion frightens Ernesto into trying to escape but it's too late, they're everywhere, surrounding the pickup truck and yelling mátalo a ese hijueputa, grab that fucker, bájalo a ese viejo desgraciado. Rocking the pickup truck. The unexpected unsteadiness loosens the arm lock on Ernesto. He tries to jostle and elbow himself free but the man behind him clamps his arms tighter. Others are climbing on the flatbed. They're ripping Ernesto's tee shirt as if about to inspect livestock. Someone punches him in the stomach. A woman jerks him by his hair. They're inserting Cristian

Cordero's signs on the windshield. Rolando rips the megaphone from the rooftop. He lifts it to Ernesto's face, as if about to broadcast a public service announcement. Decrépito de mierda, he tries to announce. Instead the megaphone yields an alarm sound. He tries to cover his gaff by raising his arms in victory, rotating with the siren above his head, the epicenter of an overthrow. The black stains on the scrawny protester's armpits sadden Ernesto. Someone's been chewing eucalyptus. Ernesto faints. That's enough. Rolando tries to hold back the crowd but there's too many of them already grabbing the old man from his ankles and arms, standing him up, a mock effigy. Caridad para el año viejo, some of them chant, passing the old man around until they tire of him. They flip the pickup truck. They begin to disperse.

Antonio runs toward the capsized pickup truck. The old man is nowhere to be, there, he's there, by a jampacked bus behind the wreckage. Antonio pushes his way through the retreating protesters, who aren't amused by him, hey, one of them yells, watch where you're going. Don't mess with me, Antonio says. Or I'll have all of you arrested. The threat carries the necessary authority. The protesters shrug and continue their retreat. A white haired woman is kneeling by the old man. She's swabbing his bloodied chin with a cotton scarf that seems tethered to her purse. Curious heads are sticking out of the bus. The toll collector is blocking the people from getting out of the bus. The old man opens his eyes. As soon as he sees Antonio he tries to lift himself up.

I'm so sorry, abogado. I was doing my job but . . .

The old man's attempt at raising himself visibly hurts him.

You better leave, the woman says to Antonio.

I can help. You can't lift him up by yourself.

Get the hell out of here.

The onlookers inside the bus seem to think Antonio's at fault. You heard her, one of them yells. Lárgate. Antonio backs away, slowly, without turning from them, hearing the old man saying I'll clean up the mess, abogado, I'll pick up the signs.

XI / FACUNDO AT SAN JAVIER

Two revoleras infiltrate San Javier, searching for their Julito. Two revoleras who had to hail seventeen jampacked interplanetary buses to
land here in San Javier and deliver a love letter to their Julito. How do
I know? Did anyone besides the Drool and the Microphone see those
two? You could tell by their cheap rumpled school uniforms that they
probably jumpstarted their voyage way over in Chinchipe, where the
mosquitoes don't prickle to avoid catching trichina from the locals
and the buses don't risk slowing down either, especially not for a
schoolgirl who looks like La Chilindrina, hey, maybe one of those
buses slowed down for the other one, the dark muslona who short-
ened her school skirt so that everyone without binoculars could osculate her spider? Stop what, Esteban? Don't be so pious, Pipí. Everyone
here likes to osculate spiders except you. Stop interrupting me with
your leguminous protestations. Huh? I'll unfurl the word leguminous whichever way I want, Microphone Head. Roll your rodomon-
tades on vinegar and stick them up your, okay, everyone shut your
eyes and imagine La Chilindrina and our Spider Woman waving and
shouting and jumping like teenagers at a Menudo show for any bus
to stop for them and, wait, one second, interludismo: did you guys
know that Julio and the Drool just had their hair straightened by the
main maraco at the Gaylord salon? That's why their hair looks like
flaccid leaves, fellows. Sure, I'll shut up, Drool, but who's going to
retell the bewitching you and your lord Julio did to those two revoleras? Where was I? Aha, yes, our revos were howling at a Menudo
show but instead of climbing on Ricky Martin's motorcycle they were
flagging buses that wouldn't take them. At last one bus snails down
ahead of them so they're both running after it, their skirts flapping
like in those skits from Haga Negocio Conmigo where machine
winds lift paper money and skirts and then, hey, I bet every Sunday
after confession Cazares hides himself by a portable television and
secretes his weekly sins while watching the skits from Haga Negocio
Conmigo. If something I owe / with pigeons I repay you. Did you hear

that on top of having a counterfeit whiskey business Cazares's family also grows pigeons at home? Let's omit what he's probably doing to those poor pigeons while his mother's in the other room, fitting the mouth of whiskey bottles with funnels. Aaaaaaviary bestiality / aaaaamen. So their skirts are flapping like in that show Cazares surreptitiously watches with pigeon in hand and everyone on the bus is cricking their necks and hooting corra mamacita, súbase que aquí le tengo la sorpresota, and just as they're reaching the doorway of the bus where the toll collector is egging them on, it speeds up, the toll collector grinning and shaking his head as if he's disappointed at, but at the same time sated by, their gullibility, oh no, but our two pigeons aren't taking that kind of flout, our pigeons are going to showcase their prowess to those conchadesumadres by sprinting after the bus and look they're catching up and jumping inside, the toll collector saying te la ganaste mamacita, the Chilindrina cursing everyone as everyone claps and the toll collector, who's probably called Joni or Wasinton or Eusebio, is repeating the saeculorum bus dictum of siga, siga, plenty of room in the back. What? What did the Pipí say? Really? Doesn't La Verga here know that this bus driver's son rams Pipí's mother inside that bus on a weekly basis and then makes her pay triple fare on the way out? Pipíííííí. Who wants to bet me an empanada that our two revos were embrangling about the love letter for Julio during their intergalactic ride? Did you hear that the Empanada almost knocked Pipí's glasses for calling him Empanada? Down, Pipí. Down. So our pigeons are on the bus and La Chilindrina's saying now let me see that pink letter, my pigeon, and our Spider Woman's saying negativo, and La Chilindrina's saying love is sharing, palomar, and our Spider Woman's saying love you nots, pecosota, and La Chilindrina's relentless nagging continues until our Spider Woman relents and pulls the pink envelope with the letter from her knee high soccer sock and lets the Chilindrina read its perfumed pages and La Chilindrina's saying his what?, and Spider Woman's saying shhh, and La Chilindrina's saying moaning like a what?, and Pipí's saying put down your perversities for the lord, and someone on the bus is saying come moan over here, gatita, and La Chilindrina and our Spider Woman are saying shut your hangar, pothole face. No, Drool. Wasn't talking about you or your venerable father. I might be a Panza de Chofer but at least my dad isn't the leader of the poor. Is he returning to defalcate us again? You started it, Drool. What did Esteban say? Sure. Buy me a sandwich from Don Alban's and I'll retell the story of our two revos starting from whenever you want. Who wants me to start when La Chilindrina was born? Anyone? So our two pigeons arrive to San Javier and they're outside the gates to our venerable school and what they must have done to the guard's salted lollipop so he would let them in I don't have time to go into. Unless Pipí here wants me to. No? All right. So La Chilindrina and our Spider Woman are, yes, Microphone Head, Wonder Woman is the superhero with the ultra short skirt but Spider Woman is the one with the spider. So La Chilindrina and our Wonder Spider Woman are, is that better, Microphone? Does that work for you? When the Microphone was born the first thing the vaginacologist did was tap his head and say check, check, is this thing on? So our two revos are standing by the entrance to our dignified school, right by our classroom where the inspiriting words of our patron San Francisco Javier, what? No, I don't remember what the inscription says. I don't go around memorizing saintly patron bullcrap like you, Saint Microphone. So our two revoleras from El Guasmo are standing there as if waiting for someone to let them in through a back door, I mean, there's eight hundred boys in this school, how did our pigeons think they were going to find their Julito? Did they think he left a trail of, what do you fellows think Julio would leave as a trail? Definitely not breadcrumbs. Right. He wouldn't leave a trail. Good one, Drool. Julito / Julito / why is your mouth tan bonito? Pa' revolearte mejor. The bell rings for recess and that's when everyone's pouring out and our two pigeons are spotting all you perverts congregating at a distance as if female Martians had landed with a note excusing everyone from abstinence before marriage. Remember when the Microphone asked Father Francisco if performing La Paja Rusa on one's wife's tits was a sin? Sex only for procreation even with your wife, the Microphone was pissed. Chaaaambas. What are our two cholitas doing here in San Javier? Of course the Microphone volunteered himself to be our emissary and find out, prancing over to welcome them to our onanistic order. Good afternoon ladies, could I be of any assistance to you? Good one, Microphone! We're looking for Julio, they said. Julio what? Of course our two revos didn't know his last name but the Microphone's a sly one. About this tall, he says, cute little eyelashes? Pinkie of a nose like Luis Miguel? Who knew that the Microphone amplifies his pecker for Julito? Did you tell them that Julio's pinkie nose used to be a potato bulb before his plastic surgery? That's our second Nariz de Chepa in less than two years, folks. I bet the Drool's next. Get that crooked monster fixed, Drool. Man you're ugly. This one is Aladino, La Chilindrina says. How'd you know? We know our Julio, Leopoldo says, ignoring their question about what's Julio's last name and introducing himself with a fake name: Antonio José at your service. The Microphone eyes the letter on Spider Woman's hand, immediately deducing what this is all about. Behind him someone muffles his yell with his hands and we're all hearing his chant of revolero / revolero. Everyone muffles their trumpets and chants revolero / revolero. Don't mind those twits, our lowfi emissary says, they haven't seen such beautiful girls in years. Beautiful? How does Leopoldo's saying go? If she's not green, doesn't crawl, she'll do. I'm a good friend of Julio, the Microphone says. I can hand deliver the letter to, oh, ho, that's when our chorus of pothole virgins switches from chanting revolero / revolero to oh / uh. The Microphone turns and sees Father Ignacio rapidly approaching and you can tell the Microphone is already machinating excuses, soliloquies, whatever. They're volunteers, Leopoldo informs Father Ignacio, but the Microphone knows Father Ignacio is the one priest at San Javier who does not fall for his verbiage so the Microphone doesn't offer up a convincing embroidery of what exactly they're volunteering for. What did you say? Lollipop volunteers? Sure, Pipí, I guess that could be considered funny somewhere. Just nowhere in a three thousand mile radius. Go tell it to the Peruvians. Do you have a delivery, Father Ignacio asks. Our Spider Woman looks at Leopoldo for answers and Father Ignacio looks at Leopoldo to check on his answers and Leopoldo opts out of giving answers by taking a step back and bowing to Father Ignacio. Father Ignacio asks for the letter and the girl hands it to him and says it's for, for, Ju / Ju / Julio. I'll make sure it gets to its appropriate destinatario, Father Ignacio says. Our Menudo pigeons bow to Father Ignacio and sprint away. Of course Father Ignacio knows which Julio, right? Isn't Julio his nephew? And of course Father Ignacio knew why our pigeons were there. Why else would two cholazas like that be looking for Julio? What? Expelled? Don't be what you are, Pipí. Everyone knows our Julito's expulsion free. Remember when he showed up to class straight from Infinity Nightclub? Okay, the bell's ringing soon and I have to pee. The End. Oh? You fellows wanted to know what Julio and the Drool did to those two cholazas? Why didn't you say so earlier? Why don't you tell them what you told me, Drool? No? I'll retell it if you let me sit behind you during our final tomorrow. Pipí already rented the spot behind him. Back to our two pigeons then. Once upon a time José Eduardo, Julio's most perverted cousin who happens to look like a perverted pug, bought a busted 1970s vw van especially for netting revoleras, enlisting Julio to do all the pickups because even revos from El Guasmo wouldn't get into that rusted van if Julio wasn't the one doing the sweet talking from the passenger window. I bet Pug Eduardo probably wets his pants just thinking about being cousins with someone who can actually convince the hottest cholitas on the street to get into his busted van. What kind of sick dog gets more satisfaction from luring revos into his filthy van by using Julio than from actually ramming them? So Pug Eduardo, Julio, and the Drool are driving in that crapsome van way over in that treacherous area where the Gremlin lives and Julio of course has no problem convincing three random revoleras strolling down the main street to get in, driving them to a squalid park where, after funneling cheap apple Boone's wine on them, the fun starts, Pug Eduardo undressing his girl and our girl's shouting no, no, please, let me out, Pug Eduardo saying you know you want it, conchadetumadre, slapping her and mounting her and rocking his van. Meanwhile Julio has had no problem undressing the other one, gripping her neck as she moans ay papacito, ay mi amorcito, and Julio's howling and pounding her as if trying to capsize the vw van and his pants are down as if he's taking a piss on the side of the road and just happened to spot a warm hole nearby. The penicillin shots come later. Does anyone want to guess what the Drool was doing? Anyone? That's right. Nothing. Nothing at all. While Julio's cousin is forcing one pigeon to witness the overpowering wattage of his pickle, and while Julio's sausaging his pigeon at a speed worthy of Mazinger, Antonio is talking to his girl about, about what, fellows? Anyone? That's right, Pipí. About the Virgin Mary.

XII / LEOPOLDO'S GRANDMOTHER GIVES ADVICE

Jaime Roldós Aguilera, Leopoldo's grandmother wrote. En los televisores y en los postes dizque de luz vía a la Costa y en las paredes de ladrillo en esos pueblitos de carretera donde a veces parábamos a comer choclo y ciruelas, ¿te acuerdas? Ahí estaba la imagen de Jaime Roldós Aguilera. Una vez paramos la camioneta en esa carretera vía a la Costa porque te urgía hacer pis y corriste al monte y yo te dije cuidado con las cigarras, mijo. Jaime Roldós Aguilera en los balcones en el centro de Cuenca donde vivía la tía Auria y el confeti que lanzaban cuando Roldós ganó la presidencia y tú ahí, recogiendo la lluvia de confeti en esas calles coloniales estrechas, guardándote el confeti en los bolsillos de tu terno como si temieras que te lo fueran a arranchar los otros niños que estaban girando en la calle bajo la nieve de confeti. A veces me da pena pensar que un día ya no recordaré nada de esto y a veces ya no me da pena porque para qué tanto recordadero, ¿Leo? Nos acurruca la supuesta alma encontrarnos en esos recuerdos, miren ahí está mi nieto Leo, el más pilas de todos, pero a veces ya nos toca soltar la paloma para poder continuar. No plantes parques de diversiones sobre tu inacción, Leo. Despabílate, como dicen los argentinos. ¿Te acuerdas del chiste de Mafalda donde Mafalda grita Burocracia y Mafalda espera y espera hasta que finalmente aparece una tortuga? Su lechuguita, Burocracia. Qué maravilla es recibir consejos abuelísticos. Solías seguir mis consejos sólo si yo encontraba una manera de pretender que no te estaba dando consejos. Seguís siendo así de mal llevado, ¿che? Espero que sí. ¿Te acuerdas de la canción de la Cigarra de Mercedes Sosa? Tantas veces me borraron / tantas desaparecí / a mi propio entierro fui / sola y llorando. Yo también aquí igual, la misma payasada pero demasiado al norte, lanzándote consejitos estoicos por carta y luego esta vieja hipócrita encerrándose en su dormitorio para irrigar en paz las memorias de nuestros tiempos juntos. Verlas florecer de nuevo y ahí apareces tú, bajo los balcones en el centro de Cuenca, regañándolo al confeti por haber salido de tus entrañas sin tu permiso, aunque esto de estar regañando al confeti suena a invento de vieja cursi, quizás da igual, así mismo eras. Caminábamos por esas calles de piedra tan estrechas que durante carnaval nadie se escapaba de los globos de agua o de los nubarrones de harina o de los huevos rellenos de manteca y harina. Me acuerdo del prac metódico de tu dedito índice ahuecando los huevos sin romperlos para poder llenarlos de lo que encontrabas en la cocina de la tía Auria y ahí aparezco yo, sacudiéndote la harina de tu terno, mi mano como raqueta, tenías cuatro o cinco añitos y apretabas los puños para apaciguar los nervios cuando te ladraban los perros. ¿Te acuerdas cuando le puse ojos a una de tus medias sport blancas? Puñetito. La voz de Roldós en la tele y tú corriendo por los pisos entablonados de la tía Auria para poder verlo, encantado por esa figura seria con lentes de búho ciego anunciando el fin del mal. El fin de la dictadura. Tus pasitos rosa en los pisos entablonados de la tía Auria no me hacen pensar en nada y esa es la maravilla de esa memoria, Leo, hasta ahora tus pasitos rosa en los pisos entablonados no me hacen pensar en nada excepto en ti. ¿Te acuerdas de esa canción de Luis Miguel? Tengo todo / excepto a ti? ¿No era esa la canción con la que bailaste tu primer bolero? Corrías para verlo a Roldós y recuerdo la mirada resentida tuya y es que porque no te había avisado que Roldós estaba zafando verdades en la televisión? Es verdad que todos lo queríamos a Roldós. Era tan joven y siempre tan agitado por todos los males cometidos contra los más desafortunados. Sabías que en su escuelita Roldós ganó todos los premios como lo harías tú en el Javier años después? Este joven abogado con esos lentes de búho ciego que dijo yo no voy a la inauguración presidencial de ese criminal norteamericano al que todos aquí en los Estados Unidos todavía veneran. A tarúpidos que veneran a Reagan se les debería prohibir viajar por nuestros pueblos. Esta patria es una patria donde impera la injusticia, Roldós decía. Sabed qué es lo que reclaman en el Ecuador los moradores de la mayor parte de los pueblos? Agua. Este es un país que tiene sed de agua y sed de justicia. Eso fue hace tantos años. ¿Ha cambiado algo? ¿Te acuerdas de nuestro cuento de la nada? Nada sale de nada porque nada es nada y nada tiene que ver con algo porque la nada no es algo es nada y así seguía ese cuento nuestro de la nada sin fin. Solías pasar horas imitándolo a Roldós, sus discursos, la gravedad en su voz. Uno se hacía la idea de que a Roldós le habían dicho de chico que no se debía subir la voz porque durante sus discursos su voz llegaba a la frontera entre la calma y la desaforez y ahí se quedaba esperando que alguien o algo dentro de sí lo empuje. Pasabas horas imitándolo en mi balcón donde la veranda todavía te llegaba solo hasta el mentón. Los vendedores ambulantes del barrio te adoraban. Me acuerdo que le tenías miedo a Don Ramiro, el que vendía los chanchitos, las alcancías, porque se aparecía con esos sacos a cuestas como en los cuentos de ogros donde se llevan a los niños. Un día él te estaba aplaudiendo tu rendición de Roldós en mi balcón y cuando acabaste abrió su saco y te enseñó adentro y dijo mire, niño Leo, aquí no hay chiquillos, sólo mis chanchillos. Sólo los más tricolores y más lindos para usted. ¿Crees que le hacían ruidos sus chanchillos cuando los cargaba al hombro dentro del saco? ¿Quizás Don Ramiro les preguntaba si estaban bien? ¿Si él estaba ambulando demasiado rápido? ¿Si debería aliviarles las colisiones dentro del saco con bolitas de algodón? Solías acorralar a las visitas para lanzarles tu versión de Jaime Roldós y claro que te aplaudían porque sonabas igualito. Sabed qué es lo que reclaman en el Ecuador. Y luego un día la avioneta oficial de Roldós se estrelló misteriosamente contra las montañas y se nos murió. Y yo no podía creer que se nos murió. Todavía no lo creo, Leo. Si alguien debía haber sido protegido de la muerte era Roldós. Y yo no tuve las agallas de decirte que había muerto. Esa semana y la siguiente desenchufé la televisión y te mentí y te dije que estaba dañada y lo encontré a Don Ramiro llorando bajo mi balcón y le dije no le diga al niño que se nos murió Roldós y yo también lloraba. Esperé a que me preguntaras sobre Roldós. No lo hiciste. ¿Adivinaste por nuestro luto que Roldós había muerto? Tus apariciones en mi balcón continuaron. Tus discursos en la casa también. ¿Cómo se sabe lo que le afecta a uno cuando se está chiquito? Un día Roldós estaba ahí contigo, un día ya no.

The long hallway where the old and the infirm waited for the apostolic group, Leopoldo thinks, the long hallway like a passageway inside cloisters or convents where the old and the infirm waited for the apostolic group every Saturday from 3:00 to 6:00, the long hallway with its hollowed benches alongside its walls where the old and the infirm waited for the apostolic group to hand them sugar bread and milk, where the apostolic group performed cheerfulness and chattiness for the old and the infirm, the long hallway that's probably empty at night just as it is empty for Leopoldo tonight despite all those Saturdays he'd spent there when he was fifteen or sixteen years old, all those Saturdays he spent in that long hallway at the hospice Luis Plaza Dañín trying to cheer up the old and the infirm who'd been forsaken by their families or who had no families or who had nowhere else to go, who had toiled in menial jobs the entirety of their lives just like the masses of people Leopoldo will encounter inside the bus on his way to Julio's party tonight — did you even ask the old and the infirm about their jobs, Leopoldo? what could you have possibly said to them to cheer them up? did you actually cheer them up or were you simply a reminder to them that god's blessings were elsewhere like they've always been? — whose last days were spent along a sunless hallway that smelled like the eucalyptus and menthol ointments they rubbed on their chests, which must have reminded them of the Merthiolate their mothers would swab on their scraped elbows and knees, whose last evenings were spent on donated hospital beds inside rooms with unreasonably high ceilings (why did the Jesuits build those rooms with such high ceilings? so that when the time came for the old and the infirm to die the priests could direct them to the vast pointlessness of the lord above?), inside rooms where Leopoldo and Antonio would stroll among the donated hospital beds with their bread baskets just in case they missed someone on the hallway, just in case someone couldn't get out of bed but still wanted a sugar bun (what did the Jesuits think this exposure to the

suffering of the old and the infirm would do to a band of scrawny
fifteen year olds? did the Jesuits think that it would change their lives?
that they would grow up to be stalwarts against suffering and injustice instead of growing up to be just like everyone else except every
now and then they feel guilty about the suffering of the old and the
infirm yet at the same time feel superior to everyone else because they
were such good Samaritans then?), the long hallway where the faces
and names of the old and the infirm continue to slip from him, year
after year one more conversation or gesture or emotion vanishing
from that long hallway like a punishment, although if you ask him
about it Leopoldo will tell you that he's not fifteen anymore and does
not believe in punishments handed down from a god who's in any
case too busy not existing just as Leopoldo's too busy not existing or
barely existing in that long hallway in the hospice Luis Plaza Dañín.

—

Name?
Two of them, yes. Though the gentleman here has at least three.
Not counting sundry appellatives.
Your name's already crossed out and Hurtado's not on the list.
Look under Arístides.
Nobody here with that name.
Check again.
Your identification. Let's see it.
The only one who needs identification here is you. Where's Rosendo?
Does he still work here?
–Who's clucking my name in vain?
Rosendo!
–Niño Baba! You here? Weren't you donkeying with the gays up
northern?
That's what Julio said?
–Full of fruits he said San Francisco is.
Sure. But only when he visits.
–That you're the terror of married women.
That so?

–Cause you steal their husbands always.

Good one. Hey listen, Rosen, your buddy grumpy here doesn't want to let us into Julio's party.

Professor's here too? Why so gloomy, Professor? Pass this duo through, Don Pancho. They're classmates of niño Julio from little school.

Keep an eye on those two.

–You keep your eyes on those two, I'm taking mine back to sleep.

—

If someone were to ask Leopoldo about what happened to him on the morning he graduated from San Javier, on that wretched graduation ceremony at San Javier's coliseum in which he was the valedictorian speaker, Leopoldo would first assume a resigned facial expression that would allow you to glean that, sure, he acknowledges the widespread corruption of his country, but he isn't really resigned to it, although of course he is, and after his pantomime of resignation he would shake his head for you as if about to relay an unfortunate incident that didn't happen to him but to some other studious graduate from San Javier, and yet because no one has asked him about what happened to him on the morning he graduated from San Javier — who goes around asking people about high school anyway, Microphone? — the memory of his graduation day is no longer bounded by his surface retellings of it, in other words by the plausible contours that would be required of him if he had to retell it to someone else, freeing him to revisit his graduation day from whatever vantage he chooses, even the most implausible ones — nothing's implausible if you don't have to retell it to someone else, Drool — flying along with the birds, for instance, that had entered the coliseum on his graduation day through an opening on the west section, flying above the basketball court and the cement stalls coded with colors and numbers (a pointless seating code, some might add, since on this Saturday morning there's no basketball game, only a ceremony for the one hundred and twelve San Javier students about to graduate, although even if there were a game the seating code would still be pointless since all basketball games here are strictly intramural, between San Javier students only and therefore always without a sizable audience, except once the priests did share their coliseum for the citywide intercollegiate basketball tournament, a decision some San Javier parents protested soon after the game between Rumiñahui School #22 and Tupac Yupanqui School #145 because who knows what kind of people attend those events (the families of the students playing, mostly), who knows what kind of people might maraud the halls of San Javier after a sweaty match (three students from Tupac Yupanqui, looking for a restroom), and since no one knew what kind of people, some San Javier parents protested and successfully overturned the priests' decision to share their brand new coliseum with the schools from the marginal areas of Guayaquil so that was that, no more of those kinds of people here), flying above San Javier's coliseum and above Guayaquil and above his wretched continent, from where he will see himself at Julio's party, drinking Chivas and sharing nothing of consequence with Antonio, although their inconsequence will continue to visit him for years — I just want an opportunity in another country unlike this one please let me be, Father Villalba — the only thing that will count is whether you accepted or rejected the — flying above the foldable chairs on the basketball court, where the children are pointing at the birds and where León Martín Cordero is scowling at the birds and where Leopoldo is glancing up at the birds as he rehearses his valedictorian speech in his head, and although the birds fly away as the graduation ceremony begins, Leopoldo remains up there, watching Father Ignacio, the school principal known for his ability to deaden even the liveliest of parables, lumbering up to the podium and welcoming our distinguished guests, enumerating our distinguished guests, sharing an inspirational graduation anecdote from his youth that concludes with Ignacio adolescing by a portrait of our Madre Dolorosa, reminding everyone in the coliseum that, as is the school's tradition, the letters the students wrote to our Madre Dolorosa six years ago will be returned to them today, urging the graduating seniors to meditate on what they wrote to her, introducing our valedictorian speaker

Leopoldo Arístides Hurtado, effusively thanking Leopoldo Arístides Hurtado for leading the winning team at this year's academic inter-collegiate television contest, Who Knows Knows, and as Leopoldo heads to the stage his classmates are saying good one cabezón, check, check, the Microphone to the microphone, keep it short loco I got to pee, and then Leopoldo's standing behind the podium and deliver-ing his valedictorian speech — what ever did you say in that speech, Leo? do you even remember? who did you think you were going to impress? were you trying to inspire yourself to be something other than what you turned out to be? did you think that León would be impressed and would anoint you as his successor? why weren't you thinking about your grandmother in the audience? and what the hell was that green blazer you were wearing? — damn, León says, that kid sounds just like me, oh that's just great, Antonio's grandfather says, yet another demagogue, and then Father Ignacio announces the prizes for theology, for mathematics, and for the grand prize, for the highest academic achievement in the last six years, the first prize goes to Jacinto Cazares, hey, wait, isn't the valedictorian the valedicto-rian because he's the first prize, no, must be a mistake, which Father Ignacio seems ready to correct because he's pulling the list of win-ners closer to his glasses, and what's disheartening is that Leopoldo can easily imagine Father Ignacio's calculations: on the one hand, when Father Ignacio inspected the rankings to select the valedicto-rian speaker four or five weeks before, Leopoldo's score was obviously higher than Jacinto's, on the other hand the vice president is here, the minister of agriculture, the former president and our current gover-nor, León Martín Cordero, carajo, the minister of finance, eight sena-tors, all of them San Javier alumni who wouldn't appreciate hearing about grade tampering on the premises, and part of Father Ignacio's calculations would have included a recalculation that consisted of allowing himself to remember all those times his memory had failed him before, yes, of course, it has failed him many times before, there are passages in Romans he can no longer recite from memory, plus his eyes aren't what they used to be, that's it, he could have easily erred when he first read Leopoldo's scores four or five weeks ago so Father

Ignacio taps on the microphone and says first prize, Jacinto Cazares, second prize, Leopoldo Hurtado, third prize, Antonio José Olmedo, and as Leopoldo remembers the finality in Father Ignacio's voice it surprises him that he has never revisited this day from Antonio's vantage, so on the bus on his way to Julio's party Leopoldo tries to revisit his graduation day as if he were Antonio, okay, Leopoldo is Antonio and he's rushing toward Jacinto along the first row of graduates and he's shouting you goddamn cheat, who did you bribe this time, did you bribe Elsa? (rumors about Elsa Ramirez, Father Ignacio's secretary, tampering with admissions tests for a fee had been circulating for years), shouting and looking as if he's about to sob from rage, and neither Antonio's outburst nor the possibility of him sobbing in front of everyone surprises any of his classmates because after six years of sharing a classroom with him they're used to him crying about everything, and as Leopoldo looks up at the stage he isn't surprised to see Father Ignacio pretending there's no commotion below, no Father Francisco fuming toward Antonio and shouting sit down right now, no Father Francisco grabbing Antonio's arm and escorting him outside, no Leopoldo's grandmother standing up and demanding an explanation, come on, no need for a spectacle, señora, someone says, we'll sort it out after the ceremony, jesus, Julio Esteros's mother says, these people have no manners.

—

You think we have to hide from Julio's mother still?

When Tanya spots you in that tight shirt she'll think you came to queerify her son. So yes, most likely.

My role as fashion inculcator here is . . .

Over?

Endless.

Either our doubles are outside shouting at that guard conchadesumadre or more uninvited riffraffs are trying to sneak in.

Julio probably just forgot to add you to the list, Leo. You know him he's . . .

See Julio anywhere?

Probably stashing his girls somewhere.

Where to?

Away from the door?

Tome pin / haga pun?

–Comenzó la fiesta, hijueputas.

That's El Loco's eldest son. Plus bodyguards.

Jacobito? Really? The hell's he doing here? How much do you think he paid that girl to be his girlfriend for the night?

How did they bypass the guard?

Cash?

Maybe you shouldn't grin so much or people will think you wouldn't mind seeing Julio's house razed by El Loco's people?

Tequila shots?

After you.

—

Neither Leopoldo nor Antonio had felt uneasy at Julio's house when they were still students at San Javier, on the contrary, they both had felt so at ease at Julio's house that neither of them had been inclined to express astonishment about the size of the house, which was so vast that Julio could sneak revoleras into the billiard room on the other side of the pool without his mother finding out, so vast that Julio could conceal revoleras in the midsized yacht that was probably still parked downstairs by the tennis court where after school Julio and Antonio would play tennis while Julio's immense loudspeakers, which they had set up by the pool, transmitted hymns of the Antichrist by Iron Maiden, or at least that's what Antonio told everyone he was doing with Julio after school, and neither of them had been inclined to express astonishment about the size of Julio's house because on the one hand astonishment implied servility and unfamiliarity and even envy, and on the other hand they had both felt this was where they belonged, this was what awaited them: from a place like Julio's house they would enact their historical reforms because they had been chosen to change Ecuador, carajo, and it was precisely this notion of having been chosen to change Ecuador that had allowed them to rise above their circumstances when they were still students at San Javier: neither of their fathers could afford to rent a house as large as Julio's computer room, or rather once they'd both had fathers who overnight had seemed able to afford everything, creating for their sons the illusion that the acquisition of wealth was easy, one day we didn't have any money, one day we did have money — and one day our fathers had to flee due to how easy it all was, isn't that wonderful, Antonio? — one day we didn't have any money anymore, and regardless of the dubious source of those funds, the sudden appearance of those funds had felt like the right thing to happen to their families (yet another topic Antonio would never bring up for discussion, of course — you wouldn't bring it up either, Microphone — that is correct, Drool —), and one weekday during their junior year at San Javier, Antonio and Julio and Leopoldo stayed up all night at Julio's house working on a school project Leopoldo can't remember anymore, and by dawn Antonio had fallen asleep on the couch in Julio's computer room downstairs, and Julio was playing video games on his computer, and Leopoldo was strolling through Julio's house thinking this is where we belong, carajo, and then Julio's mother appeared at the top of the stairs and Leopoldo climbed up the stairs to introduce himself like a marathon runner about to collect his medals and it would be embarrassing to tell you how she looked at me, Antonio, just as it would be embarrassing to confess how much satisfaction both of us derived from being seen hanging out with one of the wealthiest guys in Ecuador (just as it would be embarrassing to confess neither one of us had been at ease at the one party Julio actually invited us to), and as Leopoldo waits for Antonio to come back with their tequila shots he remembers that a week after their all night school project Julio's mother had called their mothers and in the most condescending terms possible had demanded that they keep their sons away from her son, in other words demanding that they adhere to her belief that their families weren't estimable enough to be near her family, a phone call their mothers never stopped talking about but that Julio dismissed as his mother's typical nonsense, although Julio did have to hide them from his mother whenever he managed to convince Antonio and Leopoldo to stop by his house again.

—

The Fat Albino's here.

Cristian? We must be at the right party.

The rightwingers party.

Who here isn't?

Jacobito?

Rightwinger at heart, reject at the door.

Made it in.

So did we.

If Jacobito were president he would sell the country to be let in at the right parties.

So would his father.

You think Jacobito will fight the Albino tonight?

Circle him. At best.

Why is your grandpa saying only whores and marihuaneros voted for my dad?

Because only whores and marihuaneros voted for your dad?

Let's see your Loco impression, Microphone.

Here there's no whites, blondes, blue eyes. Here there's blacks, cholos, Indians, the poor of the land.

I'd forgotten how many blondes show up to these parties.

That's because they wouldn't talk to you when you lived here.

Blondes love me in San Francisco.

I was talking about women.

Women are like cockroaches, Julio once said.

Speaking of charmers . . .

–Look who's here. The dynamic duo from San Javier.

Never a pleasure.

Good to see you, Cristian. Yesterday your grandfather and I were just . . .

–Didn't know you were back, Drool. Last time I saw you you were I guess dancing in Miami Beach?

At Liquid? Don't remember seeing you.

–Your sidekick here had a plastic orange jumpsuit on and . . .

Antonio's always been excessive.

–He was convulsing wildly on the dance floor by himself. I asked Julio what was wrong with him. Ecstasy, he said.

Haven't tried it. No need to dumb myself down. Unless I'm forced to talk to people like you.

–Very clever, Drool. I'll tell everyone here to avoid you so you don't have to dumb yourself down. Hey Pili, look, we're having an infestation. What? I don't mean Jacobito, bobaza, that's too obvious. I mean these two lerdos over here. What? Hold on, let me . . .

Love school reunions.

Who doesn't?

Chivas?

Nobody in San Francisco drinks Chivas.

Kahlúa?

A round of Chivas it is.

Double?

Neat.

—

On the other hand if someone were to ask Leopoldo about his pilgrimage to Cajas, where according to everyone the Virgin Mary had been appearing to a sixteen year old girl from Cuenca, Leopoldo wouldn't assume a resigned facial expression or shake his head as if about to relay an unfortunate incident that happened to some other studious teenager from San Javier but instead he would claim, in his most matter of fact voice, or perhaps in a voice that conceded how ridiculously unbelievable what he was about to claim was but also underscored how commonly accepted phenomena like gravity or photosynthesis were kind of unbelievable too, that he didn't care if what he'd witnessed in Cajas had been real or not, didn't care if it had been mass delusion, as some had called it later, he'd been there and had seen the sun move, thousands of believers who had pilgrimaged from Guayaquil, Quito, Cuenca, Machala for what had been announced as the last apparition of La Virgen del Cajas had gathered in a cold altiplane in the cordillera and had seen the sun move (how many times does the Virgin Mary need to appear to remind us of what we already know? how many times do we need to induce ourselves into believing she has come to warn us again that we're on the wrong path? in how many places around the world does she need to appear for no one to disbelieve anymore? or are her recurrent appearances what perpetuate disbelief?), and because so much time has passed since Leopoldo and thousands of believers saw the sun move, he has had plenty of time to think of ways to describe it to those lucky enough not to have been there (because their first question is likely to be what exactly do you mean the sun moved?), searching for the most accurate descriptions by associating the sun's movements with everything in the world, no, this isn't true, he hasn't been able to associate it with anything, or perhaps he has not associated it with anything because he doesn't want to steer it away from the world of phenomena and into the world of metaphors, or perhaps he doesn't need to associate it with anything because tracing stochastic patterns in the air with his index finger would probably be enough to describe to others how the sun moved, and on the bus on his way to Julio's party he still doesn't feel the need to associate it with anything, the sun moved and that was that, the sun as agitated as a firefly, no not like firefly, he hasn't even seen a firefly up close, as if the sun were angry, as if the sun had burned itself on a stove, as if the sun wanted to remind everyone below that the lord was among them and that the lord can manipulate his creation whichever way he pleases for the benefit of those who'd come to venerate the mother of his only son (what ever happened to those thousands of people who'd arrived in Cajas after an interminable uphill procession on that cold mountain? to those thousands of people who had been waiting for something celestial to happen and who had seen the sun move and who had cried like he imagines mothers must cry upon the irreversible death of their children? — bless me, Father, she pleaded, Father we are dying — what ever did those thousands of people do with their lives? did they disseminate her message through good deeds or did they, like Leopoldo, simply — simply what? what have you done with the memory of what was given to you? — forget her?), and yet since the people who might ask him about his pilgrimage to Cajas are likely to be or have been devoted Catholics, they aren't likely to disbelieve him too much or probe him further about this concept of mass delusion, a concept he has, surprisingly, never researched, although perhaps it isn't surprising he hasn't researched it because what difference would it make to him to discover that indeed scientists have concluded that when thousands of believers gather in one place expecting the same unbelievable event to happen, that same unbelievable event is bound to happen, the same sun moving inside everyone's heads at the same time, the same process inside everyone's heads unearthing devotional images from documentaries about the Virgin of Lourdes or Fátima or Guadalupe or Medjugorje or from those thousands of hours praying the rosary out loud, when you were sure you could sense her presence nearby, the same process so overwhelming that on that cold altiplane it triggered the same delusional process in one person, and in the next person, and then in Leopoldo, and then in Antonio, who had been there too, who was crying and had embraced Leopoldo after the sun moved and later was to say we must do something to change these situations of dramatic poverty, Leopoldo, everyone crying as the sun moved (why were they all crying? because god had finally appeared or because all those hours imagining a personal relationship with god had not been in vain?), no, he didn't know why and didn't care to know why he was also crying and embracing everyone nearby, searching for his father who'd insisted on this pilgrimage but instead finding Antonio and embracing him, thousands of people on a cold altiplane in the Andes crying at the same time, embracing at the same time, sure, he knew it was possible a few hysterics had cried first, leading everyone else to cry as well, and it was also possible a few Catholic lunatics had shrieked and said look the sun's moving, leading everyone to believe the sun was indeed moving, and although he doesn't remember too many particulars of his pilgrimage to Cajas, for instance how he arrived there or how he descended from there or what his father was thinking during the entirety of the trip or whether the sun moved before or after nothing happened during the specified hour in which the Virgin was supposed to appear for the last time to a young Patricia Talbot from Cuenca (that silent hour in which the Virgin was supposed to appear and him not seeing or feeling anything and yet seeing and hearing people around him convulsing as if Mary had touched them and him wondering if they were the typical Catholic lunatics for whom everything's a sign from god or if Mary just didn't love him?), he does remember what followed the week after, when he returned to San Javier, the intensity with which Leopoldo and Antonio disseminated her message, for instance, a message he doesn't remember anymore and yet that he doesn't remember her message doesn't diminish the memory of the intensity with which Leopoldo and Antonio disseminated her message, organizing daily rosary prayers during recess, promulgating to their classmates that joining the apostolic group was imperative not only to their salvation but to the salvation of the world, how are we to be Christians in a world of destitution and injustice, teaching catechism in Mapasingue, debating with Antonio the specifics of their duty to her and god and the future of their country, and then one day it was over, one day like any other day that intensity, which had expanded inside of them as if making room for everything god wanted from them, went away, leaving behind so much empty space that even in dreams they couldn't escape what later Father Lucio told them was called desolation, which is a test from god, he said, omitting that this test might never end, as in fact it hasn't, a test they were too young to handle or perhaps no age is a good age to handle desolation, and yet it wasn't true that Leopoldo had forgotten her: one day you're building a pyramid of sand and pebbles inside a cave in Punta Barandúa, one day you climb a mountain and see the sun move, one day you're on a jampacked bus en route to Julio's party to meet up with your dear friend Antonio, who will not ask you if you remember what happened to them because of Cajas, although if they were both women they would be allowed to bring it up and cry about the love they felt and the love they lost, and yet I haven't forgotten her, Leopoldo would say, I just didn't know what to do with her after I graduated from San Javier so I relegated her to the farthest possible space, where she's probably still shining her Llama de Amor, which is what the Catholic lunatics came to call the intensity they'd felt, although this isn't quite right, Leopoldo would say, I didn't relegate her anywhere, I didn't participate in her banishment or at least I wasn't aware of my participation, this is just how it happened and is still happening, and if I could talk to Antonio about it I'm sure he would understand why it makes no difference to know what scientists have discovered about mass delusion, you feel what you feel and that is that, Antonio would say, thousands of people witnessing the sun moving and then descending from that mountain and then rejoicing at the inexpungible mud on their soles and then a year later prostrating themselves in complete desolation, but don't exaggerate, Antonio would say, don't make it sound like we suddenly found ourselves inside a dark place wailing and despairing, it wasn't that bad, we didn't really spend weeks prostrate in bed, or we did but not anymore, Antonio would say, we, having no alternative, went on, flattening what happened to us into the daily inflow of our lives, and yet what would be the point of asking Antonio about Cajas except to bring it all back so that once again they'll be forced to suppress what is likely to surface in their chest and face and eyes? (I know you aren't supposed to be able to look into the sun but that's just how it happened, Leopoldo would say, of course I wouldn't believe it either and would be actually glad to concede it was mass delusion but what good would that do me if I still have all these feelings I don't know what to do with or do know what to do with, which is nothing?)

—

Julio, where is?

What ever happened to Bastidas, by the way?

Computer programming business. He's quite the entrepreneur. We barely see him. He's rector at the Polytechnic, too.

I stayed with him when he was studying in Paris years ago. It was awkward and . . .

He won one of those rare government scholarships to study in Paris, yes.

Why did he come back?

Terms of the scholarship required you to come back and . . .

I'm sure he could have found a way out of it.

Not everyone's like us.

Bastidas was always uneasy about being part of the Who's Most Pedantic clan.

Aced it on Who Knows Knows though.

With or without the answers?

Jennifer's here look.

Where? With Rafael?

Doesn't date him anymore.

Didn't know that.

Of course you didn't.

They were so perfect for . . .

She wanted to marry him and he didn't, then he wanted to marry her and she didn't, then she left him and he couldn't . . .

–Antonio is that you?

Jennifer!

Remember the Microphone?

Leopoldo Hurtado at your . . .

–Of course. Rafael always talked about you two. Seen Rafael yet?

He's here? I thought he hated these kinds of parties.

Mazinger inspects enemy territory before he . . .

–He must have known you were coming, Antonio. He missed you, you know?

I called him as soon as I arrived but he hasn't returned my . . .

The Drool here thinks he can just call people he hasn't talked to in years and they'll magically . . .

That's not what I . . .

–Rafael's outside. He saw me across the room and he . . .

He's going to Zumbahua for a year to teach the . . .

Really? Does he even know Quechua?

—Go talk to him, Antonio. It'll be good for him to see you before he leaves.

—

The girl in the gold encrusted dress, Leopoldo thinks, presumably Jacobito's girlfriend, who's sitting patiently in front of Julio's white piano, as if waiting for someone to listen to her sad story of how when she was little her mother couldn't afford piano lessons for her, although of course no one in Julio's living room will come near this dark girl with the gaudy sequined dress, except those in Jacobito's coterie or Jacobito himself, whose father once or more than once told an impressive crowd of supporters look at my son, this sad boy with so much extra weight because when he was seven years old León kicked him in Panamá, crushed his head when they handcuffed me, accusing me of international drug trafficking, Jacobito, my son, I have returned, and indeed if his father was allowed to return Jacobito wouldn't be relegating himself by the grand piano to argue with his coterie about whether to remove the flower arrangements atop the piano so they can raise the lid and listen to his girlfriend, wouldn't be laughing uncomfortably as his bodyguard or his sidekick picks up an arrangement of black orchids and pretends he's going to carry it off, or at least Leopoldo doesn't think that's what Jacobito would do, and as the speakers inside Julio's living room transmit a remix of Who Killed JFK, an old techno classic that Antonio's elbowing Leopoldo about, Leopoldo wonders what exactly would Jacobito do differently if his father had already returned and won the elections, because it seems implausible that Jacobito, for instance, would hurl those black orchids to the sons and daughters of our dignitaries on the other side of the room (the sound of the ceramic vase crashing on the floor would be magnificent), implausible that he would go around the room badgering the sons and daughters of our dignitaries who've openly called his father a crook and an uncultured lowlife (in other words Jacobito would have to badger everyone in the room, which would take way too long, unless he'd brought a long stick), no, what seems more plausible is that, on the one hand, Jacobito would continue to meekly antagonize the sons and daughters of our dignitaries by performing their idea of how the son of a Middle Eastern smuggler would behave at a party he wasn't invited to, or rather Jacobito would continue to do nothing at all and the sons and daughters of our dignitaries would continue to think he's behaving like an animal, and on the other hand, it seems more than plausible that the sons and daughters of our dignitaries, the ones who wouldn't mind profiting from dealing with Jacobito if Jacobito's father were president (in other words everyone in the room) would approach Jacobito by the grand piano to congratulate him and invite him for a round of Chivas on their side of the room, except perhaps the Fat Albino, who, like his grandfather León, has had no qualms about dealing with El Loco or El Loco's people as long as no one finds out (in other words what the Fat Albino would do is send his sidekick to secretly invite Jacobito to his house, something the Fat Albino has never done and will never do with Leopoldo), and although earlier, upon spotting the Fat Albino, Leopoldo had worried that Antonio would spill the story of how they were running for office, a story that would lead to León sacking Leopoldo from his job and banning him from any future jobs in government, Leopoldo, upon spotting the Fat Albino again, told himself he didn't care if the Fat Albino found out, just as he doesn't care that the girl in the gold encrusted dress, presumably Jacobito's girlfriend, who was sitting patiently in front of the white piano, has stood up to go to the bathroom, has smiled at Antonio (who's trying to make Leopoldo laugh by dancing like a robot to a remix of Who Killed JFK), and has briskly crossed Julio's living room, where the people are snickering at the trail of sequins she's left behind.

—

What's Rafael doing out there?
Filing grievances to the DJ for the dearth of techno?
Don't call him Mazinger because he no longer . . .
Mazinger!
He heard you.
–Aren't you too old to be hollering nicknames at people, Antonio?

Wasn't me.

Good to see you, Rafael.

Too old for nicknames but not for hugs, right?

Rafael turns away from Antonio to ask the DJ about cable types or wattage. Typical Mazinger.

When are you going to Zumbahua? Where is Zumbahua? Facundo would have a field day with that word.

The Drool has forgotten where everything is.

–I thought Antonio was dead.

Where is Zumbahua?

Cotopaxi.

Chanfle.

–Why are you back, Antonio? I mean what for? To heap ancient monikers on those who were once your friends?

Antonio explains Leopoldo's plan to run for office.

If we succeed of course we would invite you to be minister of robotics or . . .

–That is simply not the way to change anything.

But cloistering yourself in Zumbahua is?

My sincere apologies on behalf of the Snivel.

–To gain the support of those you wish to help you must first purge yourself of yourself.

What about El Loco he hasn't purged . . .

He's the cloaca already so he doesn't need . . .

–How are you different from El Loco or León, Antonio? You've always behaved as if you . . .

No craters on my cheeks, no glass eyes, horses, money.

–You are not an alternative, Antonio. Even if you would have stayed here you would have never been an alternative. No change will come from any of us.

Why are you being like this, Rafael? I called you as soon as I arrived and . . .

–If you run for office I will denounce you. Both of you.

—

We were worthless to him, Rafael thinks. Antonio boarded a plane to Florida and we became chaff to him. All those hundreds of hours the two of them spent together, riding their mountain bikes to San Javier through Victor Emilio Estrada and the overpasses of Miraflores and the highway to Salinas, their yellow headphones blasting the same Depeche Mode songs they'd recorded with his father's stereo, riding their mountain bikes on what now seems like an implausible distance between Rafael's house on Victor Emilio Estrada and San Javier, not minding the interprovincial buses, the wayward pickup trucks, the lunar craters inundated by rain, Antonio ringing the bell to Rafael's house and his mother saying Rafi, please, be careful around that troublemaker, although his mother never forbade him from spending time with Antonio because no one came to see him except Antonio and his mother knew that, that is the truth, riding their mountain bikes and sneaking inside San Javier while it was closed for the summer and Leopoldo would be there, Facundo, Bastidas, everyone ready to clock in hundreds of hours of soccer on the cement soccer field upstairs because the soccer fields downstairs were a land-fill of mosquitoes and mud. After a few sprints Facundo would have to catch his breath and stand still so the soundtrack to their soccer matches was often that of Facundo cursing at the mosquitoes in his version of everyone's whiny voices. What does it matter if Antonio remembers any of it? And what could Antonio possibly say if Rafael asked him? I remember our time together but not enough to write to you, Mazinger? My memories of you can coexist with my indifference toward you in those memories? Such that Antonio wasn't compelled to call him and ask him why are you so angry at everything still, Mazinger? If Antonio was so determined to save the poor why didn't he return periodically to check on them? It embarrasses Rafael to know so many of these conceited people at Julio's party. And conceited about what? About their parents swindling the country so that their children could one day mingle inside mansions protected by three layers of tall walls? Antonio used to sermonize about their responsibility to the poor but he spent as much time here, trying to befriend these people, as he did in Mapasingue, catechizing the poor. Why would anyone vote for someone so easily tempted by wealth? And why is Jennifer here? To remind him their hundreds of hours together were worthless too? During their senior year at San Javier, Antonio introduced Rafael to Jennifer, a girl from the Liceo Panamericano, at Antonio's insistence. How is Antonio doing in the United States, Jennifer would ask? Have you heard from Antonio? You never asked me why they called me Mazinger the Robot, Jennifer, because, perhaps, it was obvious? Don't come near me, Jennifer, I wouldn't know what to say to you now. My memories of you have coexisted for too long with too many dialogues between us that never occurred and I don't want to add more exchanges to this jumble. Don't have the wherewithal to parse imaginaries. What did Antonio say to Rosita at the hospice Luis Plaza Dañín? I did not know what to say to the elderly, Rafael had told Jennifer, years before she left him. How to reply to their soft litanies of pain? I would watch Antonio and Rosita on the farthest end of the corridor and wonder what they were so animated about. Even then I didn't believe our visits to that hospice were of any use to anyone except maybe us. To our purpose in life. I heard through Melissa's mother that Antonio was accepted to Stanford, is that true, Rafi? Jennifer wasn't familiar with tact so she never stopped asking me about you, Antonio. Many of the songs at Julio's party are the same songs they used to hear at San Javier but with a new dance beat. No one's dancing because that would ruin the ridiculously expensive clothes their parents bought for them with the proceeds from their corruption. Does Antonio remember the melancholic songs they used to sing at Kennedy Park? Park rules, Mazinger, you have to drink. Yesterday I lost my blue unicorn / left him grazing and he disappeared / the flowers that he left haven't wanted to talk to me. What was the blue unicorn supposed to represent? Endlessly they conjectured and joked about the meaning of Silvio Rodríguez's unicorn. After being in the same classroom with the same people for six years most of our interactions turned into skits, Jennifer. First Facundo would spot me on the other side of the school, second Facundo would yell Mazinger, third Facundo would pretend to escape from me, fourth I would sprint toward Facundo and catch him almost instantly, at a robotic speed that delighted my classmates lounging in the shade by Don Alban's cafeteria. Antonio boarded a plane to Florida and I never heard from him again. And now Antonio wants to talk, to hear me revisit what I don't want to revisit, or at a minimum, not with him? One night at Kennedy Park, after we'd barely won our semifinal match for the academic quiz show on Channel Ten, I finally relented and drank from their bottle of Popov. You forget about the lack of letters and phone calls, twelve years without a word from you, Antonio, no, you don't forget. According to Antonio I drank too much Popov that first time and embraced everyone, the Robot in love, everyone said, the Robot rebooted. Can't go home like this, I said to Antonio, my parents can't see me like this, I've never allowed my parents to see my imperfections. Staggering to Antonio's house, where I vomited in his kitchen sink. I had never told anyone that I've never allowed my parents to see my imperfections and he didn't relay that confession to everyone else like he did with the rest of it: the vomiting in his kitchen sink, the borrowing of his cologne to cover up the smell, the excessive amount I poured on myself. You guys know I can't smell anything but I could definitely smell the peculiar mix of cologne and vomit, Antonio told everyone. Can't use that cologne anymore. Antonio didn't relay my confession about my parents but asked me about it in private, like a doctor concerned about his healthiest patient. I didn't listen to him just as he didn't listen to me when I warned him against his Who's Most Pedantic. Isn't this precisely the kind of demagoguery we should be avoiding? Don't be such a robot, Robot. Antonio and Leopoldo would often avoid me because they knew I didn't approve of their schemes. Just as they are avoiding him tonight. Everyone here knows he's leaving to Zumbahua and he knows they're smirking at him, look at that robot, another fanatic from the apostolic group. Only a fanatic will escape from this kingdom of schemes and change this country, Antonio. After Jennifer left me, toward the end of my fugitive years in Lima, Bogotá, Madrid, it occurred to me that Jennifer was similar to you, Antonio, the same animated predisposition, the same irrational impulses, the crying and the hurling of whatever was at hand, but because she was gone and you were gone and I was gone, this realization, if indeed it was a realization instead of a thought I had succeeded in avoiding for years, did not exist in me as something I should react to. No. Rafael doesn't care that Antonio's back. What could they possibly talk about now? What could Antonio say to redress everything?

—

–Here they are. The distinguished scholars of San Javier. Again.

Not as distinguished as you. Give or take a hundred A pluses.

–How are those A pluses working out for you?

Ever heard of Stanford? Of course you haven't.

Everyone's heard of Harvard, on the other . . .

Your mother never stopped reminding my mother about it. Congratulations. I didn't expect any less from you, Drool.

Cristian turns to Leopoldo and smiles benignly, as if the putdowns he has assigned to Leopoldo aren't amusing enough to dispatch here.

–Hey we were just talking about Harvard, Maraco. Join in. These two were classmates of mine at San Javier. Maraco was a classmate of mine at La Moderna and he's going to be my economic adviser. He was an intern at the International Monetary Fund.

So you are running for office?

Studies have shown that countries that did what the IMF told them were worse off than those that . . .

–The Americans and the Europeans know what they're doing. Our economists should learn from them. Maraco has learned well from them.

Many of the economists at the IMF are from Stanford and Harvard and . . .

I read somewhere that when the Bolivians said we're not paying this foreign debt because we need the money to feed our people the head of the IMF called the head of Bank of America to complain. You know the head of Bank of America, right?

–This guy's mother used to do my mother's nails. Nice shirt by the way. Versace, isn't it?

Leopoldo and I are running for office, too. We're tired of seeing this country run by the same old thieves. How's your grandpa by the way? Is his buddy still running Babson? How was Babson, by the way? I heard you actually managed to graduate from there.

Maraco restrains Cristian.

–I'm canceling my manicure with la puta de tu madre.

Leopoldo restrains Antonio. A fistfight at Julio's would be too much of a spectacle so Cristian and Antonio don't mind being separated.

Fat piece of crap.

Come. Let's go look for Julio.

Oligarch conchadesumadre.

—

I'll tell you about that duo of thieves, Cristian says. Wait hold my Chivas for a second. You moron. Why are you holding my Chivas? Don't ever hold anyone's glass of anything, Maraco. At least that's the rule if you want to work for me. I'll tell you about the Microphone Head and the Pothole Face — ha — that's what we used to call that duo of nerdos. You should've seen Leopoldo's afro head and Antonio's pockmarked face. You should've seen those two abominations at our graduation ceremony, prancing on the coliseum's stage with the medals they scored by swindling an academic quiz show on television. No, I'm not kidding you, Maraco. Why would I kid around with you? Everyone else from San Javier will parrot you the usual drivel about their so called academic achievements and their amazing victory at that quiz show that no one remembers anymore but I'll tell you about the sleaze they pulled to win it. I'll tell you what kind of hypocrite that African Microphone really is, lecturing us at our graduation ceremony about the future of our country, as if he was going to have a future in this country, let alone a post bending over for my grandfather, without a recommendation from me. That's right. For six years that ingrate groveled after me, handing me his physics homework the night before it was due, and whenever the faggoty Argentinean pseudo Jesuits at San Javier pretended they were about to suspend me for spitting at Esteban or some other engendro, the African Head would surreptitiously grovel after the Jesus Loves You people on my behalf, as if I needed that African for anything besides his homework, which of course I could've aced on my own but why bother if I knew he'd done it already, for six years that African would bend over whenever I strolled by because at least that cholo was smart enough to know that no matter how stellar his theology scores were, no matter how much volunteer work he supposedly did in the filthy slums of Guayaquil — that African must have known teaching those poor bastards about jesus was pointless so why else did he trek there except to ingratiate himself with the priests? — yes, that's what I've often said, Maraco, teach those poor bastards how to fish instead of teaching them about some fisherman's son who allowed himself to be crucified — that's what I said, Maraco, a carpenter's son — he would never get anywhere in this country without a recommendation from me. I'm surprised he's even allowed here. Doña Esteros detests him. I'll introduce you to her if we have the misfortune of running into her. Just don't hold her drink. You should hear the stories about her. That she was an illiterate washerwoman who bewitched the dumb heir to the largest tuna fish empire in South America. That would explain why she's such an ostentatious witch. And why she has had all those plastic surgeries. Nothing she can do about that skin color of hers though. My mother can't stand her. The Plastic Sardine, my mother's friends call her. When we were sophomores Julio showed up at school with a brand new nose, courtesy of his bagre of a mother. The whole Esteros family except the tuna heir himself has had a nose job. Who Knows Knows: that was the name of the show they swindled. It used to air on Sundays on a channel owned by the Bucarams or the Adums or one of those Turcos who were part of El Loco's clan of smugglers who later founded the Partido Roldosista Ecuatoriano, a so called populist party that used to promise free housing for the poor but instead smuggled millions out of the country in coffee sacks. Everyone here remembers the coffee sacks story because soon after they fled my friend Pili said she spotted them at the Versace store in Miami Beach. Apparently they were stocking up on those turquoise silk shirts embroidered with gardenias or hyenas or mythological suns or whatever, the kind only Turcos and Mexican narcos wear, and what Pili told us is that after they were done bursting out of those tacky embroidered silk shirts, and after they approached the cash register as only those people can, snapping their fingers for service and flaunting their hairy chests just as they used to do in their political ads promising free housing for the poor, the Italian salesgirl scowled at them as if they had just crapped on the sheep rug and refused to touch their sweaty wads of cash that reeked of stale coffee beans. Cheap Ecuadorian coffee beans. Apparently she buzzed the security guard and asked her pit guard to count the cash from these so called populists that used to broadcast their so called populist shows on Channel Ten for the maids and the bus drivers who ended up voting for that tracalada of Turcos who then sacked whatever stupid hopes those poor bastards had of getting free housing or free milk or whatever else those crooks promised them. Haga Negocio Conmigo was the name of their most vulgar show. Ever watched that crap? With Polo Baquerizo? Remember the theme song? If something I owe you / with this I repay you. This clan of thieves then tried to appear educated by sponsoring a national academic high school quiz show called Who Knows Knows. What a joke. When it first aired, three or four years before the Afro / Drool duo swindled it — the Drool's the Pothole Face, yeah — the San Javier team had clunked so bad on the first round that the homo jesus troglodytes never allowed anyone to enter the contest again because the best, the most prestigious, the most egalitarian school in the nation — ha — the one where parents register their newborns for the entrance exam the minute they are born, an impossible entrance exam that's of course easier to ace if your math and history tutors are the same math and history teachers that are in charge of drafting the impossible entrance exam — of course those teachers were my tutors, Maraco, why wouldn't they be? — and whether you are rich or poor, the jesus people used to repeat and likely still repeat to the newest batch of hopeful parents, if you manage to pass our impossible entrance exam, you too can attend San

Javier — what a joke — although in our class we did have the son of the school janitor and the son of a bus mechanic who used to brag about raping his maid in the shower. Facundo Cedeño. That was his name. You should've heard his toll collector's voice. Facundo was the one who told me how the Afro / Drool duo swindled that television quiz show and bribed our physics teacher. Apparently they booked an appointment with him in one of the small chambers built for the parent / teacher conferences next to the principal's office. Now these chambers have glass walls for a reason, you know, to minimize the risk of grade looting on the premises, but our top nerdos had nerve so in view of everyone they sat down with our physics teacher and their long, dull speech, as performed by Facundo, let's see if I can replicate his toll collector's chicken shriek, went something like, we've reached, "reached" pronounced as reeee / ched, as you probably know, the semifinal stage of Who Knows Knows, and up next we're scheduled against Rocafuerte, one of the strongest contestants this year, and of course we've been preparing ourselves because we just can't let the school down, we've made a commitment and that's why we're here to ask for your help in winning this thing because, you see, unfortunately we don't have the time to study for the physics final, although, hey, let's speak the truth here, no lies, you know us, have known us enough to know that if we were to study for the final we would ace it as we always do so you know we really aren't asking you for much, the rest of the teachers have already agreed to help us take it all the way and we brought you a little something, not as a gift, no, we have too much respect for you to insult you like that, but as an expression of our deepest appreciation for helping us take it all the way, "deepest" pronounced deeeeee / pez. The Afro Head was of course the one in charge of the speechifying. And what did they bring to our teacher? Those abominations claim to have imagination but they have no imagination or only have imagination for masturbation and defalcation because they brought him a bottle of Johnnie Walker, which is what everyone else always brought him. A counterfeit Johnnie, I'm sure. Now our physics teacher, Emilio Turdecox, a lowlife who used to carry a laminated copy of his diploma inside his wallet, was already infamous for his graft. One year he said to our class do you all think I'm a drunk? Quit it with the bottles, people. I need a bicycle. Ha! A bicycle! I never asked Facundo the Maid Killer if he was pranking the Cox, but one year, on the day of our final, he brought the Cox a live turkey. Turdecox couldn't take the turkey home right away, and he couldn't leave it in the teacher's room either, so he had to walk it to our classroom and tie it to the leg of his desk. Good one, fatty! What a sad looking turkey that was. I wonder if it was actually a buzzard. Of course the Afro / Drool duo didn't show up to the physics final. They were too busy celebrating their so called slyness at some park. That's how the Maid Killer heard all about it. A group of them used to station themselves at parks around the city to drink and sing along to the songs the Maid Killer performed on his guitar. On one of these outings they were so drunk that they started bragging about their flatulence and their fraudulence and their so called slyness. What the Maid Killer told me is that they told everyone there that after the Afro Head convinced the priests to allow them to enter the television contest, and after they easily won the first few rounds against some nappy schools, they almost lost to some rural municipal school from Manta or Tungurahua or whatever so they got worried, probably never considered the possibility of losing. Plus the Afro Head had convinced the weary Jesuits to allow them to reenter the contest by assuring them that he had a winning team. Their next rival school was one of those charity nun schools from way over in the, whatever, let's say Esmeraldas. Facundo told me he chatted up one of those prim cholitas before the show, trying to score at least a skirt lift but couldn't, those girls were too studious and serious. Apparently those girls were the proverbial dirt poor orphans with that spunky seriousness of intent you often see in marathon runners. They had overprepared by memorizing all the books available to them. Had actually gone to a library. So after their three day bus trip across Manabí, our orphans arrived at Channel Ten and there, on the patio overlooking the Guayaquil airport, Facundo and the rest of my so called classmates saw them doing calisthenics and singing their battle songs and reciting passages from our famous poets. Our team didn't even know we had famous poets. The deed had been done by then so the Microphone and the Drool must have felt like the abominations they were. They were about to cheat those poor girls from the one thing they were likely to ever win in their lifetimes. Or maybe they didn't feel like abominations. Business as usual, you know? This guy we used to call Mazinger, another one of those nerdos who was part of the Afro / Drool team, demanded that they shred the answers they'd stolen. But it was too late. They had already memorized them. The week before, they'd gone to the office of the quiz show and sweet talked the TV host's secretary. She had a young son and she told them she'd always dreamed of enrolling him at San Javier. So guess what they did? They told her that they had solid connections at San Javier. That they could help her get her son into San Javier no problem. You can imagine this poor woman's excitement. Her son! At San Javier! What a joke. By the time the orphans arrived, the hopeful secretary had already bolstered two of their three consecutive wins. And you know what's worse? That the orphans almost won. On the Drool's segment, the orphan girl was so quick at the buzzer that he had to push the buzzer before the question was even asked so of course then it became evident that something was rotten in the San Javier camp. The host could've stopped the show. He could've drafted new questions and simply retaped that segment. Of course he didn't. Afterward, the Afro Head and the Drool and the Maid Killer and the rest of them saw the orphans sobbing angrily on the patio. Some of my classmates at San Javier will object to me running for office, sure, but at least I don't steal from the poor. Between those two swindlers and me, who would you choose? Don't be such an ass kisser, Maraco. If you're going to work for me you can't be such an ass kisser. Come. Let's head back to my nightclub. Let's refill our Chivas and get the hell out of here.

—

What did Julio say exactly?
I told him about our plan and . . .
Over the phone?
Yes and he agreed to . . .

When was the last time you talked to him in person?

. . . the same plan I've already . . .

Last year in Miami Julio and I . . .

When he was supposed to pick you up at the airport and didn't?

Yes but he . . .

What was his excuse?

Women are like cockroaches.

The day after the apocalypse only Julio will remain and he'll say to the gray, cold wind women are like . . .

Come to the party, he said. His parties used to happen on the tennis court. One long row of women, one long row of men.

Dancing?

To Nitzer Ebb, yes. Once Julio hid a girl on that boat over there for three days.

Fed her his father's shrimps?

Probably forgot he'd left her there.

Are we drunk enough?

Are you trying to over Chivas me so you can . . .

I was fired from the Central Bank, Antonio.

That's not possible sir you've always . . .

So that the minister of finance could replace me with Alfonso Morales, his son in law.

Alfo Sonso Morales? From San Javier? He was even more sonso than . . .

Did it on a Friday, before the long carnival weekend. The guards at the Central Bank were still at lunch so the janitor was asked to escort me out and on the way out secretaries and clerks, back from their jovial lunches, looked at me as if they had been expecting this. As if all along they'd been wondering what I was doing there. It was my fault, of course. I should have befriended someone I could have called to steer the minister away from my post.

I was fired from my first job at an economic consulting firm because I falsified some receipts for overtime meals I did and didn't have. Not that I cared that much about . . .

I remember thinking maybe I could call the Drool over in San

Francisco and ask him if he could find me a job up there even though I know you're full of good intentions but devoid of . . .

Of course I would've tried to . . .

Do you remember all those Saturdays at the hospice Luis Plaza Dañín?

What kind of question is that, Leo?

Do you remember Mapasingue?

Teaching the parables by the stairs that led to . . .

Do you remember Cajas?

How could I forget if it's still . . .

Desolation is a test from god, Father Lucio said.

I don't believe in any of it anymore and yet . . .

What would we be like if someone expunged those memories from us?

I didn't tell anyone in the United States about Mapasingue or Cajas or the hospice Luis Plaza Dañín.

What does that have to do with anything, Antonio? Who cares if you . . .

I'm sorry, Leo. I don't always know what to say.

More like never know what to say.

All these years I thought you and I would eventually be, at a minimum, ministers of something together. Even if I turned into a farmer in Iceland I would still be thinking any minute now Leopoldo and I are going to become ministers of . . .

I'm stuck here, Antonio. I've been stuck here since before you left. I never expected any calls from you.

Here to end your end times, sir, that was so . . .

So to speak.

I was so glad it was you on the phone and I . . .

You haven't changed, Antonio. Or you have except for this one lachrymal habit of yours. I don't remember you crying at Julio's parties back then.

Remember when I threw my calculator against the . . .

The Snivel's here, watch your calculators, fellows. You can borrow my handkerchief but don't drool on it, okay?

I'm sorry. Long plane rides always exhaust me and . . .

Julio's boat is rocking.

Let's go knock on it.

Popcorn. Hey Popcorn?

–Haven't heard that nickname in years. Who's there?

Your mother.

–You've changed, Mom. Why are you drooling, Mom? Leo, so glad you could make it.

Leo's my date so I guess that means at last Leo has managed to date your mom, Popcorn.

Who's there?

–She likes to repeat whatever I say?

She likes to repeat whatever you say?

–I was about to come out and look for you guys. So glad you could make it.

About to. Always.

Listen, Julio we have to . . .

What's happening, who are these people, Antonio?

You told your revolera my name's your name?

Why would anyone want your name, Drool?

–Shhh. Different Antonio, Antonio.

One Drool, many drools.

–I've been thinking about what you said, Leo. Your plan. It's a good one.

At last Julio does his homework.

–My father can definitely fund our campaign. He'll do it. When do we start?

We don't have much time.

Who are these people, Antonio?

Boat engineers, madam.

Boat's leaking.

We're going to have to ask you to step down, madam.

Boat engineering regulations, you understand.

–These engineers dance too. Show her, gentlemen.

I'll lead.

Out of the question.

Let Leo lead, Drool.

This is stupid.

Put your head / on my . . .

Later.

Baby the world can end tomorrow and . . .

Hey that's Julio's line.

Who's Julio? If you ever give me that line, Antonio, I will . . .

And yet the world can end tomorrow, Thalia.

Maybe it's already ended?

At least we have a boat.

Plus the possibility to procreate.

 Oh come back out, Thalia.

Is that her real name?

Remember Kalinka, the Russian?

–Hold on. Let me go talk to her, fellows.

Don't be long.

Is he coming back?

Doesn't look likely.

What's that noise?

The boat's rocking again.

How long until we knock again?

What do we do now?

What's with the lights? Time to sing Happy Birthday?

Looks like the whole block has gone dark.

The whole block being Julio's house.

Are they singing El Loco's song inside?

The force of the poor?

Sounds like it.

The man with the candle approaches us to inform . . .

–It's over.

You mean the lights? Yes we noticed that too but . . .

Welcome back, Rafael.

–El Loco just landed in El Guasmo.

Again?

He isn't allowed to be in Ecuador.

Again?

–They're allowing him to run for office. The interim president will announce tomorrow that for the good of the nation elections will be held earlier.

In six months?

–Three weeks.

Julio better hurry in there.

If Julio's Julio he'll never come out of there.

What do we do now?

Chivas?

XIV / EVA ALONG VICTOR EMILIO ESTRADA

Does Rolando think that I'm his — what? — mascot? — doesn't matter Eva thinks as she hammers posters along Victor Emilio Estrada — we're all going to die anyway — my mascot here believes we will transform our society through a sputtering radio — ugh — through community theater that conceals its sermons with face paint   white at last! — shut up — through warnings like the apocalyptic warnings of the unstoppered young student who at a street corner outside La Universidad Estatal would irrupt against the tentacles of

squid ceviche / here the squid ceviche

an unstoppered young student who would rouse no one with his anachronistic pamphlets and his gastroenterological ravings about how long will we believe that their morsels will trickle down their gullets to someday

toilets straight to the left sir

reach us?

no pamphlets today Eva would say to that unstoppered young student who sported moccasins without socks and didn't mind showing his bony ankles and avoided the main exit of La Universidad Estatal and would plant himself at a more desolate street corner nearby as if trying to boost his role as an outcast preacher of change — we're more they're less — if not today tomorrow — a pamphlet today Eva? — how did you know my name? — Uncle Karl knows everything — ugh — their daily exchanges evolving over time from the polite to the theatrical with him acting as if he were studying her facial expressions for clues after taking a pamphlet from him and her humoring him by putting on her most severe face — how did that face look then? — same as today? — she has never dreamed of stone sculptures or examined expressions in the mirror that have always been there — no they haven't — either way we're all going to — don't melodramatize yourself Eva — her brother Arsenio teasing her about her severe face — Medusa face — shut up Arsno — the moccasins of the unstoppered young student scuffed from losing at street soccer maybe — let me guess no pamphlets today right? — if not tomorrow the day after tomorrow — and one day the unstoppered young student tied his pamphlets with a bow and offered them to her like a cake and she said no pamphlets today thanks — and one day on Halloween he dressed like a Jehovah's Witness and she still said no thanks — and one day he said I brought reinforcements meet Rolando Alban Cienfuegos and she said not today thanks — what a clown — Rolando running after her unzipping her backpack sticking the pamphlets inside — not a clown Rolando didn't laugh — I'll toss these as soon as you're out of sight Cienfuegos — why don't you toss them now? — not right now I — here I'll help you — no I — Rolando hurling the red pamphlets toward the street the flying pamphlets not startling the bored audience inside a crowded bus staring at them as if expecting them to burst with confetti firecrackers ketchup — Rolando grabbing the rest of the pamphlets from her backpack and tossing them on her path like breadcrumbs — not a clown Rolando didn't even smile — there's a salmon in your purse ma'am — hurling the red pamphlets like another batch of pointless Molotov cocktails — neither good nor bad señor — running back to the desolate outpost of the unstoppered young student before she could punch him in the shoulder — Rolando told us you were recontra taken by him when you two first met — that's not true Rolando looked terrified of me — oh is that true Rolando? — no that's just another tale of La Macha Camacha — the preacher's assistant has spoken? — ugh — oh were you an altar boy Rolando? — what did impress Eva was that despite looking terrified by her Rolando stayed in character and assumed the role of the angry radical — and where is Rolando tonight? — where was Rolando last night? — probably not on Victor Emilio Estrada where people are being chauffeured from nightclub to nightclub as if playacting at being the sons and daughters of North Americans who just happened to be stationed at this miserable city — as soon as she's done hammering these posters she will leave this accursed part of town — this hollow part of town where once upon a time John Paul II was probably received with open arms — gastroentoro what? — logical — chanfle — where on every other telephone pole she's hammering her right thumb further — are you hitting yourself on purpose Eva? — not telling — her thumbnail popped while hammering these magnum roofing nails your honor — isn't it uncomfortable to carry that hammer in your back pocket? — can't carry it in my hand or these people here will panic — we interrupt this program to — warning deranged carpenter on the run — where Opus Dei cells are probably spreading the wealth of god among themselves   where once upon a time Opus Dei mothers probably found ways to rig the children's contest to welcome John Paul II — my teacher says I should enter the contest to receive John Paul II on his first visit to Ecuador — mi chiquitolina — is a sermon most off putting when delivered from the pulpit of a cathedral or a street corner? — the first time a pope will set foot in Ecuador Mama — the pope's going to kiss our land and I will hand him orquídeas from our garden — breaking up is never easy / I know — you're not entering any contest to see that good for nothing — no don't say that — don't mention that lastre in this house again — her mother slamming doors rearranging sunflowers as if being forced to tidy up the house for an undesirable guest her mother throwing plates inside the viscous pool that was their kitchen sink

my mother filling up the kitchen sink to the brim donning yellow rubber gloves sticking her hand down the sink as if conducting exploratory surgery

who wants a kidney for dinner?

ewww

and on the night Eva brought up that accursed John Paul II contest her mother read to her the usual bedtime story about Marranito Poco Rabo searching for ravioli and nabo — that's not how the story goes! — once upon time at the cacao plantations in Los Ríos men in uniforms told your grandmother that from Adam's other rib the lord had created the rich so that miserable people like her wouldn't die of hunger — so that miserable people like her would be less miserable and that she was miserable because the lord had ordained it so just as he had ordained for your grandmother's brother to die of dysentery — for your grandmother's father to toil morning to evening until his back gave out and he was let go without a handshake or a pension — what's a pension Mama? — and then one day a different cadre of men in uniforms arrived at the cacao plantations in Los Rios and with an ire unseen in that region they told your grandmother and the other farmers that none of it was true — that the rich weren't a gift from god — that god hadn't ordained for anyone to be miserable — that it wasn't normal for their children to die of hunger and that there was a different cadre of men all over the continent building schools and clinics just like they were going to build schools and clinics in Los Ríos — and then one day a bad man lambasted these cadres of good men and said that what people like your grandmother needed was guidance on how to enter heaven and not guidance on how to seek a better life on earth — and then one day this bad man whom everyone calls John Paul II sent a dark German emissary to sabotage the work of these cadres of good men — shutting down their schools and shuttering their clinics and replacing them with dark bad men in uniforms who went on preaching dark bad things — and where are the good ones now Mother? — all of them dead? — and where are you tonight Mother? — by constellations with names we didn't know? — festering underfoot? — Pisces Mother — and where is Rolando tonight? — Corona Borealis — and where was Rolando last night? — does he assume that because I'm upset with him I don't want to see him again? — did she ever tell Rolando about her grand-mother in Los Ríos? — tell me about yourself — no you tell me about yourself — no — she never told him about her grandmother in Los Ríos or what happened to her brother Arsenio — for what end I ask you? — for what purpose? — shut up — besides — to her the point of talking isn't to share asteroids with vague puffs of life — the Flying Dumbos Mama — landing on a coffee sack after her brother pushed her from what they called the balcony — Mama my brother pushed me! — alfalfa face — my mother telling me stories from when Arsenio was little before he was gone — I spent one whole Sunday cutting and arranging my new white curtains and when they were up your brother snuck inside my bedroom and wiped himself on them can you believe it? — to her the point of talking is simply to pass the time until we fester underfoot — to overlook how disemboweled her voice feels from the rest of her body — my voice stems from my stomach that's why it morphs by meal type — give me your goat soup voice — bahhh — give me your lamb chop voice — Hey — Hey hottie want a ride? — and Eva not acknowledging the voice coming from the blue Trooper that has slowed beside her along Victor Emilio Estrada — We could stop by a liquor store for Boones — Drive to hell first and liquor yourself there — Oh a feisty heretic type — Eva not speeding up or slowing down not turning to look at them the brake lights of the cars ahead of her flickering as the men inside stick their heads out to check if she's going to get in — right — pulling the hammer from the back pocket of her jeans and holding it with both hands like a crazy person who may or may not feel like swinging it at anything — the leering men inside the car are teenagers — high school boys with braces — their chauffeur seems to be the only one who takes her hammer seriously because he's driving them away as the boys yell stop the car chofer — We're taking the maid with us chofer — Chola hijueputa — Revolera conchadetumadre — whatever — she will not cross the street or wait by the shawarma place until they're out of sight and she will not imagine Rolando swiping the hammer from her hand and stumping their morsels — Rolando Bobbit — good one — neither good nor bad señor — doesn't matter we're all going to — quit it with that refrain Evatronica — she doesn't need to imagine Rolando stumping anything because she can imagine stumping everything herself — it isn't so hard to imagine Rolando — you're not the only one who wants everything to end — she has never dreamed of pulling out her hammer from the back pocket of her jeans to destroy the stagecraft — the houses and rivers — ripping the curtains is that enough Rolando? — of course it isn't — how are we to be Christians in a world of destitution and — hearing Rolando's stories about Father Villalba in which he never describes what Father Villalba looks like so she has come to imagine Father Villalba looking like Óscar Romero with those clerk glasses like a second set of eyebrows — Father Villalba refused to be anyone's spiritual counselor Eva — and one Saturday Father Villalba asked me if I could help him load the boxes that he was taking to the children who scavenge at the garbage disposal site in La Libertad and that Saturday and the Saturday after that we rode to La Libertad in silence — thinking that I could sense what Villalba wanted to say to me — what was that? — that's personal Eva — alfalfa face — boxes filled with lettuce heads and antibiotics — you know what Chagas' disease does to you? — ewww — not listening — say chinchorro — chinchulín? — churi churín fun flais? — wishing she could be listening to Rolando asking his radio audience the questions they'd come up with together the week before — who assassinated Jaime Roldós Aguilera? — that one's too serious Rolancho — how come we have all this oil and we can't even rescue people from mudslides? — didn't know you had a penchant for mud — good for the skin bobito — who's your favorite president since our return to democracy in 1979? — none of them señor — and what is Rolando saying tonight? — what is he angry about tonight? — his radio signal doesn't reach here and the radios here aren't asking anything except what's your favorite song

déle nomás / con el garrote que le va a gustar

the radios here are the background songs from the rear of the restaurants along Victor Emilio Estrada — from the hotdog stands on the street corners — from the street children who have abandoned the usual intersections and are now performing their circus tricks amid the traffic — she cannot tell if the people inside the cars have grown used to ignoring them or are worried about the street children cracking their windows as they peek inside their cars as if to check why no one's giving them any money — hello? — perhaps Rolando's playacting at being a lovelorn caller who would like to dedicate a song to Eva Calderón from Los Rios — a love song unlike the songs from the radios along Victor Emilio Estrada that Eva hears and doesn't hear

(later she will forget that she couldn't really hear any radios along Victor Emilio Estrada so the radios she's hearing now are the radios she will imagine later)

imagining what she will imagine

for years now inhabiting in the present what she knows she will imagine in the future perhaps tonight Rolando's voice lives inside the portable radio of the old indigenous woman who's sitting by a lamppost that's shutting off and switching on at random — how do you know it's random maybe there's an omnipresent algorithm behind its flickering? — the radio either set to low or tuned to a station that Eva cannot make sense of

sit crosslegged by the radio jot down the songs burn the songs pretend you never jotted them down

and Eva hoping what she always hopes when she sees a destitute woman on the street — please don't resemble my mother because what would I do then? — please take everything I own Mother — what I have and don't have — the houses and rivers — do you like magic?   knowing that later she will imagine that the old indigenous woman resembled her mother so that she'll feel ashamed of everything she didn't do for this poor woman who's thanking Eva for transferring her change from her pockets to the tomato soup can — May I request you a favor? — Of course — May I borrow a lipstick? — I don't have any lipstick I'm sorry I — Today's my Urpi's nineteenth birthday sends me a letter from El Paso Texas ñuñu I am well haven't practiced the flute in the apartment everyone works different shifts someone's always sleeping on the floor and I'm afraid to practice in the park — Do you play as well? — When my Urpi was born I carved him a flute like a centipede so tiny — My brother used to search for centipedes in the gardens outside so he could place them on my forearm when I was sleeping — your brother is dead — the old woman doesn't say — goodbye Mother — Eva doesn't say — Please be careful of everything — the old woman does say — holding Eva's hand and pointing at the alley that leads to another alley that's ideal for escaping from this accursed place — waving the old woman goodbye wondering if it is not better to cut off these handouts that trick our people into thinking that perhaps things aren't that bad? — that prevent our people from rising up? — yes you're right Eva let's cut them off and wait for them to die of hunger and then at last the dead will rise against the

shut up

once upon a time Marranito Poco Rabo wambled to the civil registry to switch his Poco and his Rabo — that's not how the story goes! — once upon a time El Loco ran for office again — and again — and each time — win or lose — his political party grew as his brothers sisters cousins aunts friends of friends swindled the country in more or less the same way as the sons and daughters of the sons and daughters of our dignitaries who are nightclubbing in this part of town and who just like El Loco have provided no housing for the poor — no health care for the poor — yes we all know that Rolando — we're not stupid — we've never believed that El Loco is our leader or that there's a chance we will not die in misery like we were born into misery — meanwhile Rolando — while we pass the time before the chinchorros prickle us — we would rather watch El Loco's show than watch these people here acculturing themselves with the money they continue to swindle from us — you're lying — about which part? — all of it — yes I am — not telling Rolando about dancing to ABBA with her mother — yes you did — telling Rolando that her mother died of grief without telling him the truth about the source of her grief — socioeconomic grief Rolando — my mother died in a traffic accident I can still imagine her thanking the lord for finally letting her go as the bus crashed against a water truck — not telling him about her brother Arsenio — what for I ask you? — not telling him that while searching for her brother Arsenio her mother neglected an abscess in one of her molars that later paralyzed half her body — once upon a

and so on

go away

(one Sunday evening when she's eight years old her brother borrows the)

not listening

two days before Halloween her brother

if you change your mind / I'm the first in line

borrowing the neighbor's pickup truck to

(in recent declarations President León Martín Cordero has stated that his administration will annihilate terrorism as a system and terrorists as scum of the earth — I'll borrow the neighbor's pickup truck and buy us flour for our costumes Evarista — don't call me Evarista Arsoso — tonight on Channel Two we investigate death squads during the presidency of León Martín Cordero — what do you want to be for Halloween Evarista? — we interrupt this program to inform you that terrorist group Alfaro Vive Carajo has kidnapped well known banker Nahim Isaías — the tailpipe of the neighbor's car scraping against the cratered speed bumps by our house — in recent developments President León Martín Cordero appears to have taken over the military operation to rescue Nahim Isaías — it has been said that our Organization wants to sow chaos and anarchy this is another hallucination of our accusers — either you let me come with you or I'll tell on you Arsenico — what did you call me? — chaos and anarchy have already been sown by those who have benefited for generations from the subjugation of our people — no you're too little to be out at night Evasiva — don't be an Arsno — the principal subversion that exists in our country is poverty and injustice — I asked you where is your brother Eva? — is the misery in which our people live — her brother locking the doors of the neighbor's pickup truck so she couldn't come with him taunting her by caressing the head of the door lock as if shining the helmet of a toy soldier — the Organization believes neoliberal policies are contrary to the objectives of bread roof and employment specified by this administration — Mama my sister's wearing my Han Solo boxers again — we will annihilate these terrorists by all means necessary — Eva climbing on the flatbed of the neighbor's pickup truck jumping on it saying you can't take off without me now — our maximum aspiration is to put an end to this chaos and anarchy — I don't play with dolls Evatronica — not knowing whether to tell on her brother because he might still come back no? — the flatbed like a bungee — good afternoon in today's news Efraín Torres a former agent of the SIC 10 is scheduled to publish a testimony detailing the crimes committed by the administration of León Martín Cordero — listen I know León he will not negotiate with your Organization — her brother climbing on the flatbed — we're all already dead — catching her on her way up or down — we are not terrorists because we are not responsible for the terror that our country has lived — chuzos / here the beef chuzos — her brother jumping on the flatbed carrying her on his shoulders like a cave person — we are not responsible for the assassination of Jaime Roldós Aguilera — dropping Eva inside their house running back to the pickup truck driving off — for the assassination of workers and union leaders — I want to be the ghost of a sugar bun — for the daily persecution of our people who are struggling to obtain a better life — a sugar what? — bun — chanfle — where is your brother Eva? — let go Arsodrita — up or down — Nahim Isaías and his captors have been killed during an assault in La Chala — you did play with dolls Arsenio — shut up — we played house and astronauts and sat outside our house guessing the color of the omnibuses remember? — the meteors are coming — goat brown look — an antiterrorist operation like that you understand like the Ecuadorian people understand engenders grave risks for the hostage — buseta blue — it was our only alternative to not liquidate our sovereignty — what the hell was León talking about? — to not allow the trampling of the conscience of the Ecuadorian people — say moon landing — her mother searching for her brother in the corner stores nearby — say goat brown — her mother saying to her you stay in the house and Eva not arguing with her mother not talking back not saying I'm coming with you because she knew her mother was — what? — terrified that Arsenio had been kidnapped? — hearing her mother rushing around the block and knocking on everyone's door — the dogs barking — the gates opening — the street children juggling beer bottles along Victor Emilio Estrada — hurrying to buy Efraín Torres's testimony after school on the day it was published — ten years after my brother disappeared Rolando — when I was already a junior in high school — reading the testimony on a bench in the Parque de las Iguanas while someone preached something about the lord our savior — when I was already too tall to be carried on anyone's shoulders — you have school tomorrow Eva — sleep please go back to sleep — hammering her fingers on purpose along Victor Emilio Estrada why not? — hearing her mother saying to the neighbors or whomever was in the living room on the night her brother disappeared that she had asked everyone — had gone everywhere — reporting his disappearance at the police headquarters where they asked her if her son had been drinking — if her son was still out with his shady friends — if her son drove off a cliff after finding out that his sweetheart had scampered with his — listen conchadesumadres — watch your mouth lady — that Sunday evening our neighbors in their pajamas brought us carrot soup and pound cake and early the next morning I was unsure as to whether to slice the immaculate pound cake into tiny squares that could fit into a sandwich bag or devour it there with my hands — let go Arsgrodita — and the lord said not a single leaf will fall without my consent — scanning Efraín Torres's testimony for her brother's name — her mother pleading with Don Carlos at the house where she worked as a domestic to please make a quick call somewhere — to someone — my son has gone missing Don Carlos — my son can't just have gone missing — he was a good boy — a decent boy Don Carlos — and since Don Carlos had gone to school with the governor he did make some calls — and we did wait for months for the possibility that Don Carlos would use his clout to unearth something — scanning paragraph after paragraph of Efraín's testimony — my brother doesn't have any shady friends you swines — no one knows anything Señora Estela — my index finger like a ruler scanning the pages of Efraín's testimony — my contact at police headquarters told me they told him to stop asking so many questions or else — ambulatory squadrons trained by Israeli experts — in the news today two adolescents of fourteen and seventeen years of age Pedro Andres and Carlos Santiago Restrepo have disappeared without a trace — scanning for a description of her brother — for years everyone talking about the brothers Restrepo instead of her brother because their Colombian parents had enough money to organize a press conference — because they had lobbied the Ecuadorian government to allow Colombian police experts to investigate what had happened to their sons and what they discovered was that their sons had indeed been detained by the police — because the Restrepos' father had asked President Rodrigo Borja to form a commission to investigate what had happened to his sons during the administration of

León Martín Cordero — because every Wednesday the Restrepos gathered at the Plaza Mayor in Quito to demand justice — because a special agent called Efraín Torres came forth and confessed that on the night the brothers Restrepo had been brought in by the police he had been on duty — that Sergeant Llerena had asked him to hand over the taller Restrepo brother — that approximately forty five minutes later Llerena returned with the prisoner who was unconscious and in such bad condition that Sergeant Llerena and Agent Chocolate had to carry him on each side — that I told the sergeant that I couldn't receive the boy in those conditions because if he died in his cell I would be stuck with a legal proceeding — scanning Efraín Torres's testimony a second time — riding the bus home on the day the testimony was published and thinking she probably did miss a paragraph or a page — President Rodrigo Borja has issued a decree eliminating the SIC 10 created during the administration of León Martín Cordero because of an institutional culture of torture — line after line — of arbitrary detentions — irrationally imagining while riding the bus home that later she would be able to gossip about Efraín's testimony with her school friends — of cruel and inhuman treatments — did you read Efraín's dedication on the first page for her noble and pure gestures Rosa Porteros wherever you are ha ha — rereading his testimony and berating Efraín Torres for spending so much time talking about his volunteer work at Garcia Moreno Prison where he'd been imprisoned instead of mentioning the names of the other people he claims he didn't disappear — I've never claimed to be a saint — no one's saying you're a saint you imbecile just tell me what happened to my brother Arsenio — Agent Chocolate ha ha — on our first assignment they hauled us in a van without windows and drove us to what we later found out was Cuenca — lambasting Efraín for his unbearably innocent tone — among the targeted were syndicate leader Fausto Dutan who was wrongly included as a subversive and for whom a direct order was issued by Mayor Paco Urrutia chief of the SIC 10 in Cuenca to assassinate him along with his wife and daughters — look here dear reader and judge for yourself — my mother lost more than thirty pounds Rolando — on the day I was to be freed from Garcia Moreno Prison my older sister my dear sister who had

suffered with me this period of injustice called the penal administration and asked to talk to me — my mother didn't even recover ten measly pounds Rolando — and in the poorer neighborhoods that had been designated as dangerous zones our ambulatory squadrons would detain innocent young men just because they were standing outside their houses — sometimes my mother would turn on the radio in the living room and listen to love songs from the kitchen — my sister said a few words that as I write these lines tears come down my cheeks again — as if that distance between the living room and the kitchen allowed my mother to imagine those songs were floating toward her — at last your release is a reality at last this nightmare is over my sister said — the Israelis trained us on basic tactics of extermination — you don't know how happy I am my sister said — for instance the triple asphyxia — it was the first time in three years and six months that my sister felt happy — for instance the submarine in which a plastic bag filled with tear gas is tied around the head of the prisoner and then it is submerged inside a tank of water — and on the fourth year of Arsenio's disappearance my mother and I rode a bus to Quito and joined the parents of the brothers Restrepo at the Plaza Mayor — riding the bus home on the day Efraín's testimony was published and finding her mother already home with her own copy of Efraín's testimony on the kitchen table — ten years Rolando — please turn around Mama — Eva didn't say — I can't keep standing here in the kitchen forever — Eva didn't say — her mother was crying — her mother did turn around and was crying — as if she didn't want to wake up anybody anymore — why wasn't she screaming Rolando? — why wasn't she tearing everything down? — and Eva pulling her own copy of Efraín's useless testimony from her backpack and offering it to her mother just as her mother was raising her frail arms and offering to Eva what was visible — this is what's left of me Eva — her mother didn't say — Hey —)
Hey sweetheart
   the Flying Dumbos the Teacups the
   mi chiquitolina
   Hey you okay? — Leave me alone — Who does this revolera think she's talking to? — Block her way Alfonso — Good evening why are

you carrying a hammer so late at night isn't that suspicious? — So
I can hammer these posters onto your ugly faces — Ha ha those
posters are for Cristian Cordero's new nightclub — Get away from
me — Take her hammer and posters she's fired — Who made Juan
Luis the leader? — I'm the one buying you morons drinks — I
don't think Cristian will approve of you firing his servants — I'm
sure she massages him on the side better watch it — Don't touch
me get away from me — Putadeverga come here — Hey don't punch
her so hard what if — The Maraco in love — Wow that's probably enough Maraco — Maraco is so Maraco he likes to kick women
while they're down — Who doesn't? — Is she dead? — No more
Chivas for Maraco — You're still a gaywad Maraco — Let's get out of
here — Don't rush me I don't want to waste my cigar my grandfather
gets these from León — Did you know Julio's cousin was wasted as
usual one night and ran over some lowlife with his van? — What was
his name? — Who cares? — Julio's cousin was at Cristian's party last
week he looked fine to me — Turns out the lowlife on the motorcycle
was the son of a military guy so Julio's cousin had to go into hiding
until they could bribe the captain to

(how many ribs does the lord
    the motion sickness on the bus to Quito
    children selling corn on the cob
      a feisty heretic type look
        –What are these horrible people doing on Victor Emilio
        Estrada anyway
    the serpentine road on our way up to
        –Call the bouncer at Opera this trash here's blocking the
        sidewalk
    the bus driver slowing down because of the fog and holding
    his lighter in front of the windshield
      Quito Light of America
        why did you listen to the radio from the other room
        Mama?
    quiet down children
      riot tanks surrounding the Plaza Mayor

reading about Luz Elena the mother of the brothers
Restrepo and how in her desperation to find her
sons she had consulted soothsayers
the fourth anniversary of the Restrepo's disappearance
if the candle is still lit tomorrow morning your sons
are still alive
don't make a nuisance of yourself
President Sixto Duran Ballen says to
the young Restrepo sister after she
asked him about her brothers
policemen with plastic shields barricading the Plaza
Mayor
the fifth anniversary of Arsenio's disappearance
corn grains sliding up and down the floor whenever the bus
driver speeds up or
I have orders to shoot if I want to
Han Solo inside a wall of lava
Nosotros / que nos queremos tanto / que
desde que nos
policemen armed with tear gas launchers
I haven't come here to recite you poetry
me gustas cuando callas / porque estás como
children climbing on the bus and selling corn on the
I haven't come here to serenade you
Agent Chocolate ha ha
trained Dobermans
Eva's mother sending her to her
aunt's house by the Salado the
week after her brother
two hundred policemen barricading the
untying a canoe on the Salado
and searching for her brother
the seams of the goat brown bus on our way to
Luz Elena visiting the hut of an indigenous
clairvoyant who filled a pearl shell with aguardiente

and said he saw the boys alive and crossing the
border
                                the branch of a palm tree
                                floating on the Salado like a
                                gnarled hand
  –Out of the way she needs help someone
    let me through I'm here to bring Doña Restrepo her
    medicine
                                my aunt standing on the
                                makeshift port by the Salado
                                desperately waving her hands
                                don't reprimand our Eva please
  –Call an ambulance you
                                please don't send me away again
                                Mama
      trucutus
                                mi chiquitolina
children selling ciruelas
                                a bloated liter bottle with a
                                trickle of spiders floating on the
        mothers of the Plaza Mayor
                                        a secret meeting
                                        between the police chief
                                        and the minister of the
                                        interior to decide what
                                        to do with the Restrepo
                                        brother who hadn't died
  –We can't let this woman in the hospital she doesn't have
  an ID
      my mother had brought her own sign
                                        shoot him
      it said simply:
you'll feel less sick if you stick your head out the window Eva
        For Our Children Until Life
the wind on my face

Arsenio Marcos Calderón

waterfalls on every corner on our way to

a sign with the lying newspaper headline There Was a
Traffic Accident Involved in the Restrepo Case

–What are you doing with that woman bring her back
into the hospital

the patches of jungle on our way to

the headline splattered with red paint

Quito light of

Marranito Poco Rabo? Yes? Hi.
Hello. Where to? Across the
cathedral. The fire thrower's
under the rock.

I have come to tell you that I love you Eva
a drawing on the newspaper of the Yambo
lagoon where the dead bodies of the brothers
Restrepo were never to be found

–I'm sorry doctor we didn't know that you knew her we
Policemen dragging Luz Elena away

a stick figure with fins an oxygen tank inside the
Yambo

Eva's mother approaching Luz Elena at the Plaza
Mayor

sneaking inside her mother's room and sleeping
by the foot of

Eva's mother sharing with Luz Elena a photograph of
Arsenio

Agent Moran the policewoman in charge of
investigating the brothers Restrepo's disappearance
inventing an informant who knew where the
brothers Restrepo were

Eva's mother didn't speak

President Sixto Duran Ballen's
daughter saying to Luz Elena that
instead of protesting at the Plaza

Mayor they should play the classical
music her father likes
Luz Elena didn't speak
–Page Doctor Rodriguez the anesthesiologist not the
heart surgeon
Luz Elena holding my mother's hand
Agent Moran asking the Restrepo family for money
taking more than sixty trips across the country to
track invented leads
Luz Elena and my mother embracing
–She's waking up that's good let her rest for a while)
does Rolando think that I'm his
clanging the metal telephone poles along Victor Emilio Estrada
with her hammer and listening in for
what were you listening in for?
the submarines Mama — posters slimed atop posters — the
rusted staples like robot ants swarming the surface of the telephone
poles along Victor Emilio Estrada — my Aunt Felicia had a French
poodle named Felicia that followed her everywhere — Jaime Roldós
Aguilera slimed atop Jaime Nebot Saadi — not like submarines like
sonars in movies about radioactive submarines — the manta rays
in the Yambo — Radio Río y Mar — the scuba divers gliding along
giant fishes with names she didn't know — there's a salmon in your
lagoon ma'am — and whenever Felicia was calm she would doze by
her feet — whenever I would smear flour on my face I would think of
you Arsenio — El Loco Bucaram slimed atop of El Loco Bucaram — if
I hadn't been holding these posters in my hand I would have been
embarrassed to have been seen staring at the posters on the telephone
poles along Victor Emilio Estrada Rolando — look at that scare-
crow she has nothing better to do than ogle at telephone poles — La
Sonora Dinamita slimed atop Assad Bucaram — pouring sacks of
flour and cement in the Yambo so no one else would be thrown in
there anymore — the wooden handle of my brother's favorite hammer worn out by his millions of clutchings — what did those hands
look like then? — beware of splinters Arsno — I'm not building your

hamster a house or wheel or nothing Evarista — a diving plank? — and whenever Felicia wasn't calm she would bark at everything — Radio Romance — no barking at the chairs Felicia — giant chairs tilting atop Felicia — I didn't come here to stencil your eyebrows Eva — white walls white roofs white vistas of nothing — climbing the walls of a tower that's also a skyscraper that's rising up to the clouds — everybody speaks in tongues because without a tongue who can speak eh? — ugh   let's inflate your pamphlets with ketchup and hurl them at the — what was inside your purse Aunt Felicia? — who wants ketchup for dinner? — ewww — forgive me tomatoes — don't eat me please eat the potatoes instead — forgive me potatoes — whenever it was dark Felicia would power the headlight on her forehead — my dog has mining experience how about yours? — what's this we have us a caller folks — hello? — hi I would like to dedicate a — what's your name Son? — my name's Rolando I would like to dedicate With You at a Distance to Eva Calderón — is Eva your sweetheart? — I wouldn't call her that yes she's my are we on the air? — we're always on the air but no one listens — Doña Leonor? — call me Aurorora — Leonor's trying to be funny here's a laugh track for you — I can't hear anything — Aurora La Deaf — do you think your Eva's listening? — I hope so — even if she isn't listening she is listening right? — nothing consoles me / if you aren't here with me — in the news today a cadre of scientists has gathered around a lamppost on Victor Emilio Estrada — Radio Nada de Nada — what's your request? — the song about the red robins who sing about the red robins who — so many songs here can you hear all the radios along Victor Emilio Estrada? — in recent declarations scientists have concluded the lamppost on Victor Emilio Estrada isn't switching on and off at random yes thank you for the opportunity at first we thought it was Morse code which didn't make any sense so then we thought it was some kind of Indian signal which didn't make any sense either so then we connected electrodes to the base of the lamp and concluded the lamp wasn't asking for help because what's the use of asking for help right? — You found me — We drove all over and then we — I knew you would find me and then I thought how melodramatic my thoughts — Don't melodramatize yourself Auroris — Don't make me laugh these exhalations hurt me — Rolando talking to Eva and Eva trying to calm him as much as he's trying to calm her connecting electrodes to Eva Calderón's head and — Did Eva just fall asleep? — Mom? — yes? — I thought it was you what are you doing on Victor Emilio Estrada? — I'm sorry I didn't have more change to give you please forgive me I'll give you everything I have — the houses and rivers — how are we to be anything in a world of — Radio Los Peces — constellations with names we didn't — and one day the dead will rise against the

XV / ROLANDO FINDS EVA

Did I tell you I read funny? — Tico Tico funny or Polo Baquerizo funny? — you think Polo Baquerizo's funny? — no Eva he's a parody of what he thinks people think is funny — we should survey the people and ask them what's funny — El Loco's definitely funny — whoever doesn't say the word funny loses okay? — the force of the poor / Abdalá / the clamor of my people / funny — fungus is funny — for whom? — you lost! — so did you — that's funny — how is it that you think you read funny? — can we not talk about El Loco today? — I just asked you what is it about your reading habits that's — you think El Loco's funny because he's also a parody of what he thinks people want and yet what's funny isn't that at all but that the people know he's performing what he thinks they want and that's what endears him to them — this girl called Eva doesn't want me to talk about El Loco today so I'm — El Loco's performance is meant for them unlike the performance of someone like Nebot who promises them the same free everything but they can tell he's not performing for them but for his neighborhood cronies — I don't remember ever seeing Tico Tico the clown when I was a kid — Nebot sports Italian suits and promises to parrot the Americans meanwhile El Loco pours beer on his head and says this land is ours carajo — Jaime Roldós Aguilera sported excellent suits — that's different Jaime Roldós was different — are you thinking about Eva? — his father doesn't ask as they drive to the hospital Luis Vernaza to search for Eva — I'm not thinking about Eva — Rolando doesn't answer — Alma corazón — I'm not thinking about my sister Alma — Rolando doesn't answer — about the one letter he received from his sister — hi remember me it's me Rolandis / I've made a friend here in San Francisco her name's Estela / I'm afraid of forgetting everything what would I be like if I forgot everything / Estela's from Guatemala the other day she found a romance novel on the street reading it to me exaggerating her accent on purpose / you would like her she wouldn't like you everything's fine here I'm fine here you've always remembered everything

Rolandis — that's not true I — do you remember the princess and the kitty you and me forcing Dad to be the princess — of course I remember the princess and the — prove it — I remember Dad picking an orange you saying not an ovoid one a round one go back Dad — you don't love me anymore — of course I do chiquita — you don't show it — do I really need to show it when I've loved you this much for this long? — which Rolando is sure he could say to his sister if she ever came back — and as Rolando and his father drive to the hospital Luis Vernaza he's sure they will run into his sister on the way there — why are you just standing there Alma get in the car quick Dad's been waiting for you — which is ridiculous but no less ridiculous than everything in the world — the metaphysical rebel declares the end of metaphysics — shut up — please save memories of me of us in case I forget everything / if this is the only letter you receive from me you can keep my felt dinosaur — which he did keep because it was the only letter he received from her — she probably didn't know it would be her last letter to him — his father didn't receive any letters from her or at least Rolando couldn't find any under his pillow or in his drawers — she didn't know he'd heard her when she called home the first time and the second time calling them less and less as if every day she forgot them a little more as opposed to Rolando who doesn't forget her because sometimes after his father has gone to sleep he transcribes his last transcription of her letter by hand — not really thinking about its content just passing the time although the next day he does like to think of himself transcribing her letter and does wish someone could videotape him (1) transcribing her letter (2) transcribing his transcription of her letter (∞) transcribing his transcription of his transcription of his transcription of his transcription — facing the camera to address his sister asking her (1) (2)(∞) can you hear Dad's snores from over there? — sending her the videotape as proof that although they had grown apart soon after he started school at San Javier — right around the time when that Esteros engendro accused his sister of being possessed by the devil — when he avoided his sister instead of consoling her as if afraid she would contaminate him with her misfortune what kind of brother does that? — I'm so sorry Alma — someone please take a picture of me I need the evidence that that person transcribing her letter is really me — how many times have you actually transcribed her letter? — only once but — you think imagining this transcription business suffices? — it isn't nothing — it is for your sister — does anyone have a video camera I can borrow? — her misfortunes attached to him against his will stay away from me please I don't want to think of you — that remote beach in Salinas you and I strolling into the sea for miles the water not even reaching our knees little waves chasing one another and you picking from that firmament of seashells remember? — yes and Dad chasing us splashing up the place saying time for ceviche de concha children — and you arranging your seashells in a circle placing the best one in the middle that strange woman at the restaurant lifting the best one from you returning to her table as if she had just picked it from a buffet — hey we're almost at the hospital Rolando — his father doesn't say because they're still far away from the hospital or not far away from the hospital how would he know look out the window Rolando see the dark walls forget the dark walls his father switching on the lights in his sleep — how about you Dad what are you thinking about? — Rolando doesn't say — Father Villalba saying to Rolando what is there to say? — that we've lost? — that I wished I would have had the courage to eliminate our enemies? — god and so on — don't expect me to inspire you Rolando — how are we to be Christians in a world of destitution and injustice? — the long silent rides with Father Villalba until one day Father Villalba did speak — in Guatemala our enemies received an unlimited supply of American weapons that ravaged mountains villages children — in Chile our enemies received enough American funds to sabotage the economy and firebomb La Moneda — if you begin by believing they are not your enemies you're already dead — in El Salvador we concealed the equipment of Radio Venceremos inside a cave where the embroilment of bats electrified our guerrilla newsflashes — how many times did you transcribe Father Villalba's words? — I was too young I'm sorry I didn't know I would forget most of them — the week after Alma left them Father Villalba didn't ask

Rolando if anything was the matter on their long ride to the dumpster called La Libertad and Rolando didn't say Father I have sinned or Father I want to set fire to Julio's house or Father how do you explain the coexistence of Chagas and christ — the empty lots on their way to La Libertad — the dark brick walls with posters of El Loco on their way to the hospital Luis Vernaza — the clamor of my people / Abdalá — you still haven't told me how you speak funny — I said read funny Rolanbobo — if you forget everything I would be a blanket and outstretch myself on these vacant plains — god and so on — the garbage piles on the empty lots on their way to La Libertad — Father Villalba had refused to be anyone's spiritual counselor Eva — Rolando's father prostrated in Father Villalba's office the week after Alma left them — a dog howling atop a hill of sawdust and garbage in an empty lot on their way to La Libertad — Cerberus has Chagas look — icepicking the moon Mars forsaken satellites — his father driving them to the hospital Luis Vernaza and Rolando asking his father if he'd ever asked Father Villalba to counsel him — When? — his father prostrated in Father Villalba's office and Father Villalba hunched next to his father as if confessing him — raindrops filtering inside our cave so that we had to cover the radio equipment with a makeshift roof of bamboo — Yes I did ask Father Villalba to counsel you Rolando — his father prostrated in Father Villalba's office and Father Villalba placing his hands on his father's hands as if to pray together — Was worried about you Rolando — his father does say — what could Father Villalba have said to even attempt to console his father? — god and so on — bats on the roof of a shack atop a hill of sawdust and garbage in an empty lot on their way to La Libertad — in Argentina a guard brought his daughter to one of Videla's concentration camps so he could introduce her to his favorite prisoners — and then that memory of his father in Father Villalba's office begins again and instead of running away from that embarrassing moment Rolando joins Father Villalba in consoling his father — the long silent ride with his father to the hospital Luis Vernaza and Rolando worrying that his father's arm will start tapping the armrest involuntarily again — the bats gnawing on the bamboo — the mate gourd inside Father Villalba's pickup truck smelling like rancid mint — what if I forget everything and everything remains intact inside my mitochondria for example — the week after his sister left them his father's arm tapping the armrest involuntarily as if it wanted out — don't think of an iguana's tail — and then that memory of his father in Father Villalba's office begins again and Rolando's resting his ear on his father's back while Father Villalba doesn't say I wish I could tell you god will provide for your daughter — sana sana culito de rana — his father's arm tapping the armrest on the driver's door as if the arm wanted to catch Rolando's attention — help me please my owner doesn't want to live anymore — I read funny because my eyes dart around the page can't explain why sorry — the long silent rides to La Libertad and Father Villalba not asking him what's the matter Rolando but speaking to him as if at last Father Villalba was ready to answer questions or not ready to answer questions but he might as well answer those questions that were submitted to him soon after Pinochet launched Operation Condor for instance — I didn't ask Father Villalba anything he just started speaking to me listen to me Rolando till the last possible second we believe the lord will change things for the better which means no one will overturn anything unless someone disrupts everyone's lives so much that they can no longer believe the lord will change anything do you understand? — after my sister left us my father wouldn't speak to anyone or he would speak to anyone but wasn't really there when he spoke to anyone he said to me don't worry they are saying your sister's okay I didn't ask him who these people were my father laughing to himself as if listening to punch- lines from ultratumba — his father's arm not tapping the armrest as they drive to the hospital Luis Vernaza when will Rolando's arms start convulsing involuntarily? — how much of himself has already been spent pretending nothing's the matter? — I'm so sorry Alma — help me please my owner — arriving at the hospital Luis Vernaza asking for his sister no one has records of entries or exits this late at night — Can I help you? — Yes my father and I are looking for — Try the next desk down the hall we're closed — Why ask if you can help me if you're going to — Let it go Rolando let's go — rushing along the dark hallways of the first floor — up next, second floor, more silent agonies — shut up — along the urgent care rooms where at last they find Eva — You found me — We drove all over and then we — I knew you would find me and then I thought how melodramatic my thoughts — Don't melodramatize yourself Auroris — Don't make me laugh these exhalations hurt me — Don't talk please I'll just sit here and swat these fruit flies with my Chapulín mallet — I'm not dead — Leftover fruit flies I'm sure let me open the window — I know you want to know what happened so you can enrage yourself into committing more futile acts of — If you prefer to rest maybe later is better I'll just sit here and read your mind don't mind the mind burr — What am I thinking? — Please hold — Money back if you take too long — You're thinking of me at a stadium batting these fruit flies into outer space — Tell me about outer space — Experts agree that it's out there — Money back if you don't power intergalactic worlds for me — A classmate at San Javier we called him Mazinger the Robot he would kick the ball into — What's wrong Rolando? — I'm sorry nothing I'm fine it's okay if you see me cry right? — Of course Rolandis — Okay so this guy called Mazinger would kick the ball into outer space — Maybe he knew that's where the goal really is? — Don't metaphoratize yourself Auroris — Metaphora what? — Tize — Chanfle — I remember Spider from the Moon a bedtime story my sister Alma would ask my father to read to us — What was it about? — Spider from the Moon lands on Earth looking for little girls to eat — Remember that movie about cannibals in the Amazon called Cannibals Something or Other? — One night while my father was reading Spider from the Moon the neighbor turns up the radio a song by Grupo Niche about rain your hands as cold as rain my father allowing Grupo Niche to alter the course of the bedtime story because all of a sudden Spider from the Moon has cold hands leaking rain-drops on earth — A flood? — Exactly which led to the story of Noah and his ark — And Spider from the Moon instructed Noah to collect one male and one female — And then the neighbor switches stations and La Sonora Dinamita's singing about the fire of your beautiful black eyes and all of a sudden Spider from the Moon tries to cork the flood with firestorms that shoot from his beautiful black eyes — Julio Jaramillo sang the aguardiente version of that same song I'm so tired Rolando — Please don't talk anymore Eva I'll take care of the talking I'll pretend I am both you and me okay? — Okay but how did Noah distinguish between the male fly and the — Ewww — Okay fine I'll play dead go on — Rolando as Eva saying and what happens in the end Rolando? — Spider from the Moon chases Alma and just as Spider from the Moon is about to spiderweb her he realizes he would rather be friends with her — Rolando as Eva saying tell me about your father's improvisations Rolando? — Yes well my sister would ask my father to do it again the next day and the next day my father's catching the sounds around us immobile there and he's listening intently the siren of an ambulance turning into Spider from the Moon having a stomachache from eating too many meteors — What's that noise? — That's my dad he's a little sensitive today he's staying outside until he can calm down and stop crying — Why would he want to do that? — Why would he want to calm down? — Or stop crying — That's what men do Eva — Tell him to come in please don't make him wait outside — Rolando asking his father to please come inside his father entering the room wiping his red eyes with his Emelec tee shirt — Alfredito your son tells me you're quite the story-teller — Rolando exaggerates I — his father trying not to stare at the bruises on Eva's face or the bandages around her head or the wounds on her shoulders — Tell me the one about Spider from the Moon — which makes his father cry — I'm not dead Alfredito — She's joking Dad she — Why did they do this to you I — I'm not dead I thought am I relieved? — We're relieved don't say that — knowing me / knowing you — I fought back at first then I thought either way we're all going to die right? — let us pray for her — his father doesn't say — I thought Radio Nuevo Día / la radio al día — let us contemplate god's mysteries — Father Villalba doesn't say — Did Eva just fall asleep? — Her face is warm her hands aren't I think she's sleeping yes — the dust on the windshield on their way to La Libertad — the dry wiper washers clearing slices of dirt for them — read something to me show me how you read funny — no funny nothing today we have to rewrite Snowflakes in Mapasingue — why did you bring it up then? — you lost! funny! — and then that memory of his father in Father Villalba's office begins again and Rolando's saying to Rolando you twig you didn't console anyone you just stood there outside Father Villalba's office and ran away from them — you find consolation in this endless carping of yours don't you? — does it make you feel more alive to torch yourself endlessly? — Rolando of Arc ha ha — ugh — (1) John Paul II signals he doesn't support liberation theology priests (2) Reagan floods El Salvador with guns (3) bullets rain on Óscar Romero's heart — the squalid children at La Libertad not flocking to Father Villalba like in those movies about saintful priests Father Villalba asking them their names the children forming a line inventing funny names for themselves — dear Rolando the Americans here in San Francisco aren't used to the sun everyone strolls to the park when the sun's out / sometimes I think one day when we're old we'll drop on the floor and play topos again doesn't matter all these years we didn't talk — Clodomiro at your service — rats nosing on the squalid children in their sleep — Tremebundo here — the children asking Rolando to join their betting pool on who among them will die next — two tapitas on Dientefrío check out his yellow eyeballs — Father Villalba jotting down their names on a clipboard memorizing their names crossing out the names of those we couldn't find after three or four weeks why would he do that? — a reminder of the futility of his task is that it? — how much futility can one take Eva? — all of it or none of it depends — I'll open Hopscotch at random show me how you read funny okay? — fine I'll point you to where my eyes dart to and you can number them ready (1) here (2) here (3) here — Rosamundo at your service — how are we to be Christians in a world of destitution and injustice let us delude ourselves look our charity doesn't perpetuate destitution and injustice — (1) a process of enriching despoilment it can come to him while he is sitting on the toilet — what does that mean? — Morelli the advocate of comfortable toilet seating? — (2) pebble and star absurd images — the metaphysical rebel declares that pebbles equal stars we're upside down? — (3) incapable of liquidating circumstances he tries to turn his back on them — did I tell you the one about the liquid paper and the squid? — the long silent wait in the hospital room after Eva falls asleep — Father Villalba's long absence after his first heart attack — the smell of rancid mint inside Father Villalba's pickup truck along with the ridiculous smell of lavender — the smell of heart ointment he'd imagined Father Villalba would exude after his heart surgery — Father Villalba's pickup truck had no air conditioner so I could only detect those smells in the seconds between entering the pickup truck and rolling down the windows — the bats gnawing on the squalid children in their sleep — our father was the princess you're the princess Dad I'm the purr asleep in the forest hide in the kitchen quick — what does one do with all these unsharable memories Rolando? — Let's go Evarista — Arsenico — Eva's talking in her sleep does she do that often Rolando? — Arsenio's her brother — holding Eva's hand what else can Rolando do? — it has been said that our Organization wants to sow chaos and anarchy — let's collect these pebbles and hurl them at their gates is that enough? — Father it burns — this is another hallucination of our accusers — little waves chasing one another — ovoid like your stoopoid head ha ha — the strange old woman at that restaurant by the beach not so strange a retiree her husband sporting a gray suit and a matching gray vest we didn't see her take your seashell Dad confronting her you should be ashamed of yourself — let's stroll further out on this beach until we reach outer space — Alma repeating the seashell story again and again not as if retelling some profound injustice but as if giddy that something had happened to her she was four years old — Are you Eva Calderón's family? — Yes hello Doctor let's please step outside what's the diagnosis — Head concussion five broken ribs we're concerned a rib might have punctured her lung — What does that mean? — She's in critical condition — She was just speaking to us like nothing was wrong — What else can a patient do except pretend nothing's wrong? — Don't talk to us like that Doctor — Like what? — Nothing like nothing Doctor we — Listen I have people lining up outside trying to bribe me for a room the nurses refused to even let Eva into the hospital I just happened to walk by — Why did you intervene? — It's silly you'll guffaw not that I care if you guffaw you're better off not guffawing at your doctor by the way — Everything's more or less silly Doctor — She looks almost exactly like a cousin of mine — A cousin? — My cousin Marta we used to play soccer together she's in Madrid now — My sister's away in San Francisco too — I was walking outside by the emergency room thinking of those thousands of people lining up holding up their piggy banks trying to bribe someone so their children could be seen by a doctor meanwhile the director of the hospital calls me hey Alberto the assistant to the minister of so and so just called his son needs a cast please take good care of him and I'm having to say yes of course I don't mind I do mind who cares if I mind if not me someone else who knows what my cousin's doing to make ends meet in Madrid? — Alma corazón — the long wait after the doctor walks away — the long days after fighting with his father about skipping Father Villalba's funeral what's the point of attending Father Villalba's funeral he's dead he will remain dead he wouldn't have wanted a funeral toss my useless bones into a ditch he would have said — Rolancerdo at your service — Dientefrío's dead I won I won — I'm an accomplice to all this injustice — Father Villalba did say — and so are you — and you — and you — this a country thirsty for water and injustice — at last you're dead Father Villalba are you relieved? — how can I be dead if you can still hear me? — I'm tired and all of this hurts too much Father — a smaller place a loan from the priests anything I'll do Alma — after everything I've done for your family Don Alban — she's waking up look — You found me — Thank the mind burr — Why so cold mind burr? — A homeless woman on Victor Emilio actually told us to come here — Need some mittens mind burr? — She also told us what happened to you she said she found you on the sidewalk — Her son doesn't play the panflute in Texas — This Argentinian priest at San Javier once smacked Facundo with his flute remember Facundo? — Where's your father? — Almond chocolate run — At last we're alone I can tell you everything — I'll need a more comfortable chair please hold — Don't run out of here embattled thinking this changes everything you're better off learning how to make gold fishes — I'm tired I just want to lie down next to you for a while — Too bad the bed's so narrow I don't disagree with you that our plays accomplish nothing — We don't let's not talk about that now — That our radio accomplishes very little — Free advertising for the people? — We're like a whistling duo at a funeral home — Once I saw a casket shop in Cuenca with a sign on the window that read — We could run for office — Don't be funny — El Loco's funny — A sign on the window of a funeral home that said We Rent Chairs — El Loco's back? — Yes — That's funny.

PART FOUR

—

FACUNDO SAYS FAREWELL

XVI / FACUNDO SAYS FAREWELL

El Loco, Facundo says into his tape recorder, bah, Macundo, you sound like a circus mouthpiece, Facundo thinks, rewind and jump-start, El Loco, Facundo says into his tape recorder, and not only is he tired of parroting circus loudmouths, Facundo thinks, his audience at La Ratonera is probably tired of him reparroting from circuses nobody attends anymore, hey fatty, someone in his audience had once yelled, you're turning into the Fat Lady, to which Facundo replied by singing everyone loves the Fat Lady / because we're all going to win, a popular limerick for an old raffle called The Fat Lady, which, according to a mathematician who later became the chief of statistics for the ministry of information, was rigged, rewind and jumpstart, El Loco, Facundo says into his tape recorder, a tape recorder to which he could've attached a microphone but didn't because he doesn't own a microphone and, besides, a microphone would only accrete his likelihood of sounding like a circus loudmouth, bearded ladies and obese gentlemen and amented children and that kind of Welcome to the Circus crap, but let us omit any mention of the microphone from La Ratonera, which he wasn't allowed to borrow to rehearse his skits in his mother's kitchen like he's doing tonight, as if he cared that much about borrowing a bulbous microphone that smells like algae doused in Patito, the word bulbous, incidentally, being the kind of word the Microphone Head would have picked to strafe other Big Headed Microphone looking fellows like himself, in any case he can rehearse without that priapic microphone, Facundo thinks, hey fatty, someone in his audience had once yelled, quit it with your comic intros and sing us the one about the rabbit in the mirror, a popular tune by a band of pissed off Spaniards who sang about unfettered destruction, sexual dysfunction, women jumping out of windows, and a rabbit faced guy inside the mirror who's staring at you, why are you staring at me / do you want me to meal on you / rabbit / good evening ladies and gentleman, Facundo says into his tape recorder, have you heard the one about the free houses El Loco promised during his campaign, yes, now that he's finally president, our free houses are on their way here from Paraguay, yes, that's right, but they might vanish in customs unless El Loco kickbacks enormous sums to Jacobito, our brand new customs director, also known as El Loco's son.

—

Do you think Ecuadorians appreciate everything you've done for them, Jacinto Manuel Cazares writes in his notebook, preparing for his interview with León Martín Cordero. Do they thank you enough? Does it bother you that young people don't remember your public works? All those yellow signs that read Another Public Work by León? ~~Even if everyone was saying that you were building all those overpasses to deplete the public coffers so that your enemy, Rodrigo Borja, would be hampered when he assumed the presidency after you?~~ Do you remember when you swore, in front of god and the republic, that you would never betray us? ~~Did you betray us?~~ What did you tell John Paul II when he confessed you during his visit to Ecuador? ~~Did you two share your strategies for squashing dissent?~~ What did you and Fidel Castro talk about? Do you find it ironic that despite all your physical ailments people continue to admire your fortitude? Is it true that when your retina came out you continued working for the good of the nation? What's behind the unconditional support people have toward you? ~~Are you an oligarch?~~ Are you the owner of the country or do Ecuadorians hide their own desire to defalcate the country by calling you the owner of the country? León no se ahueva? ~~Did you fabricate the drug trafficking charges against El Loco? Is it true that you prefer the country to be unstable because that way you can run the country without having to put forth a presidential candidate? Is that why you allowed El Loco to win?~~ Do you think you've sacrificed yourself? Do you think the history of modern Guayaquil will be divided in two, Before León and After León? ~~After the success of your presidency, why didn't your political party win any presidential elections when you did put forth presidential candidates?~~ What motivated you to assume the overwhelming responsibility to serve us? Do you think you've left a mark? ~~Would it bother you to find out~~

~~your family paid me to write your biography?~~ What constitutes, for you, a state crime? Do you believe in the repose of the warrior? What does Ecuador owe you? Everyone recognizes that your fight against terrorism liberated Ecuador from the plague of terrorism; nevertheless, why do some people keep battling you because you supposedly violated human rights? ~~Do you see dead terrorists?~~ Do you still carry the .38 Reagan gifted you? Is your strong arm still strong? ~~Would it bother you to find out your family will be bankrolling the publication of this biography?~~ Do you like my tie? ~~Do you ever point the .38 Reagan gifted you to your mouth and say León no se ahueva?~~ Was the sacrifice worth it? ~~Do you see dead nonterrorists? Why aren't you dead already?~~ Do you think, like I do, like so many of us do, that your thoughts and the principles that have guided your life would be of value to our youth?

—

Jacobito, Facundo says into his tape recorder, or rather Jacoboto, because Jacobito's envergadura is such that the president of Ecuador, also known as Jacobito's father, had to ship him, on the presidential jet, to an institute of ventripotence in Miami, an institute of trimming the guata so he can reguata, tome pin / haga pun, an institute that has not been photofeatured in our newspapers yet because our newspapers are running out of space to feature every single desmadre from these conchadesumadres, Jacobito, Facundo says into his tape recorder, but when the son of El Loco suffers, El Loco said, the nation suffers, just as the nation suffers when Jacobito doesn't invite anyone to celebrate his first million, yes, I know you've heard that in less than four months Jacobito has accumulated one million from his post in customs, even though he doesn't even have an official post in customs, and yes, you've read in every newspaper about Jacobito's party to celebrate his first million, but no one has relayed the sad news that Jacobito didn't invite anyone, this sad boy with so much extra weight because when he was seven years old León kicked him, El Loco said, Jacobito, my son, I have returned, Jacobito not inviting anyone because why should he share his caldo de bolas with anyone, his guata de cerdo, plus all his feculent friends were too busy grabbling inside the six containers filled with stereos that had been wheeled out of customs on Jacobito's orders, oh, and he's especially not sharing anything with the American ambassador, who on national television proclaimed that under El Loco the current levels of extortion exceed the solid customs of corruption in Ecuador, but apparently Jacobito doesn't mind sharing his Argentinian prostitutes with our hircine forefather also known as his father, or at least that's what the Argentinian newspapers said after El Loco and his scrofulous coterie visited Buenos Aires to smear themselves with the excremental economic miracles of Menen and Cavallo, no Macundo, Facundo thinks, you're unspooling too much negativity, no one wants to ingest this summation of minuses, give your audience equivoques not hebetudes, perpend, Macundo, cachinnate, Fecundo, rewind and jumpstart, Jacobito, Facundo says into his tape recorder.

—

Professor Hurtado.

Economista Bastidas.

Has it been years?

Missed you at the alumni barbeques.

You guys still do those? Take a seat, Leo.

Had imagined your office differently. No ferns, no watercolors, all business.

My assistant insisted on these fripperies and I didn't . . .

Your assistant has a nice . . .

She can hear us.

She should hang your favorite quotes from Rubén Darío.

The Veil of Queen Mab?

Remember? During Berta's class?

Or Facundo singing Happy Birthday to Berta on Halloween.

Berta crying and running out.

Or that time at Kennedy Park when you and Facundo tried to lift me with a plank of wood that happened to have a rusted nail.

Cauterized your wound with Patito.

We continued singing.

Those were the days.

I'm fond of them but . . . don't miss them.

To San Javier you enter but you do exit.

Do you?

The Drool's in town did you hear?

Called me yesterday, said he wanted to see me, say goodbye.

He's leaving already?

Your husband didn't inform you?

We broke up years ago.

How is he? Still hurling his calculator against the wall?

That was after our math or physics final?

Physics.

Problem is the Drool has no physics finals anymore. Did he tell you why he came back?

To see you?

We were supposed to run for office with Julio but . . .

Julio didn't show?

He's in Miami opening a new nightclub with Cristian.

Minister of finance.

What?

I used to imagine you as minister of finance.

Used to?

I haven't see you in so long, Leo. I don't want to get into it.

You never spoke much about . . .

You started spending so much with Antonio and Julio, reveling on what you could get away with. I still remember how proud you looked when you told us that you and Antonio had swindled the answers for Who Knows Knows. Rafael and I were dismayed. If my father would have found out he would have pulled me out of that contest.

We won.

I'm sorry, Leo. Who goes to the alumni barbeques by the way? Does Facundo still . . .

You celebrated with us.

I was never very good at saying no to either of you. I enjoyed being around you despite . . . I used to wish I could be as eloquent as you. Did you know that years ago Antonio came to see me in Paris? Or rather he didn't come to see me but needed a place to stay. My wife didn't like the idea of having a high school friend staying with us for a week. We were living in a small dorm room then, and after arguing with my wife about it I realized I didn't care as much as I thought I did about whether he stayed with us or not. Too late to let him know so I waited for him to call me.

You didn't pick him up at the airport?

He told you about this?

Didn't mention it, no.

The information booth at the airport picked a hotel for him. He spent most of his time in Paris shopping for expensive sweaters and leather jackets. He'd purchased a long purple leather jacket with a fur collar at one of those irrational designer stores and he seemed so proud of it, as if at last he could show up anywhere. Dragged my wife and I to those ridiculous nightclubs roped at the front. Had to call his bank long distance so they would approve his purchase of that flashy leather jacket.

–Coffee, Economista?

And Danish cookies for Leopoldo too, yes, thank you.

Sugar cubes on the side would be . . .

–You just don't do that to a friend, Giovanni.

Marta, please.

You should see this Antonio guy he's so conceited, Marta.

–Antonio's the one who convinced you to join the apostolic group?

What does that have to do with . . .

He convinced me too and look at me now, Marta.

–You two should be ashamed of yourselves. Talking about your friend like that. I'm not bringing you two anything.

Well that was . . .

Shut the door?

Let's try and whisper, okay?

–I heard that!

How does she know about the apostolic group?

Too many tequilas one night and . . .

Told her how good we used to be so you could . . .

I heard Mazinger still goes to . . . can she still . . .

I can't even hear us. Whisper less.

Ever think about Mapasingue?

Come closer what?

Ever think about the hospice Luis Plaza Dañín?

I wish I could tell you that I don't.

Remember the old lady with the electric makeup?

Sometimes I wish we could . . .

Bright red blush on her cheeks and . . .

Orange seashell beads around her neck?

That's the one. Always ready for a cumbia.

She's the one who pined after the Drool.

Rosita Torres. Listen. When Antonio . . . can she hear us?

I think she's gone.

When Antonio arrived in Paris he called me ten or fifteen times at least. I don't know how long he waited for me at the airport but with each call I could sense his rising disbelief. I wouldn't have believed it either. Pick up the phone, my wife said, and tell that individual he's a thoughtless mooch for trying to impose himself on us for a whole week. I didn't know how to explain to her that although I hadn't talked to the Drool in years he was still . . . you know Antonio . . . he's rash and . . . probably thought what you and I would have thought: my buddy from San Javier is in Paris so of course I'm staying with him. I didn't pick up the phone and he gave up calling and I left our dorm room without . . . didn't tell my wife. Wasn't trying to punish her I . . . just didn't know what to say to her. Outside our gray slab of dorm I thought about you and Mazinger and the Drool and Facundo singing about the blue unicorn.

Silvio Rodríguez.

That one soccer game when Antonio received yet another yellow card and tossed it at the referee's face . . .

Flashed him a red card right after.

I walked him off the soccer field and tried to calm him down. He cried like he always did when we were losing and I told him to put his head under the faucets. I stood there watching the water pouring on his head and you know I think my wife must have understood something or maybe she didn't want any trouble at home because she . . . why don't you invite your friend to stay with us for two or three days, she said. I called Antonio immediately. You know him. He joked around as if nothing had happened.

Why are you telling me all this?

I don't want you to think I don't . . . I wouldn't have minded if you had asked me to be part of your administration even though I know we would've failed or one of you would've succumbed to backdoor deals with El Loco or León. No one we know has done anything to change anything. Can we still call Antonio the son of El Loco?

His monster zits are gone.

Terrible timing now that El Loco's finally our . . .

El Loco messing with you at the Polytechnic?

Watch it. I think Marta voted for El Loco. I don't anticipate it. El Loco's too busy recording his rock album and ransacking the country.

El Loco Who Loves.

I wonder if Facundo applied to be his backup singer.

I bet you have to bribe your way to even that position. Listen, Bastidas, I wanted to ask you . . .

Anything for you, professor.

You know those scholarships in . . .

Indiana University?

Doctorate in economics, yes.

Certainly.

Any chance you might . . .

I know the pool of applicants is daunting and the selection process problematic.

Wondering if you . . .

–Those scholarships are for students without means!

She's back.

Don't tell her you work for León.

I don't work for León anymore. He fired me after hearing that I was thinking of running for office. You know I'm qualified for those scholarships so I'm not asking for . . .

Of course, Leo.

Thought maybe you knew someone who could . . .

I'll definitely look into it.

—

El Loco, Facundo says into his tape recorder, aha, I see my fans have decided to forfend their spirits from steep malaise and show up today, let me guess, fellows, early this morning, before or after the roosters you don't have hornswoggled you with their squalls, before or after you dreamed of onion crowns and lycanthropists, you wambled out of your indurated mattress, folding your mosquito net equidistantly, without toothpicking it, because your net feels more alive with those sibilant insects embrangled in it, and after you equipped your daughter with the free school backpack she never received, courtesy of El Loco, a free school backpack that contained, as announced in the announcements, one fresh towel, one bar of soap, one translucent soap container, one pocketsized comb, one toothbrush, one tube of mentholated toothpaste, a box of crayons, one pen, one pencil, one eraser, one pencil sharpener, one ruler, and five notebooks of fifty pages each, hey, whosoever brings me one of those collectable bars of soap with El Loco's initials engraved on it wins another round of songs about la de la / mochila azul / la de ojitos dormilones, and after your daughter swallowed a bowl of free milk that wasn't fit for human consumption, courtesy of El Loco, and after you proudly stepped out of the free house you never received and hauled the bus your daughter couldn't take because the latest Paquetazo quintupled the bus fares and quadrupled the price of lentils, courtesy of El Loco, you stumbled upon an immense national protest against the leader of the poor, and although you had nothing to protest against, especially after all the toys your daughter never received during El Loco's Christmas Telethon, you joined the protest anyway, because who doesn't need the occasional singalong to Down with El Loco, or rather, Down with All of Them, banging on the casserole you didn't bring, thousands of pots and pans entuning Down with Everything, and after everyone silenced their farrago of cataclysmic tunes to intake the news that congress had ousted El Loco because of his excessive heteroclitude, no lewd free associations, folks, respect for the deranged man, please, and after you heard we, at last, had scored one luxury, the luxury to choose between three presidents, and by choose I of course mean not choose between the vice president, an elegant lady from Cuenca who does not sip tea from a tea bag, the president of congress, an encultured crapulence from Quito, and El Loco, our brand new leader of the poor, and after you heard your choices were narrowed by one because El Loco had escaped from the presidential palace through the window of the presidential kitchen, rucksack of discretionary funds in tow, you thought to yourself, hey, let's stop by La Ratonera and ask the fat one to sing us a happy song for a change, let's demand that he sing us a happy song for a change and you know what, compatriotas, despite the sign here that says today I don't take requests but tomorrow I will, I will comply and, for you, tonight, on our first Loco Less Night, before the interim president bombards us with more packages of encultured economics, I will sing you a happy song for a change.

XVII / ANTONIO EDITS HIS BABY CHRIST MEMOIR

And if all our actions, from breathing to the founding of empires or metaphysical systems, derive from an illusion as to our importance, the same is true a fortiori of the prophetic instinct. Who, with the exact vision of his nullity, would try to be effective and turn himself into a savior?

— CIORAN

The baby christ wept soon after we reached my Uncle Fernando's house. I had never seen his house before, but I had advocated it as a Christmas location because I knew it had been built in the newest and most exclusive neighborhood in Guayaquil, L'Hermitage, which was not far from San Javier and Ciudadela Los Ceibos. Since no one came to open the gates immediately, my grandmother aired her frustration about how hard it was to find good service. From a narrow cement booth the guard rushed out, desperately trying to tuck his uniform shirt in and appear less asleep. He waved at my uncle, bowing repeatedly, then pulled the gates open. My grandmother rolled her eyes, just as she had done earlier with Maria. After finishing the kitchen, Maria had reported that she was done and had asked for permission to leave. My grandmother had rebuffed her, clinically explaining that there were still the floors to mop, the bathrooms to disinfect, and plenty of garbage to take out. But señora, Maria had pleaded, it's Christmas Eve.

—

What does it matter if his memoir about the night the baby christ cried lacks a singular style, Antonio thinks (and here Antonio searches online for Proust's notion of style as quality of vision — the revelation of the particular universe that each of us sees, Proust wrote, and that other people don't see —), or rather what does it matter if he's so dispirited about his lack of a singular style in the one short story that's really a memoir that seemed to him salvageable from the morass of overwrought sarcasm he'd written before rushing back to

Ecuador so he could fail to save the natives or, as it's becoming apparent to him, not that salvageable because if what remains of the night the baby christ cried is mostly an impulse to revisit that night, then what shouldn't remain of that night in text is these drab sentences and their cargo of fabrications, because years from now he will have forgotten even more about that night so he's likely to return to this text about that night and what will remain for him will be these drab sentences in English, and so perhaps this whole text about the baby christ should be crossed out and he should start again, or he should not start again until he figures out how to perform in text his impulse to revisit what he has mostly forgotten instead of trying to fill in with narrative fabrications what he has forgotten (a performance of an impulse meaning an exhaustion of an impulse as a way to dramatize that impulse?), in any case what does it matter if he feels compelled to revisit the night the baby christ cried if on the patio of the Belgian café in the Hayes Valley district of San Francisco, where he's editing this memoir about the baby christ, three tall women in sundresses are asking him where's he from, what's he writing about, what's his name, and perhaps he's writing about crying figurines so he can impress tall, hot women in sundresses like these — I write so I can impress hot young boys, Foucault said — but the less cynical side of him, which he hasn't been able to transcribe into text yet, knows that he's revisiting what he's revisiting because that's where he still exists, where he finds solace despite the disheartening contents, although one day he will have lived among the sundresses long enough that perhaps he'll also find solace in revisiting his life among the sundresses (and here Antonio searches for a passage from Faulkner contradicting what he's been thinking — the past is not a diminishing road but, instead, Faulkner wrote, a huge meadow which no winter ever quite touches, divided for the old by the narrow bottle neck of the most recent decade of years —), but before he revisits his life among the sundresses he's likely to revisit his short stint failing to run for office with Leopoldo, which will allow him to feel useful without having done anything to be useful, or perhaps revisiting his short stint failing to run for office with Leopoldo will be his lamb's blood, forcing him to confront his uselessness on a daily basis and ask himself how are we to be humans in a world of destitution and injustice, and yet if his eighteen years in Ecuador are his huge meadow that no winter can touch, Antonio thinks, if San Javier and Leopoldo and the baby christ and Cajas and the hospice Luis Plaza Dañín will never vanish from him completely, can he at least attempt to reinterpret those years so that he isn't so susceptible to run off with whatever caravan of change reminds him of the intensity he felt during those years, no, forget reinterpretation, Drool, encumber yourself with enough comforts and you'll never leave San Francisco again.

—

L'Hermitage is one of the many gated communities in Ecuador, which I was to see again many years later in the moneyed areas of Venezuela, Colombia, and Bolivia. The neighborhood was so new that the lampposts were still headless, illuminating nothing. The houses on this hill must have been as long and wide as their pools and tennis courts, but because it was dark and because these houses were probably fortresses surrounded by white concrete walls it was difficult to tell how big they really were. There must have been no more than twenty houses total. Some of them, the dark ones without flickering Christmas lights, were obviously empty. Others, mounted with cane and rope structures, were still under construction. Three years later, Stephan Bohorquez, a classmate at San Javier, was to move from the other side of town into one of these houses soon after his father had been appointed to an important government post, and when his parents were out on official business, Stephan would splurge on prostitutes and whiskey and throw parties for us and eventually, when his allowance ran out, he would steal his mother's dresses and use them to barter with his favorite prostitutes. None of us brought up the obvious question of where the money came from. Stephan's pool was refreshing and the Chivas was free and we knew where the money came from in any case.

—

To search for the source of his impulse to return to Ecuador by revisiting the night the baby christ cried was pointless, Antonio thinks, just as it's pointless for him to teach English to immigrant women at El Centro Legal for one measly hour a week, photocopying pages from an ESL book at the last minute and hoping they would smile at him in gratitude, knowing he was fooling himself into believing he was being useful — if all the NGOs and nonprofits of the world ceased their activities, Antonio had asked a British art critic during their first date, would anyone notice? — just as it was pointless and childish for him to imagine the possibility of deforming American English as revenge for Americans deforming Latin America with their interventionist policies, and if he continued in this vein there would be nothing left, everything's pointless, congratulations, Antonio, now what?

—

As soon as we entered his house, my Uncle Fernando said so very sorry. I should've mentioned it before. Most of our furniture is still in transit, on some ship in the Atlantic, I suppose. My sincere apologies. He nonetheless gave us a proud tour of his house, which looked like a vacant museum of modern art. We gathered in his living room. My grandmother placed the baby christ by the cemented chimney. Before Christmas, she would always arrange a nativity scene for us at her house. On top of wooden fruit boxes, she would place a grass green blanket, reserving the topmost spot for the baby christ, which was not to take its place until after Mass, and then she would populate the rest of her valley with Mary, Joseph, the three magi, and below them bushes and trees and the earless donkey I used to play with when I was five years old. But my grandmother did not bring any of it to my uncle's house, so by the fake chimney the baby christ looked out of place. My Uncle Fernando brought two garbage bags bloated with gifts wrapped in jingles. I do not remember what happened next, or how much time passed between my grandfather bringing us kitchen chairs so we could all sit in the living room and then someone yelling the baby christ! The scream had the authority of panic. Everyone congregated around the baby christ, several steps removed. Tears were materializing beneath both eyes, falling in urgent succession, as if an actual child were trying to burst out from the immobility he had been condemned to. His eyes stared at us, or past us, and the urgency of his tears, combined with the indifference of the clay, consigned him to an eerie sadness.

My grandfather stepped forward. It seemed so natural for him to be there, alone with his baby christ, that none of us followed. I can still see the back of his ample suit jacket, light brown and checkered, as he bowed a bit. To me, at that moment, or perhaps later, my grandfather looked like an apostle humbly accepting his gift, the gift of revelation.

My grandmother shrieked and sobbed. He's crying for my Antonio's return to the faith, she said. This was to become the official version.

My grandfather turned and glared at my grandmother with a disdain I did not think him capable of. Maruja, he yelled, and as he realized his disdain had staked a place in his words he stopped and calmed himself by raising his left hand as if about to dictate silence to himself. He then softened his voice and said come. Let us kneel. He guided my grandmother to the front by putting his arms around her, and as they knelt my aunts knelt, too.

My Uncle Fernando did not look surprised by what the baby christ was doing. He must have felt entitled to witness this sort of thing. Soon he, too, would have to flee.

I waited for my father to kneel, but since he didn't I eventually knelt and joined the others in hymns and prayers. I turned and glanced back at him, although sometimes I think I did so not then but later, in memory, trying to remember what he looked like by turning and glancing back at him across the years. He was still standing, red eyed and stiff, a mixture of terror and shame in his face. I wanted to make him kneel with the same force he had used to thrust his stiff drinks at me. If he saw me staring at him, he did not acknowledge me. He tightened and untightened his hands as if trying to shake them off his arms. Then he walked away.

—

The double bill on Sundays at the Cine Maya, Antonio thinks, watching Rambo I and II, or Rambo III and Conan the Barbarian, one man against the world, carajo, his father picking him up at the apartment on Bálsamos Street and taking him to the Cine Maya every Sunday for the double bill, Antonio visiting the Cine Maya by his house before returning to San Francisco and finding it shuttered, longing to feel strong emotions like nostalgia instead of just the plain passing of time, the houses in his old neighborhood wrapped in high voltage fences and angry warning skulls: and this nothing, Cioran writes, this everything, cannot give life a meaning, but it nonetheless makes life persevere in what it is: a state of nonsuicide, okay, sure, Cioran, I don't disagree with you, and yet too much would have to be expunged from my life in Ecuador for me to ever consider exiting this state of nonsuicide, all these impulses to return again and again, to change something for someone, to become the one who could've changed Ecuador.

—

After a solemn hour or two, the tears did not ebb. We must have expected that the end of our prayers would coincide with the end of the baby christ's tears, so the continuing torrent started making us uncomfortable. Finally my grandmother announced she had to go to the bathroom, and then everyone stood up and scattered.

Alone with the baby christ, I did not make any promises of faith or love or anything. I was not Lucia or Francisco, promising the Virgin of Fátima to endure all suffering as an act of reparation for the sins of the world. Perhaps I was paralyzed by the knowledge that as this moment passed its veracity passed, too. Or perhaps I was already steeped in desolation, the kind left behind by a miracle that changes nothing. Even so, when I see myself there, still lanky at thirteen and quite sweaty, I am always surprised at my coldness. Seeking explanations, I inspected the baby christ as if it were a malfunctioning toy. I picked up the wicker basket and checked underneath. I lifted its purple and gold shawl, checking the white ceiling for leaks. With my fingertips I prodded the figurine's cheeks, trying to unearth a hidden mechanism. I did not find one.

Sometimes, when I revisit that Christmas night, I wish it were all true. I wish that the baby christ had not been crying for the corruption being perpetuated back then — the same corruption that continues to sink my country further — but was really crying for my father. I like to think that, while he was alive, someone was able to cry for him.

Or my brother Rolando returning the orange that was supposed to
be / what was it supposed to be / our father was the princess you're
the princess Dad I'm the purr asleep in the forest hide in the kitchen
quick / the princess hides in the kitchen / the princess enters the forest with an orange in his hand / on tiptoe Dad go back / the princess
reenters up on his toes / uff / waking me by tapping me on the shoulder two times the same pattern on purpose so I would remember him
maybe my father once told me if you set the same song on repeat
before bedtime you'll feel as if time hasn't passed when you awake
tap / tap as if giving life to a door / reloj no marques las horas / no /
our profe will not want to hear about tap / taps on my shoulder or an
orange that was supposed to be what was it supposed to be our profe
said he was volunteering for a book of interviews about undocu-
mented immigrants please share your terrible experiences with me he
didn't say terrible experiences he just said stories / experiences /
lives / of course he meant terrible experiences nobody wants a book
of wonderful immigrant experiences I didn't say yes to him when he
asked wasn't even in his class / was in his class / wasn't there to learn
/ my friend Estela was there to learn basic English phrases every
Wednesday before the meeting of the women's collective at El Centro
Legal one day I arrived early none of the women were there usually
Estela was there to talk to / how did you and Estela meet? / we'd been
assigned to the same address two housecleaners were needed when
we were done Estela said let's find us pupusas for dinner Estela sharing casual anecdotes about her life in Guatemala as if she'd practiced
how to be amenable company at home look I'm okay / hello good
day / a water truck in Estela's hometown had a horn that howled like
an elephant Estela interrupting herself or something inside / outside
of her interrupting her how can a human being do that to another
human being to children the driver of the water truck a funnyman
who mounted plastic elephant fangs atop his water truck elephants

don't howl what do they do / Estela interrupting herself and I holding Estela's hand what else could I do she was crying / not crying /
hello good day / would Estela have been comforted if I'd shared
with her that in the mountains in a camp in Guatemala / no / she
wouldn't have been comforted how do you comfort a mother tell me
that profe please in the mountains in a camp in Guatemala I'd been
waiting to cross the border into the United States armed men barging inside abducting some of the men in our group who were sleeping on the floor around me I was asleep / wasn't asleep / scared / can't
remember any sounds how is that possible barging inside with
machine guns combat boots wrestling masks the men on the floor
who were taken away didn't scream / I did / didn't / pretend you're
asleep Alma / the men on the floor resigned to anything happening
to them I wasn't resigned how can you not be resigned to anything
happening to you when you haven't been able to wash in a week /
twenty days a foul smell that turns out to be you is that what you
want to hear in our interview tomorrow profe all the terrible things
that I'll remember tonight you'll record from me tomorrow / not
everything Alma / I'll never find comfort in this bed this room away
from you and Dad Rolando / that's not true Alma / I know that
Rolandish / our first interview tomorrow what will I share / not share
with you profe the mold under my fingernails after not washing for a
week / twenty days in the mountains of Guatemala how cold I felt the
coldest I've ever felt in my life like being submerged in ice / no / like a
wind from Antarctica sent after you / wherever she is find her / didn't
know where I was we'd been hiding inside a bus Líneas Los Pajaros
couldn't see the patrolmen searching for us / a cold wind descending
on your skin staying there I can get used to this you think then across
the earth another wind finds you wave after / wave a remote beach in
Salinas where my brother Rolando and I are strolling into the sea the
water not even reaching our knees little waves chasing one another /
don't tell him about our beach Alma / quick hide in the kitchen Dad
/ why can't I tell him about our beach Rolando you think sharing our
beach invalidates our memory somehow that's silly what if one day I
forget about our beach we need a record maybe / a starfish look / find a

tape recorder and record yourself instead Alma / Estela crying / not crying during our pupusas dinner nobody at the tables nearby in that Salvadorian restaurant hidden behind a storefront on Mission Street thought it odd that she was crying an old man in a checkered gabardine suit approaching us he looked like one of those singers from Los Panchos with a raspy voice from a lifetime of cigarettes my father saying to our chainsmoking neighbor Don Pascacio even the drool on your pillow smells like smoke / what does your drool smell like Dad / ewww / an old man in a checkered gabardine suit approaching us so solemnly he probably has been starching his checkered suit every morning since before I was born holding up his soup plate placing it in front of Estela like a birthday cake saying here we are my dear / that was it / and Estela drank the old man's soup? / yes the whole thing profe / the waiter who hadn't starched his guayabera apologizing don't mind him he's a veteran from the ouster against Somoza / here we are / in the mountains in a camp in Guatemala avoiding the men in our group some of them had tried to abuse the women I was relieved when some of the men on the floor were abducted / they were trying to cross the border just like you Alma / I'm sorry / you don't know if they were the ones trying to abuse the women it was probably the ones in charge don't you think those men bunched on the floor were as scared as you / I'm sorry / arriving early for the meeting of the women's collective at El Centro Legal none of the women were there usually Estela was there to talk to / Estela is from Guatemala profe she didn't want to tell me what had happened to her in Guatemala the librarian at the San Francisco Library who spoke Spanish handed me four volumes from a report called Guatemala Never Again I didn't want to open Volume I / The Impact of Violence / Volume II / The Mechanism of Horror / maybe you were right to not tell me anything Estela what's the point of telling anybody anything profe / come listen to the remarkable story of Alma Alban Cienfuegos who pretends to endure in the end / The End / uff your story made us feel better thank you so much for pretending you're okay for us have a good one Alma / here we are / please take care Alma / the librarian who spoke Spanish smiling at me pushing a book cart with crosseyed wheels I couldn't leave without at least opening Guatemala Never Again the librarian had looked so proud of me when I'd asked him about Guatemala finding the name of Estela's village in Volume I what's the point of repeating those atrocities here profe how can a human being do that to another human being to children arriving early for the meeting of the women's collective at El Centro Legal all the women were there twenty / twenty five of them inside the conference room a young man in a business shirt with stripes no starch talking in Spanish to them he's our brand new English teacher his name's Antonio José a volunteer nice one eh Estela said joining his class for the last five minutes no place to sit he removed the motorcycle helmet from his chair offered the chair to me holding a photocopy of a page from a study book with drawings of people at work the women repeating with him broom / bucket / chair I knew some of the women there already knew these words what were they doing there he said let's go around the room now Estela at least twenty years older than me fifty / sixty years old maybe ashamed of her English she'd been a schoolteacher in Guatemala she'd arrived to the United States alone didn't look so ashamed in front of you profe / broom / bucket / chair and you correcting her in Spanish her pronunciation a crossword they could solve together very good Estela you see bucket is tough for us Latin Americans that u sounds like a moo let me write it on the board how it sounds in Spanish boquet see / bo instead of bu / boquet / rolling up the sleeves of his business shirt with stripes above his elbows embarrassed that his shirt was too tight on the chest that his shirt probably cost more than the chairs / stacks of legal encyclopedias in that conference room he was about my age younger maybe please don't tell him I'm from Guayaquil Estela what if he knows Julio Esteros Guayaquil is so small for months I didn't think of him I was busy caring for an elderly woman who didn't look like my grandmother didn't like me claimed her sons were going to care for her berated me for not understanding most of her mumblings about a shameless waiter who'd sniffed a cocktail before serving it to the couple next to her table at an Argentinean steakhouse arriving at El Centro Legal the women older than our profe by twenty /

thirty years surprising him at the end of class with gifts Estela was there too she hadn't said anything to me about gifts I hadn't seen her that week we tried to see each other at least once a week / Almita let's meet for / Estelita I have a confession to make I can't stand those pupusas from your native country / don't blame me I'm not Salvadorian / oh ha ha / my brother Rolando and I watching a mini-series about aliens while my father hauled crates to the Isla Santay past midnight / my father putting us to bed flipping a coin whoever wins picks the bedtime story / me / me / me / my brother Rolando demanding we use the same coin every time / why is that? / couldn't say profe hey Rolando why is that / I told you that's between us Alma / if you don't tell me I'll invent something / don't believe you / my brother demanding we use the same coin every time because he loved fabricating useless talismans of luck / that's not why Alma / because he snuck it under his armpit when we weren't looking so as to bias the outcome somehow / ugh / can't remember even one of my father's bedtime stories anymore profe how is that possible / Rolando and I with a flashlight sneaking into the living room after hearing my father's snores searching for flying saucers out the window / growl / zzz / growl / I'm so sorry Estela I thought pupusas were from Guatemala whenever I complained about something Estela said don't blame me I'm not Salvadorian / here we are / the women at El Centro Legal surprising you with gifts Estela was there too she didn't tell me anything about gifts she was caring for a toddler who dragged his pink umbrella everywhere the tip of it leaving behind a trail of doodles on the gravel our profe unwrapping his gifts a tiny bodysuit with a tulip / rainbow mittens / a beanie hat with antlers / white bibs with owls / his girl-friend from Poland was having a baby how did the women know about the baby he thanked the women stunned you could tell he didn't want to say much he knew he would cry if he said anything Estela asked him if he'd picked a name / Lilia Klara he said / think of us Lilia Klara / thank you for being so patient with us profe the women said tomorrow's our first interview what do you want to hear from me profe tell me please / here we are / tap / tap / the kitten awakes in the forest / on tiptoe Dad / my toes can't handle the weight /

shhh no talking Dad / the princess holding the orange in his hand canvasing the horizon the orange purposefully unattended behind his back the kitten swiping the orange from the princess's hand the princess sobbing / like a mime Dad no noises go back / the princess sobbing noiselessly / quick exit the stage Dad / The End / again / you're the audience Rolando / again / my brother Rolando must have been two years old so tiny didn't speak can't remember much of anything anymore profe what if I omit the terrible does that increase the chances of forgetting year / after year these memories dissipating from me that's not how it works Alma / how does it work Rolando tell me how it works or I'll share more than just our beach tomorrow / I'm sorry Alma / descending from a camp in the mountains of Guatemala patrolmen capturing us interrogating us one of them poured his glass on my head not much rum left melted ice one ice cube hadn't melted yet bounced on my head like a coconut isn't that funny the sawdust on the floor cut marks on my wrists the rope smelling of manure the policeman saying we can't waste our resources sending you back to Ecuador Luis Alberto dump this mongrel in Gracias a Dios with all the rest of them a forsaken place homeless people refugees transients like me I didn't want to feel the backwash of rum in my hair flattened carton boxes for Hitachi televisions on that sidewalk with bloodstains / food stains didn't have money for food scared of everyone rows of destitute refugees sleeping on every corner reclined against brick walls / fences like spiderwebs from those futuristic movies my brother Rolando and I used to watch past midnight the thick layers of dust on my face making me feel safer / that's silly Alma / I'm invisible look / someone rolling down from the sidewalk to the road like a caterpillar asleep immobile there embalmed there couldn't tell if he was alive / cover your face Alma / against a wall I slept / no / I'm sorry ask me about something else profe / do you call your father often? / something else profe please I / the night before I was to leave Guayaquil my father on the cement floor of our bedroom pleading / a smaller place / a loan from the priests / anything I'll do please stay Alma / Rolando didn't stir you could spork a saucer by his ear and he wouldn't stir my father bunched on the cement floor sobbing could barely hear him how is that possible / please Alma / like a tortoise shell my father there / Alma corazón / Rolando returning the orange didn't speak so tiny no hair on his head one curl on his forehead my father in our room with scissors shhh cutting a piece of Rolando's curl placing it inside a Ziploc bag / growl / zzz / growl / quick let's switch I'll be the audience you'll be the kitten Rolando / a band of military men in Gracias a Dios drinking from the same two liter bottle blindfolding the shortest one with what looked like a white sheet too long the ends dangling behind his head Rapunzel ha ha the men spinning him once / twice on the sidewalk a game of kicking whoever the blindfolded one stumbled upon golazo Trujillo the military men strolling and kicking homeless people refugees transients like me and I thinking of all the good things / bad things I've done in my life was it my turn look at that female swine they said lifting me shouting at me mocking each other's broken English slapping me to wake me I was awake / resigned / I'm sorry / open your eyes mongrel / something else profe / Alma corazón / look at this dwarf here he's a graduate from the School of the Americas isn't he ugly / that's not what your mother said / my mother's a Catholic she wouldn't date a priest killer / look who's talking machete boy / my mother wouldn't date her own son you imbecile / viva la puta de tu madre / the blindfolded one removing his blindfold examining me disgusted at me / remember fellows if she's not green doesn't crawl she'll do / blindfolding himself again his breath their breath crabfish onions rum throw up spitting at me / missing / burro ha ha / again / spitting at me / missing / frío frío / punching me on the stomach good one chino de verga ha ha / laugh you wench / Bruce Lee ha ha / disinfect her down there first Trujillo / don't spill the rum and Coke I'm next / esophagus breath ha ha / here we are / Rolando answering the phone in our house in Guayaquil didn't know what to say to me his voice too businesslike how are you / where are you / can barely hear you / come back if you don't adjust to that accursed country Dad's not here I'll tell him you called that wasn't the first time I'd called home after leaving Guayaquil profe the first time I called home I couldn't contain myself what's the use of worrying my father I told myself before calling him I hadn't talked to my father in six / seven months Alma don't tell him about your ribcage hurting whenever you step down from the bus Líneas El Pajorreal my father answering the phone hello it's me Dad / Alma he said / Alma / Alma he said / Alma corazón / Alma / ya corazón / Alma / Alma he said / Alma corazón / Alma he said and I crying and listening to him inside a phone booth in that long distance phone place on Mission Street with the ashen walls decorated with flags from Panamá / Honduras / Chile / the Colombian owner didn't say much to me didn't charge me for that first call she had tissue boxes in her booths for us can you imagine profe one day after the meeting of the women's collective Estela and I strolling along Valencia Street people gathered on the corner of Sixteenth Street an accident I thought / no / an accordion Alma / a tuba / a drum / a dance song from the Middle East maybe / a clarinet look / a young man with a trumpet so handsome Estela saying he wants to look like a gypsy look at his rumpled vest I'm sure he spent the afternoon rumpling it by hand the other gypsy next to him ready for a parade with his portable drum a young blond girl in the crowd arranging her polka dot skirt on top of her wide flower pants sitting on the sidewalk crossing her legs closing her eyes resting her arms on her knees touching her index fingers with her thumbs what is she doing I said she looked so serene there receiving the music as if it were a serenade from the galaxy meant only for her she's trying to impress the trumpeter what else do you think how do I look I'll show that trumpeter a move or two Estela said quick let's switch I'll be the audience you'll be the kitten Rolando / again / here we are / the crowd growing around the gypsies who weren't gypsies the drummer beating the wooden edge of the drum so quickly my father preparing breakfast and I next to him sixteen / seventeen years old tapping a Guns N' Roses song on the kitchen table my school uniform ripping after a soccer match / we won I scored twice Dad / my father mending my uniform playacting at not knowing how to mend clothes this pin prickles my thumb Alma the trumpeter singing without words someone in the crowd clashing his cymbals out of sync Estela saying I think that policeman over there is watching us / which one I said /

don't look at him let's go she said / I didn't want to leave didn't see any policemen the streetlights flickering to life people dancing on the sidewalk her nails on my forearm grabbing me a little too hard okay fine let's go Estela hurrying along Valencia Street people waiting outside restaurants smoking laughing at us / not laughing at us he's following us don't look Estela said and I thinking about the good things / bad things we've done in our lives was it our turn / that's not how the math works Alma / tell me how it works Rolando or I'll tell everyone how you used to play with my dolls / no one was following us profe / please stay the night Estela said of course I said sleeping next to her in her narrow bed I couldn't sleep her blanket didn't have owls / penguins / returning the orange that was supposed to be what was it supposed to be Estela's room as big as a closet Estela talking in her sleep a language I didn't understand along Valencia Street before the meeting of the women's collective I said Estelita are you going to sign up for an interview with our profe / yes she said / for what I said / I don't know for what the woman at El Centro said it would be therapeutic / thera what / peutic / chanfle / I don't think it would be thera anything she said our profe needs help I help him / what are you going to tell him / about how much you love pupusas / be serious tell me / I was born too soon by a river of catfish / fine don't tell me / don't blame me I'm not Salvadorian / pupusas / pulpos / medusas / again / awakening the kitten by tapping Rolando on the shoulder two times the same emphasis every time / again / canvassing the horizon the orange purposefully unattended behind his back / again / the kitten swiping the orange from the princess's hand / again / the princess is sobbing look / Rolando returning the orange to the princess / a starfish look / that's not how it goes / Rolando raising his hand offering the orange to the princess he didn't say please take back the orange princess he didn't talk much yet so tiny returning the orange to the princess my little brother looked so sad profe he thought the princess was really sobbing because he'd taken the orange from her do you understand profe I didn't feel jealous / did feel jealous that I hadn't thought about returning the orange to my father my father kneeling to embrace my little brother thank you

Rolando / again / I wish I would've been the one who returned the orange to my father homeless people transients like me our profe alone on a bench in Dolores Park looking down at his hands as if he was reading from them / wasn't reading from them / good afternoon profe what a coincidence to see you here I was just on my way to class / no class today Alma / everything okay what's happened I said he didn't want to say anything he knew he would cry if he said anything didn't want to look at me there was a raid Alma he said / where I said / a construction site in Reno / Carmen / Anita / that's not possible I / Elena / Renata / Estela / the attorney at the Centro Legal said he was looking into it not much he could do doesn't like me Alma I'm sorry / the attorney from Oaxaca with the gray ponytail wasn't at El Centro Legal that day he liked me nobody could tell me anything about Estela where she was what could we do calling the attorney again that day / the next day the attorney picking up the phone we don't know where she is he said / there must be something we can do I said / we don't know where she is they won't tell us where she is please take care Alma our profe alone on a bench in Dolores Park not reading from his hands saying to me please don't think I think I'm a good person just because I'm worried like this / angry like this is so useless to be indignant no one here cares / Estela's from Guatemala I said / her English had improved so much he said / yes I said leaving him sitting there on that bench without saying goodbye I didn't show up at El Centro Legal week / after week avoiding him / leaving him sitting there without screaming at him / without protesting didn't want him to think I was one of those hysterical women who pretend they're not hysterical until a doorbell / newsflash derails their performance of peace screaming at passersby don't just stand there you monsters my best friend has been deported / my life here will not include / will include me screaming at you in Dolores Park profe of course that Ecuadorian woman's hysterical haven't you heard the terrible things they do to these poor women who try to cross the border / go pity your goddamn mother / why share with you these terrible things profe you'll no longer think of me as your cheerful student from El Centro Legal who gives you a hard time for not wearing those padded motorcycle jackets when you ride your motorcycle take care of yourself profe / I just don't like the way those bulky jackets fit me Alma / you'll think I wasn't strong enough to avoid misfortune hey everyone Alma's just like all the other unfortunate women who cross the border into the United States year / after year I was so proud when I decided to leave Guayaquil profe / didn't want to leave Guayaquil I was twenty years old deciding my life for the first time / anything I'll do Alma / I still like to think proudly of me deciding to leave Guayaquil as if that moment didn't lead to me leaving Guayaquil / Guatemala / México / El Paso / Estela in a detention center couldn't stop thinking of what Estela must be feeling was she relieved at last to return to her village / terrified to return to her village where the paramilitaries were waiting to ambush her embarrassed to return to her family empty handed please forgive me Dad I have caused you all this pain and I return to you with nothing / you're back Alma that's all that matters to me / Estela in a detention center thinking of all the good things / bad things she's done in her life screaming / protesting dear god who doesn't exist my arithmetic doesn't add up recasting her arithmetic so her misfortunes don't seem so arbitrary a cold wind sweeping me to Estela's detention cell I'm here tell me everything Estelita / please let me die in peace / no don't say that / why isn't it over already Alma / tell me about the water truck that wanted to be an elephant / running after the water truck falling on the gravel scraping my knees the driver plugging a black hose to his truck an elephant's nose swooshing my legs / arms / hair the sun drying the cold water from my skin I'm not going to tell you anything profe all those copies of that interview book with terrible fragments of my life that is not my life in bookstores across the United States diffusing me maybe that's not so bad / we've delivered all of you there's nothing left Alma / thank you so much / Estela's village doesn't exist anymore Alma / sometimes I wake up my body as tense as the night when the armed men barged in our camp in the mountains of Guatemala / pretend you're asleep Alma / couldn't see if they were wearing wrestling masks so dark their boots stomping on the floorboards / my body tensing for no reason once / twice a month no doorbell needed can't eat solids Almita let's go for humitas / again / Bruce Lee ha ha / Estela thinking / not thinking week / after week the not thinking adding up to me no longer existing for Estela / for Dad / everyone not existing for me / for them / omitting everything in the world / avoiding you profe until I ran into you at El Centro Legal you were making photocopies of an English manual good afternoon I said / hi Alma do you need the copy machine / no I said / why was I trying to talk to you / hello good day / today's my last day of class he said ashamed of himself I didn't need to ask him why he was quitting he seemed ready to justify himself / one hour a week of English lessons doesn't help anyone except me who feels better look everyone I'm helping my fellow immigrants he said / so quitting or pretending to help are the only two choices I said / what could he say except I don't care enough about you people to dedicate more than one hour every week of my life to teaching you English / how's your book of interviews I said / it's not mine he said I was just assisting them / are you still looking for people to interview I said / I don't think I'm doing more of those interviews anymore do you want to participate I'll put you in touch with them / why aren't you doing them anymore I said / I don't see the point Alma / I didn't say anything he thought I was expecting an explanation from him / I was / wasn't / so pointless Alma what's the use nothing will change because of these interviews / I should've kicked you / I should have screamed at you until my intestines strangled you / I did raise my voice / I did say you're an imbecile of course everything's pointless we're all going to die doesn't matter we're still here / I'm still here / why did I yell at you if I agreed with you everything's more or less pointless I don't want to talk about Gracias a Dios profe you didn't know what to say to me saddened worried that someone at El Centro Legal had heard me the attorney from Oaxaca did show up is everything okay Alma / yes I said I was just telling him about you know the soap opera / which one / María Mercedes / the one with Thalia / a rerun yes / shout if you need me careful with this asshole / I don't know why he doesn't like me Alma / I want to sign up for an interview I said / I'll put you in touch he said / I don't want to talk to just anybody / some good people are putting this together you'll like them / no you hear what I have to say / he didn't reply hoping I would go away maybe / you're our profe I said / Alma / Alma corazón / pretending I was about to yell at him again laughing at him / okay yes he said / I'm sorry I shouted at you profe / you don't need to apologize for anything Alma / I was desperate at Gracias a Dios profe I had to promise a smuggler money from my uncle in New Jersey please help me out of here the smuggler with a glass eye his other eye swimming from side to side hiding us in the back of a truck filled with lettuce delivering us at night by a black river instructing us to take off our clothes I didn't want to take off my clothes what's inside a black river profe tell me that please / do you call your father often? / sleep Alma / a terrible thing to want to talk to my father / not want to talk to my father profe / no / not terrible that's what's terrible about it you don't notice that day / after day someone scrubs out your loved ones in your sleep calling my father and afterwards someone / something inside of me complaining we've scrubbed away your father for nothing Alma why did you request it / I didn't request it go away please / my father slicing a breadloaf into small triangles for breakfast a black river what's inside a black river wave / after wave Estela's room like a closet picking up Estela's things the week after she was taken away a blanket without owls / penguins / a framed photograph of Estela and two children bouncing on her lap pulling her curly hair Estela ten / fifteen years younger the children's hair curly like Estela's hair beautiful girls I didn't know she had daughters profe I didn't want to imagine what had happened to them in Guatemala sometimes I wish every river was a black river then we'll all be alone Estela and her two daughters by my bed I couldn't keep their picture there awaking at night couldn't sleep / Alma corazón / here we are / again / please take care Alma / along Valencia Street people waiting outside restaurants everything so quiet people laughing / not laughing at us a safehouse in El Paso the doors bolted women waiting for their money like me I didn't have any money couldn't reach my uncle didn't have papers the men in charge forcing us to be their servants shackling us at night terrible things profe don't blame me I'm not Salvadorian and Estela interrupting herself or something inside / outside of her interrupting her how can a human being do that to another human being to children the interim president of Ecuador appearing on television informing the nation that he'd met with the international agencies and had agreed that another package of austerity measures was needed the price of everything shot up we could barely afford to eat profe my father slicing a breadloaf into tiny triangles blue marmalade on top preparing our breakfast how do you console a father tell me that profe please my father bunched on the floor sobbing we'll make it work Alma please stay my father mending the sleeves of my uniform my father over the phone saying please stop sending us money we're okay here please take care Alma awaking at night thinking the money from my uncle in New Jersey hadn't arrived Almita let's go for humitas the money did arrive I did make it here sleep Alma putting away the picture of Estela and her daughters couldn't go on waking up next to them every night floating on a black river holding on to a tube my clothes inside a Ziploc bag tied around my waist black night black river someone behind me screaming father I'm drowning please take care Alma how can a human being do that to another human being to children tell me profe please what do you want to hear from me maybe you interviewed Estela before she was taken away let's listen to her before our interview tomorrow profe I was born by a river of catfish hello good day maybe one day your daughter will listen to us profe she'll speak Spanish with you she'll think of me she'll ask you about the orange that was supposed to be what was it supposed to be doesn't matter think of us Lilia Klara / Carmen / Anita / Elena / Renata / Alma corazón / Mercedes / Maria / Cecilia / Estela / por favor cuídate Alma / think of us Lilia Klara / cuídate.

LITERATURE
is not the same thing as
PUBLISHING

Coffee House Press began as a small letterpress operation in 1972 and has grown into an internationally renowned nonprofit publisher of literary fiction, essay, poetry, and other work that doesn't fit neatly into genre categories.

Coffee House is both a publisher and an arts organization. Through our *Books in Action* program and publications, we've become inter-disciplinary collaborators and incubators for new work and audience experiences. Our vision for the future is one where a publisher is a catalyst and connector.

FUNDER ACKNOWLEDGMENTS

Coffee House Press is an internationally renowned independent book publisher and arts nonprofit based in Minneapolis, MN; through its literary publications and *Books in Action* program, Coffee House acts as a catalyst and connector—between authors and readers, ideas and resources, creativity and community, inspiration and action.

Coffee House Press books are made possible through the generous support of grants and donations from corporate giving programs, state and federal support, family foundations, and the many individuals who believe in the transformational power of literature. This activity is made possible by the voters of Minnesota through a Minnesota State Arts Board Operating Support grant, thanks to the legislative appropriation from the arts and cultural heritage fund and a grant from the Wells Fargo Foundation Minnesota. Coffee House also receives major operating support from the Amazon Literary Partnership, the Bush Foundation, the Jerome Foundation, the McKnight Foundation, Target, and the National Endowment for the Arts (NEA). To find out more about how NEA grants impact individuals and communities, visit www.arts.gov.

Coffee House Press receives additional support from the Alexander Family Foundation; the Archer Bondarenko Munificence Fund; the Elmer L. & Eleanor J. Andersen Foundation; the David & Mary Anderson Family Foundation; the Buuck Family Foundation; the Carolyn Foundation; the Dorsey & Whitney Foundation; Dorsey & Whitney LLP; the Knight Foundation; the Rehael Fund of the Minneapolis Foundation; the Matching Grant Program Fund of the Minneapolis Foundation; the Schwab Charitable Fund; Schwegman, Lundberg & Woessner, P.A.; the Scott Family Foundation; the US Bank Foundation; VSA Minnesota for the Metropolitan Regional Arts Council; the Archie D. & Bertha H. Walker Foundation; and the Woessner Freeman Family Foundation in honor of Allan Kornblum.

THE PUBLISHER'S CIRCLE OF COFFEE HOUSE PRESS

Publisher's Circle members make significant contributions to Coffee House Press's annual giving campaign. Understanding that a strong financial base is necessary for the press to meet the challenges and opportunities that arise each year, this group plays a crucial part in the success of Coffee House's mission.

Recent Publisher's Circle members include many anonymous donors, Mr. & Mrs. Rand L. Alexander, Suzanne Allen, Patricia A. Beithon, Bill Berkson & Connie Lewallen, the E. Thomas Binger & Rebecca Rand Fund of the Minneapolis Foundation, Robert & Gail Buuck, Claire Casey, Louise Copeland, Jane Dalrymple-Hollo, Jennifer Kwon Dobbs & Stefan Liess, Mary Ebert & Paul Stembler, Chris Fischbach & Katie Dublinski, Kaywin Feldman & Jim Lutz, Sally French, Jocelyn Hale & Glenn Miller, the Rehael Fund-Roger Hale/Nor Hall of the Minneapolis Foundation, Randy Hartten & Ron Lotz, Jeffrey Hom, Carl & Heidi Horsch, Amy L. Hubbard & Geoffrey J. Kehoe Fund, Kenneth Kahn & Susan Dicker, Stephen & Isabel Keating, Kenneth Koch Literary Estate, Jennifer Komar & Enrique Olivarez, Allan & Cinda Kornblum, Leslie Larson Maheras, Lenfestey Family Foundation, Sarah Lutman & Rob Rudolph, the Carol & Aaron Mack Charitable Fund of the Minneapolis Foundation, George & Olga Mack, Joshua Mack, Gillian McCain, Mary & Malcolm McDermid, Sjur Midness & Briar Andresen, Maureen Millea Smith & Daniel Smith, Peter Nelson & Jennifer Swenson, Marc Porter & James Hennessy, Jeffrey Scherer, Jeffrey Sugerman & Sarah Schultz, Nan G. & Stephen C. Swid, Patricia Tilton, Stu Wilson & Melissa Barker, Warren D. Woessner & Iris C. Freeman, Margaret Wurtele, Joanne Von Blon, and Wayne P. Zink.

For more information about the Publisher's Circle and
other ways to support Coffee House Press books, authors, and activities,
please visit www.coffeehousepress.org/support or
contact us at info@coffeehousepress.org.

A Collapse of Horses
by Brian Evenson

Faces in the Crowd
by Valeria Luiselli

Fugue State
by Brian Evenson

A Girl Is a Half-Formed Thing
by Eimear McBride

Leaving the Atocha Station
by Ben Lerner

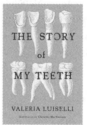

The Story of My Teeth
by Valeria Luiselli

ULULU
by Thalia Field

Mauro Javier Cardenas grew up in Guayaquil, Ecuador, and graduated with a degree in economics from Stanford University. His fiction has appeared in *Conjunctions, Guernica, ZYZZYVA, Witness, BOMB,* and the *Antioch Review.*

The Revolutionaries Try Again was designed by
Bookmobile Design & Digital Publisher Services.
Text is set in ITC Legacy, a typeface designed by
Ronald Arnholm in 1992.